MEMORY

Books by Linda Nagata

Tech-Heaven
The Bohr Maker
Deception Well
Vast
*Limit of Vision
*Memory

*A Tor Book

MEMORY

LINDA NAGATA

TOR®

A TOM DOHERTY ASSOCIATES BOOK
NEW YORK

MEMORY

Copyright © 2003 by Linda Nagata

Edited by Patrick Nielsen Hayden

This book is printed on acid-free paper.

Book design by Michael Collica

A Tor Book
Published by Tom Doherty Associates, LLC
175 Fifth Avenue
New York, NY 10010

www.tor.com

Tor® is a registered trademark of Tom Doherty Associates, LLC.

Library of Congress Cataloging-in-Publication Data

Nagata, Linda.
Memory / Linda Nagata.—1st ed.
p. cm.
"A Tom Doherty Associates book."
ISBN 0-312-87721-8
1. Life on other planets—Fiction. 2. Brothers and sisters—Fiction.
3. Missing persons—Fiction. I. Title.

PS3564.A34 M4 2003
813'.6—dc21
2002043581

First Edition: April 2003

Printed in the United States of America

0 9 8 7 6 5 4 3 2 1

For Junzo—
A Quest, a Puzzle
And Multiple Lives

MEMORY

Chapter

1

When I was ten I had a blanket that was smooth and dark, with no light of its own until I moved and then its folds would glitter with thousands of tiny stars in all the colors of the stars in the night sky. But the pale arch that appears at the zenith on clear nights and that we call the Bow of Heaven never would appear on my blanket— and for that I was glad. For if there was no Heaven, I reasoned, then the dead would always be reborn in this world and not the next, no matter how wise they became in life.

This was always a great concern for me, for my mother was the wisest person I knew and I feared for her. More than once I schemed to make her look foolish, just to be sure she would not get into Heaven when her time came. When my antics grew too much she would turn to my father. With a dark frown and her strong arms crossed over her chest she would say, "We have been so very fortunate to have such a wild and reckless daughter as Jubilee. Obviously, she was sent to teach us wisdom." My father would laugh, but I would pout, knowing I had lost another round, and that I must try harder next time.

I seldom suffered a guilty conscience. I knew it was my role to be wild—even my mother agreed to that—but on the night my story begins I was troubled by the thought that perhaps this time I had gone too far.

I lived then in the temple founded by my mother, Temple Huacho, a remote outpost in the Kavasphir Hills, a wild land of open woods and rolling heights, infamous for the frequency of its silver floods.

As often as three nights in ten the silver would come, rising from the ground, looking like a luminous fog as it filled all the vales, to make an island of our hilltop home. I would watch its deadly advance from my bedroom window, and many times I saw it lap at the top of the perimeter wall that enclosed the temple grounds.

That wall was my mother's first line of defense against the rise of silver and she maintained it well. Only twice had I seen a silver flood reach past it, and both times the chemical defenses of the temple kobolds that lived within the wall stripped the silver of its menace before it could do us harm. True silver is heavy and will always sink to fill the low ground. But the remnant silver that made it past the wall spired like luminous smoke, tangling harmlessly in the limbs of the orchard trees.

Because silver was so common in that region no one dared to live near us. Only a temple, with its protective kobolds, could offer shelter from the nocturnal floods, and Temple Huacho was the only one that had been established anywhere in Kavasphir. So the mineral wealth the silver brought was ours to exploit, while the temple well was famous for producing new and mysterious strains of the beetle-like metabolic machines called kobolds. My mother harvested the kobolds while my father prospected, and eight or nine times a year small convoys of truckers would visit us to collect what we had to trade.

On that evening, two trucks had arrived from distant Xahiclan and the drivers had with them a boy named Tico who was also a lesson in wisdom for his parents. Naturally I loved him on sight, and so did my brother Jolly who was a year older than me but not nearly so useful to our parents. We abandoned our younger siblings (who we were supposed to watch) to play wild games in the orchard. After dinner—a magnificent feast that my parents had prepared and that we did not appreciate except for the sweets at the end—we disappeared again, this time on a special quest.

In the old enclaves like Xahiclan the temples all had long histories. Thousands of players depended on their protective powers, and so they had become sacred places. Children were not allowed to play on the grounds, and only the temple keepers were permitted inside the buildings. None of this solemnity was attached to Temple Huacho. Our outpost was not thirty years old; it was home to no one but our own family; and it was the only playground my brothers and sisters and I had ever known.

Jolly and I were oldest, so we could go where we wanted within the confines of the temple wall, though perhaps not to the well room, not without supervision. But Tico wanted to see the well of the kobolds. He told us he had never seen a kobold well before. Jolly and I were so astonished to hear this that it took only a moment for us to reason that the rule about not visiting the well room was an old one, and that if we were to ask, our mother and father would surely say we were old enough now to go there on our own . . . but of course we couldn't ask: they were busy with the truckers and would not want to be bothered, while it was up to us to keep Tico entertained.

So we crept quietly through the halls, accompanied by Jolly's little dog, Moki—a sharp-faced hound with large upright ears, a short back, lush red fur, and a long tail. Moki had been Jolly's pet for as long as I could remember. He stood only knee-high, but he followed my brother everywhere. Now he trotted beside us, his nails clicking against the tiled floor.

Temple Huacho was a house of stone, made from the abundant minerals of Kavasphir. The floor tiles were a cream-colored marble laced with gold; the walls were of lettered stone, in a shade of green like malachite with the letters compressed into barely readable veins of black print; the ceilings were made of translucent slices of a lighter green stone bearing the image of fossilized forests. Lights shone behind the ceiling panels, giving the effect of walking through a woodland on a cloudy day. Tico was much impressed by this decor. On the way to the well room he kept whispering about how wealthy we must be until I decided that perhaps I didn't like him quite as much as I had thought.

The entrance to the well room was framed by the trunks of two trees fossilized in white jade. Jolly held on to Moki while I leaned past the nearest trunk, taking a quick, cautious look around the room, confirming that it was empty. Then I motioned Tico and Jolly forward.

The well room was a round chamber, its walls lined with cabinets holding hundreds of tiny, airtight drawers where mature kobolds were stored. On the right-hand side, in front of these cabinets, was the broad jade table that served as my mother's workbench. Her microscopes and analytical equipment were shapeless lumps beneath a white dust cover. On the left side of the room another workbench supported stacks of transparent boxes—test chambers for uncataloged kobolds—but they were empty.

At the center of the room was the temple well. A thigh-high mound of fine soil surrounded its throat. Over the years I had watched this mound grow until now it spilled onto the tiles around it, where its soil was scuffed and crushed to a fine brown powder by passing feet.

Tico did not wait for further invitation. He strode past me to the mound's edge, where he looked over the embankment of dirt, and down, into the dark, jagged hole that was the throat of the well.

A kobold well is made wherever a plume of nutrients chances to rise from the steaming core of the world, a bounty that awakens the kobold motes, tiny as dust, that lie dormant everywhere in the soil.

I felt proud when I saw the awe on Tico's face. The well was the heart of Temple Huacho. It was the reason my mother had settled there. It was the source of our security, and our wealth. So I was surprised when Tico's expression changed. Awe became confusion. And then confusion gave way to a wicked scowl. "Is that it?" he asked. "A dirty hole in the ground?"

I frowned down at the fine, loose soil, wanting desperately to impress him. "There are kobolds," I said, and I pointed at the well's throat where two newly emerged kobolds were using their weak limbs to claw free of the hard-packed ground. These were large metallophores—metal eaters—as big as my father's thumb and beetlelike in appearance, their color as dull as the soil that nourished them.

Kobolds were a kind of mechanic, a machine creature, and like any machine they were created by the labor of other machines: the kobold motes, to be specific. That was the essential division among the animate creatures of the world: mechanics were made, so that they began existence in finished form, while organic life had to strive for existence through the complexities of birth and growth and change.

Mechanics were living tools. The metallophores that I pointed out to Tico could be configured to make many kinds of simple metal parts. As a spider eats and secretes a web, so kobolds could take in raw material, metabolize it so that it took on a new form, and secrete it. But where spiders secreted only webs, kobolds could produce things as diverse as medicine or machine parts, depending on the strain. The common metallophores of our well did their work inside a metabolic foam, which they would excrete in layer upon layer for many days depending on the size of the artifact they had been programmed to make. When the project was complete the foam would be washed away, revealing the fan blade, or bracket, or truck body that the configuration had called for.

All players were dependent upon mechanics, but we were especially dependent on the kobolds. We could not have survived without them, so it was easy to believe the legends that said they had been made for us.

But Tico showed no sign of being impressed by the large metallophores, so I hurried to look for other kobolds, and soon I spotted some that were tiny, the size of a grain of wheat or even smaller, moving through the mound's soft soil. "See those?" I asked Tico. "There. Where the soil quivers? Those are probably the kind that make platinum circuits. My mother's been trying to improve that strain."

He shrugged. "Who cares about kobolds? I've seen thousands. I thought you were going to show me a well like the ones in Xahiclan. They're a hundred feet across, with crystal walls crawling with rare kobolds no one's ever seen before."

A hundred feet across? I wondered if it could be true. I looked at Jolly. He had circled around to the well's other side where he stood with his hands clasped behind his back, a sure sign he was getting angry. Moki sat beside him, his alert ears listening for any familiar words in our conversation. Jolly said, "At Temple Huacho we find lots of kobolds no one's ever seen before. More than in all of Xahiclan, because this temple is new."

I smiled, pleased at my brother's parry. But now the line had been drawn and Tico had territory to defend. "New kobolds out of this little hole? I don't believe it!"

It took me a moment to understand that he had just called my brother a liar. When I did, my cheeks grew hot. "Why do you think your dad comes all the way out here?" I demanded. "It's because our kobolds are special."

"Uh-uh!" Tico countered. "It's for the minerals."

Jolly smiled his signature half smile. I saw it, and took a step back from Tico. In a quiet voice Jolly said, "You forget where you are, Tico. This is the Kavasphir Hills. You're not in an old, tame enclave like Xahiclan. We don't need a big well, because the silver here is powerful."

Jolly was a beautiful child, smooth-skinned and bright-eyed, his blue-black hair sprouting in unruly spikes—but he was eleven, and the easy cheerfulness of his early years had already begun to fade under the pressure of a growing self-doubt, for no talent from his past lives had ever returned to him. Every new skill had to be learned with great labor, as if for the first time. Though I was younger, I was far ahead of him in reading and math, because for me each new lesson only wakened a knowledge I already had, while Jolly had to earn it. He would grow frustrated, and rail that he must have been the stupidest player in existence, to have learned nothing from his past lives.

That night though, he was a player. He told Tico, "This land belongs to the silver. It's in the ground. It's in the well." He stomped his shoe softly. "It's here, right under our feet."

Tico didn't like this idea. He took a step back. "It's not."

"Oh, yes it is," I said, rising to my brother's aid—though the idea of silver lying in wait underground was new to me, and deeply unsettling . . . because it made sense. Questions I had never thought to ask were suddenly answered, and I echoed them aloud: "Where do you think kobold motes come from?" (As if I knew!) "The silver makes them, that's where. It's in the land."

"It is not!" Tico said. He was becoming desperately angry now. "My uncle's a stone mason. I've been to a quarry where stones are cut out of the ground, and there's never been any silver underneath any of them."

"This is a temple," Jolly said.

Well it certainly was and Tico had never been in a temple before. What did he know about temples? Nothing except the silly rumors he'd heard in Xahiclan of wells a hundred feet across. But Tico was proud of his ignorance. He shrugged; his lip thrust out in a pout. "Your well is still boring to look at."

This was too much for me. To belittle the well was to belittle the life my mother had made for all of us and that I could not bear. "Come with me, then," I said, and I started to climb carefully over the mound. "If you want some excitement, then come with me and see the silver—unless you're afraid."

Jolly's eyes widened when he saw what I was doing. "Jubilee!" But the well lay between us, and he could not stop me.

I looked over my shoulder at Tico. "What's the matter? Don't you want to come?"

Warily he asked, "What are you going to do?"

"I'm going to climb down the well. That's what you have to do to see the silver."

"But I can see the silver outside any window. It's rising tonight. My dad said so."

I edged closer to the well's dark throat, placing my feet carefully so as not to crush the lumpy shapes of dormant kobolds that lay buried beneath the surface of the mound. "But it's in the well too. Always. Night or day. Don't you want to see it?"

I didn't expect him to follow me. I thought fear (or wisdom) would get the better of him, and he would run away and then Jolly and I could have a good laugh together. But Tico was a gift to his parents, and to me. "Okay," he said. "You go first."

Of course I had never climbed down the well. I had no idea if the silver really could be seen at the bottom, or even if there was a bottom, but Tico was watching me with a wicked smile. He knew I was lying. He was only waiting for me to give up and admit it, but how could I? I glanced at Jolly. He was my big brother. He was supposed to keep me out of trouble, but he only looked at me with merry eyes, saying, "The chimney bends about ten feet down, but if you wriggle past that, you can keep going for almost thirty feet."

I could not hide my astonishment. "You've been down the well?"

"Sure. How do you think I know about the silver?" He looked past my shoulder and his smile widened to a grin. I turned to see Tico fleeing the well room. The sound of his footfalls faded in the direction of the dining hall. "He won't tell on us," Jolly said. "He'd only get himself in trouble."

Tico was already forgotten. I turned back, to glare at my brother. "Have you really been down the well?" I didn't want to believe it. I didn't want to believe he'd done something so momentous without me. And he didn't want to admit it. I could see that at once. "You *have* gone down it!" I accused.

He looked askance. "Only one time. When you went with Dad to Halibury."

That was the time my father had taken me to see the match-maker. Jolly was oldest and he should have gone first but our father wouldn't take him—not until he knew what Jolly's talents were. My own special talent was languages. I had a knack for them that had been clear by the time I was six. Naturally my brother had been jealous, and he must have been bored too in the days I was away—but that was months ago! He should have forgiven me, and confessed. I wondered what other secrets he kept. "You should have told me."

"Why? You would only want to go yourself."

"So?"

"So it's dangerous. You really *can* see hints of the silver down there."

"I'm not afraid."

"Jubilee—"

He was only a year older than me. I knew I could keep up with him. I always had. "You can follow me, Jolly, if you want to, but I'm going."

I lowered myself into the well's dark throat. The shaft sweated a cold dew. Knobs of jade stuck out from the narrow walls as if they had been put there on purpose to make a ladder. I moved cautiously from one to the next. Jolly and I had climbed every tree in the orchard; we had scaled the wall around the temple at a hundred different points; and we had even climbed up to the roof once, when my father was away and my mother was busy with the new baby. But the shaft was a new experience for me, and I didn't like it.

I could feel my shirt getting wet, and crumbles of dirt trickling past my collar. The smell of dirt was strong. Beneath that though, there was something else: a sharp scent that made me think of knives, or melting glass. The walls were tiled with the shapes of dormant kobolds. I could see their legs folded against their machine bodies, and their scaled abdomens, but the complex mouthparts that decorated their beetle faces were only half-formed.

I had never seen an unfinished kobold before. I stroked the back of one. Then I pried my fingers into the dirt around its pupal shape to see if it could be freed. It popped loose with surprising ease. I almost dropped it, but managed to catch it with my left hand, while my legs held me propped against the wall.

"You shouldn't do that," Jolly said.

I looked up at his foreshortened figure braced across the well's throat, and I made a face. Out of sight in the well room, Moki was whining anxiously, wondering where we had gone. It was a lonely sound, and did not help my mood, but I had things to prove. So the pupal kobold went into my pocket and I continued down.

The bend in the well shaft was just as Jolly had described. I wriggled past it, leaving behind the friendly light of the well room. I felt the shaft open out around me and I had the feeling I'd entered a secret chamber. It was warmer here, and it was dark enough to make me breathe hard. I couldn't see the shapes of the pupal kobolds in the walls anymore, but I could feel them, bumpy-smooth, like river rocks under my hand. The sharp, glassy scent had grown stronger.

Jolly was wriggling past the bend now, so I started down again to get out of his way. "Where's the silver?" I asked softly.

"Farther down. It's trapped in the walls."

"It can't get out, can it?"

"I don't know."

My hands trembled. The temple protected us from the silver. But it was night—the time when silver rose. And I wasn't exactly in the temple; I was *under* it.

"Did you climb down at night?" I asked Jolly. "Or during the day?"

"At night."

Okay. I bit my lower lip. It was only thirty feet or so to the bottom. That's what Jolly had said. I climbed faster. The sooner I touched bottom, the sooner I could come back up.

It was too dark to see anything.

I couldn't believe Jolly had climbed down here by himself.

Or maybe I could believe it. Jolly was like that. I would never have done this alone—and that was a hard knowledge to bear.

I slipped. I slid only a few inches and then I caught myself on a knobby rock. But now my eyes were playing tricks on me. Was there a gleam in the walls of the shaft? Yes . . . like threads of light beneath the black soil, but not silver threads. Their color was bronze. I brushed my fingers over them and some of the covering soil crumbled away. The light grew brighter, and closer to silver in color, but the texture was wrong. "Jolly?"

"Yeah?"

"Is this what you meant? Is this the silver?" It didn't look much like silver to me.

"Tiny veins in the wall?"

"Uh-huh."

"That's it."

I felt a little calmer. I could handle this. I started again for the bottom, moving faster now. I wanted this adventure to be over. I wanted to be out in the temple's sweet artificial light. But to get there, I had to touch bottom first.

The well came to an abrupt end. Still clinging to the walls, I felt around with the thin soles of my shoes, but I could not discover any further passage. I was a bit disappointed. Despite my fear, it would have been fun to find a new passage, and venture just a little farther than Jolly.

"Where are you?" Jolly called. His voice sounded far away. I glanced up, and saw him silhouetted against a patch of gray. He had come only halfway down from the bend. His black shape hung there like a giant spider.

"I'm at the bottom."

"Then come back. And hurry. Mama's going to be looking for us soon."

"In a minute." Gingerly, I lowered my weight to the floor. Something brittle crunched under my feet and I half expected the shaft to give way and drop me all the way through the world to the ocean.

Nothing so dramatic happened. All around me I could see the tiny veins of embedded light glowing in the walls. They were everywhere at the bottom of the shaft, like luminous spiderwebs under the dirt. Or maybe they were just easier to see there, so deep down inside the world. I traced their tangled paths with my fingers. "This doesn't look like silver," I said. I looked up at Jolly. "Are you sure it's not just a mineral?"

"I didn't dig it out."

My father had once shown me a grotto near our home where silver could be seen even in the daytime. He had not allowed me to go inside, but standing at the grotto's entrance I could clearly see the silver tucked into the crevices and the hollows of the rock. It had looked just like silver looks in the night: cottony tufts of luminous fog. These gleaming veins didn't look anything like that. Instead, they looked like strands of metal. "I don't think this is silver."

"Jubilee, come back up."

I scraped experimentally at the dirt. I was still angry with Jolly. How I would love to prove him wrong! I scraped harder, but it hurt my fingernails. That was when I remembered the pupal kobold in my pocket. My fingers slipped around it, exploring its hard shape, and the way its abdomen came to a sharp point like a tiny pick. I pulled it out, and—gently at first, but with more force at every stroke—I used it to scrape at a vein.

Jolly must have guessed what I was doing. "Jubilee!" He started down toward me.

I kept scraping. Little streams of dirt rattled to the floor. The line of light beneath my excavation brightened. Encouraged, I stabbed my little weapon hard into the vein, and something popped. It was a tiny sound, like a clucking tongue, far away. Then a spurt of glowing silver slurry shot out across my hand like a pulse of blood. Or acid. My hand burned as if someone had laid a wire of red-hot metal across its back. I dropped the pupa and screamed a little half scream, bit off at once because worse than a burn would be Mama finding out what I had done.

"Jubilee?" Jolly whispered, a note of panic in his voice. "Where are you? What's wrong?"

"I'm okay!" I said. "Go back up. Go back up." My hand hurt so badly. I whimpered, expecting a cloud of silver to ooze out of the wall at any moment to engulf me. The traceries of light still gleamed, while the vein I had attacked wept tiny drops like luminous quicksilver.

"Jubilee?"

"I'm coming!" I climbed frantically toward his voice, knocking loose the pupal cases of several half-formed kobolds in my haste.

I kept my hand hidden from Mama. The wound was a livid red trench that ran from the knuckle of my little finger to the base of my thumb. After a few minutes it stopped hurting, but I could hardly bear to look at it and I certainly didn't want to explain where it had come from. So I said good night with my hand thrust deep in my pocket. Then I hurried to the room I shared with Jolly, shut the door firmly, and crawled under my blanket of stars. I lay in the dark, staring at the trees beyond the open window, their leafy branches bathed in a pale gleam. I was terribly tired, but my guilty conscience would not let me sleep. After a few minutes, Jolly came in, with Moki following at his heels.

"You okay?" he asked.

"Yes."

He walked to the window. Pale light shone across his face. "The silver's deep tonight. It's almost over the wall."

I crawled to the foot of the bed to look. Kneeling beside him, I leaned out the window.

Temple Huacho was built at the summit of a softly rounded hill. I looked down that slope, past the orchard my mother had planted, to see a luminous ocean lapping at the top of the perimeter wall. The silver's light filled all the vales so that once again our hilltop had become an island, one of many in an archipelago of hills set in a silvery sea, though all the other islands were wooded. Ours was the only one where any players lived.

The oldest stories in existence, the ones brought forward again and again through time, tell us that in our first lives we came from beyond the world. A goddess created this place for us and the silver was her thought: a force of creation and destruction that could build the bones of the world or melt them away. She brought us out of darkness to live in her new world, for it was her hope that each of us might gain talents in our successive lives so that someday we would grow beyond this world and ascend to Heaven too.

The goddess had made the world in defiance of darkness, but the darkness was an angry god and he pursued her and sought to slay her world. A great war fell out between them and while he was cast back into the void, she was broken, her existence reduced to a fever dream with the silver the only visible remnant of her creative power.

We call it silver, but other languages have named it better. In one ancient tongue it is the "breath-of-creation." In another it is "the fog of souls," and in a third, "the dreaming goddess."

That was how my mother spoke of it. When the silver rose she would say that the goddess was dreaming again of the glorious days of creation, and certainly the silver brought with it both the beauty and the madness of dreams. It was an incoherent force, wantonly powerful, that entered our world at twilight and stayed until dawn, reshaping what it touched. In the course of a single night it might dissolve a hundred miles of highway, or the outer buildings of a failing enclave, or a player unlucky enough to be caught out after dark. In the same night it might build new structures within the veils of its gleaming fog, so that a columned mansion would be discovered in an uninhabited valley, or a statue of glass would be found standing in meditation amid a field of maize. But while the silver could both dissolve away the structures of our civilization and build them anew, it acted always as an impersonal force, never seeming aware that this *was* our world, or that we existed in it.

So we walled it out.

A silver flood might get past the protection of the temple kobolds that lived within the perimeter wall, but not without losing most of its strength. More temple kobolds guarded the orchard, and more existed in the temple itself so that the silver could never reach us. So my mother promised.

Every temple was an enclave, an island of safety in the chaotic wilderness of the world. The truckers had brought their vehicles into the courtyard; my father had closed the gate behind them. They would sleep in the guest rooms tonight, and we would all be safe.

I watched the silver lapping at the top of the wall, somehow eerily alive that night. I watched the first tendrils reach over the wall's flat top. When they encountered the chemical defenses of the temple kobolds they smoked and steamed, rising as a fine mist into the air. But the advance of the silver did not stop. More tendrils spilled over the wall, and these were not turned back so easily. I watched first one, then many more, flow down the face of the wall, gathering against the ground like smoke on a cool morning.

I retreated from the window.

My fear must have shone because Jolly said, "It's okay. It won't come inside the temple. It can't."

That's what Mama would say—but she didn't know about my adventure in the well. She didn't know I'd disturbed what was there.

Jolly left the window to sit beside me on the bed. Moki followed him, snuggling in between us. "How's your hand?"

"Better."

He was silent for a minute. I could smell the silver: a fresh, strong scent as I imagined the ocean would smell. "Do you . . . ever feel like you're having a dream?" Jolly asked. "Even though you're awake?"

I puzzled over his question, wondering where it had come from. "You mean like a daydream?"

"No."

"Then what?"

I could see he was already regretting saying anything. "Never mind."

"Are you having a dream right now?" I asked him.

Silver light glittered in his eyes.

"So what do you dream about?"

But he looked away. "Never mind. Go to sleep."

I *was* tired, so I lay down again, wriggling about for a minute so the stars on my blanket gleamed brightly. I looked at Jolly, still sitting at the foot of my bed, gazing out the window at the silver, his hand moving slowly as he stroked Moki, who had fallen asleep in his lap. I wasn't sure, but I thought I saw faint motes of silver sparkling over his hand. Then I was asleep, before even the stars in my blanket had begun to fade.

Moki woke me, his sharp high bark like an electric shock. I sat up. Jolly had fallen asleep where he'd been sitting. Now his head jerked up. I was astonished to see motes of silver dancing in his hair and over his hands and in the folds of his clothes. He turned to the window.

The silver light was brighter than I had ever seen it. Jolly was silhouetted in its glow. He rose slowly to his knees, staring out the window like someone mesmerized.

"Jolly!" I spoke past Moki's frantic yipping. "There is silver on you."

He looked at his hands. Then he swiped them against his pants as if to wipe the evidence of silver away, but the motes would not leave. "It's too late," he whispered. "I called it, and now it's coming."

At first I didn't know what he meant. Then Moki went ominously silent, and a moment later the silver rose over the windowsill. It had rolled up through the orchard all the way to the temple. Now it spilled through the window and into the room: a luminous stream that spread in a smoky pool across the floor. Its fresh, crisp scent filled my lungs and planted a quiet terror in my heart.

I crept backward, to the far corner of my bed, pulling my blanket of stars with me until I felt the wall against my shoulders. I could see no way to escape, for the silver had already rolled up against the door.

"Mommy!" I whispered it like a spell, a word with magical warding powers. *"Mommy."* Too frightened to shout.

The silver started to rise. It inflated in ghostly tendrils that swirled toward Jolly, who seemed hypnotized by it, for he didn't move. I reached out, grabbing a fold of his shirt where the silver motes were thinnest, and I yanked him backward. "Get away from it!" I whispered. "Move back. Move back."

He seemed to wake up. Had he still been asleep? He scrambled into my corner. Moki came with him, barking frantically again. I put my hand over his muzzle and hissed at him to *hush!* I did not want Mama to wake. What would happen if she hurried to our room, if she threw open the door? She would be taken.

"Go away!" Jolly whispered. *"I didn't mean it."*

He had boxed me into the corner, put himself between me and the looming silver fog. Never had I seen silver so close. I peered past him, in terror, in wonder. It looked grainy. As if it were a cloud made of millions of tiny particles just like the silver motes that clung to him.

The cloud touched the edge of my bed.

Jolly started to creep away from me, moving toward it. "No," I whimpered. "Don't go."

I grabbed his shirt again and tried to drag him back, but he turned on me in fury. "Don't touch me! If the silver takes one of us, it'll take the other too if we make a bridge for it to cross."

"I don't care!" I started to cry, but I didn't touch him again. I held on to Moki instead, who was trembling in my lap. *"I want Mama. I want Dad."*

"I do too," Jolly said in a soft, shaky voice. Then a tendril of silver slipped across the bed and touched his knee. For a moment the tendril glowed brighter. Then it flashed over him, expanding across his legs, his torso, his arms, his face, all of him, in a raw second. For one more second he knelt on the bed like a statue of a boy cast in silver. Then the cloud rolled over him, hiding his terrible shape within a curtain of perfect silence.

I couldn't breathe. Air wouldn't come into my chest. I pressed myself against the wall and held on to Moki, wanting to scream, wanting it almost as badly as I wanted air, but I didn't dare because I didn't want Mama to come into the room and be stolen by the silver too. Even when the glittering mist began to retreat, leaving the foot of the bed empty, with ancient letters newly written in gold on the bed frame and on the stone floor, I stayed silent in my corner. I waited until the cloud had drifted out of the room—not out of the window, for the window was gone, and most of the bedroom's wall with it, dissolved in the silver, just like Jolly.

I stared out at the orchard, wondering why the trees had remained unchanged, but silver was like that: sometimes it would leave things and sometimes it would change them, but it always took the players it touched, and animals too. I waited, until the last wisp still clinging to the ruined wall evaporated from existence. Then I screamed.

Chapter

2

If a child should ask, *What is the world?* a parent might answer, "It is a ring-shaped island of life made by the goddess in defiance of the frozen dark between the stars. On the outer rim of this ring there is mostly land, and that is where we live. On the inner rim there is only ocean. We have day and night because the world-ring spins around its own imaginary axis. At the same time it follows another, greater circle around the sun so that we see different stars in different seasons." These are the simple facts everyone accepts.

But if a child should ask, *What is the silver?* the answer might take many forms.

"It is a fog of glowing particles that arises at night to rebuild the world."

"It is a remnant of the world's creation."

"It is the memory of the world."

"It is the dreaming mind of the wounded goddess and you must never go near her! Her dreams will swallow any player they touch. Do you want to be swallowed up by the silver? No? Then stay inside at night. Never wander."

What is the silver? After Jolly was taken, that question was never far from my mind. I interviewed my mother, I consulted libraries for their opinions, and I asked the passing truckers what they thought. It was from the truckers I first heard the rumor that the silver was rising. The oldest among them had lived more than two hundred years, and they swore it was a different world from the one in which they'd been born: *"The roads were safer in those days. The silver did not come so often, nor flood so deep."*

Sometimes their younger companions would scoff, but as I grew older, even the youths insisted they had seen a change. *"The silver is rising, higher every year, as if it would drown the world."*

I began to keep records. I noted the nights on which the silver appeared, how often it touched the temple's perimeter wall, and how often it passed over. That first year I kept count, it reached the orchard only once, but in the second year it breached the wall three times, and seven times in the year after that.

I was fifteen when I showed these notes to my mother. Her expression was grim as she studied them. "Kavasphir is a wild land," she admitted, handing the notes back to me.

"Do you think the silver is rising?"

She was hesitant in her answer. "All things move in cycles."

"I have heard the silver moves in a cycle of a thousand years. That it grows more abundant with time, until the world seems on the verge of drowning in it . . . and then it is driven back until there is almost no silver left and that is almost as bad."

My mother said, "I have heard that too."

I waited for her to elaborate, to explain why this was a foolish rumor, but she was lost in thought. It was night, and we sat together in her bedroom, the only sound that of the fountain playing in the garden beyond the open window.

At last I spoke again, my voice hushed. "Do you think it's true?"

"It's hard to know for sure."

"But it could be?"

"The world is old, and most of our past forgotten. But fragments remain. In the libraries . . . and in the lettered stone and the follies the silver makes. There is enough to convince most scholars that the world has passed through many ages of history. Sometimes the silver was common. Other times it was rare. No one can say why."

"No one has explained it?"

She shrugged. "Many have tried to explain it, but none in a manner to convince me. Players love stories, but they do not always love facts." We traded a smile. "Don't be afraid, Jubilee. Perhaps the silver *is* rising, but I don't think we are on the verge of drowning just yet."

What is the silver? Eventually I decided it must be all the things players claimed it to be. It was a remnant of the world's creation: that was how it was able to disassemble solid objects, breaking them down into its gleaming fog while it compiled new objects in their places. It was the memory of the world, mapping the structure of everything it touched, so that it could bring ancient objects forward in time—to create meaningless follies in the wilderness, or to deposit veins of valuable ore in the exposed rock of the Kavasphir Hills. And it was the mind of a dreaming goddess, or at least of some savant of an ancient world far more learned than ours. This I allowed only because of a handful of legends. Mostly the silver acted in a way that seemed random, and unaware. Now and then though, there were stories of some tool or talisman brought forward through time, delivered at a crucial moment, as if someone beyond the silver sought to move the pieces . . .

But why only now and then?

I would look at the scar on the back of my hand, remembering the night Jolly was taken, and I would wonder.

I never told my mother how I got that scar. It was a strange mark: an intricate ridge of reddish tissue that didn't fade as any normal scar would. I would look at it, and wonder: Had I caused Jolly's death with my adventure in the kobold well? For neither I nor anyone else could explain why the silver had been able to breach the temple that night.

But if ever I got to thinking it might be my fault, I would remember what Jolly had said, a moment before the silver spilled over the windowsill: *I called it, and now it's coming.* Those words were engraved in my memory, though how he—or anyone—could summon the wild chaos of silver I didn't know.

There was much I didn't know, but I swore it would not always be so.

I was never lonely in those years. By the time I was seventeen, the count of my younger siblings had grown to six and I had long since corrupted my nearest sister, Emia, and our oldest brother after her, Rizal, and made them my companions in many adventures that our parents did not approve. But I abandoned them that year, when my father's brother came to live with us.

I haven't said much about my father. In a sense, there isn't much to say. He was a wayfarer who had traveled a third of the way around the ring of the world to find his destined lover, and during his years on the road he had many adventures, and many narrow escapes. Then one sunny day he found his way to the enclave of Halibury, and as he'd done in hundreds of enclaves before, he went to see the matchmaker.

That self-righteous old man wanted nothing more than to send this foreign ruffian on his way. But against all expectation, this Kedato Panandi turned out to possess the blood pattern that matched my mother's. The matchmaker sent a note to her at Temple Huacho, giving the worst description.

My mother was not a young woman. She'd given up wayfaring ten years before. Having reached her late forties, she'd settled her mind to a single life. Now she read the matchmaker's description and was afraid. The body speaks its own language. What if this stranger truly was a wicked man? And what if she loved him anyway? Such things happened. This was no perfect world.

So she dithered in her answer, until finally Kedato bribed the matchmaker's assistant and got her name. The body speaks its own language. They were married on the day they met, and though she was twenty years older than her husband and far more learned, Kedato Panandi was a gentle, intelligent man, and together they were able to make a marriage of love and of respect. Theirs was the same story told in a thousand romantic tales out of history. (No one tells the stories with bad endings.) Read any of these to understand my father.

Like his older brother, Liam Panandi too had traveled alone a third of the way around the ring of the world, stopping at every enclave he passed to visit the matchmaker and enter his blood pattern into the local market pool. But he had not found a lover yet.

Who hasn't paused to wonder why the world is made this way? Our dogs, and the animals that run wild, are all able to mate freely: any male and any female of their species together stand a good chance of producing offspring. So why is life harder for men and women? Why do our bodies speak in individual languages that almost no one else can understand?

"Because the goddess who left us here was wicked and cruel." That's what Liam growled, that first night he was with us, still surly from the road, and I thought he might be right. Who else but a wantonly powerful goddess could find romance in the notion that only one lover exists for all of us, in all the vast world?

There was no question of Liam and I becoming lovers. We were not a match. But he was only twenty-five while I was already seventeen, and we soon became good friends, hunting and exploring the wilderness around Temple Huacho until my sister complained I had forgotten her name.

Late in that year my father announced a plan to journey to Xahiclan. He liked to travel, so three or four times a year he would take the truck to Halibury or Xahiclan, bringing one of the children along with him each time. I whispered to Liam that we should grab the seats.

I'd heard a rumor in the market that there had been a great flood of silver on the Jowádela Plateau, and that truckers from Xahiclan had since sighted a vast field of newly deposited ruins north of the highway. The site was nearly three hundred miles from Temple Huacho, but Liam and I had fared as far as a hundred miles over roadless wilderness, camping overnight on hilltops before returning home. So three hundred miles didn't sound so far, especially if we could ride most of the way in the truck.

My father was agreeable. So we loaded our off-road bikes onto the truck, shoved our savants in beside them, then climbed into the cab, waving good-bye to my jealous siblings and promising to bring them trophies from the ruins, if there were any to be found.

The morning was brilliant, the air steamy after a night of hard rain. We set off down the hill on a switchback road that had been rebuilt six times in the last year alone, after being destroyed by the night fogs. By contrast, the bramble of sweet raspberries surrounding the road never seemed to change.

That was the fickle nature of the silver: no one could say what its particles would seize and transform, and what would emerge unchanged from its fog, except that animate creatures could not survive the least contact with it—not the deer of the forest or the cats that hunted them, the birds or the insects or the players—and no living thing had ever been returned by it to the world.

That is why in some languages the silver is called *"the fog of souls."* It is true that in their last exhalations the dying breathe forth clouds of silver that sink to the bedding or the floor, and then quickly vanish. This silver is said to contain the memory of the life that has passed, but I have done the math, and in a thousand years there are not enough dead to explain the silver that arises in just one night. So it would seem that human souls are but a small part of the memory of a world.

At the bottom of the hill the brambles came to an end, and shortly after that so did the pavement. For the next sixty miles we made our own road, driving through shallow vales filled with nodding fields of shoulder-high grass.

Long before I was born, a crew of engineers had passed through Kavasphir, laying out a route for an army of road-building kobolds to follow. For three months a smooth ribbon of pavement linked Temple Huacho to the Xahiclan highway. Then the silver rose, and in one night erased the road. What impressed me most about this story was that the road had lasted ninety days. In my lifetime I would expect it to be gone in less than ten.

So there were no roads in Kavasphir, but I didn't mind. The slopes were gentle, and riding in the truck on its gliding suspension, propelled by silent engines through oceans of grass as high as the windows, I would pretend I was a bird, skimming the valleys on my smooth wings, free.

We stopped once in late morning, on a rise of land between two wide vales where a folly had been deposited by a recent flood of silver. It was an arched gateway of blue lapis lazuli sprouting between the rock outcroppings that stood watch in the narrow pass. The gateway's two decorated pillars held up a sloping roof studded with stone dragons peeking out from under the shingle. The surrounding rocks were also decorated, with a frieze depicting a busy enclave populated by thousands of fanciful animals carrying on at tasks of trade and entertainment as if they were players.

My father frowned at the lovely obstruction, and offered his mundane assessment: "It's too narrow to get the truck through." And there was no way to drive around.

But it was early in the day so I wasn't worried. "Out," I said to Liam, pushing him toward the door. "I want to read the inscriptions."

"I can read them from here," Liam said as he slid off the seat and dropped to the ground. "It says, 'Luck and goodwill.' It's what these follies always say."

But Kedato didn't agree. "It's neither one for us if we can't get through."

"We'll get through," I said as I scrambled out of the truck. Then I hurried to read the inscriptions while I still could.

The language was a version of the Ano syllabary: spiky symbols carved deep in the mottled blue stone and painted in gold leaf to make them stand out. I made out "luck" and "prosperity" so Liam was not far wrong. But there was far more that I could not read just yet, so I went to the back of the truck to retrieve my savant.

Kedato and Liam were there, arguing over which kobolds to use against the gate. My father glanced up at me, and smiled. He knew what I had come for. My savant was already unloaded, floating beside him at shoulder height. "Hurry and make your pictures," he said. "We need to be on our way."

"A minute," I assured him. "No more."

I crooked a finger at the device. The savant was a feather-light aerostat, held up by the low pressure of air within its slender wing. Gel lenses at the wing tips gave it sight, and fine wires embedded in its paper-thin shell acted as antennas so it could link to the market. Its surface was mimic, so it could assume the blue color of the day sky and disappear from sight, or drop to ground level and act as a video window when I wished to visit the market at night. The intelligence within it was based on a scholar of ancient languages who had lived in an enclave called Pesmir that was abandoned six hundred years ago when the silver began to encroach upon its borders.

Under my direction the savant surveyed the folly, recording both the carvings and the gateway from every side while Liam made jokes about what the symbols might mean. "This column here," he said, pointing to stacked symbols on the inside of the gateway, "means 'give us a kiss and you can go past.'"

"Give us a bite, more likely," Kedato said. "The silver has left us a pretty gate, but it's in the wrong place. If a trucker making the run to Huacho found himself stopped by this in the late afternoon, it could be his death gate."

That was the hazard of travel: the silver changed things unpredictably. It could build a folly to block a narrow pass, or re-lay a road in a false direction, or leave a wilderness of towering stone where a road used to be. Truckers passed news of changes into the market— assuming the hilltop antennas were still standing, which wasn't always true. Temple Huacho was cut off from the market several times every year when silver broke our chain of communication.

My father had selected his kobolds. They were a model of lithophores, stone eaters. Tiny as termites, they worked in much the same way. He emptied a vial of the little mechanics along both sides of the gateway. Their gray bodies crawled off in random directions until one stumbled into the stone. It must have emitted a signal, because all the others instantly turned and joined it. They set to work, chewing passages into the lapis rock, so that after a few seconds all that could be seen of them was a fine stream of dust dribbling out of a hundred tiny holes.

We sat on the ground beyond the gate and had a light lunch and waited.

From this ridge we could look ahead into the next valley. It was much like the one we had just left, carpeted in green shoulder-high grass, with broad-leafed trees owning the higher slopes. I watched a herd of antelope foraging on the western side; only the sharp points of their long horns were visible above the grass.

"It must have been a major flood to reach this high," Liam said.

I glanced back at the lapis gate, then up at the hilltops and saw what he meant. Silver flowed downhill, which meant that both valleys must have been flooded to several hundred feet before the tide could drown this pass. Only the peaks of the rocks that framed the gate could have remained above it . . . unless the flood had started here on the ridge?

Kedato said, "It was a flood like this that took Jolly."

I glanced at my scar, and frowned.

My father spoke again, in a voice soft and thoughtful, while I watched the antelope leave the grass to disappear one by one into the forest. "In all my traveling, I've never seen a land as turbulent as these hills. They say it's worse in the high mountains or in the basin of the Iraliad, but no one wants to live in those places. This"—his hand swept in a gesture that took in the valley before us—"it's a beautiful land, but never at rest. Never safe."

This was the silver as a creative force, one that reworked the shape of the land, creating new landforms and bringing veins of pure metals and semiprecious building stone writhing into existence.

More fascinating to me was the silver as memory, the dreaming goddess who remembered the past, trading it sometimes for the present, so that an ancient, undisturbed forest might stand for centuries on a high mesa, until some great silver flood washed it away, rearing a ruined enclave in its place—one that had disappeared into the silver thousands of years before, or so we told ourselves.

But even when the silver brought forward objects from the past, it did not rebuild them exactly as they must have been.

The folly that blocked our road might truly have been made of lapis lazuli in its first life, but I have seen newly laid roads of jade running for miles from nowhere to nowhere. I have seen walls of sulphur and statues of salt, or quartz-lined pools in wilderness vales, connected to no other structure.

The silver returned ancient texts too, but most often as fossilized lettered stone in which the writing was compressed, and illegible. Only in rare specimens could fragments be read—though I was always happy to try my skill. Languages came easily to me. They were my talent. Not that I was quick to figure them out. It was just that I already knew them, and only had to struggle to recover the memory, no doubt carried forward from my past lives.

As I sat on that ridge, with the sun climbing toward noon and a soft breeze whispering in the grass below us, I tried to imagine what it would be like to live in a quieter time, when silver came rarely and then only in shallow tides that rejuvenated the lowland soil but did little more. What would it be like to be alive in a time when things did not change? When there was no danger, no threat of anything new? I could not imagine it. In the Kavasphir Hills the past was always erupting, while at the same time everything was kept fresh and new by the silver's flood. When I thought about what had happened to Jolly I hated the silver, but I could not envision a world without it.

We waited an hour, then we climbed back into the truck. The lapis gateway looked the same, but it was not. My father ordered the truck forward. "Brace yourselves," he said. I grabbed the dash. Liam held on to the door. The wide front bumper struck the two pillars and the truck shuddered. Kedato ordered it to reverse. As we wheeled backward the pillars crumbled, launching a dense cloud of blue dust into the air as they collapsed in twin heaps of rotten stone. We put the windows up as Kedato drove the truck forward again, the fat tires climbing easily over debris that collapsed like chalk under our weight. The kobolds we had released would continue to process the rock to powder, so there would be no barrier to block the next convoy that came this way.

North of the Kavasphir Hills the land rose gradually through a country of dense brush bright with purple flowers and swarms of bees that kept pinging against the truck's windshield as we followed a grassy track toward the highway. Copses of small-leaved trees grew in the gullies, their highest branches barely rising above the general grade of the land so that it looked as if they were hunkering down against an expected storm. The wind could blow fiercely off the Jowádela Plateau, but that day the air was hot and still. It was an ancient, weather-worn land, less subject to silver storms than either the plateau or the Kavasphir Hills—which was why it hosted the highway between Halibury and Xahiclan.

We reached the highway—a ribbon of textured white concrete just wide enough for two trucks to pass—near noon, and turned east, running at forty miles an hour on an easy grade. We slowed when a herd of pygmy horses bolted out of the brush and across the highway just in front of us, and again, when a jackal wandered onto the edge of the concrete, standing in the baking heat to watch us pass.

The jackal reminded me of Moki. Both dogs were the same size, though Moki, with his short back and red coat, was much handsomer. He'd become my dog since Jolly was taken, and I felt a pang of guilt for leaving him home, but ruins were often filled with hazards and I didn't want him getting in trouble.

"Look," Liam said, pointing ahead to where the road could be seen through a heat haze, swinging north in a wide loop as it climbed toward the Jowádela Plateau. A flash of sunlight on metal caught my eye.

"A convoy," my father said.

Liam squinted past the windshield. "Three trucks, I'd say."

My father nodded. "They'll be on their way to Halibury, with a stay at Temple Kevillin tonight."

My father would be staying at Temple Nathé. He expected to be in Xahiclan by early afternoon on the following day.

We watched the convoy approach and as it drew near we stopped for a quick exchange of news. The other drivers wanted to know if we'd had trouble. That was always the first question my father was asked because he didn't drive in a convoy. Professional truckers won't go out alone because a breakdown could leave them stranded on the road overnight, a predicament that would be fatal if the silver came. My father assured them we were fine, and invited them to stop at Temple Huacho, if they ever came that way again. They had stayed at Temple Nathé the night before, and they reported the highway to be in good condition all the way to Xahiclan.

We said good-bye, and a few minutes later the truck downshifted as we began the climb to the Jowádela Plateau. A call came in. I answered, and found my mother looking up at me in surprise from the mimic panel on the dash. "Jubilee? You're still there?"

I nodded. My father planned to drop us off at the edge of Jowádela, another half hour at most. "We're a little behind schedule," I said. "There was a folly in the road. It took time to clear." It occurred to me that she had called expecting me to be gone.

She looked over at Kedato. "Where are you, then?"

"Climbing to the plateau. Don't worry, love. There's plenty of daylight left. It's these two"—he nodded at Liam and me—"who will be taking their chances."

My mother looked at me again, her manner almost furtive. "Are you and Liam still going to see the ruins?"

"Of course. Mama, what's wrong?"

She bit her lip. Then she looked again at Kedato and said, "We need to talk."

Her worry leaped to him. "Tola, is something wrong? Are the children—"

"They're fine. Nothing's wrong. Kedato, I'll call again later—"

"No. Jubilee, hand me the headphones."

I didn't like it, but I did as I was told, retrieving the headphones from a dash compartment and passing them to my father. He put them on. Then he shut off the mimic panel and stared grimly ahead at the white road, listening. Liam put his hand on my shoulder while I searched my father's expression for some hint of what this call might be about. The last thing I expected to see was the grin that spread like dawn across his somber face. He said, "I'm *not* laughing."

Liam and I exchanged a look of raised eyebrows.

"Tola," Kedato went on, "this is not bad news . . . Yes, yes, of course . . . Yes, I'm going to tell her . . . No, I'm not worried. She's a sensible girl, and there's time . . . All right. I'll have her call you later. I love you too. Good-bye." He pulled off the headphones and tossed them on the dash, wearing a grin like a man who has just conceived his first baby.

"What?" Liam and I spoke the question at the same time.

Kedato shrugged, enjoying his moment. "The matchmaker has found a lover for Jubilee, that's all." Then he did laugh, while Liam and I stared, too stunned to speak.

His name was Yaphet Harorele and he was exactly my age, seventeen. My mother had seen a picture of him and reported that he was handsome. Most young men are.

"Your mother was reluctant to tell you the news," Kedato explained, "because she was afraid you would take it into your stubborn head to run away, and it's a dangerous journey. So the news is not all good. Though this boy is young and handsome, he lives very far away. Seventeen hundred miles away, in an enclave called Vesarevi. The northern reaches of the Plain of the Iraliad lie between you, and beyond that the Reflection Mountains. Crossing those wastes would make the shortest journey, but not the safest. The silver storms in the Iraliad are legendary. The worst in the world, some say. Better to journey north, to the coastal road. The way is long, but most of that road is reportedly in good shape . . . though at some points you'd have to travel by sea." He sighed. "I traveled by sea only once. I would not want to do it again."

"Neither would I," Liam said darkly. "There's no shelter from the silver there."

Kedato nodded. His smile returned. "Well. You're young, Jubilee. Too young, your mother says, and she's right. We won't allow you to go. Not now. And the boy's father . . ." Kedato hesitated, a flush warming his dark cheeks. "Well, apparently the boy's father is unwilling to let him travel at all. He has only this child—"

"Only one child?" I interrupted. I had never heard of any family with only one child.

"It's what we were told. The mother is deceased. Some kind of accident, not long after the boy was born."

"You mean after *Yaphet* was born," Liam said, startling me with the sullen anger in his voice. "His name is Yaphet."

Kedato looked at him, his expression carefully neutral. "You are happy for us, Liam?"

I felt my cheeks heat, and I did not want to be sitting between them just then. But Liam answered as he should. "Yes. Of course."

"You'll find your lover," Kedato told him. "It's only a matter of time."

Liam turned to stare out the side window. I looked at the road ahead, conscious of his stiff back and my own fear.

My father was puzzled by our gloomy moods. "This is something to celebrate!" he insisted. "You should both come into Xahiclan with me. Jubilee? You're a woman now. Come. Have fun."

But Liam was already shaking his head, and I . . . Though I didn't want to make my father unhappy, I could not bear the thought of facing the crowds in Xahiclan, and my father telling everyone I had a lover and the endless grins and the congratulations because I had won a boy I didn't want and had never seen before. "I think . . . I think I need time to settle my mind, Daddy. Besides, I really did want to see these ruins before anyone else."

Kedato chuckled. "You look as worried as your mother." Then he squeezed my hand. "You're a lucky girl, Jubilee. So lucky. I hope you know that."

"*I do.*" Then I kissed his smooth cheek, and everything was right between us.

As we topped out on the plateau, the ruins came into view for the first time, and we all got out to look. The site was still many miles away across a rolling grassland, but there was no mistaking it. "Look at that!" my father exclaimed. "It's an actual *city*."

There was no other word for it. Standing on the bumper of the truck, I could see hundreds of low white buildings surrounding two white towers that thrust their spires up above the shimmering heat waves of midafternoon. Even Xahiclan was not two-thirds this size.

"Now I wish I was going with you," Kedato said. "I've never heard of the silver returning a ruin so large."

"So stay," I urged him, suddenly aware we would not have many more years together.

"I can't. There are shipments to make, and appointments to keep. Reputation is everything."

Liam was rolling his bike down the ramp at the back of the truck. "So if there's anything worth looking at, we'll all three return here, as soon as you get back."

"Yes," I said. "That's what we'll do. You'll come, won't you, Dad?"

"Of course." He put his arm around my shoulder. Liam had returned to the truck to get my bike. "I'll miss you when you finally go, Jubilee."

"Dad! I'm not going yet."

"You'd better not." We hugged. Then he spoke softly, so that Liam couldn't overhear. "Your mother will send you Yaphet's market address. He has yours. It's only fair."

I nodded. Then he was back in the truck, waving good-bye and ordering us to be careful. "I'll be home in a week," he promised, and I believed him, though I've learned since that promises are not always possible to keep.

Chapter

3

"Liam, are you angry?"

He was astride his bike, his sunglasses on so I couldn't see his eyes.

He shrugged. "So. Maybe a little." We had talked of wayfaring together when he was ready to return to the road. Now he would have to go on alone.

The afternoon was hot and still. There were no clouds, and the sky had been baked to a pale, pale blue. "It wasn't supposed to happen like this," I said. "I don't think I'm ready."

"Don't you dare complain, Jubilee. You've won the prize."

So I had.

I looked out across the rolling plain of grass to the distant city shimmering in the heat. "I've never been anywhere, Liam. I've never done anything."

"So go visit him. Go to live with him! That journey should give you all the adventure you'll ever want."

"I wish the matchmaker had found a lover for you instead."

He sighed. "So maybe I'll go with you when the time comes. Maybe there'll even be someone there for me, and you and I, we'll live close together. Kedato's right, Jubilee. You have a lot of luck about you. Do you think it could stretch that far?"

"I don't know. I hope so." It was a strange kind of luck I had; a kind that didn't make me happy.

"Come on," Liam said. "Let's get going. It's later than I like."

He nodded toward the city. "If those towers are accessible, we can stay in them tonight. But if not, it's going to be a long run to Olino Mesa."

I nodded. We would need to be in some kind of sanctuary by nightfall, in case the silver should rise. High ground was safest. If we could get into one of the towers we could camp on an upper floor, where we'd be beyond the reach of all but the worst silver storms. But if the towers were closed to us, we'd have to cross a hundred miles of wilderness to reach Olino Mesa, the only significant eminence on the plateau. Of course, even if we were forced to camp on the plain, the odds favored us, for in this country the silver still came only an average of one night in ten. But when it's your life being gambled, one in ten odds are not so good.

I climbed onto my bike, balanced it, then kicked up the stand. "I hope Yaphet stays home, and that I'm the one to do the traveling."

Liam grinned. "Your mother knew you'd feel that way. It's why she didn't want to tell you about Yaphet." He touched his ignition and his bike whispered to life, a soft purr of pumps. "I don't know anything about this boy of yours, Jubilee, but I can tell you that no father of mine would have been able to keep me home if I found a lover like you."

I blushed, then looked down, fumbling at the ignition switch to start my bike.

"Put your glasses on," Liam said.

I did. Then, in a small voice, I whispered my greatest fear. "What if I hate him?"

"It won't matter."

"Liam! Don't say that."

He studied me a moment through his dark sunglasses. Then he turned back to the city. "It'll be all right for you, Jubilee. Don't worry. But it's late. We need to go."

The plateau was a softly undulating land, covered in crisp brown, waist-high grasses that hid the dry streambeds riddling its surface like cracks in the glaze of a dropped dinner plate. We followed the drainages when we could—that way at least we couldn't fall into them—but the dry streams meandered in lazy paths while we knew our destination. So we spent the better part of an hour stirring up clouds of dust as we slid in or climbed out of a chaos of shallow gullies. We disturbed a few rabbits and a small herd of ankle deer, but it was a blue hawk, drifting overhead, that marked our arrival at the city.

We stopped just short of a stark boundary. The grasslands of the plateau ran up against the gleaming white stone of low buildings separated by equally white streets that looked as if they had been sliced off from outlying neighborhoods by some great knife. Stark, brilliant white was the color of every surface, even the shingled rooftops, which caught the sunlight and split it apart, so that the buildings were haloed in a rainbow glow. Despite its weight, despite its great size—the city was larger by far than the enclaves of Halibury and Xahiclan together—it had about it a sense of impermanence as if it might melt in a rain, or crumble in a drying wind, or vanish overnight into another silver flood like the one that had created it. It made me think of some gigantic fancy of sugar crystal. I wondered if it might really be sugar, or salt. When we advanced to the city's edge I tasted a wall, but it was not.

Many of the buildings looked as if they'd been reworked by silver, perhaps many times, before the whole city was finally taken. Their walls were melted, the white stone puddled in round lenses that sent dancing heat shimmers rising into the baking air. Liam looked grim as he surveyed the damage. "If the silver touched only the outlying buildings at first, then the residents might have had time to get away before the final flood came."

That was the way history described the erosion of an enclave. A failing temple could not produce enough kobolds to ward off the silver. As the defensive perimeter thinned, silver would creep over the walls, licking first at the outlying buildings, then moving deeper into the city's heart on each subsequent night. Only someone with a death wish would stay to meet it.

Our world had existed for thousands upon thousands of years.

That was clear from the fragmented histories that had come down to us, but most of the past was lost, washed away by time and silver floods. Uncounted enclaves have vanished from the world and no one now remembers their names. I could not guess what city this might have been, or how long its memory had been preserved in the silver before it was finally rebuilt by the flood. Perhaps it had been swallowed up only yesterday, in some far land on the other side of the world. Or perhaps it had existed in an epoch recalled by no one for a thousand years.

I walked along the city's perimeter, gazing down the narrow streets, each much like the one before it. Nothing moved among the buildings that I could see, not even birds.

Choosing a street at random we entered the city, walking our bikes between ornate buildings three and four stories high, their arched windows sealed with panes of clear glass. Heat reflecting off the street and the buildings had sent the temperature soaring, even above the oppressive heat of the open plateau. It might have been a hundred ten degrees in that little street. Sweat shone on my bare arms and shoulders, and my sunglasses weren't nearly dark enough.

We tried the doors on several buildings, but none of them could be opened. They were like decorative panels—imitation doors cast in the same pour of stone that had made the walls. We peered through the windows but saw only barren rooms. There was no furniture, no shelves, no art of any kind. No books. Each sealed room appeared empty and pristine. "As if no one ever lived here," Liam muttered.

Then we found a building with double doors standing open. They were false doors like all the others, part of the solid block of the house so that they could not be swung shut, but at least we could get inside.

I entered, hoping the open doors would mean this house had a different history from all the rest, but I was disappointed. The rooms were as empty as those we'd seen through windows. We wandered the house, looking into every open room and climbing the stairs. All the walls, all the floors, and even the ceiling were made of the same white stone. The only other element was the glass in the windows, but the windows would not open. There were no plumbing fixtures, no panels for lights, no mechanism for electricity. The monotony was unsettling, as if we had stumbled onto a stage set being prepared for some terrible drama.

"There's no point in doing a house-to-house," Liam said, "if all the houses are like this."

I nodded. Already I was hungering for some color other than white. "Let's find the towers." We needed to know if we could spend the night here, or if we would have to move on.

So we returned to the street, and rode swiftly for the city center.

The engines of our bikes made only a soft hum, and the sound of their tires was like the sound of gentle rain, but in that empty city even these slight noises reverberated like the carousing of vandals.

We rode for a mile, until our street ended suddenly at a wide square, at least two acres in size, surrounded on all sides by decaying buildings that must have once been beautiful. Most had wide stairs and columns and graceful balconies, but all of them were badly damaged. Many had collapsed roofs. Some had fallen walls that had spilled white rubble into the square, each fragment a perfect cube. But it wasn't the buildings that commanded my attention.

At the center of the square was a working fountain. Thin jets of clear water rose from all around its edge, arching inward for a few feet before falling back to the pool in a splashing rainbow of light. In the center of this pool was a large circular platform raised a foot above the water. It was perhaps a hundred feet in diameter, and rising from its center was a white mast.

The mast was a gigantic structure. It dominated the square, reaching at least ten stories high, and I knew at once that this was the smaller tower we had seen from the highway. A cross pole branched from it at half its height, with arms as wide as the island platform. A second cross pole, half as wide, branched at right angles above the first, and two successively smaller spars split off near the top. White ropes trailed from these arms, their ends touching the stone like the broken strands of some abandoned spiderweb.

I could not imagine what purpose such a structure might serve. I tried to picture it as an antenna, but why give an antenna a position of such prominence in the city? Maybe it was to display banners? But it looked too massive, too powerfully built for that purpose. "Perhaps it's a folly of the silver," I said softly.

Liam shook his head. "I don't think that's it." He squinted at the mast, like an artist bent on seeing a scene in its essential shapes. "I think I've seen something like this before . . . in a picture maybe."

"I don't like it. It gives me a bad feeling."

"This whole city is a nasty place. Have you noticed we haven't passed a single temple?"

I hadn't noticed, but now that he mentioned it, I knew it was true. Temples have a distinctive architecture, with their sprawling walls and one-story structures. We'd seen nothing like that since entering the city. I nodded at the monstrosity in the square: "So what do you think this is?"

"I don't know. I just feel like I *should* know." He swung off his bike, kicked down the stand, then opened one of the compartments behind the seat. His savant was there, packed within the thin cushion of his sleeping bag. He took it out, unfolded its narrow wing, and released it. It drifted before him, its silver skin shimmering. "Find a match for this scene if you can," Liam instructed it. Then he turned to me. "Let's get out of the sun."

We drank water and ate chocolate on a veranda held up by tall columns carved to resemble the trunks of royal palms. Our water supply was dwindling rapidly, so I took the filter and walked out into the sun again, filling all our empty water cells from the fountain. There was no wind at all to stir the air and the heat had become overwhelming. Actually frightening. I had never felt anything like it before and I dreaded returning to the narrow streets where the temperature was sure to be even higher. But we would have to move on soon. We needed to know if the second tower could offer us refuge for the night, or if we would have to make the long run to Olino Mesa.

Whether it was the heat or the anxiety this city wakened in me I cannot say, but as I returned to the veranda's shade I was conscious of my heart fluttering in a weak and rapid beat like the heart of a frightened bird. Liam was sitting cross-legged on the floor of the veranda, studying the mimic screen of his savant. "Did you find something?" I asked as I collapsed beside him.

"Yes. I know where we are now." He nodded at the screen.

I wiped the sweat out of my eyes and leaned forward. Displayed on his mimic screen was a ghastly painting. I could see the texture of the paint, so I knew it was not a true image, but that did little to assuage my horror. Pictured there was the very square where we found ourselves, but changed. The white buildings were all of dark gray stone. Thousands of people crowded the pavement, most of them men in uniforms of black and red. Black banners were draped from the balconies of the encircling buildings, while black flags flew from the top of the mast and from the ends of its cross poles. The purpose of the mast was quite clear. At least a hundred tiny figures hung from the cross poles, suspended by black ropes tied about their necks. Their faces were covered, but their legs were shown in postures of kicking, twisting agony. All of them had their hands tied behind their backs.

"Mother of all!" I whispered, and turned away, wishing I had not looked, and that I didn't know.

Liam cleared the mimic screen. "The painting is ancient. It's supposed to be an illustration of the crusade of Fiaccomo."

"Fiaccomo?" I knew that name. Everyone did, for Fiaccomo was a legendary figure.

It was said that in the beginning of the world the silver obeyed the will of players and all was paradise. Then the dark god came, and the goddess withdrew from the world to wage war against him. The silver vanished with her, and players were left without food or tools or clothing or the simplest pleasures, for all such things had come to them through the silver. Great armies formed to fight over what remained. Hunger and war were everywhere, and so many players died that none of those left could find a lover and there were no children. The world lay on the edge of ruin.

Fiaccomo had been trained as a warrior, but he loved life, and could not bear to see the world die. So he gathered about him brave players, and together they fought their way past the scavenging armies and ventured into the high mountains, where it was said traces of the goddess might still be found.

The goddess had won her victory over the dark god, but not without cost. The battle had left her wounded and delirious. When Fiaccomo's entreaties caused her to turn her mind again to the world she was horrified to behold her beautiful land all in ruins and her beloved players sunk in wickedness and war. She came upon the band of heroes in a fury, and in the guise of a silver flood she swept all those good players away. Among them, only Fiaccomo kept his wits. Even as his mind dissolved in the silver, he whispered to the goddess all the desires of his heart, and his passion was so like hers that she loved him, and their minds entwined in a kind of lovemaking never known in the world before and never since, and in those moments of union Fiaccomo seized the creative power of the silver and dreamed the first kobolds into existence.

The goddess gave Fiaccomo back his life, and more, she gave him a gift that he could pass through the silver unscathed, and command its flow when he had need. He returned to the world bringing with him both the silver and the kobolds, and prosperity followed after him, and peace.

That was the legend as I knew it, but the painting Liam had found did not show a time of prosperity or of peace.

"It doesn't make sense, Liam. This city is a real place. But Fiaccomo is a myth . . . isn't he?"

"I wouldn't know."

"No one can survive the silver," I insisted. "No one can pass through it unscathed."

"I won't argue it with you, Jubilee. I have only told you what the painting is supposed to show."

I looked out across the brilliant white square, but it was the dark painting I saw.

The past is deep and jumbled and more than half-counterfeited, or so I believe, and we, even with the help of our savants, can recall it only as we recall our dreams, in fragments detached from beginnings and ends. This city had gone through the silver and it was clean to look upon, but it did not feel clean. "Was Fiaccomo supposed to be one of those hanging from the mast?"

"The document didn't say. But it occurs to me, Jubilee, that in an age without silver or kobolds, there would be no reason to build temples."

I thought about that, until Liam insisted we move on.

A wide, straight boulevard on the far side of the square led directly to the second tower. It rose high into the cloudless blue sky, its smooth white walls tapering to a narrow summit. Arched windows looked out from a dozen different floors. They did not appear to have glass in them. "If we can get up to the top," Liam said, "we should be safe."

A low flight of broad steps led up to the tower's entrance. We rode our bikes up, the tires bending around the angles of the stairs so that our ride remained smooth and secure. Great double doors stood open, as if inviting us to enter. The first floor was surrounded by the arched windows we had seen from the street. As we had guessed, they were without glass, so light and air passed freely to the inside.

The interior was a single room that encircled a central column where another set of huge doors—I suspected they were elevator doors—looked back at us, but these were closed. "Want to bet we can't get them open?" Liam asked.

"No thank you."

We stopped briefly to inspect them, but Liam was right: the closed doors were purely ornamental, like all the others we had seen in this city. "Maybe there's another way up?" I suggested, trying to sound more confident than I felt. The afternoon was waning, and I did not want to be caught on the open plateau when evening fell.

"Stairs, you're thinking?" Liam asked.

"It's worth looking."

So we rode our bikes around the column, and there it was: a stairwell, with its door standing ajar, just wide enough to allow a bike to pass.

I stopped beside it, and looked in. Daylight reached just far enough to show me a short flight of white stairs that turned back on themselves at a narrow landing. I was surprised to feel a hot breeze flowing over my shoulders and tugging at the strands of my hair, blowing *into* the stairwell as if it were a great chimney piping hot air up. "Feel that wind?" I asked. "There must be an opening somewhere above." Then I backed up my bike, and gave him a chance to look.

He peered inside. Then, "Awfully convenient," he said, turning to look at me over his shoulder.

I nodded. "Like we were expected. Does the silver have a sense of humor?"

"Oh, yes," Liam said. "Sharpest in the world."

He flicked on his headlight. Then he eased his bike through the door while I followed after him.

The stair rose in a zigzag column beside the elevator shaft, with a tight, 180-degree turn at the end of each flight. I had to put a foot down for balance and skid the back tire of my bike at every landing while my headlight glittered crazily across white walls. After three flights we found a door, but it was closed and useless. Three flights higher there was another door, also closed. But we could still feel hot air rushing up the stairwell, so we kept going.

We went up past nine floors until finally, on the tenth story, we found an open door. Sunlight spilled onto the landing, but there were no dust motes drifting in the air and that absence seemed as strange as anything I had seen that day.

I followed Liam into the room. It circled the tower's central column just as the room on the first floor had, though this one was much smaller. Not surprisingly, it was also empty.

I stopped at a window and looked down on the city, blazing white in the afternoon light, with a rainbow iridescence above the rooftops that gave it the aura of a mirage. "It's too clean," I said softly. "Too perfect. There's no dirt. No insects. No birds." I shook my head, groping to explain what was troubling me. "Even if this city came out of the silver looking like this, it should be showing some wear by now. Some dust or bird dung at least."

"But there's nothing," Liam said.

"It's like some invisible curator has been keeping it tidy."

"Don't scare yourself."

I raised my chin. I didn't want him to think I was afraid. "Do you want to spend the night here? We're high enough. It should be safe."

I was half hoping he would say no, and instead opt for the long sprint to Olino Mesa. But he kicked down the stand of his bike and dismounted. "It's so late now, we don't really have a choice."

Chapter

4

We were not quite at the top of the tower. There was one more floor above us, but the door to it was closed and sealed, and we did not have the proper tools or kobolds to take it down. So we returned to our room, where a cool breeze soughed through arched windows.

We shared a chilled water cell. Liam splashed some of the water on his face, leaving dark streaks of dust. "Do you want to go out again?" he asked.

We had at least two hours before sunset, but I was afraid to face the heat of the streets, so I shook my head. "It's too hot. I'm going to rest."

"Good. I feel the same."

I looked out the window, at the sheets of rainbow light shimmering over the rooftops. "Anyway, it's not like we've found anything."

"Finding the square was something." He pulled a sleeping bag from his saddle bin. "I wonder how old this city is? Ten thousand years? More?"

Who could say? History is deeper than anyone can measure, and as chaotic as the silver. The past is carried forward into the present, while the present is washed away, to be used again in some other age, or so it seemed to me.

"Let's look around some more tomorrow," I said. "We can stay until it gets hot. Then head for home."

We inflated our sleeping bags and Liam fell asleep immediately, but my mind was restless. I lay staring at the blue sky, thinking about the square, and the tiny bodies suspended on ropes. My mind could not cease a lurid speculation on the details of life in an age without silver, or kobolds, or any temple to shelter them. I tried to imagine Fiaccomo as something more than a myth, but I could not. Players cannot pass through the silver unscathed, any more than they can breathe the salty water of the ocean. Living things never emerge from the luminous fogs.

After a while I sat up and gazed out the window again, but southeast this time, to the highway, where I thought I saw the gleam of a passing truck. It was late though, and no truck should have been on that part of the highway at such an hour, so perhaps it was only imagination.

It seemed a long time since we'd said good-bye to my father. I wondered where he was. And I wondered too about the boy, Yaphet Harorele, who I had never seen and never met and who was to be my lover. What was he doing now in faraway Vesarevi? What was he thinking? Would he approve of our expedition to this city? Or would he judge it a dangerous waste of time? I wondered, and before long I decided that the answer to such a question would reveal a lot about a person. Maybe, it would reveal everything that mattered.

Our savants had already been unpacked, their narrow wings unfolded and set adrift near the doorway. I beckoned to mine, signaling it to follow me around to the other side of the room, where the central pillar would lie between me and Liam.

I sat down on the floor next to the window, my elbow resting on the sill while the savant floated before me, awaiting instructions. "Are there messages?" I asked in a hushed voice, not wanting Liam to waken.

I was expecting only one message from my mother with Yaphet's market address, but there was another, and that was from Yaphet himself. I immediately sent it to the savant's mimic screen, intensely curious to know what he had written.

The message displayed in a formal script:

Dear Jubilee,

My father celebrates, but I need to know who you are. Will you meet me? If you will, come soon. There is only one channel open between us as I write, and night is coming.

Yaphet

I smiled. It was a terse note, but it was one I might have written myself and I liked him—or the idea of him—better after reading it. I tapped the market address that was attached to the note, signaling my savant to find a link. That took some time, and I began to worry that the last channel had indeed gone down. Yaphet lived beyond the Plain of the Iraliad and the Reflection Mountains, all of it dangerous land where only a few relay antennas were maintained. If one crucial tower fell to the silver there might not be another link to Vesarevi for weeks to come.

I had nearly given up hope of getting through when the mimic screen flashed with a yellow warning placard. At least it wasn't red! I leaned forward to read it:

Automatic Notice
Inadequate system resources require market
time to be rationed in five-minute segments.
Tap to begin.

I drew a deep breath. Five minutes. Maybe I wouldn't want to talk to him longer than that anyway. I listened for Liam's breathing, to be sure he was still asleep, then I tapped the placard. It minimized to a tiny clock in the mimic screen's lower corner, counting down the time as a view opened onto a dimly lit room furnished in wood and dark colors. A young man was standing beside a night-black window, his figure half-hidden in shadow. Yaphet? I assumed it must be him. Stars blazed beyond him, bisected by the white shimmer of the Bow of Heaven rising up from the horizon.

Yaphet turned. He approached me, and as he did a warm light from somewhere behind my point of view fell across him.

My mother had reported Yaphet to be pretty and I could not disagree. His build was lean, and that was attractive to me though he did not seem tall. I guessed he was no taller than me. He had thick black hair in a heavy braid down his back; unruly bangs; skin like toast. He wore a green shirt that was almost black, and a necklace of white beads that were probably pearls. All this I took in at a glance, before his eyes seized my attention. Deep blue they were, like the sky at sunset but hard, like a gem a kobold has made. Memory whispered through me, reechoing from the past lives we must have shared together, and I shivered, for I sensed an obsession in him, a dreadful vision that would own him.

I can safely say that Yaphet did not see anything so interesting in me. He studied me for several seconds, his so-serious eyes veneered darkly with distaste, until I remembered myself, my flushed and dirty face, my hair wound into dreads by wind and sweat. I had not washed, or even bothered to smooth my hair, and yet here I was, facing for the first time the boy who would likely be my life mate. It was an absurd introduction. Too absurd for me to do anything but tip my head back and laugh, gulping and gasping as softly as I could so as not to waken Liam.

"This is a wrong address, isn't it?" Yaphet asked in a flat voice that did not hide his anger.

"No." I ran my fingers over my tangled hair, suddenly afraid he would leave. I wiped at my sticky face with the back of my hand. "I'm Jubilee Huacho." Maybe I should not have admitted it? "I'm not always this bad," I added softly, listening for any sound of Liam stirring.

Yaphet frowned and looked past me at the arched window and the sky beyond. "It's still afternoon there."

I nodded, remembering the night sky outside his window. The world is a ring that spins in the plane of the sun and Yaphet was far to the east, so night came sooner for him.

"You're high up, aren't you?" he asked. "Are you at home?"

"No." In a furtive voice, I told him about Liam and the city, the strange square and the painting, and our plans to spend the night here above the reach of any common silver flood. As I spoke I turned the savant to the window so Yaphet could see the city—it was a nice view, and the less time he spent looking at me, the better. That was my opinion.

He spoke too, telling me that in the market at Vesarevi there were respected historians who thought Fiaccomo might have been a real player. When our eyes met again he looked at me with more respect.

"Are you thinking of coming here?" he asked suddenly.

His bluntness caught me by surprise, and I blurted out an honest answer: "I don't know. I—I've thought about it . . . but it's happened so fast . . ."

Yaphet nodded "I understand. I didn't plan on finding a lover this soon. I'm sure you didn't either."

True enough. "At least you're not an idiot," I said with real gratitude—and that was the first time I saw him smile. It was only a little smile, one that might have gone unnoticed on anyone else, but I had already gathered that for Yaphet, smiles were rare.

"Only twenty seconds left," he said. "Will you call me later?"

A glance at the clock showed he was right. "I'll call tomorrow night, after I get home, if the channel's still—" His image vanished, replaced by a yellow placard announcing our time was over.

At twilight Liam and I went out again. We wandered the empty streets for over an hour, marveling at the heat still radiating from the walls. It felt strange to be wandering about so close to nightfall, but this was our last chance to escape the tower before dawn. We stayed out longer than we should have, but we returned safely, with the stars blazing in a sky of deepest blue. I sat by an eastern window, watching the Bow of Heaven brighten and remembering how it had looked outside Yaphet's window. It was brilliant tonight: a narrow, gossamer bridge of white light rising from the horizon to the zenith, passing out of sight beyond the tower's roof.

"I haven't seen the Bow so bright in at least a year," Liam said as he sat down beside me, with a couple of ration packs in hand for our dinner. He asked his savant to give us some light, and we talked together, about anything but Yaphet. Then I called my mother to let her know we were well and sometime after that I fell asleep.

I awoke in the night with the feeling of being watched.

We had left our savants on alert, one by the door, and one set to slowly circle around the room. Neither had called an alarm, and yet somehow I knew we were no longer alone in our tower room. I lay in my sleeping bag, staring wide-eyed at arched shadows cast by starlight against the chamber's smooth inner wall. Why was every surface in this ancient city so clean, so perfect? Was it possible that some unseen curator had accompanied the ruins down through time?

Liam breathed beside me and from far overhead a passing night bird called an eerie song but nothing else stirred. Nothing I could directly sense, yet my feeling of unease did not go away. After a few minutes I sat up, and leaning on the windowsill, I looked out at the city. It gleamed faintly under the press of starlight like a diaphanous, half-imagined thing. A city of mist that might disintegrate on the least breeze. I searched the streets for silver, but I could see none.

A puff of warm air brushed my ear, like a breath. I whirled around to face the room, sure I had heard a whisper, a question that was a single word, though the language was not one I knew.

But the room was as it had been. The only sound was Liam's soft breathing.

I slipped out of my sleeping bag and I searched the chamber. I examined the walls and the ceiling on the chance that there might be a lens or a hidden doorway. In this way I circled the entire chamber before I finally saw it: a shape on the inside wall, a white shadow, barely brighter than the wall itself. It was almost human in outline, though the legs were too long and slim, the waist too narrow. It looked like a lithe woman in caricature, though she was only four feet tall. The gleam of her disappeared if I looked at her directly. I could see her only when I turned my head and looked from the corner of my eye, but when I did that I could clearly see she was gazing down at Liam.

I shivered, and nudged him gently with my toe. *"Liam."* Then I called his name louder, *"Liam!"*

He woke suddenly, raising himself on an elbow. "Jubilee? What . . . ?"

"Look at that wall before you. Do you see anything there?"

For a moment I feared the shape was only in my imagination, or at most a stain that marked the place where a picture had once hung. But then Liam's gaze fixed on it. He shoved off his sleeping bag and got to his feet, padding past me to the wall. He touched the shape, his fingers following the line of its petite shoulder. It shifted away from his hand, and vanished.

"Liam!"

"It's all right, Jubilee."

Of course it was. I let go a slow breath. "Deep silver, that scared me." I tried to laugh. "These must be mimic walls, partly recharging in the day's heat, and playing some old program—"

"No, that's not it." He gestured to his savant, and it drew near. "Give us some light," he ordered. It lit slowly, casting a warm glow through the room. Liam ran his fingers through his chestnut hair. "What woke you?" he asked.

"I thought I heard a . . . whisper. A question." I had felt a warm breath.

"It was a bogy." He brushed the wall where the shape had been, stroking it with his fingertips as if seeking out some secret message encoded in its texture. "Come out, little one," he crooned. "You have something to say. So show yourself."

"Liam, what's a bogy?"

"A mechanic."

An artificial creature. "Like a savant?" I asked.

"No. Nothing like that. More like a watcher. A place spirit. Some are horrible. Many are very beautiful. But they're not alive, so sometimes they get returned by the silver . . . and it's said some players made them for just that purpose—to hold the memory of a favorite place, when it seemed sure the silver would take it.

"But from all I've heard most have a darker nature, guardians created to keep intruders away or to complete some unwholesome task their owners left unfinished."

I caught a flash of motion to the left and turned. Liam followed my gaze.

There she was—and no faint shadow this time. She had gained definition in the light, and as her tiny hand moved, her fingers—so strangely long and slender—*emerged* from the wall like fingers breaking the surface of water. Liam stepped in front of me. "Stand away," he warned. "It's coming out."

The hand reached from the suddenly fluid wall as if it were pushing a curtain aside. Then the creature leaned forward, and a delicate woman's face peered into the room. Her gaze settled on us as she stepped forth onto the floor.

She was as white as the walls, with eyes that were saved by a small film of iridescence from being as white and blind as a statue's. Her hair was sculpted and fixed in an upswept coiffure. Her body was sculpted too, appearing white and unshadowed and terribly slender as she slipped free of the wall. But she was no starveling: no bones showed through her skin, though nothing else was hidden. She was nude, with long, long legs in no human proportion and small breasts and a sculpted patch of white pubic hair. She smiled coquettishly at Liam. Then she whispered a syllable, the same syllable I had heard before, and again I felt the warmth of her breath.

"Do you know that word?" Liam asked.

I shook my head. The wall behind her looked intact, as if it had given up nothing of its structure. I wanted to knock against it to see if it was still solid, but Liam raised his arm protectively in front of me as if this little mechanic might be a threat. So I went instead to fetch my savant.

There are people who claim to remember the details of their past lives: who they were, what they did, where they lived, and who they loved and hated. Perhaps their claims are true, but I had no such specific memories. The best evidence of my past was a knack for ancient languages. There were nine I could speak and understand in full, and several more in pieces. All of them had come to me easily the first time I heard them spoken, so I can only think they were languages I had used in other lives. I was sure many others still lay undiscovered in my mind, and I hoped to find one that night.

I retrieved my savant from its post at the door. Then I turned to the bogy, and in our own language I asked her, "Can you understand any of the words we say?"

She fixed me with her iridescent eyes, answering in a strange, harsh tongue. I didn't recognize any of her words, and neither did my savant. So I switched to another language, and repeated my question, and when that didn't work I switched to another. That was the charm. The bogy drew back in startled surprise. Then she spoke: not in the language I had just used, but in one somewhat similar.

It was as if a channel had come into focus. Her words suddenly made sense within my mind. She had asked: *"Do you know this one?"*

I did. It was an archaic language, one I had learned from my savant, so old that its origin had been forgotten even in the time of that ancient sage. *"Yes,"* I said. *"I know this tongue."*

The bogy drew herself up. Though she was scarcely four feet tall, she somehow contrived to look down on me with a haughty gaze. *"It is a slave's language."*

I turned a puzzled frown on my savant. "What is this word?"

In its cultured voice the savant explained the meaning of "slave."

Liam's expression became grim. "Translate for me," he said.

I nodded at my savant to convey the order. Then I turned back to the bogy, and speaking her "slave language" in a tone that was none-too-friendly, I said, *"You are from a time very long ago. Much has changed in the world."*

She paid no attention to my words. Instead she listened as my savant whispered its translation to Liam. I had no doubt she understood the implication, for she turned to Liam with a crafty smile. *"Your slave has been plotting against you."* With a nod of her head she indicated me, while the savant dutifully provided Liam with a translation. *"She has been in contact with another slave. Punish her now, and perhaps she can be made to serve properly. If you do not take a strong hand, you will surely have to kill her in the end."*

I knew at once that she was referring to my conversation with Yaphet, and I felt a surge of guilt for it was true that I hadn't mentioned it to Liam.

He glared at the bogy. His face had taken on a dark, rosy flush. His hands were clenched in tight fists and I couldn't tell if he was about to erupt in fury or in laughter.

"I was talking to Yaphet," I said quickly, feeling an irrational need to make this confession. "While you were asleep."

His gaze shifted to me. "Were you?" His voice sounded strained. A smile flitted around his mouth, then disappeared. "Best you behave, Jubilee. Your daddy might not like it if I had to do you harm." He winked at me. Then he turned to the bogy and spoke to it, while my savant translated his words into the "slave's tongue." "You came here to tell me something, didn't you, little one?"

"Your words are not polluted by this slave's dialect."

Quickly I asked, *"How would you say that in your own tongue?"*

I didn't expect the bogy to respond. She obviously thought me beneath her notice, so I was surprised when she spoke her language again, though she addressed her words to Liam, not to me. I repeated her strange words, speaking them softly to myself and immediately I felt a resonance deep in my mind. Liam watched me expectantly. "I think I have it in memory," I told him, "but I need more words."

Liam got them for me. He questioned the bogy, commanding her to respond first in the slave's language, and then to repeat the same thing in the master's dialect, and to my surprise she obeyed, though when I remarked on this, Liam only shrugged. "Calling bogies is a talent of mine. This is the fifth one I've seen."

"You never mentioned it before."

"It's not a talent I would have chosen. They're mostly wicked things, left behind to guard a place or perform a task too distasteful for true players."

That was certainly true of this one. We learned she was a persona based on the ancient queen of this city, though I think she was only a shallow reflection of that evil, without much wisdom or cunning. Despite what I had told her, she believed that only a few days had passed since the silver had drifted over her city. She thought she knew Liam as one of her warlords. This angered him. None of us can be held responsible for our past lives, but it's never pleasant to think of the evil we might have done. She told us that the aristocracy of this city had been supplemented with children who fell within a certain genetic range. They were taken from their slave mothers and made into warriors. Liam was of this class.

But what did it mean that I was quickly learning to speak the language of such a people?

The bogy believed it was Fiaccomo himself who had brought the silver into this city.

All that last week before the silver came there had been public executions of his followers. On the final evening, as the executions progressed, a report arrived from a scout in the hills north of the city. Fiaccomo had been seen. Warriors were sent after him in flying machines—

(Flying machines! I could hardly contain my surprise. Flying machines were like tinder made to ignite a silver storm. Any mechanical device rising into the atmosphere could not go long without attracting an outburst of silver, even in the bright light of noon. But the bogy spoke of flying machines as if they were common devices, and safe.)

The warriors searched until full dark, when all communication with them abruptly failed. Minutes later the silver was sighted, flowing out of the northern hills and down onto the plain. The queen's anger reverberated in the bogy's fierce voice: *"It was Fiaccomo who stirred up this legendary weapon against us, dredging it up from the dead past. We had no defense. Those who mattered escaped in flying machines, but the slaves—Fiaccomo's own people—they all succumbed. I heard them screaming in the streets below and then a silence.*

"But it was not over. Trespassers had gotten into the tower. They crept up the stairs, to this very room, but their insolence did not save them. The silver rose, flooding my windows, floor by floor, until it rolled into this chamber. How they screamed! And well deserved it was, for trespassing in my private rooms.

"The fog lingered for an hour or so past dawn. No one remained when it finally went away. That was nine days ago. Fiaccomo thought he could destroy us with this ancient curse, but now you have come back. Have you found Fiaccomo? Is it time for our counterattack?"

Liam's face was more grim than I had ever seen it. "There will be no counterattack, little one. Not ever. This city is dead and you are a powerless ghost, and I hope you vanish into the silver again, and for all time. Now begone."

Her face contorted in fury at his words, but somehow she could not disobey him. She stumbled sideways, toward the central wall, thrusting a hand out to keep from falling. "You will hang too," she growled. "Traitor."

"Go!" Liam shouted. "Vanish!"

And she did. Her substance flowed back into the wall until not even a shadow of her remained . . . except the shadow she had left on our minds. I could hear her voice speaking in its master's tongue the death sentences of hundreds and it made me dizzy. My head buzzed and I sat down before I could fall.

"Jubilee, are you all right?"

Next thing I knew Liam was crouched beside me with his arm around my shoulders. My skin felt clammy and I didn't know how to answer. "Is it dawn?" I whispered.

"It's close enough."

"Then let's go home."

We packed our things as quickly as we could and we left that city when the sun's light was only a glimmer in the east.

Chapter

5

"Wake up, Yaphet. Yaphet?"

I could see him asleep on his bed beneath the dim glow of a hanging lamp, its globe worked in tiles of colored glass to make flowers purple and yellow in color. The variegated light fell over him, illuminating the high points of his face, accenting the shadows. Sleep gives to some people a look of peace so profound it is almost inhuman. Yaphet had that look. In the shadows he seemed more a memory of an idealized past than a young man of this world.

"Yaphet."

A week had passed since my adventure in the city and in that time I had been able to talk to Yaphet only twice. The market connection to Vesarevi was intermittent and rationed, and tonight the channels were especially bad. My father had called that morning to say he was leaving Xahiclan at last. He was to have called again from Temple Nathé where he would stay the night, but an antenna must have gone down along the highway because we'd had no word from him. So it was a wonder I'd reached Yaphet at all.

"Yaphet!"

He sat up abruptly, the peace on his face replaced by fear as he stared wide-eyed at the door of his room.

"Yaphet, it's me. Jubilee."

He turned to the sound of my voice. His gaze found the mimic screen of his savant, and as he focused on me, the tension went out of him. "Jubilee. I was dreaming. What time is it?"

"Late. It's past midnight here."

"Are you outside?"

I nodded. I'd come to sit on the lettered-stone wall that surrounds Temple Huacho. Silver filled all the vales that night, making islands of each hill. The gleaming surface of that nocturnal sea lay a hundred feet below me, disturbed by currents and restless waves that moved in no concerted direction, but it wasn't rising. I breathed its fresh, invigorating scent (like newly made air, I thought). Its cool, clear light lit the night, spilling over the wall to touch the shapes of the trees in the orchard. Through their whispering leaves I could just see the pink glow of a lantern in the temple courtyard. Moki had come out with me. He lay now with his chin in my lap, breathing softly in a dreamless sleep. Overhead, the Bow of Heaven arched in faint luminescence across the stars.

Yaphet glanced again at his bedroom door. Then he spoke in a low voice. "I wish I were with you. Now."

"Don't come," I warned him. "Not yet." I was frightened at how quickly his feelings were changing. He'd been wary at our first meeting, but he'd been hungry at our second. After that there had been a row with his father, and by the anxious way he watched his door I guessed there had been another, but I didn't ask.

"Don't you want to be with me, Jubilee?"

In truth, I wasn't sure. I liked Yaphet. I liked talking to him, and I would stay up hours for the chance of a few minutes of conversation. He was a puzzle to me, a fascination: How could it be that of all the players in the world, he was for me? Why should it be so? I wanted to understand this strange rule almost as much as I wanted to understand the silver.

But I also knew that if Yaphet left Vesarevi he would be taking away from me the years I had planned to spend wayfaring. I would be forced to wait for him at Temple Huacho and that I did not want to do.

So I mumbled some reassuring sentiment—"We'll be together in time"—and went on to another subject. Yaphet had many interests, and it wasn't hard yet to turn his mind onto other tracks.

I told him about the archaeologist from Halibury who had gone out to the ruined city. "I saw the report in the market—he came too late. There had been silver floods since I was there and they'd eaten away at the buildings. The base of the tower and the execution tree in the square were so badly eroded they'd toppled."

I had seen pictures. The tower resembled a log drizzled with sugar frosting while the execution tree had become a long, thin, branching mound of no discernible purpose. I remembered my first impression of the city, the ephemeral feel of the pristine white buildings, and how I had wondered if they were made of salt. Now they were melting like salt structures lapped by a rising tide. It was strange—even disturbing—to think that Liam and I might have been the only players to see the city intact. Even my mother had never heard of a ruin so large, brought forth by the silver and consumed again with such speed. Everyone agreed we were lucky to have seen it, but I wondered . . . was it luck? The silver was said to act sometimes as if with a purpose: the dreaming goddess, waking briefly to accomplish some small task in the world. I was young enough to wonder if the goddess had somehow guided our visit to those ancient ruins.

"You were lucky it was quiet the night you were there," Yaphet said.

I shrugged. "It's a quiet region. There are only three or four floods a year."

"It sounds like there were that many just in this last week."

Was he criticizing me? I didn't like the idea. "So I *was* lucky. I'm a lucky player. It's what everyone says."

He didn't seem to notice my change of tone. "I wonder if there's something in the ruins that draws the silver?"

"That bogy," I suggested, only half facetiously. "Fiaccomo's ghost probably wants it lost again."

That drew a faint smile, but already our time was up. "Be safe," he whispered. He raised his hand as if to touch me, and the link closed.

I lingered awhile on the wall, wondering at myself. Why didn't I feel more grateful for my luck? To find a lover like Yaphet so easily, and so soon—it was unheard of. But my gratitude was mixed with resentment, and I began to worry that my ambivalence would extract some terrible price of its own.

I was immersed in these gloomy thoughts when Moki came suddenly awake. He raised his chin from my lap, his jackal ears pricked forward and a low growl in his throat. I turned to follow the direction of his gaze and was startled to see a dark figure walking up the switchback road from the vale. It was a man, but I knew at a glance it wasn't Liam. The walk was wrong, the span of the shoulders, the manner of dress. This was a stranger.

But that wasn't possible.

The silver lay only a few dozen feet behind him. All night it had encircled the hill. There was nowhere this man could have come from, unless he had been hiding in the brambles since nightfall.

Moki stood, growling again, louder and more menacing than before. I laid a hand on his back and felt his red fur standing stiff. "Quiet," I whispered. "Let's see who he is."

I watched the stranger come up the path. The color of his skin was lost against the glow of the fog, but I could see he was a man of medium build, near my own height. He was dressed strangely, in wide, starched pants and a long tunic with starched sleeves. At first I thought he was wearing an odd hat, but as he drew nearer I saw it was his hair, long and thick and folded on itself in sleek black waves, pinned in place by silver clips.

I was sure he glimpsed me as he rounded the switchback but he did not call out a greeting. Neither did I. Little Moki gave up on his defense. He slunk behind me and lay down, his chin pressed against the lettered stone of the wall. The night was quiet, so that I could hear the stranger's footsteps as he advanced up the road.

He bypassed the gate and walked across the grass until he drew even with me. Then, standing below the wall, he looked up.

The silver was behind him and I could not make out his features in any detail, but I thought his skin was pale. Certainly his eyes were dark, and his clothing too. Tiny silver sparkles danced about his eyes and in the dark spaces between his fingers. Horror touched me, for they were exactly like the silver sparkles that had hovered around Jolly in the seconds before he was taken. For a wild moment I wondered if this could be Jolly, grown into a man, for there was something hauntingly familiar about this stranger, as if I had known him before, in some other time, or some other life.

But he was not Jolly.

My heart beat faster, remembering a fear my mind had long forgotten. I started to rise.

He spoke then, in my own language, though it was not his native tongue. His voice was low, crisp, his words a distorted echo of my own thoughts: "I have come for your brother, Jolly. Command him to come forth now."

I froze, half crouched upon the wall, the fine hairs of my neck standing on end just as Moki's had. *Jolly . . . ?* I could not think who this man might be, to ask after my brother. I could not think how to answer. Moki stirred, and I picked him up, cradling him close to my chest. "He's gone." It was all I could find to say.

"Lately gone?" the stranger inquired. Though he spoke softly, there was menace in his voice and the motes that danced about his hands grew brighter, so that a silver storm seemed ready to ignite around him . . . but surely that was impossible? If the motes were true silver, he should have already been consumed.

Perhaps it was the hour, or the dreadful sense of familiarity he stirred in me, but I felt the world shift, a crack in the boundaries of the possible opening the way for forbidden things to slip into the world. "Do I speak to a bogy?" I whispered. "Or a ghost?"

His teeth flashed white as he grinned. "Not a bogy," he said, stepping closer to the wall. "But a ghost all right, dressed in flesh.

Now tell me, girl, where is Jolly? Why does he hide from me? He should know that I am his father now."

I rose to my feet, Moki clutched in one arm, and my savant in the other. I didn't know who this stranger was or how he had come to Temple Huacho, but I did not like his tone or his manner. I didn't like his cruel, taunting questions. And most of all, I didn't like the strange, hot fear brewing in my chest. "Your manners are very poor," I said, in the best imitation of my mother I could muster. "But if you would know, Jolly isn't here."

"Not here?" He cocked his head to one side, so that some trace of reflected light illuminated his face. I could just make out his thin, dark brows and his graceful cheeks above a goatee of black beard, though there was no mustache. Perhaps the truth of what I said showed on my face for he turned half away, looking dejected. "So he is lost again."

He made as if to leave by the same road he had come despite the sea of silver that filled all the vale. "Wait!" I stepped along the wall to follow after him. "Who are you? Why have you come asking after my brother?"

He looked back over his shoulder, his face once again a mask of darkness. "Will you come find out?" He held his hand out to me.

Some traitorous part of me was tempted. "Come where?"

He nodded downslope. I followed his gaze, to see the silver washing up the path where he had walked only a minute before, moving toward him in a swift tide. Moki whined and wriggled in my arms so that I had to stoop to put him down. He jumped off the wall and disappeared toward the temple. "You must come inside," I said. "Quickly. Come in through the gate before the silver reaches it."

"It's too late, I think." He raised his arm to the silver, and the shimmering motes that danced about his hand brightened again. Then the silver rushed to him. Never had I seen it move so quickly. It flowed like water released from a dam, sweeping across the grass to wash past his calves, his hips, rising up around him in a great halo of gleaming light that revealed his cold smile, but only for a moment. The silver rushed over his body, sheathing him in a second skin just as it had done to Jolly long ago, but he was still alive under that terrible armor, because his shape *reached* for me, and I thought I heard his voice, speaking in a lower octave than before, so low it was barely audible. It was as if the world itself were speaking, *Come find out.*

"Jubilee!"

It was my mother, shouting from the temple. The sound of her voice broke whatever trance had held me on the wall. The silver was only a few feet away and rising fast. I stumbled back, forgetting for a moment where I stood so that I half fell, half jumped off the wall. It was six feet down on the uphill side and I hit hard. Pain lanced my ankle. I hissed and glanced over my shoulder to see silver pouring over the wall where I had just been, and flowing unimpeded through the open gate.

"Run!" my mother screamed. "Hurry! Hurry!"

She was racing down the hill to meet me. I could not bear that. I could not bear to think of her being taken by the silver. So I broke for the temple, ignoring the pain in my ankle and running hard. She met me and we ran together for the courtyard, illuminated by crossing lines of paper lanterns. Liam was there and he swung the gate shut as we entered. It closed with a sigh and a click, making a perfect seal.

In the courtyard the air was sweet with the scent of the guardian kobolds that were spawned each day in our well, living out their single night of existence in the ground or in the temple walls. Their vapor protected us. It had a mechanism about it that would not let the silver pass. I breathed it in gratefully, my heart beating hard.

But my mother was furious. "What were you doing out there? Did you fall asleep on the wall? Didn't you see the silver rising? Jubilee, you could be dead."

"But there was—" I stopped as tears started in her eyes. *Tears?* But there was nothing to cry over. I was safe inside the temple.

Then Liam touched my arm. "We have had news of your

father." He said it in a voice hardly more than a whisper. "He was taken by the silver this evening, outside Temple Nathé on the highway from Xahiclan."

"*No.*" I shook my head. I would not believe it, but my mother nodded and the tears spilled from her eyes so I knew it must be true. She held me, and we cried together, until Liam finally made us go inside.

I sat up with my mother all that night. She was a silhouette beside her bedroom window, listening to the glassy tinkle of the fountain in the courtyard. I sat in the rocking chair. The runners whispered against the floor as I rocked myself in a slow, even rhythm. "I nursed you in that chair," she said, without turning her head.

"You nursed each one of us."

Starlight glimmered in her eyes. I caught the soft exhalation of her sigh. "Lie down on the bed, Jubilee. Try to sleep."

I lay down, but sleep did not come. My mind would not rest. The same questions kept returning to me, over and over again: How had my father come to be on the road at dusk? Who was the stranger beyond the wall? Why had he given himself to the silver on the same night my father was taken? And why had he asked about my brother as if he were still alive?

Jolly should know that I am his father now.

It wasn't possible to survive the silver. Was it?

Was the legend of Fiaccomo real?

By dawn all these mysteries had become one in my mind. Somehow the stranger had caused my father's death. I was sure of it. And maybe he had caused Jolly's too, and perhaps . . . it wasn't over yet? Should I tell my mother what I had seen?

Or what I thought I had seen. When I tried to put it into words it sounded absurd. My mother would certainly say I'd been asleep on the wall, that I'd been dreaming, but it had been no dream.

Real then. It had been real and reality leaves tracks—but where to look for them? Where else but in the experience of others? I would visit the market, and inquire.

With this resolution made, I sat up. My mother turned from her post in the window. Behind her the sky was just beginning to lighten. *"Jubilee,"* she whispered, fear carried in a high overnote.

I went to her, and I took her hands. "Mama?"

"Jubilee, don't—"

Don't go. I knew that was what she wanted to say. Don't go wayfaring. Stay home. Stay away from the silver. Be safe. *Don't make me sit this vigil for you.* But she did not say it. She kissed my forehead and told me instead, "Wake your brothers and sisters. All but the baby. Send them to me."

I nodded. My mother was wise.

Chapter

6

I had no time to visit the market that day, or the next, caught up in the preparations for my father's memorial ceremony. But on the third day, when all the notices had gone out and the food had been ordered, I found myself with a free hour in the early afternoon. My mother was napping with the baby and all the other children were quiet, so I took my savant and a folding chair and went out to the orchard with Moki, finding a shady site in a hollow between three trees.

I sat down with the savant in my lap and thought for a moment about strategy. What if Yaphet was in the market? His profile was linked to mine, but I didn't want him to know I was about. I didn't want anyone to know. So I stripped all identifiers from my market presence—name, face, notifiers, history. I reduced myself to a blank face within a portrait frame, and then I linked.

I went first to the library and, using a synthesized voice, asked my question of the resident savant: "Has anyone ever survived the silver?"

An oval portrait in the corner of the screen showed me what this savant had looked like when her persona was copied: a dark and wrinkled old woman with wide, bright eyes and white hair, but it was only a still portrait, bordered in black for she had died centuries ago. The intelligence I spoke to was not her. It was only a mechanic that mimicked her thought patterns.

The savant answered me in a low voice, each syllable carefully controlled. "There are several million references associated with your question. The most promising are on-screen now. They refer to a character named Fiaccomo. Fiaccomo is widely regarded as a legend in most markets, but there is evidence to suggest a historical basis—"

"Stop," I said, scrolling quickly through the list of references. "Let's try this again. Has anyone besides Fiaccomo survived the silver? Limit references to . . . the past seven years." The years since Jolly was taken.

"This search yields only a few works of children's fantasy from Ano. Do you wish to see?"

"No."

I closed the link and thought some more. Perhaps the library wasn't the right place to look. The library was a sanctuary of reliable information, but I was chasing ghosts. I shivered, remembering my exchange with the stranger:

Do I speak to a ghost?

A ghost all right, dressed in flesh. Now tell me, girl, where is Jolly?

I looked about me, at the insects drifting golden above the grass and the patterns of the leaves overhead against bright sunshine and none of it seemed real. Not nearly so real as my memories.

I entered the market again, but I did not go to the library this time. I put my face back on (though not my name) and wandered through the truckers' clubs instead. That market linked three distant enclaves into the couplet of Halibury and Xahiclan. The players who walked in those streets or lingered in the clubs might in real life be as far away as Ano, or as close as a truck on the highway north of Temple Huacho, but they came together here, to share news and to gossip. If someone among them had seen a stranger haunting the silver I had no doubt it would be discussed here, and that the rumor of it could be uncovered with only a few questions.

But the time of day was against me. It was still early in the afternoon, and most drivers were on the road. I looked into several clubs, only to find them empty, or nearly so.

MEMORY

I have known many truckers, and they range from intellectuals engaged with every aspect of the world to automatons whose only interests are chemical euphoria and machine sex. I soon discovered that in the daytime the second variety is far more common in the clubs. In half an hour I did not find a single player I dared approach.

And still I continued from one club to the next, my progress tracked by position sensors that brought the sleepy buildings to life with lights and video as I passed. One display in particular caught my eye. It framed a doorway, and the sights exhibited there were so bizarre my brain took many seconds just to puzzle out the parts.

Someone came up behind me as I hesitated in front of that club, though I was not aware of her until she spoke. "Ah, now, Jubilee Huacho, isn't it? I remember *you*. But aren't you a little young for what goes on in there? Hmm. You should let me show you a happier place."

I jumped at the first mention of my name and turned, but without earphones it was hard to tell the direction of sound within the market. I toggled my viewpoint to the left, but the only players I saw there were well down the street. So I continued to rotate my viewpoint. I'd gone almost full circle when I finally discovered a diminutive old woman, hardly taller than my chest and scrawny, though what little muscle she carried looked tough and well used to hard work. She wore the bright canvas colors that many truckers favor, and though the wrinkles around her eyes and her cloud-white hair testified to an age well over a hundred, her back was straight and her eyes were bright.

Unlike me, she wore a profile, and it gave her name: Lita. I did not recognize it. Nor was her face familiar to me, and yet somehow she knew me, or at least she knew my name. Judging by the span of her grin, Lita was finding my confusion most amusing. "Now, Jubilee," she scolded, "what would your mother say if she knew you were visiting a place like this?"

Certainly my mother would have found more words than I possessed at that moment. *Lita.* Who was Lita? I was desperately trying to dredge up some remembrance of her. She must have stopped at Temple Huacho sometime over the years, but I could not recall her. The names and faces of the truckers who had visited us were blurred in my memory and I could not say if I had ever seen her before.

She cocked her head and gave me a coy smile. "You don't remember me?"

It was the worst manners to admit it, but I had not the wit to hide behind a polite lie. "No. I'm sorry."

My apology was waved away. "No offense taken! You were a child when I saw you last. No higher than this." She held her hand at the level of her rib cage. But then her face grew stern. "You're growing up too fast, I think, if you're already coming here for entertainment."

My cheeks warmed. "Oh, but I'm not—"

Lita cut me off with another wave of her hand. "No explanation is owed! But if you're going to play here, you should know better than to go in without a name. It implies things. Things you don't mean, or so I would guess by the warmth of that blush on your cheeks."

"But I wasn't—"

"It's all right," she said with a laugh. "We're all curious. But if you want some diversion I'll show you a better place—quieter—where the real players log in." She ushered me up the street with gestures and nods that were almost physical, chattering as we progressed. "So how is your mother? Tola was always such a determined woman. Has she kept Kedato in line?"

I could not help myself. A little pained noise escaped me and I stopped—so abruptly that Lita's avatar brushed mine and disappeared for a moment, before jerking back into existence a step ahead of me. She turned about immediately, her gaze full of concern.

"I've said something wrong?"

My voice was not steady. "My father . . . he was taken by the silver."

"Oh, no." Her face seemed to shrink then, becoming something small and wrinkled as if her age had stepped forward to claim her. *"Too soon,"* she whispered. Then louder, "When?"

"Ah"—I did not want to answer—"a few days past."

And what was I doing about on this street at such a time? I could see her wondering, and I felt the flush of my cheeks deepen. I was very young still, and I could not bear the thought that she would draw the wrong conclusion. "I'm not here for the clubs. It's not that. I came because . . . because something strange happened and . . . there was nothing in the library, and I—" Her disapproving eyes did not make it easy to find the proper words so finally I just blurted what I had come to ask: "Is there any talk of a man who can survive the silver? Not Fiaccomo, but one that is alive today?"

The transformation was stunning. Lita's eyes grew wide. She took a step back, glancing behind and to both sides before she spoke in a voice that had gone low and hoarse. "You came here to ask *that* question?"

I nodded.

"And have you?" she whispered. "Have you asked it of anyone else?"

"No," I confessed. "There was no one who seemed . . . savory."

That stirred a tiny smile, but fear huddled behind it and she continued to speak so that no passerby might overhear. "In that case we cannot altogether despise the filthy habits of this street. They've kept you from an attention you would not want. But, Jubilee, you are a young girl from a good family. What would move you to ask a thing like that?"

"I did not know it was a scandalous thing," I whispered. Then I thrust my doubt aside. "I have seen him."

All expression vanished from her face, and for several seconds she did not speak. Then she shook her head. "It's lucky I saw you here. You're lucky. The goddess must have her eye on you." She sighed. "I don't know much about him. The less known, the healthier for me, that's how I see it. There are some who don't react kindly to talk of him. They want him to be their secret, and it's only lately I've heard of him myself."

"Heard what? Of who?"

She glanced around again. "Not here." With a sweep of her hand she gestured me up the street. We fell into step, resuming our journey toward the unnamed destination where she had decided to deliver me. As we advanced, she searched the street, her gaze darting to take in the face of every player who came into sight. She spoke under her breath. "I've set it up. She's agreed to see you. That's good. She won't often talk, but you can trust her. I've known her a long time. What she said of the war in Phau . . . it made my hair stand on end. But the silver is rising, and she said we may soon grow used to such news—"

"What's Phau?" I asked. "Is it an enclave?"

"Hush! Don't say it so loud." Now Lita spoke even more softly, so that I had to cock my head close to hear. "What happened in Phau was no accident. It was not bad luck. He *called the silver.* It's what she said, and I believe her. The truth is in her eyes. They look like yours do now, bright and fragile with a vision they were never meant to see. Come. Come in here."

She turned abruptly onto a tiny side street. Placing her hand against a wall of mortared basalt, she made a door appear where none had been before. When she pushed the latch, the door swung open onto a dimly lit room. "Enter quickly."

I hesitated. Was this some bizarre game? Or might Lita be the very enemy she warned me against? I glanced back the way we had come—perhaps to see if an accomplice was following, I don't know. My attention was caught by an open-air restaurant just across the street. Several players were seated at the scattered tables, talking, eating, engaging in their own business—except for one. He watched us. His gaze met mine: a smallish, stoop-shouldered man without hair on his shiny scalp. He gave me a cool smile.

"Damn it," Lita whispered when she saw where I looked. *"When* will I learn to mind my own business?" Then she hustled me inside.

I found myself in a dignified club room projected in textures of dark wood, with candles burning on the tables and a slow-moving fan turning overhead. When the door closed Lita and I were the only occupants, but another player joined us, appearing suddenly in one of the chairs surrounding a central table.

"Here she is," Lita said, and I could not tell if she meant me, or the woman who sat regarding me with a gaze that took my measure. How had Lita described her eyes? Bright, and fragile. I knew at once this was the player she had spoken of.

She was a small woman, and lean, very like Lita in her build, but much younger than the aged trucker. Still, I could see lines of gray in the black hair she wore in a neat bun at her neck. She was dressed in a worn gray-green shirt and gray trousers. Black, fingerless gloves protected her hands. Her eyes were narrowed as if she squinted against sunlight, and there was dust on her face.

Lita did not introduce us.

"Please sit down," the woman said in a rich, cultured voice that contrasted with her vagabond appearance. She indicated a second seat at her table.

I glanced at Lita for reassurance, only to discover her avatar had disappeared. I thought about leaving too. All that held me in that room was a market link—and my curiosity. The player watched me, waiting patiently as I decided what I would do.

Finally I pulled out a chair. I had come here for a reason, after all. I made my avatar sit. "I want to know if there is a man who can survive the silver."

"I was told you saw such a man."

"I don't know what I saw."

She nodded. "There is sometimes a gap between what our senses tell us, and what we are willing to accept. Will you tell me what you think you saw?"

"Have you seen him too?"

"Yes."

"And if I speak, you'll tell me in turn what you know?"

"I'll tell you what I feel is safe for you to know."

I thought this over. The offer did not seem fair. Still, there was something in this player's steady gaze that made me want to trust her. So in halting words I described the stranger and his impossible appearance on the road beyond the temple wall, when the land all around had been drowned in silver. "I saw him gesture at the silver and it came hurrying to him. He did not try to run. He stood there, and it swallowed him."

"You did not see him come out of the silver?"

"No. I didn't see him after that. But his manner was not the manner of a man who goes to his death."

She asked me some questions about the stranger's appearance, and his clothing. I answered as I could, but I said nothing about my conversation with him. I could not speak of that. I would not take the chance.

"When did this happen?"

"Three nights ago."

She looked startled at this news. "The same night your father was taken?"

"Lita told you that? Did she tell you my name too?"

The player nodded.

"It was the same night," I admitted. "But my father was on the road. He was not at home."

"I'm truly sorry for your loss. I can't tell you if it was coincidence or not, but I can say that you have seen Kaphiri himself, and that you are lucky to be alive."

That was not what I wanted to hear. "People are always telling me I'm lucky, but my father is dead. If that's luck, it's a treacherous kind and I'm sorry I have it."

She nodded. "It's true that luck is not always good. Sometimes, it only softens an evil result."

My gaze fell, for I felt ashamed. As hurt and angry as I was, I knew others had seen far worse, and faced it. So in a contrite voice I asked, "This . . . Kaphiri? Will you tell me about him? What is he? Why do you know of him?"

"What is he? That's the key question, and I have no answer for that. But what he does—I've seen it. So have you. He commands the silver. Have you heard of Phau?"

"Only now, when Lita mentioned that name."

"Phau was an enclave, an old one, far to the east in the district of Lish, close to the Reflection Mountains. Some fifty-five years ago a cessant cult formed in the district. They had the luck to found a new temple, very close to Phau. You've heard of cessant cults?"

"Yes." Cessants are those who have given up the search for a mate. I guessed that this player was herself a cessant. They have no children, so they turn their minds to other things: art, science, business, history. Life. But some are bitter, and of these, a few form cults that are dedicated to celibacy and it is said they will lure young players into their ranks, persuading them to give up the search for a lover even before it's begun.

"The families of Phau were naturally concerned," the player continued. "They got up a posse to confront this cult and they tore down the new temple and poured acid in the temple well. The cultists spoke the name of their absent leader, Kaphiri, and they promised he would bring revenge.

"They did not lie. That very night he came. He appeared in the lower streets of Phau and a flood of silver rolled in behind him, consuming the outlying neighborhoods. More floods arrived on the next night, and the next, until the fourth night came. All the people who had not been taken and who had not yet run away were huddled within the sanctuary of the temples. They should have been safe there, but when dawn came and the night's flood receded, only one temple remained in a wasteland of barren soil. Phau was gone."

For a moment I was not in that club. I was on the wall again, with the stranger looking up at me, his face still lost in shadow. What could such a creature do to us at Temple Huacho? What had he already done?

"Is it really the same man?" I whispered. "Can it be, after so many years?"

"He is very old—very much older than he seems—and clever. He has learned to use the kobolds to extend his life far beyond any natural limit. He is certainly the oldest player alive in the world today."

"You know this?"

She nodded. "His history can be traced back almost four hundred years. There is no doubt it is the same man, in the same life. Since Phau he has been seen many times—and far more often, this last half year. But his interest lies with the cessant cults. I can't guess why he came to Temple Huacho."

I nodded, more frightened now than I had been on that night. "I have to go."

The player's eyes were grave as she regarded me. "Perhaps it's best. But if you want to find me again, come back to this room." She tapped the table. "Leave a message here. My name is Udondi Halal."

I started to close the link . . . but there was one more question I had to ask. "This Kaphiri . . . does he ever have another with him? A young man who can survive the silver too?"

Udondi Halal saw through me then. She knew I'd told her only part of my story. Though her expression did not change, I felt suddenly cold before her gaze. "That is a strange question." She glanced at my scarred hand, which in life was poised to tap the link off. Then she met my gaze once again. "This is truth, Jubilee Huacho. Kaphiri makes many promises, but I've never heard of anyone following him out of death."

I nodded, my thank you barely escaping my dry throat.

Then I closed the link.

When I looked again at the orchard the sunshine seemed to me only a fleeting promise. In just a few hours dusk would come, the time of silver. And then Kaphiri might return too.

Chapter

7

In the days that followed I lived in a state of nervous terror, jumping at any odd noise in the night, or the sweep of an unexpected shadow. I didn't talk to Yaphet, though my mother must have notified his family because he sent me a formal letter of condolence.

We waited seven days to hold the memorial ceremony, as custom advises for those taken by the silver. This is to allow time for friends to gather from neighboring enclaves. But travel is dangerous as my father's fate showed, and I did not expect many guests—revealing how little I knew of Kedato Panandi.

My father had traveled often and made many friends. In the end, forty-two players risked the journey to Temple Huacho, many from far away Xahiclan, and if they hadn't thought to bring gifts of food and drink and their own bedding we would have been hard-pressed to provide for them all. Among them were merchants and truckers and hoteliers and librarians and even the matchmaker from Halibury who had changed his opinion of my father over the past nineteen years.

The night before the service I went with my mother to the well room. She wore her green evening gown, and I wore a new dress of dark blue, for this was a formal occasion.

Stored in tiny, airtight drawers along the walls were the dormant kobolds she'd collected since the founding of Temple Huacho. Most of the little mechanics had been gathered from the mouth of our well, but many had been received from other temples, and some very rare specimens had been traded from hand to hand, traveling to us in slow steps from far around the ring of the world.

Our well produced kobolds in four different series: one of metallo-lithophores that specialized in mining; another of metallo-lithophores dedicated to building many rare objects of metal and glass; a third, unique series that produced the organic stones from which our orchard had been grown; and of course the series that encompassed the temple guardians, which were found in every well. For everything else we had to trade.

My mother approached the wide cabinet that housed the temple series. She knelt beside it, examining the drawers before choosing one at knee height. It rolled out to its full length of two feet. Inside were many small, transparent boxes. She selected one from the back, closed the drawer, then carried the box to her workbench.

The box was a complicated device used to store dormant kobolds. It was divided into two horizontal sections with a trapdoor between them. In the upper chamber were six kobolds. They looked very much like the guardian kobolds that lived within the walls and grounds of the temple, exuding their sweet, protective scent whenever the silver drew near. Like the guardians, these had membranes resembling petals on their backs, so that each looked like a blossom, but not a simple blossom like a cherry. Their petals were thicker and more numerous and they overlapped one another like the petals of a rose, hiding the degenerate legs beneath them. But where the temple guardians were white, these kobolds were a dusky red touched with tones of purple. A warning color.

My mother manipulated a bar built within the box, using it to push one of the kobolds onto the trapdoor. Then she pressed a lever, and the kobold was sucked into the lower level with a pop of pressurized air. After that she opened the bottom of the box and the kobold spilled onto the workbench, its useless legs already twitching as the touch of oxygen brought it out of hibernation.

"We'll need two," my mother said as she handed me the box.

"But it's best to do one at a time. So return this to the drawer for now, and be sure you close it tightly."

I did as I was told. When I returned to the bench my mother had turned the kobold onto its back. Its legs waved in the air as she bent over it, studying its configuration code with her magnifying goggles. Then, using a tiny pick, she pressed at its belly, manipulating the digits. Sometimes configuration codes are fixed, but most kobolds have a range of functions that can be selected by adjusting the readout on their bellies.

"Have you memorized the setting?" I asked.

"It's displayed on the screen of my goggles."

"How can you keep your hand so steady?"

Her lips twitched in a faint smile, though she did not look away from her work. "It's my talent. Steadiness."

Her tears were long gone, her mood calm as she used the pick to tick off changes in the code.

"You did this for Jolly too, didn't you?" I asked.

The thought came out of nowhere, taking me by surprise. I had blurted it out without thinking and immediately I was sorry. She didn't need to be reminded of that other grief now— but I should have known my mother better. "How much do you remember of Jolly?" she asked without pausing in her work.

I remembered every detail of his last night. "I haven't forgotten anything."

She nodded her approval. "You must remember your father too. If we embrace the memory of those we love, they'll continue inside us."

I nodded, though I didn't speak right away. Steadiness was not *my* talent.

Philosophers tell us to take comfort in the thought that those who are gone are born again into new lives but this was no comfort to me, for the memories we are made of are not reborn, and though my father might have already found new life in the womb of a woman somewhere in the world he would never be my father again.

But as they had for a week now, my thoughts slid from the fate of my father to the problem of the stranger beyond the wall. Neither my mother nor Liam had seen Kaphiri that night (if indeed it was him), for he had been standing beneath the wall, out of view of the temple—and I had said nothing.

I didn't know what to say. I would go over it in my mind—*Mama, I saw a magic man beyond the wall that night. He came out of the silver looking for your dead son.*

She already had grief enough.

But I could not stop thinking about Kaphiri, and the way he had asked after Jolly as if Jolly were still alive. *He should know that I am his father now.*

These words, they haunted me. The possibilities they implied . . . it was almost more than I could bear.

So I watched my mother as she ticked off each of the hundreds of digits in the kobold's code, and when I was sure my voice would be steady I asked, "Mama? Have you ever heard of a player called Kaphiri?"

She did not hesitate in her work. "No. I don't know that name."

"It's said he can survive the silver."

A smile touched her lips. "Has that rumor started again?"

I shrugged, though she wasn't looking at me.

"No one can survive the silver, Jubilee. Don't wish for it. You'll only hurt yourself wishing for things that will never be."

"It's said Fiaccomo could pass through the silver."

"It's said he *died* in the silver and only the special favor of the goddess restored him. But that's just a story."

"I'm not so sure."

My mother ticked off several more digits on the kobold before she answered. "All right. I thought Fiaccomo was a myth, but what you found in the ruined city suggests there really was a player by that name. That doesn't mean he had supernatural powers. That city fell because the silver behaved then as it does now."

I didn't see it that way. "But why did the silver come in such a great flood on that one night, when no one in that city had even seen silver before?"

"Jubilee, I just don't know."

"I think I do." I hesitated. I'd never told my mother this before: "That night Jolly was taken . . . he told me he'd called the silver, and it's said Fiaccomo could do the same."

"Jubilee!" This time she did stop her work. She laid down the pick and took off her goggles and looked at me so that I immediately regretted saying anything. *Jubilee.*

"I'm sorry," I whispered. "It's what he said, but he didn't mean to do it."

"He didn't do it. Stories are not the same as life. No one can call the silver."

But Kaphiri could. I'd seen that with my own eyes.

My gaze shifted to the kobold on the table. "This kobold you're preparing, it'll call the silver tomorrow. If it can—"

"No." She shook her head. "That's not a thing any player can do. Jubilee, have you believed all these years that Jolly brought on his own death . . . ?"

I shrugged again. I didn't know what I believed.

"You should have told me."

There was a lot more I should have told her, but I didn't. My mother was very wise, and I was afraid she would find a way to explain everything that puzzled me—a clever and logical explanation that might have nothing to do with the truth.

She put her goggles back on and retrieved her pick, but when she returned to her task her hands were not as steady as before.

The procession set out the next morning on foot. It was a glorious morning, with the sun bright and warm and only a few fluffy clouds. A hawk floated high in the air, while songbirds hid in the brush and trees so that it seemed as if the woodland itself was singing.

We followed a path Liam had cleared in the grass, around to the back of the hill, and from there a game trail led down to a quiet stream where I'd spent many pleasant hours swimming. Liam led the way. I followed behind him, carrying my youngest brother,

Zeyen, who was only two. We were a subdued party as we picked our way along the stream for nearly a mile, but it was pleasant to walk under the shade of the trees, and to witness my brother's delight with everything he saw.

The look of a puppy can be accurately predicted by looking at its parents, but it's different with players. We don't resemble our parents at all, for our parents change from one life to the next, while we remain the same person, only grown a little in experience. That is the usual rule, but Zeyen was the exception. Whether it was chance or the whimsy of the goddess I cannot say, but he looked very much like my father, and for that I kissed him often.

At last we reached our destination: a grotto where silver lingered even in the daytime. Here the stream had cut a shallow cave into the high, rocky bank on the farside. The cave was bordered in ferns and broad-leafed shrubs that bore small white flowers, and its floor was of coarse sand. At its mouth Liam and I had built a low platform of river rock to serve as a shrine. If there had been a body, it would have been laid there, but today we would leave only offerings.

The shrine was reached by a simple footbridge, made by my father when Jolly was taken. Yesterday Liam and I had repaired and repainted the bridge. I approached the site hesitantly, half expecting to see Kaphiri in the shadows, but of course he wasn't there.

I took up a post at the near end of the bridge, while our guests gathered. My little brother had been in fine spirits all morning, so it surprised me to see his mood dim. He grew subdued, and turned his head from the grotto, resting it on my shoulder while holding himself perfectly still, just as a frightened fawn will huddle unmoving in the grass. My nearest sister, Emia, saw this and came running. "Give Zeyen to me, Jubilee. You shouldn't bring him so close."

"He's all right," I insisted.

But of course her worried face and her words convinced him there was something to fear. He started kicking and wriggling, reaching for her and crying so I had no choice but to hand him over. Babies are like that, but I felt stung—though it was a well-deserved rejection. Emia had spent far more time caring for the younger children than I had, especially since Liam came.

I watched her carry Zeyen away from the bridge and up the hill to where our guests were gathering. Herds of small deer commonly browse in Kavasphir and on this side of the stream their feeding had opened up the woodland, so that grass grew between the trees. My mother directed her guests to seat themselves here on mats and low folding chairs that had been brought for this purpose. I stayed at my post, making sure no children went across the bridge or into the water, though at this time of day there was really no danger—not until the kobolds were released.

When all was settled my mother spoke to her guests of my father's life, and then Liam spoke, and then one by one many there came forward to tell what they had known of Kedato and why they had loved him. And as I stood at the foot of the bridge my father had built, I learned many things about him I had never heard before and felt a sharp pang of regret that I had not known him better.

Two of my brothers and my nearest sister also spoke, but words were beyond me. I listened to the soft voice of the stream and waited for the pain in my throat to subside.

When the speaking was over I crossed the bridge. I had carried a gold cloth with me, and I laid that now on the rock platform. My nearest brother, Rizal, came next and lit incense that filled the air with the sweet scent of citrus flowers. Then one by one my siblings crossed the bridge and left offerings on the shrine, gifts they had made for my father, or things that had belonged to him. Jacio brought his favorite bow. Emia brought a shirt he liked to wear that she had embroidered with flowers. Tezoé left her favorite kite.

Beside the other gifts I laid a spray of cherries from the orchard, and a figurine of a hawk that had belonged to Jolly. It's said that in other times and places the youngest child was left on the shrine or if there were no children then the distraught lover might offer herself instead.

Thankfully, we lived in a kinder age.

My mother was last. She laid a handwritten letter on the shrine, and a strand of hair from each of us, made into a braid. Then she looked at me with dry eyes and nodded. I sent my siblings back across the bridge to join our guests on the hill. Everyone stood. Some of those who were older and slower, or who had small children with them, began to migrate toward the hilltop.

I stepped within the shadow of the cave, my mother beside me. The dazzle of sunlight had prevented us from seeing inside the cave before, but now we could look to the back wall where tufts of silver gleamed in narrow crevices running in rough angles from floor to ceiling.

"The silver won't last long in the sunlight," my mother said in a low voice. "But it will rise quickly. Don't stumble as you cross the bridge."

"I won't."

Then we bowed our heads to the silver and spoke together the ancient words credited to Fiaccomo:

> *"Within the silver all begins*
> *Blood of the world*
> *Breath of the world*
> *Dream of the world*
> *and death*
> *Beginning again."*

I could hear Zeyen crying far away across the stream. My mother listened a moment. Then she took two tiny, transparent boxes from the pocket of her gown: the boxes that contained the kobolds she had prepared last night. In their airtight chambers they had gone dormant again but that would not last long. She gave one to me, saying, "Now we will ask the goddess to visit us."

We returned together to the sunlight, placing the boxes on either side of the shrine. I waited for my mother's signal. She nodded, and together we pressed the spring latches and our boxes fell open. Oxygen brushed the kobolds' thick petals. I glanced back into the cave, thinking I had seen a shadow move within the shadows, but the sun was too bright and I could see nothing.

"Come," my mother said, holding her hand out to me. "We'll walk together. Quickly. But walk. And don't look back until we've joined the others."

I took her hand and we crossed the bridge together and climbed the hill. I did not look back, though I wanted to. I imagined Kaphiri emerging from the cave. I imagined his dark eyes, and his disquieting questions: *Where is Jolly? Why does he hide from me?* His presence filled my mind, so that when a murmur arose from our guests I knew Kaphiri was the cause. He had been seen. I started to turn, but my mother gripped my hand more tightly. "Wait," she whispered. "Don't turn back until we reach the top."

I nodded. This day I was determined to obey her, no matter what.

Our guests had retreated ahead of us to the hilltop. As they looked past us I could see excitement in the faces of the children, but in their mothers' eyes I saw anxiety. I could hardly bear not knowing. I hurried the last few steps. Then I let go of my mother's hand and turned back.

The trees were widely spaced so it was easy to see down the grassy slope and across the stream to the cave, but I saw no sign of Kaphiri there. Our guests were mesmerized instead by the appearance of silver in daylight.

The kobolds had wakened the dormant silver. It billowed out of the grotto's dark mouth, looking thin and almost white in the sunlight, floating higher than silver should, as if it had become light as a cloud. It drifted over the shrine, hiding our offerings. It rolled to the water where some of it was caught by the current and carried downstream in steaming clouds, but the main bank of silver crossed the water, filling the little vale and climbing the slope of the hill. An anxious, excited murmur ran through our gathering as the silver drew nearer. I could smell its fresh and lively scent. My heart beat faster. Instinct warned me to run away, to flee over the hill, and I knew everyone around me felt the same. But we stayed, and in a moment the sunlight did its work. The silver broke up into iridescent tendrils that rose like steam among the branches of the trees, vanishing utterly as they passed above the canopy.

In a few minutes it was all over. The silver was gone, and the streambed was as it had been except the gifts on the shrine and the cloth I had left there were gone. Taken by the goddess in her dream? It's what my mother would say.

The bare river rock glistened now with flecks of gold. More flecks decorated the bridge, but that was all. The silver had not lasted long enough to bring about any real change.

Chapter

8

Kaphiri seemed to forget us. For twenty days there was no sign of him, though I remained vigilant, spending many nights on the wall. No one questioned me. They knew I had a lover, and it was only natural I would want to be alone with him; when the market link was down, it was just as natural for me to choose to be alone in my grief. I was of the age of restlessness and melancholia, and my behavior was easily explained.

That was why I was on the wall one dreary evening, when clouds lay low and heavy over the land. Night was falling early. The vale had become a wide gray shadow and the horizon had taken on the color of old steel, when the headlight of a bike appeared in the distance, racing through the dusk for the shelter of Temple Huacho.

There was no sign of silver that night; no hint that this rider might be a servant of Kaphiri, but I'd been on edge so long I started to my feet, expecting the worst. I wished furiously that I had my hunting rifle in hand, but it was locked up safe in my room. (My mother was accepting of my seclusion, but she would have wanted an explanation for a rifle laid across my lap.)

Then from across the vale I heard a high-pitched cry, *"Jubi-lee!"* and I was glad I didn't have a weapon.

"Auntie Som!" I shouted in return. I whooped and waved, and she waved back at me, the headlight on her bike bright as a star in the gloom. *"Auntie Som!"* We hadn't expected her until tomorrow afternoon.

Auntie Som was my mother's older sister. She was a cessant who'd made a life for herself teaching school in the Ano marketplace. She'd visited us before, first when my brother Jacio was born, and three times since, as each new baby came. This time she had come to stay.

I leaped off the wall and ran to open the gate, while my brothers and sisters bubbled out of the temple, racing one another down through the orchard while Moki dashed, barking, about their feet. My mother followed, carrying Zeyen. She met her sister at the gate and hugged her; and while there were tears in her eyes, there was also a smile on her face.

I closed the gate, then turned to watch them all as they walked back up the hill. Liam had stayed behind too, though I wasn't aware of him in the deep shadows until he spoke. "I think it'll rain tonight."

I jumped, but then I forced myself to laugh at my own edginess. Liam wasn't fooled. "Jubilee, are you planning to run away?"

"No!"

The dusk had passed into full night and I could barely see him, though I could feel him thinking, thinking. At last he spoke, his voice hardly more than a whisper, "Anyway, you're free to go, now that you know your mother won't be alone."

I didn't want anyone up the hill to overhear, so I whispered too. "Do you want to go? Are you ready?"

"None of us ever knows how much time we'll have."

I nodded, though I don't think he could see me in the dark. "I've been worried . . . about Mama."

"You can stay here," he said quickly. "You don't have to go with me."

"It's not that."

He hesitated. "Saying good-bye is the hardest."

"Liam, will you wait a few more days. Please? Until Auntie Som is settled." Until I could convince myself Kaphiri would not come again. Why should he come? Jolly was long gone, and there was nothing else here he could want.

Liam sighed. "You've been spending so much time out here, I thought you were on the edge of leaving."

"I wouldn't run away."

"All right. I'm sorry."

"You'll wait then?"

"A few days. Not longer."

A drop of rain struck my cheek, and then another.

"Come on," Liam said. "This is not a night to stay out and wait for ghosts."

Is that what I'd been doing?

I retrieved my savant from the wall, while the rain became a steady drizzle. Moki dashed after us as we jogged through the orchard, toward the friendly glow of the lanterns that hung in the courtyard.

It was the last night I would spend at home.

I fell asleep listening to the rain and heard it again when I awoke in the morning. A glance out my window showed gray veils drifting over the hills but the clouds that trailed them had grown thin. I guessed there would be abundant sun before the morning was far gone. So I dressed in shorts, a field shirt, and ankle-high shoes. I'd decided to search the hills around Temple Huacho; see what turned up. If I found no sign of spies or wanderers, maybe it would be easier to believe Kaphiri had forgotten us; that he'd sent none of his followers to interfere in our lives; and that my father's death that night had been a terrible coincidence and nothing more.

I grabbed a jacket and made my way to the kitchen. My mother was there, helping Zeyen and four-year-old Arial with their breakfast, while she chatted with Auntie Som and Emia. Liam was breakfasting at the far corner of the table. He saw me first. "Are you going out?"

The others turned, and suddenly I felt guilty for wanting to spend the day away from them. I gave a little shrug. "I was thinking about it."

"Eat breakfast first," my mother said. "And take Liam with you. He's about to go crazy trapped inside these walls."

I had just sat down when Jacio came bursting in, with Moki prancing at his heels. "Jubilee! Jubilee! There's a machine in the forest."

I was on my feet in an instant. "What kind of machine? Where?"

At the same time my mother demanded to know, "Jacio, what were you doing past the wall?"

Jacio wisely chose to answer me. "It's a savant," he panted, his dark hair tousled and his pale cheeks flushed red. "But the shape's different. It's not one of ours."

Jacio was ten, the same age I'd been when Jolly was taken. I'd enlisted him to look for "strange things"—it was the kind of imaginative game he enjoyed, though I'd never expected him to be the first to find a sign of Kaphiri.

I shrugged into my jacket and ran after him out the door, while Liam abandoned his breakfast to follow.

Rain fell in a soft mist as we galloped down through the orchard, all the way to the closed gate. My eight-year-old sister Tezoé had climbed to the top, where she balanced on elbows and belly, her sodden hair lying against her back, glistening with rain. Jacio boosted himself up beside her and I climbed up on her other side. "It's there," Tezoé said softly, pointing down at the forest that covered the western side of the hill.

"I don't see it."

"It's on mimic," Jacio explained. "Here. I'll show you." He swung over the gate and dropped to the other side. I jumped after him, rainwater splashing up around my feet. Behind me I heard Liam warning Tezoé to stay inside the wall, and then a heavy thump as he dropped to the ground.

Jacio had found a path through the brambles. He ran silently, half bent over as if he were stalking bush deer. I raced to catch up with him, but Moki was faster. He must have taken his favorite path over the wall, along the branch of a large lychee tree that lay atop the stone. He darted past me, his jackal shape a blur of red as he chased Jacio.

I ran hard in pursuit. The rain pelted my eyes and raspberry thorns raked at my legs, but Jacio still reached the woods ahead of me. He knelt to scoop up a handful of leaves and rain-soaked humus and then, before I could cry out, he flung it into a cluster of low branches.

The dirt wrapped around a quadrangle of reality, a separate world of sharp edges hanging seven feet above the ground. I stared at it, breathing hard, trying to make sense of this vision; and then the shape dipped as the weight of the soil unbalanced it, and suddenly I could see it for what it was: the delta wing of a camouflaged savant. "Do you see it?" Jacio shouted.

"Yes."

It was only a few feet away. One jump and I could have grabbed it, but that's not what I wanted—and in that moment of hesitation it slipped away. I sprang after it, and Moki followed. "Go back!" I shouted over my shoulder at Jacio. "Tell Liam to bring the bikes!"

Jacio didn't listen. I could hear him a few paces behind me, running hard, and Liam behind him, shouting, "Jubilee! What's going on?"

I had no time to answer.

Liam didn't know about Kaphiri. He could not guess what was at stake.

Moki kept pace with me, but after a few minutes Jacio fell behind. I think he waylaid Liam and finally delivered my message because after that there was only silence behind me.

I ran on, ducking beneath branches and weaving between trees, with Moki sometimes ahead of me, sometimes behind. I was determined to keep the savant in sight. I had no doubt of its purpose: it was here to spy on my family. And I knew as well who had sent it.

I plunged across a deer-chewed lawn while the savant retreated, its delta wing flickering in shades of dappled green as it glided beneath the branches. The rain was already yielding to bright sunshine, and in that unforgiving light the savant's mimic skin could not change fast enough to hide it. I trailed it through a stand of bracken, then across a tiny stream and up the farther slope. The ground began to steam around me, and I shed my jacket, tying it around my waist.

How far? I wondered. How far to the master of this machine?

I wanted to find him. Now. This very morning. Early on a day that promised abundant sun. On such a day it would not matter if he summoned the silver. The sun would burn it away before it could harm me; but there would be time for my anger.

I rounded the side of the hill, clambering over a spine of glittering white crystals that thrust out of the ground like the bones of a glass beast. On the other side there lay a swale, filled with the feathery gray foliage of wormwood. The savant became a gray shadow as it glided above the shrubs.

Savants are not known for their speed. Still, they can glide as fast as I can run, so I was surprised to find this one still in sight. Maybe Jacio had damaged it when he'd hit it with the dirt. As I watched, it slipped again under the shelter of trees.

Moki had figured out that I followed the savant. He plunged into the wormwood, but I went around.

My world grew small and tightly focused. I strove to keep the savant in sight, at the same time gauging the ground ahead and dodging the branches that tried to slap me. I'd hunted deer on foot since I was twelve and I was a strong runner, but deer grow tired, while machines do not. Three times I lost my quarry as the savant floated over short cliffs where I could not easily follow. Twice I found a way down the rock face, though I had to make a pack out of my jacket to carry Moki. The third time we blazed a path several hundred feet to the west. Moki scrambled ahead, pursuing the savant on his own, but it took me fifteen minutes just to clear the ravine. When I finally climbed out on the other side my legs were shaking and my lungs were on fire, and I despaired of finding the savant again.

Still, I knew it had been heading generally north, so I kept on that way, and after a few minutes I heard Moki barking in the distance. I hurried on, and half an hour later I broke out into a grassy vale, and there it was: a tiny chip of green, flitting out of sight as it passed over a saddle into the next vale. I could hear Moki's bark, but I couldn't see him in the shoulder-high grass.

Again I ran, using my arms to thrust the tall stalks aside, but I had little energy left, and my pace soon slowed. All around me steam rose wherever the sun touched, filling the air with such a density of moisture I could hardly breathe.

That's when Liam found me. He came over a hilltop to the east, riding his bike fast between the trees. Rizal followed, and Jacio came behind him. They intercepted me before I reached the end of the vale. I waved Liam on after the savant, relieved to see that he had brought his rifle, tucked in its sheath. "Go! Keep it in sight."

"You want to tell me why we're chasing this thing?"

"Later. Just catch up with it. Watch where it goes."

Rizal stopped beside me. He was riding my bike, and he'd remembered to bring my rifle along too. "Get on," he said.

"No. You get off. Take Jacio home."

"No way! We want to—"

"Rizal! This is not a game. Take Jacio home. I don't want him hurt."

My words frightened him. His freckles stood out against the sudden pallor of his skin. "It's just a savant," he said.

My hands were bleeding from the brambles. They were an ugly sight as I grasped the handlebar. "Get off," I repeated.

This time, he did. Jacio came up then. I seized the handlebar of his bike too, so he couldn't take it into his head to set off after Liam. I glared at Rizal until he nodded. He told Jacio, "Slide back. We're going home."

Jacio fussed of course, but Rizal was four years older, and outweighed him by fifty pounds. There wasn't much he could do. "I'll explain later," I shouted as I took off after Liam. "Just go home!"

I stopped on the rise, long enough to make sure they were heading in the right direction. Then I pushed the bike as hard as I dared all the way across the next vale.

Liam was waiting for me at the top of the next rise. He spun his bike out, blocking my way, forcing me to stop. Behind his sunglasses, his face was hard. "Why are we out here?"

I could see the savant, still half a mile ahead, gliding away across nodding plumes of grass. Moki sat nearby, his tongue lolling happily, looking at us as if he couldn't understand why we didn't push on. "To find the owner of that machine!" I shouted, trying to force a way around Liam.

He moved his bike to block me again. "Tell me why we care."

"Because I met someone on the night Kedato died, and he scared me."

"Someone threatened you?"

"You could say that."

"Why didn't you say anything?"

I shrugged. "I need to know who owns that savant, Liam." It had caught a breeze. I could see it scudding through the valley, hastening north.

"You don't think it's just a lost savant?"

"A lost savant wouldn't use its mimic function to hide from us. It wouldn't run away."

He drew a deep breath. "All right then." He rolled his bike back out of my way. I called Moki, and put him in the empty saddle box between my knees. Then I took off.

It was noon before I began to worry. When I'd set out in the morning, I'd expected to find the savant's owner close by. Now I wondered: how far away might Kaphiri be? The day was getting on. I wasn't afraid to confront him under the sun, but I didn't want to find him at twilight.

At last I pulled up on a broad ridge, almost the last outpost of the Kavasphir Hills. Liam stopped beside me. Together we watched the savant retreat across the brush like a slow-soaring owl, its color shifting to match the changing vegetation. Liam asked, "Have we gone far enough?"

"Do you have field glasses?"

He reached into his saddle box and pulled out a pair. Then he searched the land ahead of us. Finally he shook his head. "There's nothing out there. It's probably just a runaway after all."

I'd been so focused on following the savant that I'd allowed myself to think of little else, but now a new thought intruded. Was it possible the savant was deliberately luring us, drawing us out from the shelter of Temple Huacho? "Can you still see it?" I asked. "Has it slowed down?"

Liam looked, but he did not answer right away. His head turned in a slow arc as he searched the land. A minute passed. Then another, and with it went my new theory, for if the savant was a lure, surely it would have slowed down, or shown itself? Giving us some motivation to go on . . .

"There!" Liam said. "Straight ahead. At least a mile."

I squinted, trying to make it out. "Has it reached the highway?"

"Not yet. But there's no one out there. No sign of a truck or a bike."

"Okay. I'm tired of chasing it anyway. Let's change tactics. Let's try to catch it this time."

He continued to watch the savant through his field glasses. "If you want. But if we go any farther, we won't be able to get back to Temple Huacho before dark."

I thought about it. "We could camp. There should be gear in the saddle boxes." It was our habit to keep the bikes ready.

"Or we could push on to Temple Nathé. Once we're on the highway, it'll be easier to reach than Huacho."

Temple Nathé. Where my father had died. I felt suddenly frightened, but at the same time I wanted to see it. "All right." I patted Moki's head. He was still sitting contentedly in his saddle box, awaiting our decision. "Let's go then, before we lose our quarry."

The savant changed direction when it reached the highway, turning northeast to follow the line of the road. But even with a strong breeze behind it, it couldn't stay ahead of us once we were on the pavement. We pushed our bikes to seventy, and within a few minutes we caught up with it: a triangular pane of blue in the air overhead.

Then suddenly, the savant ceased to flee. We brought our bikes to a stop beneath it. It floated, twenty feet overhead. I glared at it, willing it to move on, to show us on to Kaphiri.

"Jubilee, it's going higher."

I pulled my rifle. "Don't lose sight of it." I would bring it down, before I would let it get away.

The savant was thirty feet overhead. Then fifty. A tiny blue chip, barely discernible. "Liam, it can't survive up there."

"I think that's the point."

Silver sparks began to boil around the savant's triangular wing, and then the sparks bubbled into a glinting cloud that completely enveloped its shape, a tiny, glittering silver storm that lasted only seconds before it burned away in the afternoon's brilliant light, but that was long enough. The savant was gone.

Such was the fate of flying machines. Scholars say there is some dormant form of silver floating as particles high in the atmosphere that will cling like static electricity to the wings of any flying machine. When their density rises to some trip point, these particles will boil into true silver, even in defiance of sunlight. If the flying machine is not destroyed immediately in flight, it could still ignite a silver storm on the ground, which is why no enclave will allow its citizens to even experiment with flying machines.

I sighed and sat down on the side of the road. Moki came to me, nuzzling into my lap. I felt like a fool for running so far after a machine that was (it seemed quite obvious now) lost and crazy.

Liam sat down beside me, passing a water cell into my hands. "It shouldn't take more than two hours to reach Temple Nathé," he said. "So we've got time. Why don't you tell me why we're here?"

I nodded. Certainly, I owed him that.

Chapter

9

Dread had stirred in me when Liam first mentioned the name of Temple Nathé. The feeling did not leave me all that afternoon, and still I was taken by surprise when the highway crested a ridge and suddenly we were looking down on a wide valley filled with golden knee-high grasses. There beside the highway were the grim remains of my father's truck.

Neither of us spoke as we approached the hulk. It was an eerie testament. The wheels and undercarriage, and the lower third of the truck's body, were gone, dissolved by the fickle touch of silver. The remaining shell was engraved in a language long dead in this world, though it was one I knew. I walked around the ruin, reading as I went: community news from some forgotten era—a storm, a marriage, a new temple site, a silver flood. Each word a faint echo of lives lost to the past and now my father had joined them.

Morning glories were already sending their vines over the hood of the truck and in through the windows. I checked the back. If there had been any cargo it was gone now—though whether it was taken by the silver or by some trucker who had passed through since the flood, I could not say.

The truck lay in a low swale, twelve feet from the raised roadbed. Silver had transformed the highway surface, reworking it into a folly of glass tiles that had since been crushed by passing trucks.

Thirty miles back Liam and I had overtaken an army of road-building kobolds—black, thumb-sized machines patiently transforming stone and soil to rebuild the ruined highway. In another day or two (if the silver did not come again) the kobold army would reach this valley and recycle the shattered glass, blending it into a new road of more practical material. As they passed, they would likely cannibalize the remains of my father's truck, so I was grateful we had arrived ahead of them.

Liam sat on the high shoulder of the road, gazing past the truck, toward the flowing white walls of Temple Nathé less than two-tenths of a mile away. Set on the valley's tawny slope, the temple gleamed in the mellow rays of late afternoon. "Look at it," Liam said in disgust. "How could he have been so close, and not made it?"

I shook my head. Some part of me was afraid to learn the answer.

Liam had not said much since my confession. I wasn't sure how much he believed, but his face was grim behind his dark sunglasses. He stood up, his shoes crunching on bits of colored glass. "It's time we found out."

So I called to Moki, who was bounding about in the grass, stirring up moths. Then we mounted our bikes, to ride the last few hundred yards to the temple gate.

Temple Nathé produced few kobolds, but it was famous for its healing baths. Elek Madhu was the temple keeper, presiding over a staff of a dozen cessants. She had kept Temple Nathé for nearly a hundred years, and had established two more small temples in the surrounding hills—the first step toward creating an enclave—but she still came forward to welcome each one of her guests.

The great doors of the temple gate stood open in the security of the afternoon. Elek waited for us there, dressed in a gown as white as Nathé's walls. Age had softened her flesh and brought a fullness to her curves, but she was a beauty still, endowed with a feminine grace that has always eluded me. I had met her once before, the time I'd gone with my father to Xahiclan, and I remembered her as a kindly and courteous woman. But that had been three years before and though she looked much the same, I had changed considerably. She didn't recognize me until I offered my name, and then her eyes grew wide and a little fearful. She couldn't help a quick glance at the ruined truck, sitting in front of her sanctuary like an accusation. "Come inside," she said softly. "I think we'll find much to say."

We walked our bikes up the driveway, to the temple's expansive courtyard. Two trucks were already parked there, and a battered bike, dusty from the road. "You have guests?" Liam asked.

Elek smiled, though I sensed it was only the role-playing of a practiced hostess. "Nine now, with the two of you. It's a rare night when we're without guests, but I can offer you a private bath . . ." She looked anxiously from me to Liam. "And then perhaps, we can talk?"

I nodded. "You do know how it happened? How he was caught so close to sanctuary?"

Her hands clenched in a knot against her belly. "I will tell you what I saw. Perhaps *you* can tell me what happened. But not here—" She glanced toward a flight of white stairs rising to a columned veranda. Then, in a soft undertone, "Some of my guests are strangers to me."

She gave us no chance to reply to this, for in the next breath she was speaking again in a normal voice: "I'll go now to prepare your bath. Please come up when you've gathered your things."

My things? As Elek mounted the steps I realized I had nothing. When I'd raced out of Temple Huacho that morning, I hadn't exactly prepared for an overnight expedition. Liam offered a grudging smile. "There might be a clean shirt in the saddle boxes," he offered. "Oh, and I brought your savant."

I turned to open the saddle boxes, but as I did I heard Elek's voice from the top of the stairs, sounding querulous and mistrustful: "No, they don't want to talk, I'm sure. *Please.* I thought you had come to stay the night and rest?"

I looked up, to find her on the veranda, speaking to someone inside who I could not see, though there was something familiar about the voice that answered: "I've come for many reasons, Elek, but rest is low on that list."

"Not for them. They're tired. They've requested a private bath. Perhaps tomorrow—"

"Has something happened to frighten you?"

Silence followed this question . . . though I felt more sure than ever that I knew this voice. But from where? The memory would not come.

I glanced at Liam, to find him listening too. I had told him all about Kaphiri, and the cessants who followed him. "Should we go?" he asked when he noticed my look. We could never get home before dark, but we had camped before, on hilltops in Kavasphir.

Elek answered her unseen guest before I could decide. "The truth, stranger, is that *you* frighten me."

"Ah. A flaw in my nature, I suspect."

At that, my memory finally gave up its obstinate game. *"Udondi Halal,"* I whispered. The cessant who had told me Kaphiri's name.

She appeared on the veranda, a small, lean woman dressed in weathered clothing, with fingerless black gloves on her hands, and dark hair pulled in a loose knot behind her neck. She smiled when she saw me. "Jubilee Huacho," she said as a flustered Elek hovered at her elbow. "So it is you."

I did not respond in kind. I was wary as she descended the steps. She saw this, and stopped, saying, "It's not me you need to fear."

I wanted to believe that. "Why are you here?"

"To see you of course, though I hadn't expected the pleasure until tomorrow. I was on my way to Temple Huacho."

"He hasn't come again."

"You shouldn't speak of that here."

"I don't think he will come."

"I hope that's so." She stepped forward, tentatively extending her black-gloved hand. "Well met?"

I hesitated. Should I trust her just because she had told me

Kaphiri's name? She held her hand out still, though she was disappointed, I think, at my doubt. Under her breath she said, "Know this at least: I am not his friend."

That I could believe. So I clasped her hand, and after that I introduced her to Liam, and then I reintroduced her to the perplexed Elek who, I discovered, knew her under a different name and perhaps a different purpose.

Liam and I returned then to our bikes and gathered our things, but within a few minutes we were stripped and immersed in one of the fine healing baths of Temple Nathé. At my invitation Udondi Halal shared our round pool, while the temple keeper sat beside us, hunched on a stool, her white dress held carefully above the damp floor.

Sunset light poured into our private room through a ceiling of polished glass and for a time no one seemed willing to speak. I sank into the hot water, letting it rise to my chin, and I watched Udondi past wisps of steam as the light faded and her face sank into shadow. I felt calm for the first time since that terrible night. Patient. It was the way I felt when I waited for the words of a new language to boil up to the surface of my mind.

In that prolonged silence I almost forgot about Elek. As darkness crept into the room the temple keeper became a shape without features, a frozen phantasm of the silver perched on her little stool. I was startled when she finally spoke aloud: "It was at just this time that I saw the headlights of your father's truck."

All the tension that had leeched out of me in the nurturing water returned now. I strained to see Elek through the gathering darkness, and I listened.

"I'd been expecting Kedato that afternoon, and when he didn't arrive by sunset I grew concerned. I had no other guests that night, so I went to stand on the temple wall where I could watch for his lights.

"There was no sign of silver. There had been none for many days and I told myself that even if there had been a problem with the truck, he would likely be safe camped along the road.

"Then I saw his headlights at the valley's northern end and my worries left me. The evening was so beautiful. Bats were hunting, their dark shapes flitting through the dusk, and I stayed on the wall to watch them."

She bowed her head. "The world can change so quickly. Kedato was only a half mile out when the valley floor blushed silver. Never have I seen anything like it. There was still a pale light in the sky, so at first I thought the sheen was just some strange reflection, but it was silver, seeping up from the ground, seeping up everywhere at once. Kedato drove faster, but it was no use. His tires failed in seconds and the truck skidded off the road, sliding into the low ground where it lies now.

"He climbed out of the window and stood on the roof, looking toward me. By then the silver had filled the valley floor. It lay all around him, many inches deep. He called out to me—you see, the truck's phone had already failed—he asked me to call his lover, but the silver was rising fast. I feared that if I went up to the temple, he would be gone when I returned.

"So we spoke. He talked about you, Jubilee, and your brothers and sisters, and his travels in the world. The silver lit the night and I could see him clearly. I could see everything. I have not imagined what I am about to tell you.

"I have said that Kedato stood upon the roof of the truck. The silver had risen to within a few inches of his feet when the wizard appeared. I don't know where he came from. He was just *there*, walking through the silver, following the path of the highway, which is built higher than the valley floor. The silver lapped at his waist.

"Kedato had been calm until then, but now he trembled. He called out to the wizard, but received no answer. Only when the wizard stood beside the truck did he speak. Or seem to speak. I couldn't hear him, but I heard Kedato clearly. He said, 'He is dead.' Then he asked the wizard how it was he could survive the silver, but again, if there was an answer, I didn't hear it. They spoke for a few minutes and I think Kedato asked him for help, but his voice had grown soft, and I could no longer make out his words.

"All this time the silver continued to rise. Kedato must have known he had only seconds left. He knelt on the truck's roof, and reached a hand to the wizard. The wizard met it with his own hand, and the silver rushed up, rolling over both of them and they were gone."

She sat with bowed head and hunched shoulders, a silhouette of despair in the near dark. "I have never before seen anyone taken by silver, and I hope never to see it again."

Stars had emerged in the deep blue vault beyond the glass ceiling. The Bow of Heaven lay across them. It was faint that night, a bridge of gossamer that could be seen only from the corner of the eye.

I climbed out of the hot bath and sought a towel. Footlights winked on, and water splashed as Liam and Udondi emerged behind me. I patted myself dry, half suspecting I was caught inside a dream spun from weeks of worry.

Liam was first to break the silence. "This is the second strange story I've heard today," he said as he toweled himself. "Jubilee, is this 'wizard' Kaphiri too?"

I shrugged. "Udondi will know."

"It was him," she said firmly.

"But how is that possible?" Liam asked. "How could this ghost be at Temple Nathé and then Temple Huacho on the same silver-shrouded night?"

"That is his latest art," Udondi said as she dressed in a black sweater and black pants. "For the last half year he has been sighted all over this turn of the world, vanishing at one site only to reappear moments later at another, thousands of miles away. I have records of hundreds of incidents . . . but I've never heard of anything like Kedato's death."

I pulled on a long-sleeved shirt and leggings that smelled musty from their sojourn in my saddle boxes. I could feel Udondi's gaze, though she spoke to everyone, not just me. "Kaphiri was here asking questions of Kedato. But what questions?"

Liam said, "Likely, the same questions he asked Jubilee."

"Oh?" I hadn't told Udondi of my conversation. "He spoke to you, Jubilee? What did he say?"

I shrugged, pretending it was unimportant. "He asked about my brother Jolly. He'd come to see Jolly, to *get* him . . . but it made no sense because Jolly was taken by the silver years ago and it's not possible he's still alive." My voice faltered as my real feelings broke through. "It's *not* possible . . . is it?"

"I've never heard of such a thing," Udondi said gently, "but there's much I don't know. Is he the young man you asked about before?"

I nodded. I could not speak.

Elek finally stirred on her stool. "I have never heard of this 'Kaphiri,' who seems so well known to all of you and I have to wonder at that, but I remember when this Huacho boy was taken. Players are lost to the silver all the time, but not like that. Not inside a temple. It should have been impossible, but the aftermath of evidence showed it was real."

"The reason you have not heard of Kaphiri is simple," Udondi said. "He is cautious. His followers work to ensure that word of him does not spread outside their ranks, for if he became well known, expeditions would surely be mounted against his strongholds, and he's not ready for that. I used to try to make him known in the markets, but every time I spoke I was attacked as a doomcryer, a hysteric. My posted bulletins were buried under tedious objections that sounded intelligent, but meant nothing. Several times, I was attacked on the road. So I don't speak publicly anymore." She turned to me, her expression growing thoughtful. "But this incident with your brother, Jubilee . . . I remember hearing of it. Though wasn't it long ago?"

"Seven years," I said.

Udondi nodded. "Very strange, for it's only in this past year that Kaphiri's been seen beyond the district of Lish."

"Because he has not strayed before?" Liam asked. "Or because he has not been seen?"

I shook my head. "Kaphiri was not there the night Jolly was taken!" The force of my denial surprised even myself.

Udondi spoke softly, "But you were? Jubilee?"

I remembered the way the silver had loomed over us, its smell, and the high-pitched sound of Moki's bark. "I saw it. It came for him. It reached out for *him*, not me. Just like it reached out to Kaphiri that night. It was the same."

Elek touched my cheek, summoning me back to the present. "All the puzzles of the world cannot be deciphered in one night. Come with me now. My staff has prepared a fine meal, and we are overdue."

Chapter

10

Elek had six other guests that night, five of them truckers from distant Ano who spoke in the formal style of that region, with many "ma'am's" and "Should it please-you-my-lady's" and courtly nods and smiles. We sat with them, and with Elek's staff of twelve, at a large table in Temple Nathé's dining hall. Throughout the meal—a feast centered on sage partridge, as fine as Elek had promised—the truckers entertained us with stories of the silver and of their lives on the road.

These truckers had with them a player called Mica Indevar, who they introduced as a scholar from a land even beyond Ano. This Mica Indevar was a stoop-shouldered cessant whose round face and smooth, hairless head gave little hint of his age, though his husky voice led me to suspect he was pushing ninety years. He seemed familiar to me, though I could not place him. I wondered if he had visited Temple Huacho, but Elek dashed that theory when she explained that Mica Indevar had sworn himself to a quest, to fare all the way around the ring of the world. It was his first time in that region, and he paid many compliments to the landscape.

This scholar had accompanied the Ano truckers all the way from the sea and I suppose in that long journey he had heard all their tales many times over, for he showed no interest in their talk. His curiosity was fixed instead on me and Liam.

He wanted to know why we were on the road. Liam would not

speak to him, but my mother had taught me to be polite even in the face of rudeness. So I answered him, explaining that our reasons were personal, but this did not please him.

"What *personal* reason might bring someone abroad?" he mused. Apparently the question troubled him deeply, for after dinner he came to me when I was alone in the hall.

"My lady Jubilee, if I might have a word."

To stay and speak with him was the last thing I desired. "I must return to my uncle. I promised to be back immediately."

He smiled. "No doubt he still thinks of you as a child. But I will speak swiftly. In my journeys it has been my habit to investigate tales of the silver, and none has been more striking than a story I heard even before I reached Ano, of a lost boy who appeared from out of the silver."

I do not know what expression my face showed. Horror maybe. Or hope. Whatever it was, it intrigued Mica Indevar. "I see you have heard such a story too."

"You're mistaken. I have not."

"It's a story I would have discounted, if I did not know the player who saw it happen, and if he did not make an image of this lost boy." As he spoke, he drew this printed image from his pocket and he displayed it to me in a cupped hand. It was a picture of Jolly as he had been when I was ten.

I drew back. "You would show me that?"

"I was told you would know him."

"I *don't* know him!" But as soon as the lie left my mouth I countered it with a question. "Who told you?"

He held my gaze, and while no words passed his lips, it was answer enough.

I turned away, trembling.

Indevar spoke to my retreating back. "Most players believe the goddess is nothing more than the unconscious hand of chaos, but it isn't so. Though she has been wounded in her long battle against the darkness, she is a goddess still, and her will is harsh. Still, she is not unkind. This lost boy has been sent to us to remind us of her mercy—"

I turned in sudden fury. "Do you know him?"

He drew back, a new wariness in his eyes. "No, lady. That has not been my privilege."

"Have you seen him then?" I pressed.

His gaze faltered, as if I'd caught him in a lie. "He is lost, lady." It had the sound of an apology.

"Then you have not seen him."

"I *seek* him—"

"Then you should know that you chase a ghost! That picture in your hand—it's of a boy seven years dead. If he had lived he would be a man now. Not a lost *boy*. You have been deceived."

Apparently this was not the response Mica Indevar had expected. His face grew red. His mouth opened, but words proved hard to find. "You—" he sputtered. "You don't know what—"

"Jubilee!"

We both jumped at Liam's harsh voice. I turned, to see him at the end of the hall, Udondi a step behind.

"Jubilee, has this stranger offended you?" Liam's voice was soft, but there was a chill in it that startled me. In the ruined city the bogy had mistaken him for one of the ancient queen's own warlords. It had seemed an absurd error to me, but I realized then it might not seem so absurd to a stranger. Liam was a man of size and strong bearing, with a face that fell all too easily into a grim and brooding aspect.

It was this other Liam that Mica Indevar saw. Fury flashed in his eyes, but he stepped away from me. "I have offered polite conversation only. If that gives offense, then this is a barbaric land."

"It is a barbaric land," Liam agreed. Then he looked at me. "Jubilee?"

I nodded, and the three of us left together, ceding Mica Indevar the hall.

There was no silver that night, so we left Elek to the company of her other guests and we went outside to sit on the wall. I told of my encounter, while Moki patrolled the grounds around us, keeping watch against any curious scholars who might wander close in the dark. "Kaphiri sent him," I concluded. "But why? Why do they care about Jolly? Why do they believe he is still alive?"

I wanted someone to say it was possible, that maybe Jolly *was* alive somewhere, and that was how Kaphiri knew him. But Liam was a harder man than that. "It's clear now, isn't it?" he asked. "Somehow a rumor was started about Jolly, probably because he was taken inside a temple."

Udondi nodded. "That seems likely. And Kaphiri would want to know if there was another like him. He would investigate that kind of rumor."

But the night I met Kaphiri, he had spoken as if he knew my brother: *Why does he hide from me? He should know that I am his father now.*

The white wall of Temple Nathé gleamed faintly under starlight. I stood upon it and looked for the remains of my father's truck at the bottom of the slope, but it was too dark. I could not see it. Behind me, Liam spoke to Udondi. "Will you come back with us to Temple Huacho?"

"I think not," she said. "I am known to his followers. I would not want to bring his attention back to your family."

Guilt touched me. "That's why you gave a different name to Elek, isn't it? I gave you away."

She shrugged. "This Mica Indevar likely knew of me anyway."

"I feel like I've seen him before," I mused, sitting down beside her. But I could not remember where. So I asked a new question. "What is known of Kaphiri? Udondi, do you know where he comes from? You told me before that his history goes back four hundred years. How can that be? And what is there in his past to make him hate the world?"

"There is shame," she said softly. "That is the spur, though I think the heart of it is something different. A flaw in his nature. It is my guess he was not made like the rest of us."

She hesitated. She had kept her own counsel for years, and I think it was hard for her to speak aloud the knowledge she had gathered in her long pursuit of Kaphiri. But after a few seconds, her soft voice took up the tale:

"Each of us, we have existed since the beginning of the world. We cannot remember our past lives, but we always remember the lover we were made for. For us, there is only one. But for Kaphiri it was different. His lover found another."

I felt dread stir in me then, for no reason I could define, but I said nothing.

Udondi continued to speak. "This is his story as I have pieced it together. Over two lifetimes ago, three hundred and eighty years, he was known by a different name, Owinca Najar. His parents kept the main kobold well in a large enclave that existed then in Lish, near the Reflection Mountains. He was raised in rank and privilege, and he was called lucky, for he had been wayfaring less than a year when he found his mate. He brought her home to Lish and they lived there six years, though without children. There were never any children. In the sixth year, she left him. A wayfarer had come to the enclave, and she recognized him at once as her true lover. That same day she put aside her marriage and she went away with her true mate.

"Never had anyone in that enclave heard of such a thing. Owinca Najar had taken a false lover. That was the conclusion, and the lack of children was held up as proof. I do not have to speak of the bitter shame that family must have felt. The young man fled, and it was the belief of all in that enclave that he had given up his life to the silver.

"I think he tried to. Who would not? Given the despair he must have felt . . . how tempting to leave behind the shame, even the memory of shame, and embark on a new life. So yes, I think he tried to end his life in the silver, but the silver would not have him."

A little laugh escaped her. "Did he feel like a monster then? Even more than before? Or did he feel like a god?" She shook her head. "In either case he did not return to Lish for nearly three hundred years. Where he went is not certain, though there is evidence he found a new home in the south. It was only some sixty years ago when he came again to Lish, though of course all who had known him before were long gone."

"Then how do you know it is the same man?" Liam asked.

"It is him. He is a man outside his time, with the mannerisms and habit of dress common in that ancient enclave. His face is the face of Owinca Najar that I found recorded in a library in Lish, and his anger is the same. Too, he preaches celibacy, so that he has become an icon of the cessant cults. And I have his fingerprints. They are the same as that sad young man of Lish. He has nursed his hurt for over three centuries and a half while the silver floods have grown steadily worse. It is his oath that he will see the world drown in silver."

I was keenly aware of the ruin of my father's truck in the darkness below us. "Why does he believe Jolly is alive? He must believe it. Why else would he keep watch on Temple Huacho?"

Udondi shifted, her eyes glittering in the faint starlight. "Has he been watching?"

"Not himself. Not that we've seen. But this morning Jacio surprised a savant in the forest. We pursued it all the way to the highway. It's why we're here."

"Where it self-destructed," Liam added. "And how will Kaphiri react to that? Perhaps he'll think we have something to hide after all."

Udondi leaned back against one arm. "Actually," she said, "that savant was mine."

"Yours?" I whispered it so that I would not shout. "The savant we pursued? You know about it?"

She nodded. "I was in Dalanthé that day I first spoke to you. I came as fast as I could, but it's a long journey and I was worried Kaphiri, or one of his servants, might return before I could reach you. So I had a friend, a trucker, release the savant as he passed the Kavasphir Hills. It was set to watch all comers, and it would have delivered a warning to you if anything suspicious turned up, but it was otherwise instructed to remain hidden—I didn't want to upset you without cause. That's why the savant retreated, and why it finally destroyed itself."

I couldn't think what to say. I'd been so sure the savant belonged to Kaphiri, or at best someone who served him, like Mica Indevar, or that player who had watched me in the market . . .

I slapped my thigh. "It was *him*! In the market. It was Indevar who was watching me. That time I went to see you, Udondi. He was there."

"That was many days ago," Liam said. "Kaphiri could have returned many times to Temple Huacho . . . so why wait for Indevar to come instead? Why? If it still mattered to him?"

"You're thinking Indevar may be less than he seems?" Udondi asked.

Liam grunted. "Perhaps he is not so much serving Kaphiri, as desiring to serve . . . or at least to be noticed. By his reaction I would guess he had no idea that picture of Jolly was seven years old." Liam shook his head. "Whatever it was this Kaphiri hoped to find that night at Temple Huacho, he was disappointed. He's probably forgotten us . . . and Kedato."

Udondi said, "For the sake of your family, I hope that is so."

For myself, I could make no sense of it, but there were other things I wanted to know. "Why are you hunting him, Udondi? You *are* hunting him. Is it for revenge?"

"It did start that way."

"You were in that last temple at Phau, weren't you?"

In the darkness I saw her nod. "That was a long time ago. For years after, Kaphiri was only a phantom of Lish. The players there call him a ghost and some make shrines and offerings to him so he will not bring the silver. I used to tear these down, but as my anger grew colder I started to ask myself questions instead. Was Kaphiri a man? Could a man control the silver? Had any man ever done so?"

"Fiaccomo," I whispered.

Udondi turned to me in surprise. "Have you worked that out already? You're faster than I am."

"Or luckier," Liam muttered, and he described our visit to the ruined city.

"A world without silver," Udondi said. "I'd heard such stories, but I didn't believe them. Fiaccomo was a legend, a magical hero created for the amusement of children. Then my journeys took me to a temple high in the Reflection Mountains." Her voice grew softer. "I hope neither of you ever has to visit those peaks.

"Silver is a constant hazard in those elevations. Almost every day the peaks are hidden in heavy, dark clouds that the sun cannot break through. Under that shelter, silver will often rise up from ravines even in the daytime so that traveling only a short distance is dangerous. Then, too, there are no roads and no antennas, for any structures are wiped out within days. That's why the temple I sought had no market link. It's why I had to go there in person—but it was worth the journey.

"In that mountain temple I found a brief, handwritten document, very old. The temple keeper helped me with the translation. This is what I read: *'A grievous night! It is dawn now, and I set pen to paper for no purpose I can discern, except that I would leave a remembrance of those who are gone. In all my travels I have been ever wary of the rare traces of silver fog that are found sometimes in these mountains, but my wariness failed last evening! Tomas, Jonny, and I were overcome by a sudden boiling of the grim mists. I felt myself dying. I know I became other than myself, for a new consciousness came over me, as if some part of me had wakened to a greater reality. My sight expanded, so I seemed to see somewhat of the mind of another far greater than myself, and I understood the unfathomable details of the world. But to what purpose? I have no answer to that. Nor can I guess why I have been returned to the world, while of my dear companions there is no trace. Am I mad to think of returning? For there is a hunger in me to understand it, to know why this thing happened. I struggle to be calm, to be rational, but in truth I wait only for the return of evening. I do not think I will ever write more.'*

"Fiaccomo was the author of this account. This tale of how he discovered his affinity for silver is a little different from the story we tell to children, no? Not as pretty. But the talents Fiaccomo reportedly possessed—passing unharmed through the silver, and summoning it at will—those were the same talents Kaphiri had displayed in Lish."

Liam stirred. "Are you thinking Fiaccomo *is* Kaphiri, in another lifetime?"

"It's something I've wondered."

"But Fiaccomo is known for restoring the world, and for creating the first kobolds."

Udondi said, "He is also known for bringing the silver back into the world." She shook her head. "The silver moves in cycles. In some ages it can hardly be found, but for us the silver is common, coming more often, and in deeper floods than anyone can remember. Already players have begun to wonder how bad it might be. Kaphiri tells them it will be the end of all we know.

"He has Fiaccomo's talents, but he does not speak of saving the world. Instead, he preaches that the goddess has given him the task of unmaking the world in a great flood of silver . . . and I fear he is learning how to do it. Just this year, something has changed for him. Before, he was only a ghost of Lish, preaching annihilation to a handful of unhappy cessants. Now he has been seen in far-scattered enclaves, proclaiming the wrath of the goddess and promising that all the world must soon drown in silver. Clearly, the silver *is* rising. And if all drown, none will ever be reborn again, no? So it is the bitter end. But Kaphiri offers this hope: that he will shelter those who accept his protection, and that when the final flood recedes, they will emerge from the silver into a world remade, the world the goddess had always intended for us, without the flaws of this one. A world in which birth and death have been discarded, and lifetimes go on forever, and where every player may become the lover of every other. But only those who serve him now will ever reach this place."

"*Can* he guide players through the silver?" I asked.

"No. His cessants are consumed by the silver as easily as anyone else. I have seen it. But desperate players will believe what they will. At his command they will open the gates of enclaves and allow the silver to enter. They will poison kobold wells. How hard could it be to destroy every last shelter in a world on the brink of drowning in silver? In past ages when the silver has risen, some few players have always survived. But not this time. Not if Kaphiri has his way."

In my mind I saw a night when there was no hill or tower high enough to escape a rising silver flood, and only a handful of enclaves strong enough to hold it back. But if the gates of these enclaves should be opened? If Kaphiri himself should visit each stronghold and call the silver in, even past the temple walls? Then all that is must drown.

Morning would still come to such a world. The ring of the world would turn, the sun would rise, and the silver recede, but there would be no one to see what follies had been brought forward in time, or to celebrate the renewal of the land.

"So you've set yourself to stop him," Liam said.

Udondi nodded. "I have already seen enough drowning in this world."

Chapter

11

Much later that night I was awakened by my savant, whispering my name. I opened my eyes to find it floating beside me, its wing emitting a soft, golden illumination that did not reach to the edges of the little room. "A call," it said in its old man's voice. "From Jolly."

A cold flush ran through me as I sat up on my pallet. I stared at the gleaming savant, afraid to speak, afraid that speech would shatter the dreamspell that surely held me.

"It is a time-limited channel," the savant added.

"But how could it be Jolly?"

The savant hesitated a second. Then it answered confidently: "It can be Jolly because the biometrics are correct."

"That can't be."

"Rechecking. Done. Identical results. Reminder: this is a time-limited channel."

"Answer it!"

It was not Jolly calling me. That's what I told myself. But I wanted to know who it was, and why.

A rectangular window appeared within the golden glow of the savant's wing. At first the mimic screen was dark, but a second later light stirred, rising like silver in the night to coalesce in a face half lit, half in shadow—a boy, with beautiful, dark, fearful eyes.

It was as if the years between us had been erased. Here was my brother, hardly older than when I'd lost him. *"Record,"* I whispered to my savant. Then louder, "Jolly?"

"Mama?" He cocked his head; a look of confusion crossed his brow. "You're not my mother! Where is she?"

"No, I'm not Mama. It's me, Jolly. It's Jubilee. Were you calling Mama? She's home—"

"You're not Jubilee! And this is my mother's link. Why do you have her savant?"

I caught my breath. What Jolly was saying was true. When he was alive—

(When he was *alive*? What was he now? I could not doubt it was him, yet he looked only a little older, hardly touched by seven years of time.)

—yet it was true. When he was taken, this savant had belonged to my mother. It had not become mine until I was thirteen.

My astonishment was like a keening climbing higher in intensity and pitch until I could no longer hear it. I spoke calmly. "Mama gave me the savant, Jolly. A long time ago. And it is me. I am Jubilee, but time has gone by . . . for me. I'm seventeen. We thought you were gone. Lost."

"I've been lost." Tears started in his eyes. "Jubilee?"

"Yes."

"It can't be you. You're littler than I am."

I shook my head. "I don't know how, Jolly. I don't know what's happened, but this is me. Look—" I patted my thigh, calling Moki to my side. "Here's Moki. Your dog. *He's* just the same."

Jolly stared at the little red hound, looking like a boy sinking beneath clear water, dumbfounded, drowning in confusion. *"Moki?"* His voice cracked. Moki pricked his ears, sniffing furiously. "Moki!" Jolly shouted, and Moki jumped off the bed, searching behind the savant. "Moki!"

Time was counting down in the corner of the screen. "Jolly. We only have a minute left. Tell me where you are. Tell me where I can find you, and I'll come."

"You'll tell Mama and Dad?"

I winced, but I nodded.

He licked his lips, looking uncertain. He glanced to the side, but apparently he got no counsel there. Moki returned to my lap, and Jolly's gaze fixed again on his dog. "I'm at a small temple . . . in the Iraliad. It's called Rose Island Station. Ficer is the temple keeper. He lives here, by himself. He keeps the antennas."

Time was ticking down. We had only seconds left. "How did you get there, Jolly?"

"Out of the silver."

It was the answer I'd expected, and still it rocked me. I struggled to keep my voice calm. "Send me your address, Jolly."

"How—?" Again he turned as if to ask someone offscreen.

"Tell the savant," an old, low voice advised in gruff syllables.

"Send the address," Jolly said dully.

The connection closed.

I held on to Moki and cried for several minutes. Then I wiped my face and blew my nose and got up. I walked around my little room, pinching myself, jumping up and down, stroking the walls to feel the complexity of their texture, the pain of corners pressed against my fingertips, the detail of sensation as I rubbed my face and swallowed.

Details that were never mimicked in dreams.

Only when I was sure I was awake did I call the savant back to me. "Replay the last call."

I watched Jolly and listened to my voice talking to him. *Not* a dream. I watched again.

Then I sat down on my pallet, my back braced against the wall and the savant balanced on my knees. I launched a search for Rose Island Station.

The library access took only a few seconds. It was a real place, in the Iraliad, just as Jolly had said. The station keeper was recorded as one Ficer Elmi.

Of course, someone who wanted to deceive me might easily use the name of a real place. But why try to deceive me about my brother?

My brother was not a deception.

I had talked to him and he'd been real. Impossibly real. Only a little older than the boy I remembered.

I had promised to tell his mother where he was.

I gripped the savant, not daring to even think what I would say to her.

I sent the call.

My mother's confusion and grief, and her anger: they warred with a quiet joy as I told and retold every detail of my story, many times over, each repetition making it more real. At last she asked me this question: "Jubilee, do *you* believe it's Jolly?"

"I do."

She nodded, her face reflecting a stern resolve. "We have to bring him home."

"I'll go," I said quickly, for I was afraid she would go herself. "Liam will go with me."

My mother looked doubtful. "It's the Iraliad."

"I'm not afraid."

Her hands met, palm to palm, beneath her chin. "What about Yaphet?"

Yaphet was even farther away than Jolly, though every step closer to the Iraliad would bring me closer to him. It was a thought that made me uneasy, as if I were contemplating a betrayal—but of who? I shook my head. "If that's meant to be, then it will happen," I said. "Someday. For now it's Jolly who matters most."

"I wish I could go with you."

"You can't. You have the babies to care for."

"Yes . . . Jubilee? When you are deep in the Iraliad, there may come a time when you look back and realize that your home has become too far away. Too far to ever risk returning. If that happens, I'll understand. If you want to take Jolly and push on to Vesarevi, to Yaphet . . . well . . . it might be best."

"No." I rejected the idea immediately. "No, Mama. I'll bring Jolly back to you. I will."

"If you can," my mother said firmly, for she knew the ways of the world far better than I.

I checked the time. Still two hours before sunrise. From the window of my room I could look out over the gardens and the temple wall, to the north end of the valley. There was no sign of silver, and the odds of it rising so late in the night were very slim. So I went to wake Liam.

He had the room next to mine. I slipped past his unlocked door and shook him awake. Then in a whisper I told him all that had happened. "I'm going after him," I concluded.

"Into the Iraliad?"

"Yes."

"That's not a land I ever thought to visit. It's said the silver rises there almost every night, and for much of the year the land is pummeled by terrible storms that blow in from the ocean. The antennas there come down almost before they're grown. The Iraliad's the reason the channels are limited to Vesarevi."

I nodded. "Terrible stories are told about it, but Jolly's there."

I heard something then: the crack of a stick, the rustle of a shrub. I went to the window to look, but saw only the night shapes of the garden. From my room next door I could hear Moki's nails tapping on the tiled floor, but nothing else.

Liam joined me, moving so silently I didn't know he'd stirred until he brushed against me. I flinched away, then laughed softly at my own reaction. "I'm feeling jumpy."

"I'm thinking that's good. This Kaphiri could be after us, if he learns you've found Jolly." Then he added, "If we leave now, we might leave unobserved."

"You'll go then?"

"Of course I'll go."

I gave him a quick hug. "I knew you would."

We retreated from the window. "We need supplies," I said. "Should we return to Temple Huacho?" I didn't want to. It would mean time lost, and time was crucial, for Kaphiri was looking for Jolly too. "It'd be foolhardy to set out with nothing, but—"

A faint knocking sounded from the hallway. Liam went to the door, listening as the knock repeated. *"Your room,"* he whispered. I came to look over his shoulder as he opened the door a crack.

Elek was just down the hallway, standing before my door with a flashlight glowing golden in her hand. She turned a startled gaze on Liam. Then she saw me and took a tentative step. "Jubilee," she said in a soft whisper, "your mother has just called. She has asked me to outfit you for a journey. A long journey. You are not to worry about the debt."

I breathed a silent thank you to my mother.

"Can you do this now?" Liam asked. "We'd like to be gone long before dawn."

Elek nodded. "Come. My supply room is yours. It will take only a few minutes to gather what you need."

Temple Nathé was a stop for almost every trucker making the run between Xahiclan and Halibury, and Elek's supply room looked to be stocked with samples of nearly everything that had passed on that well-traveled road. There were field clothes and jackets, machine parts and electronics, agricultural seed, precious stone, kobolds, artifacts, and objects of art, and wines from all over the world, bows and rifles and skins . . . and food. Most of the food was in bulk: huge wheels of cheese and massive sausages and sacks of grain, but one shelf held travel rations, each portion neatly sealed against time and weather. Liam made most of his selections from these, taking enough to fill our saddle boxes. He had brought our rifles from home and there were sleeping bags already on the bikes. I found a field jacket to fit me. Then I hunted down two shirts, and one pair of long pants. I already had shorts. A length of rope and an extra water cell went into Liam's sack, and already I thought it was more than we could fit on the bikes.

We wanted no light in the courtyard that might draw attention, so we worked by starlight as we loaded our saddle boxes. The courtyard gate stood open, for Elek had already gone down through the garden, to open the temple gate.

The night was clear, the stars bright and plentiful, but the Bow of Heaven had faded entirely from sight. Unlike the stars, the Bow does not rise and set but remains always at the zenith. Even when it seems to disappear, it's not really gone. With a telescope it can still be seen as a thin, black ribbon eclipsing the stars. What it truly is, no one can say. The best telescope shows no detail. Even when its light is bright, all that can be seen is a glowing, rounded surface as of some fine flawless glass. By observing the way it eclipses stars, scholars have estimated that it is two hundred thousand miles above the world—an indomitable gulf that cannot be crossed by any physical means.

As I worked to pack the saddle boxes I found myself thinking about Fiaccomo, and his tryst with the goddess. If the silver was the manifestation of her dreams in the world, did the rest of her mind dwell in that inconstant arch of light? Then a new thought came to me: Had Jolly been to Heaven? He had to have been somewhere after all . . .

What was the Bow of Heaven? I thought of it as a placeless place, not truly of this world . . . and perhaps that's why our telescopes never seemed to bring us any closer to it. Maybe the Bow was no physical thing at all, but only a boundary, bleeding the white light of some other realm. I couldn't imagine what such an other-place might be like, but in that cool predawn morning, working hurriedly under the stars, it was easy to think that time might run very differently there.

The last saddle box was full. I leaned on the lid, pressing it down until the latch clicked. Several packets remained, with no place to put them. "Do you have any room?" I asked Liam.

"No, I'm full."

I frowned at the leftover packets. I didn't want to leave even one behind, for if the weather was against us it could take days, even weeks to cross the Iraliad. I wore my new field jacket to hold back the night chill. So I started filling the pockets. "I guess I'll carry them then."

Liam came over to look at my bike. "You've got room up front," he said. He was pointing to the bin where Moki would ride.

I snorted. "I can't hold Moki in my arms the whole way."

Liam hesitated. Then he asked, "You're not planning to take the dog?"

"Of course I'm taking him . . . did you think I was going to leave him here?"

"He'll be fine here. Elek can put him on the next convoy bound for Huacho—"

"I can't turn Moki over to strangers!"

"Then Rizal can come get him! Jubilee, bringing a dog on a trip like this is only asking for trouble. If he even survives—"

"He'll survive, Liam! And he's going with us. Moki is Jolly's dog. He's the only thing left of the life Jolly used to know—"

"*Hush,*" Liam whispered. He looked past me. I turned, but saw no one. The temple stairs glimmered white and empty in the starlight. Then Liam bolted past me, dashing up the stairs, taking them three at a time before disappearing into the hall. A moment later he came stumbling back out as Udondi emerged, her arm wrapped around the chest of Mica Indevar. The stoop-shouldered scholar sagged against her, his bald head nodding and his feet dragging like the feet of a baby who has not learned to walk. His eyes fluttered open as Udondi brought him to the top of the stairs, but then his knees gave way. She laid him down, none too gently.

"What have you done to him?" Liam asked in a low voice, full of horror.

"Only made him sleep," Udondi said as she came down the stairs. "He was listening most intently just inside the door. Did he hear enough to earn the favor of his master?"

My cheeks grew hot. I had been speaking of Jolly. "He heard enough," I admitted.

"It can't be taken back," Liam said gruffly. "And that's all the more reason to leave now. Come on. Elek is waiting at the gate."

I nodded and mounted my bike. Then I called softly to Moki, who had disappeared into the garden.

Udondi gripped my handlebar. "You've had news," she said.

Liam and I traded a look. Then I whispered, "We were wrong and Kaphiri was right. My brother *is* alive. I talked to him myself this night."

Even in the darkness, I could see the surprise on her face. "Alive . . . ? Has Kaphiri found him?"

"Not yet."

"I would go with you."

"We're leaving now," Liam said.

"I can leave now."

"What about your sleeping scholar?" Liam nodded at the dark figure at the top of the stairs. I could hear Indevar's soft, sonorous breathing, like the song of some night insect.

Udondi's teeth flashed white. "We will ask Elek to see to it that he leaves this morning with the Ano truckers. He will be far away—and so shall we!—by the time he is conscious enough to protest."

At the courtyard gate I called again to Moki, and this time he came. I put him in his bin. Then we let our bikes roll through the expansive gardens propelled by gravity alone. Elek waited for us at the outer wall, ghostlike in her white robe. If she was surprised to see Udondi in our company, she showed no sign. We stopped to talk with her, and she agreed to do what she could with Indevar. Then she took my hand. "I thought I knew the rules of the world, but all that changed the night the wizard came. Now myths are coming real, and I don't know anymore what is possible and what is not. Perhaps it will be up to you to find out." Then she hugged me, and I thanked her, and we left Temple Nathé behind.

Chapter

12

At first we followed the highway south, as if to return to Temple Huacho. But once we rounded the hills that guarded the valley's end we left the road, striking east into a trackless land of low hills and scattered trees. By dawn we'd put seventy miles behind us.

Udondi had her own field glasses. When the sun was well up we stopped, and she and Liam searched our trail, but they found no sign of pursuit. "Anyway, it's too soon," Liam said.

Udondi returned her field glasses to a battered saddle box. "Only if Indevar is alone."

"Are you suspecting the Ano truckers too?"

"Better to be cautious, that's all."

Udondi had assured us that Indevar would sleep until noon, but what then? If he woke on a truck bound for Xahiclan, he might not get a ride back for many days. But if the truckers left him behind, it would be easy for him to find his way to Temple Huacho.

So I sent a message of warning to my mother, giving detailed descriptions of Mica Indevar and all the Ano truckers, and I instructed her to give no welcome to any of them should they appear at the temple gate. She surprised me with a reply even before I put my savant away: *Jubilee, I will be cautious. But when the silver rises, all travelers are welcome at Temple Huacho.*

What other answer had I expected? She was who she was, and I loved her for it, but it made me angry just the same. I felt torn. I wanted to be at Temple Huacho where I could protect my mother. But if I went home, I would be abandoning Jolly and that I could not do.

The day started bright and clear, but by midmorning clouds gathered, dark to match my mood. The land was changing too. We made good time in the gentle hills east of the highway, but our progress slowed as we entered a rising land of crumpled stone cut by steep ravines. When I looked back I was startled to see how far above the lowlands we had climbed. "Are these mountains?" I asked, looking ahead at a highland curtained by clouds.

"Not true mountains," Udondi said. "This is the western escarpment of the Kalang Crescent. This part of the Kalang runs some eight hundred miles north to south, dividing the western lands from the southern reaches of the Iraliad. We're near to its northern limit, where the escarpment swings easterly, to make a great crescent reaching far into the desert." She frowned at the heights. "The plateau is supposed to be only twenty-five hundred feet high, though it looks higher to me. Anyway, it's high enough to catch the clouds that come from the northern ocean, so it'll be wet up there, and densely forested. But it's also an empty land, and there's a good chance we can make our way along the eastern spur without being seen. Then we could descend into the Iraliad, far beyond the reach of any permanent highway."

This encyclopedic answer amazed me. "But I didn't think you'd been in these lands before. How do you know so much of what is here?"

Udondi smiled. "I am new to this region. But I try to understand the temper of the land wherever I am, even if I'm only passing through . . . just in case something happens and I find myself in quiet flight before sunrise."

I blushed, for I had not once thought to look at a map. I could not remember ever using one. There had never been a need. I knew every dell, every stream in Kavasphir, I knew how to find the highway, I knew how to follow the highway to Halibury, or Xahiclan—but every geography beyond that was only a vague reference in my mind.

By contrast, Liam had traveled a third of the way around the world and Udondi had likely wandered much farther. Her battered bike looked as if it had been all the way around the ring, though it still ran smooth and fast. I felt childish beside them, and very foolish, but also grateful I was not alone. "It's lucky for Jolly he doesn't have to count on just me to find him," I said around a sudden constriction in my throat. "Or both of us might be lost forever."

"If you got lost it would not be forever," Liam said gruffly. "Jolly would not have a worry."

I smiled my gratitude, but then I nodded again at the cloud-shrouded heights. All my life I had heard of the hazards of mountains. "Even if these are just little mountains, do we want to enter them? I have always heard there is a great danger of silver in any highland, and surely we cannot journey all the way down the eastern spur before nightfall?"

"Not unless we find a way to fly," Udondi answered with a grin. "This is a rough land."

"There's no sign at all it's settled," Liam said doubtfully.

"That's true. East and south there are no temples recorded on any maps I've seen. If we follow the Kalang Crescent we'll have to camp for several nights, but it's said silver is rarely seen in that forest. It's an old land. Very old. We could be safe from Kaphiri there, at least for a while, for he cannot appear at will in a land where there is no silver, and he cannot bring the silver to such a place unless he first travels there like an ordinary man."

"And if we go north?" Liam asked. "Following the foot of the crescent?"

"The terrain will get easier. In a hundred fifty miles or so there will even be a small highway that runs along the base of the Kalang and into the desert. There are temples there we could take shelter in, but . . ."

"But where there are temples, there are also truckers," I finished for her.

"So the wise course would be to chance the forest," Liam said, "except I have to wonder, if this land is as quiet as you say, why have we seen no sign of settlements? Safe lands are not so common that players will overlook them year after year."

Udondi turned her hands palm up. "I truly don't know. But no land is safe without a sheltering temple and there are none here."

For myself, I wanted to travel unobserved for as many days as possible and I was willing to risk mountains, albeit small ones, to do that. So after a few more minutes of discussion we agreed to try the Kalang Crescent, and we set out again on our climb toward the clouds.

There is a problem with forests where abundant rain falls. It's a matter of recursion. Dominating everything is the primary forest of tall trees, but beneath that there is a smaller forest of slender shrubs and fallen trunks, and beneath these are smaller species still, and for all I know there are greater and lesser levels of micro-forests among the mosses that grow upon the ground.

On the escarpment the vegetation soon grew so dense that only an army of highway-building kobolds would have a hope of finding a straight path through it. Being only three players on bikes, we were forced to follow winding game trails that had mostly been made by creatures much shorter than a player seated on a bike.

I leaned close against the handlebars, but branches still whipped my face and shoulders. Beneath me, the bike tires stretched and jumped and grabbed for traction, kicking up mud as they fought to keep balance, and to climb, but their vertical reach was only ten inches. Every minute or two we'd have to stop and lift the front tires of our bikes over a rock step, or onto a fallen trunk, and once we had to port all three bikes across a narrow ravine with near-vertical walls, because we could not get up the speed to jump it. It was hard work, but at least it was not hot. Clouds closed in around us just past noon, drawing curtains of fine gray mist across the last views of the lowlands, and shortly after that it began to rain.

We kept on. Several times the game trails vanished against vertical stone, or disappeared into fast white streams, or wandered back downhill where we did not want to go. At such times we struggled to turn the bikes around and then we backtracked, looking for any suggestion of an opening in the dripping vegetation.

It was very late on that dreary afternoon when we finally reached the top of the escarpment. We topped out beside a trickle of water that drained an odd little meadow of thick grasses that turned out, on closer inspection, to be a bog. It looked like paradise to me. "Let's camp here," I said, dropping the kickstand on my bike. I gave into exhaustion and tumbled to the soft ground, sure that I could not get any wetter, until I felt chill water seeping against my shoulder blades. Oh, well. Moki jumped down from his perch in the saddle bin to lick my face. Then he raced away, happy to stretch his legs.

Gigantic trees leaned over the little bog, ghostly gray silhouettes that faded in and out of the mist. I could hear birds calling in small, squeaky voices, but I could not see them.

Udondi and Liam had gone on across the clearing but they stopped when they saw I was not following. "Jubilee?" Liam called, his voice strangely muffled by the mist.

"Let's camp here," I repeated. "It's the only place we've seen all afternoon with enough room to unroll a sleeping bag."

"We can camp here if you want," Udondi said. "But come closer to the trees. It's dryer."

"There is no such thing as dry!" Just the same, I forced myself up one more time, climbed onto the bike, and trundled across the spongy ground.

I got a surprise when I reached the trees. All those layers of greater and lesser forests that we had squirmed through on the journey up the escarpment did not exist here on the plateau. Beneath the trees the ground was carpeted with moss—nothing but moss. Raindrops glittered like tiny diamonds strewn across the perfect green. I could see into the forest for maybe twenty yards before the mist closed in and it was like that everywhere: huge tree trunks and a green moss carpet. I closed my eyes and drew in a deep breath of contentment. "So, I guess we could sleep anywhere here."

And that's what I did. I rolled out my sleeping bag, switched on the heat, and crawled inside with a dinner packet, drifting off before it was half-eaten.

Moki must have finished the rest, for the packet was empty when I wakened to the old-man voice of my savant. Night had fallen, and the rain had stopped. Stars glittered to the west, where I could see past the bog to the edge of the escarpment and the vista beyond. The savant floated beside me, gleaming silver, just an inch or two above the ground. Liam must have gotten it out of my saddle bin and set it to watch.

"What is it?" I whispered, listening to the soft breathing of the others from the darkness nearby.

"A call from Yaphet."

Yaphet. I'd almost forgotten about him.

"What time is it?"

"Thirty minutes past midnight."

Ah. Our usual time of discourse. I slipped out of my sleeping bag into a night colder than any I had felt before. I drew in a sharp breath. I had always heard that mountains were cold; it snows in the mountains after all, though never in the lowlands. I wondered if it might snow on us before we crossed the Kalang.

My field jacket was still damp, but I pulled it close anyway. Moki appeared from somewhere, and with the savant soaring beside us to light the way, we stumbled toward the bog.

That night the Bow of Heaven remained invisible, but the stars were bright and I could just make out the edge of the escarpment. An exposed rock, softened by moss, sufficed for a rather soggy bench. Above and beyond and even beneath me, stars filled the black canopy of the sky. I had never looked *down* on stars before. We were that high and for several seconds all I could do was stare at them until the savant whispered again for my attention. "This is a time-limited channel."

"All right. Link. Link now. Yaphet?"

The warning placard appeared, then immediately minimized, and Yaphet was there—still at home in his room. I was surprised at the rush of relief I felt knowing he had not left home. "Jubilee." He looked at me with worried eyes. "Were you sleeping?"

"Yes."

"I didn't know if I should call."

"It's all right."

He searched my eyes, as if seeking there for some hidden truth. "You're okay?"

"A lot has happened, since we talked last."

"You're not at home, are you?"

"No." I pushed at my disheveled hair, then drew a deep breath, trying to drive away the lethargy of sleep. We had only a few minutes. "I've left home. My brother—my older brother—though he's younger than I am now—he was taken by the silver years ago. I never told you about him, Yaphet. His name was . . . *is* Jolly. We thought he was dead, but he's not. He's alive but lost. He's at a station in the Iraliad. I'm going after him. You must not tell anyone this. Yaphet? Do you understand?"

His scowl told me he did not. "This isn't funny."

"It isn't meant to be."

"You've set out for Vesarevi, haven't you? Why don't you just say so?"

"Because I haven't. And I won't. Not until I get my brother home."

He looked at me doubtfully. "You're . . . serious?"

"Yes. The ruined city, I told you about that. It was from the time of Fiaccomo."

He nodded stiffly. He still did not believe. And yet he did. I could see that conflict on his face.

"I think my brother is somehow like Fiaccomo—"

"No. That's imposs—"

"Just listen!" I hissed. "There is another who is not destroyed by the silver and he is hunting my brother too. It's why you must tell no one. *No one.*"

He looked at me in helpless confusion, before remembering himself. "Our time . . ." He gestured to the corner of the screen.

I glanced at the clock. Our time was almost up. "I'll call you when I can, and explain more."

"Where in the Iraliad?" he asked quickly. "Where are you going?"

Would he come if I told him? Would he? Did I want him to?

"Jubilee, you know I'd never do anything to bring you harm. Tell me."

And if he would harm me? I would know it now, before I ever met him. Until that time, I would still have a choice. "Rose Island Station," I whispered.

"Okay." The link closed, and he was gone.

I sighed deeply and shoved the savant away, watching its silvery wing shape bobble on the air, wondering what Yaphet would choose to do. It was Moki's soft growl that brought me back to the present.

He stood on the rock beside me, staring down the escarpment, at the track we had come up that afternoon. I leaned forward, striving to see past the darkness beneath the trees, fully expecting Kaphiri to appear on the trail we had made, a shadow walking out of the shadows, but I could see nothing. I heard nothing, but Moki growled again and when I laid a comforting hand on his back I felt his red fur raised high.

It might be a lion stalking us. And my rifle was still on my bike. "Liam!" I shouted, and my voice echoed across the escarpment.

I listened for the sound of some great creature charging through the forest below, but I heard only Liam and Udondi calling me. "Jubilee! Where are you?"

"By the escarpment. Pull the rifles. Moki thinks something's down there."

Then several things happened at once. Behind me I heard Liam bounding across the bog. Beside me Moki danced back, barking furiously—his high-pitched warning bark exactly like that night the silver came for Jolly. My heart turned over. I rose to my feet.

I saw it then: a silver-colored worm sliding uphill along the track we had followed in the afternoon. It did not gleam like a savant, but its surface caught the starlight so it looked like a faintly glittering cord of light. I guessed it to be six feet long, but very thin, probably no more than an inch in diameter. It moved with stunning speed, not slowing for rocks or the rough terrain as any organic creature would, but gliding over them as if it truly was made of light. By this unnatural locomotion I knew at once it was a mechanic, and with equal certainty I guessed it had been sent to hunt us.

Moki's barking grew more frantic and he scampered back, showing more sense than me. I should have retreated. But I'd seen the worm move and I knew I couldn't outrun it. So I scrambled higher onto the rock outcropping where I had been sitting.

I didn't see the worm reach the edge of the escarpment. It was just there, sliding out of the grass and onto the moss-slick rocks where I stood. A bullet whined, smacking the stone just ahead of the worm, throwing mud and moss and sharp rock flecks into my face.

I slipped. I went down on my side and the worm was on me. It slid over my legs, then across my chest. I grabbed at it, just as its tiny mouth flared open, exposing the glittering point of a single tiny fang. In my hands I felt cold metal scales; on my neck, a piercing pin-point of pain. I flung the worm away over the precipice. Two rifle shots followed as I regained my feet and jumped down to the bog. I was halfway back to the forest when my legs gave out beneath me.

All that night I was in a strange state, drifting in and out of consciousness. Somehow, I was back in my sleeping bag. I thought I was warm, but I wasn't sure. I couldn't move. I wasn't even certain I was breathing. Somewhere in the distance I heard Moki bark in his high, frantic voice. I heard Liam shout and Udondi answer and the rifle sounded again.

I remembered the feel of the worm's cold metal scales and thought, *This is Mica Indevar's revenge.* The worm was his. It had to be his. He'd sent it to follow our trail.

Then maybe the poison wouldn't kill me. Maybe it was no worse than the sleeping drug Udondi had used on him. Except I wasn't asleep. I was dreadfully aware.

I could not turn my head. I could not even tell if my eyes were blinking, but I could see and hear. Moki was barking again, far away, while down the wide trunk of the tree beside me something crawled. Something silvery white just like the worm.

A savant must have been gleaming behind me, because a circle of faint light fell against the tree trunk. As this thing crawled into that radiance I saw it was not the worm. Instead, it was a thing like a mantis, but larger than any insect I had ever seen, as tall as my hand is long.

It crawled headfirst down the rough bark of the tree trunk, stepping carefully on four legs while holding two front limbs close to its body. Its long neck was capped by a triangular head just large enough to hold its two wide, pale eyes. They were not animal eyes. There was no white, no iris, no pupil. Just a dry disk, striated by a circular fan of white rays, marking it as a mechanic, but one very different from the worm.

I screamed for Liam, but the sound was trapped inside my mind.

The mechanic reached the base of the tree's trunk. It stepped gingerly out onto the thick moss.

Liam!

I could hear him and Udondi in the distance, calling to one another in the sharp, staccato voices of hunters close on the prey.

The mechanic raised its forelimbs before my staring eyes. One was a large pincer, more slender than a river crab's. One was like the blades of a pair of serrated knives. From a mouth in its chest it spoke in a strange, unpracticed voice like a rusty hinge swinging: "These trees are Kalang's. To harm them is not allowed."

It waited as if for an answer. When it did not get one it turned and disappeared back up the same tree it had descended.

MEMORY

I still could not move. I could not speak. But I could feel my heartbeat racing in helpless fear.

Some long time passed. Then finally Liam came by and made me close my eyes.

Chapter

13

By dawn I had recovered enough volition to throw up when Liam tried to get some water down my throat. My thoughts fixed on Mica Indevar and they were wicked thoughts indeed.

But soon after that I got my fingers to twitch and my eyes to blink on command. Then, instead of the pleasure of feeling nothing, I endured a horrible prickly return of sensation as when the leg has fallen asleep, but it was everywhere and lasted a solid hour at least. I'm ashamed to say the first sound I uttered (and the only sound for some long time) was an agonized moan.

At last though, the torment faded. I gained some control of my muscles, especially of my tongue and throat—though I had no control at all of what I said. I began to babble, to confess. Anything and everything I had never told to Liam before poured forth: the story of how I had taken my father's rifle when I was eleven and still forbidden to use it, and how I had killed a deer then left the carcass in the forest because I was too frightened to admit what I had done; and the time I had convinced Rizal it would be a good idea to sneak a ride on the rear bumper of a truck leaving Temple Huacho, except Rizal was afraid to jump off so we went too far and it was long past dark by the time we managed to walk home and lucky for us there was no silver that night; and the time Jolly and I had climbed down the kobold well; and how I would fantasize that Liam was my lover after all.

After that confession he left me to recover on my own, and Udondi was too wise to come anywhere near me, so I had only Moki to babble my secrets to, but he already knew them all.

I have no doubt that if Mica Indevar had managed to climb the Kalang escarpment that morning, I would have happily confessed everything I knew about where to find my brother Jolly.

By noon I had mostly returned to myself. I could stand, though my legs trembled. And I could hold my tongue, which is a skill we should not take for granted. I was working my way through a sweetened oat bar when Liam ruefully informed me that the worm had escaped.

I was incredulous. "You let it get away?" Liam was an excellent shot; it had not occurred to me the worm might have escaped him.

"Not by choice. It was fast. Cunning."

"But you had Moki. You had the rifle."

"We hit it twice," Udondi said. "It broke into segments, and then re-formed."

I looked wide-eyed at the lanes of moss-covered ground between the giant trees. "So it's still out there."

"And whoever sent it could be on their way here as we speak," Udondi said. "We need to move on."

"But I saw how fast it moved. We can't outrun it."

As a mechanic, the worm would be powered by the same tiny battery chips that powered our bikes, which could run for months. If they were smarter, I'm sure it wouldn't be long before mechanics owned the world, but fortunately they have no passion for their own existences. Their only interest is the task they are given—and this worm had apparently been charged with stopping our flight, and holding us, until its master could catch up. If we left now it would certainly follow us, and give away our position once again.

Udondi shrugged. "Of course you're right, the worm will find us again, but . . ." She pulled a vial from her chest pocket. "The next time it shows itself we'll have it . . . and we'll still be far ahead of whoever sent it."

A half-dozen dormant kobolds filled the little vial. They were silver, and no bigger than the smallest housefly. "Metallophores?" I asked.

Udondi nodded. "Can you ride?"

I didn't want to. I wasn't sure I could stay on my bike, but if someone was following the worm's track up the escarpment, I did not want to be caught sitting here when they came over the top. So I forced myself up. Liam had already packed my sleeping bag and my savant, so there was nothing left to do but get on the bike, and lift Moki into his bin. That was when I remembered the second mechanic I'd seen in the night.

The memory was remarkably clear, but Liam gave me a funny look when I described what I had seen. "I was not hallucinating!" I insisted. He shrugged.

Udondi was more willing to believe me. She eyed the forest thoughtfully. "Kalang's trees, huh? They do look rather nicely tended."

So they did. I had been too tired yesterday to notice, and too sick to see it in the morning, but the trees were all straight-backed giants without dead limbs or wounds or gnarls. They looked as if they'd been carefully pruned and tended for what must be the hundreds of years they had been alive.

Udondi said, "Personally, I think I'll leave the trees unharmed and forgo any fires until we leave the Crescent. What do you say, Liam?"

What could Liam say? He nodded, and took the lead.

The moss that carpeted the forest floor was so thick and moist our bike tires hardly disturbed it; our tracks disappeared almost before we could turn around. Yesterday on the escarpment I'd expected to spend many grim days hunting a path through the forest. The reality proved suspiciously easy. The trees were planted in great lanes, with no saplings, no underbrush, and no low-hanging branches. There were no follies either; no sign at all that silver had ever been there.

Following the lanes of trees took us in a northeasterly direction:

deeper into the forest and ever farther from the western escarpment. By late afternoon we had put over eighty miles behind us. We might have gone farther, but I was still very weak, and for my sake Liam called a break every half hour or so. During these times I would let Moki run free, hoping he would alert us if the worm drew near. Then I would fling myself onto the wet moss, sleeping for five minutes, sometimes ten, while Liam and Udondi kept watch.

It was during one of these rest stops that Moki discovered a mantislike mechanic, identical to the one I had seen the night before. It clung to a tree trunk, at a height of fifteen feet or so above the ground. From its perch on the rough bark it examined us, making no comment while Moki danced and barked at the base of the tree. Udondi shooed him away. Then she looked up at the mechanic, her hands on her hips. "You see?" she called. "We are not harming the trees."

The mechanic made no response. When we continued on our way a few minutes later, it was still clinging to the tree.

Soon after we saw another, this time on the forest floor where it was busy using its clawlike appendage to snip away at tiny weeds sprouting in the moss. Moki growled at it, but I held on to his scruff so he could not give chase. These were not the mechanics we wanted him to hunt.

Late in the day the rain returned. Fat drops fell down from the distant canopy, pattering dully on the moss, while the aisles of trees were filled with drifting mists. I was overwhelmed with the certainty that this had been the pattern of life here, every day, for hundreds of years. The rain would come and the trees would grow, with no difference from one day to the next, no way to measure time passing.

Then into that stillness there burst a terrible animal scream.

I skidded my bike to a stop to listen better.

Every player is born with instinctive memories. Though I had never before heard such a horrible bellowing, I knew immediately it was the death rage of some great beast, set upon by a predator even more fierce. The hair rose on the back of my neck, while Moki cowered in his bin.

The noise came from somewhere ahead. Not far, I guessed, though nothing could be seen through the mist. The sound became higher in pitch and more frantic, waves of pain echoing through the aisles. I bowed my head and covered my ears but I could still hear it. It seemed to go on forever, though I suppose it couldn't have been more than two minutes, maybe three before silence returned to the forest.

But nothing was the same. The aisles of trees had become sinister lines leading to a dark and unknown heart. I looked back, thinking to turn and flee perhaps, I don't know, but Udondi was there and though she looked shaken she managed an encouraging smile. "At least that hunter found game before it could notice us."

Liam rolled his bike back, so that we made a small circle there under the trees. "I'd like to know what it was."

"You want to look for it?" I asked, wide-eyed.

He nodded. "It could take us two days to reach the eastern end of the Crescent. I'd rather know the hazards than not."

I glanced back once more, but there was no sanctuary that way. Mica Indevar had overheard me speak of Jolly. He would surely have gotten word to Kaphiri by now. I stroked Moki's back and whispered a few words to soothe him. Then I slipped my rifle out of its sheath and slung it over my shoulder.

Udondi did the same, but Liam eyed me doubtfully. "I'll be in front," he reminded, "so don't shoot if your hands are shaking."

They were shaking quite visibly. "Come. Let's get this done."

We came on the kill in just a few minutes. It appeared first as a mound of gleaming, scurrying metal looming in the mist. Only as we drew near did I see the great horns and hooves of a wild bull—eight feet at the shoulder in life—protruding from the mass of forest mechanics that swarmed the carcass, using their claws and blades to cut away tiny slices of meat.

Scarlet blood pooled on the moss.

The bull must have rampaged, for in places the moss was torn out down to the mud, and many trees were slashed as if by horns. A crowd of forest mechanics crouched at each of these wounds, using their feet to pat in a paste just the color of the bark. I kept my hand on Moki.

Liam said, "I think we see the reason the Kalang Crescent has not been settled. I will take your advice, Udondi, and not harm any trees."

Beyond the dead bull (at least, I hoped it was finally dead . . . a death of small cuts and slashes and slow bleeding) new movement caught my eye: a fluid cable of silver metal sliding out of the mist. *"It's there!"* I whispered. *"The worm."*

The worm. It must have been drawn by the activity of the forest mechanics. I watched it slip toward the bull's boiling carcass. It moved slowly, its tiny head raised an inch above the moss, and it did not look to either side. It seemed entranced, hypnotized by this mechanical frenzy, utterly unaware of us on our bikes, only a few dozen feet away.

I realized then that it must have been close to us all day, staying just out of sight—for how else could it have found the carcass so quickly?—and yet it had not once attacked us. Why not? Perhaps because it would be easier to let us escape the Kalang Crescent under our own power . . . ?

I dropped the kickstand on my bike. Udondi turned to stare at me. "They're waiting for us on the other side of the Crescent!" I gestured at the worm. "It's been called off. It's been told to follow us only."

Panic took me. What had I said this morning when the worm's drug had set my tongue to talking? Had I said anything more about Jolly? About where I hoped to find him? I couldn't remember, but what if I had? "They want to use me against him!" Already wet and sick and trembling in that grim forest, I could not bear this added injury. "They think they can find him first!"

I swung off my bike. Moki leaped down to follow.

"Jubilee!" Liam said, backing his bike around. "Be calm. There's nothing we can do here."

"Yes there is. Give me your vial of kobolds." He would have a stock of the metallophores too. I had not seen them, but I knew Liam.

"No. It would be too—"

I wanted no excuses. I turned from him to Udondi. I swear my intention was only to demand the kobolds, but she had come up behind me and in my weakness I stumbled against her. She reached out to catch my arms and I felt the vial in her chest pocket. In an instant I had it out and I was away, running bent over for balance, straight for the feeding frenzy, with the smell of the bull's blood in my nostrils.

The worm was still there, on the other side of the swarming mechanics. It looked like a channel of light in the blood-soaked moss, its tiny head reared up and swaying above the forest mechanics in the attitude of one entranced by an incomparable symphony. Of me, it was utterly unaware.

I drew my hand back to throw the vial—but the moss was soft. Would the vial shatter? I hesitated, and in that moment Liam caught up with me. He grabbed my hand. I cried out in wordless fury while he shouted at me, "Stop and think what you're doing!"

Then we were both shouting at once, while Moki danced around our feet barking like a mad thing.

"I'm going to kill the worm, Liam!"

"You're going to kill us all."

"Let go of me! The worm will follow us if we don't kill it now."

"Think what you're doing! If you release those kobolds here they won't just attack the worm. The forest mechanics, Jubilee! They're made just like the worm. What will happen if *they* begin to die?"

His words got under my rage at last. What would happen? Even more of the forest mechanics would come. Hundreds had swarmed together to attack the bull. How many more might come if some of their own were dying?

The fight left me. I let Liam take the vial.

The worm had been roused by our shouting. It stared at me, its tiny eyes like blind white circles. Somehow it knew I would not dare hurt it.

"Come away," Liam said.

The smell of the carcass and the churning and snipping of the mechanics intruded on my senses as sickening things. Even Moki was lapping at a pool of blood. I let Liam guide me backward. "We will not harm any trees," he murmured. "Or any mechanics." I called to Moki, and he followed, his tongue licking at the blood on his nose and chin.

The worm watched us. Listened. When we were six feet away it lowered its little head to the moss and sped off tail first into the mist almost faster than my eye could follow.

Liam was quietly furious all that afternoon—because I had been foolish, yes, but also I'm sure because he wanted to destroy the worm as much as I did and yet he had been forced to let it go. We would not get a chance like that again, and as fast as the worm could move, how could we ever escape it? I had not seen it again, but I did not doubt that it still followed.

Liam was well ahead of me, his shape on the bike only a silhouette in the mist when I saw him stop. I slowed my own bike, wary of his anger. Udondi had been following, but now she rode up beside me.

She had been silent since my escapade, but with her, as with Liam, I sensed there were words to be spoken that had only been put off for a while. "Stay close," she said. "We need each other."

A blush touched my damp cheeks and I hurried forward, to learn that Liam had found a path.

It was a narrow track, running at right angles to our heading. The moss had been worn away, revealing a maze of tree roots cradling scattered patches of thick mud. Pressed into the mud in several places was the watery impression of a very large boot.

Udondi looked up from where she had been crouching, examining the tracks, "Do we follow the path?" she asked. "Or do we leave this mysterious resident to himself?"

"Let's go on," Liam said. "I don't want to know the player who would choose to live here."

I felt the opposite. I wanted to know who would adopt this forest for a home, and the thought of sleeping under a roof, behind a closed door, was pleasant to me. But I was not going to argue again with Liam. So we crossed the path and went on, but we did not escape.

After half an hour our northeasterly trek was interrupted by a wall that marched across our way. It stood perhaps nine feet high, with a crown of moss on the top. Its bricks had the chalky look of condensed stone that grows by harvesting molecules from the air.

The wall ran off to right and left, wending between the trees until it disappeared in the mist. At several points its stonework had been shattered by the expanding girth of some massive trunk. But despite the strange setting, and the wall's poor condition, I thought I recognized its purpose, for I had climbed upon a similar fortification all my life. "This is a temple wall."

"Maybe it *was* a temple wall," Liam said. "It's a ruin now."

"But perhaps not uninhabited?" Udondi mused.

It was late. Darkness would be falling soon. I knew Liam wanted to push on into the night, but he looked at me and saw it was no use. I was exhausted, not at all recovered from the worm's bite. I played on my weakness. "If it's a temple," I said, "the players here are sure to let us stay the night." And perhaps there would be no forest mechanics within the temple building. I was developing a hearty loathing for all mechanics greater in size and intelligence than simple kobolds.

"Let's follow the wall around," Liam said, nodding to the north. "If we find the gate, maybe we'll see what goes on inside." He was hoping we would not find it, but it was my luck—my famous luck—that we did, and only a quarter mile away. The gate stood open, its panels stained with rain, and moss growing along its upper edge and piled around its hinges, so it was clear it hadn't been shut for years upon endless years.

The path we had spurned in the forest found us again at the gate. It stepped boldly through, dividing the carpet of moss in half.

Liam sat his bike, peering reluctantly within at a massive, dark shadow that was the temple building, looming in the mist. There were no lights, or any scent of dinner cooking. No voices, no gardens, nor any paths, except the one determined path leading directly to the front door.

It was Moki who decided us. He jumped from his bin before I could stop him, and trotted toward the temple, his ears pricked forward in a curious pose. "So," Udondi said, "I've been in stranger places." She followed after Moki, and I followed her, so in the end Liam had no choice.

Chapter
14

We left our bikes alongside the path and walked up the moss-covered stairs that led to the temple's open doors. I was surprised at the dull thump of our footsteps on the stair, as if it was made of hollow plastic. An angled roof covered the small stoop, sheltering it from the rain and shading the double doors so that instead of moss, their plain panels were covered with a slimy black algae that came away on my fingers when I made the mistake of touching it. The doors were pinned against the wall with blackened hooks.

Twilight was falling over the forest, but within the temple night had already come. Liam used a flashlight to chase back the shadows, revealing a modest hall bare of any furnishing. The massive trunks of two trees grew up through the floor, disappearing past neat collars set into the ceiling. Water—presumably from the rain—trickled down their rough bark and out of sight. The floor was a slick of black algae, except where that one resolute path made its way straight across the room, vanishing into a hallway beyond. Moki sniffed at the floor, his tail wagging furiously.

"Nobody home?" Liam wondered.

Udondi addressed the question to the house. "Hello? Anyone here?" Her voice reverberated from hard surfaces. There was no response.

I shrugged, too tired to feel much fear. "If there's any comfort to be found here, it'll be at the end of this path. Come on."

The floor was slick. I almost went down before I figured out how to walk flat-footed. "Hold on, Jubilee," Liam said. "Let me go first, I've got the light."

The path took us through a hallway, then into a round chamber crowded with four massive tree trunks. Rain was drumming on the roof now, and little freshets of water raced down the trunks, trickling into drains in the floor. Everything was damp, and the chamber smelled the way chronically damp things do: of mildew and moldering. Still, it was warmer in here than it had been in the hall and when we stepped past the first great tree trunk it was clear why: four huge gold coils spiraled up from battery pots set into the floor. They gave off a cheerful heat so that in the center of the room the air seemed light to breathe, though its smell reminded me of burnt mulch.

This, apparently, was where the resident had chosen to live, for between the heating coils was a bed with a sagging mattress, a bench, a battered table, a tiny stove, and an ill-designed sink served by a pipe laid right across the floor.

I collapsed onto the bench. Udondi leaned past me to touch a quartz-paned lamp that sat on the table. It blushed to life, reducing Liam's flashlight to an inconsequential role.

I looked about at the pathetic furnishings, and at last a healthy doubt began to assert itself. If this truly was a temple, why was it on no map? Why was it so empty of everything except an abject poverty? "Maybe Liam was right," I said softly. "Maybe this is only the ruin of a failed temple."

Liam answered from the darkness beyond the heaters. "A nice theory, but there's a thriving kobold well here that disputes it."

"You found a well?" I was on my feet in a moment, despite my fatigue, hobbling into the shadows where Liam was crouched beside a waist-high ring of sour-smelling soil as coarse as worm castings. The mound shivered and trembled as kobolds by the hundreds crawled aimlessly through the surface layers. Inside the ring the well was a dark, unfathomable circle. The air above it was cold.

"Listen," Udondi said softly. She stood at the doorway, Moki beside her, his ears pricked as he stared down the hall.

After a second I heard it too: a sound of low, mournful singing, just at the threshold of hearing.

Udondi said, "I think the keeper returns."

We put the light out, and returned to the front door to wait.

The mist-shrouded twilight had given way to true darkness in the few minutes we had been inside. Neither the light of any star nor the gleam of Heaven could reach down through the clouds that shrouded the Kalang Crescent that night. Neither was there any stir of wind, nor whisper of leaf against leaf, but everywhere the endless soft pattering of rain on yielding moss.

I crouched on the stoop, too tired to stand, holding Moki gently by the scruff so he would not charge. The singer's voice drifted through the trees. It was a man's voice, and the song he sang was soft and sad, and full of loneliness, though the words were of a language I did not know, and that did not move any memory in me. A light appeared through the mist, a blurred golden spot jostling along the mud path, revealing nothing of the one who held it.

We waited in silence while the light advanced to the gate, where it stopped. Had the singer seen the tracks our bikes had left on the mud path? Or had he sensed our presence some other way? A scent, or a strange warmth in the air of bodies passing . . .

How long had he been alone? How long, with his world never changing?

Udondi stepped forward then, deliberately scuffing her boots against the slick stair. "Greetings, Keeper," she called in a voice that was clear but soft.

The light rose higher in the air, as if the keeper had lifted it to extend its reach, and for the first time I could see a large, looming shadow behind it.

Udondi said, "We are three strangers on your doorstep at twilight, seeking shelter from the silver."

Those are the traditional words used in stories of old to gain entrance to a temple. I couldn't remember any visitor to Temple Huacho ever being so formal, but of course our hospitality was never in question.

"Mari?" the singer asked, his voice oddly hoarse as with some wretched hope. Then, speaking in the language we all knew, "Mari, is it you? Did you find your youth? Have you come home at last?"

Udondi answered him, "Alas, Keeper, none of us are your Mari." Then she turned to Liam and murmured, *"Hand me the flashlight."* He passed it to her. She turned it on, and held it high so its light shone down on us. "I am Udondi Halal, this is Liam Panandi, and this, Jubilee Huacho."

"Are you wayfarers?"

"It's only that we have business in the desert to the east."

He came forward then, into the gleam of the light, and I could see he was a player big enough to fill the boots whose tracks we had seen—taller than me and Liam by a head and shoulders, and almost wider than the three of us put together. He wore a hat with a great, flat brim, and a long green raincoat that whispered as he moved.

But despite his size, and despite a neatly trimmed black beard that furred the lower half of his face, he looked a boy, his features youthful and rounded and smooth. If not for that beard, I would have guessed him even younger than me, a husky adolescent just reaching his full growth. The beard looked like stage costuming.

He examined us in turn, and his confusion was that of a child. "She said she would come back." His worried eyes looked first at Udondi, and then Liam. Next he turned to me, and hope touched him. "I never saw her when she was young. Are you sure . . . ?"

"She is not Mari," Udondi said quickly. "She is Jubilee Huacho."

"And she is no wayfarer," Liam added. "She is mated."

"I am not," I snapped. "Not yet."

The boy-man chuckled at this, showing an elusive maturity, though he still did not seem convinced. He studied me, as if hoping I would reveal some habit or gesture to prove I was his lost Mari after all. This annoyed me. I was exhausted and still sick, and I didn't want to defend myself against the ghost of a woman long gone.

So I let Moki go, and rising to my feet, I said, "You don't look old enough to have ever known a lover."

"Oh, but I am." He rubbed at his damp forehead with the tips of pale white fingers, as if trying to rouse some memory. "I'm older than I look. My name, it's . . . Nuanez Li. And . . . and . . ." He frowned. "I *am* the temple keeper. I have been, since she went away. A long time, now. There are words I'm supposed to say when players come. I know there are, but . . . what were they? What?" He shook his head in utter mystification. "Anyway, all of you are welcome here. Not that there's any silver to hide from. I've never seen it here. Not once. But you're welcome . . ." He snapped his fingers, looking at us in sudden triumph. "*All travelers are welcome!* Those are the words. 'All travelers are welcome at Temple Li!' Well. It has been a very long time since any have come."

We brought the bikes inside to get them out of the rain. Then we returned to the well room, which was the only room Nuanez Li used anymore. He had gone in ahead of us, and we found him waiting there with the light turned on, looking forlorn as he stood before the open door of a small cabinet. "There's only kibble," he said softly. "It's not fresh."

Kibble is a wayfarer's food, made of a strain of kobold that can eat almost anything organic. The kobold's body swells into a marble-sized pellet of protein. Then the head and legs die and fall off, leaving a protein pellet encased in a sweetened carbohydrate shell. Kibble can last for months, and apparently that was how Nuanez cultivated it: in large batches in a back room of the temple whenever he could get the carcass of a wild calf, or gather enough fallen leaves to make a compost heap.

"We have other food," Liam said. "If you'll permit it, we'd be honored to provide dinner tonight."

Nuanez looked close to tears at this suggestion, and I could not tell if it was because he felt ashamed, or because he was moved to be with other players again. Liam nodded, pretending Nuanez had assented. Then he went to fetch our road packets from the bikes and Nuanez went with him.

When they came back Nuanez carried all the packets himself, looking as pleased as a child on his birthday. He sat beside me at the table and sorted through them again and again, admiring the labels, and the listed contents. Liam encouraged him to choose whichever he wanted and that took another ten minutes until finally I said I should cover his eyes and let him pick blindly. He agreed that would be best and afterward he ate with his eyes closed, and a look of bliss upon his face. None of us had the heart to disturb him, so it was a silent dinner, requiring only a few minutes to finish.

Afterward I forced myself up. Leaning past Liam, I put my hand on his flashlight. "I'm going to get our things off the bikes."

He looked up at me, and the look in his eyes made me remember that we had not finished our business of the afternoon. Udondi saw it too. She leaned across the table, distracting Nuanez with questions about the structure of the temple. "Oh, aye," Nuanez said. "It's all plastic, compiled of carbon harvested from the air . . ."

I took the flashlight and left. I did not look back. Shadows retreated ahead of me in the hallway and I heard Nuanez ask, "Where are they going?" Udondi answered something I could not understand and Moki's claws scrabbled at the floor as he hurried to catch up.

I listened for Liam following me, but he moved like a cat, silent. Saying nothing. When I could stand it no longer I turned about in the hall sending the shadows jumping up the mildewed walls. "I had to do something!"

He was six paces behind me, looking as angry as he'd been that afternoon, as if he'd packed the emotion away, only to pull it out again, still fresh. "You didn't think I'd do something?"

"I'm not the kind of player to wait for someone else."

"If you don't learn to think first, Jubilee, to think ahead, you're not going to last out here. It's as simple as that."

I nodded. "I made a mistake, Liam. I know that."

He watched me, as if waiting for something more. "What? No promise it won't happen again?"

"I can't promise that."

"So you're honest." He held out his hand. "Give me the flashlight."

It was his, so I handed it to him. He went past me, into the front hall where we had left the bikes. "Liam, I *am* sorry."

He was already throwing open the saddle boxes, pulling out the sleeping bags, and our savants. "I don't want to die out here. I don't want you to die."

"We aren't going to die."

"Spend a few months on the road, and you won't sound so confident when you say that."

He was in no mood to make peace. So I took my savant and went out on the stoop to call my mother, but I could not get a signal, not even when I floated the savant high on a wire line. Liam came out to watch. "No luck?"

I shook my head. "Either the district antennas are down or there *are* no district antennas."

"That last, I'd guess."

Moki was running about in the rain. I whistled for him, trying hard to hold on to an artificial calm. At Temple Huacho we had often lost our market connection, but never before had I been prevented from calling home if I was away. What was going on there? Did they need me? Would I ever know?

It came to me that I might find Jolly, and that I might take him back to Kavasphir only to find that our home, Temple Huacho, had been lost: fallen to ruins at the hands of some cessant cult, or washed away by the silver, and all that we loved in this world gone.

"She'll be all right," Liam said as if he had heard my heart. "Your mother is good at taking care of things."

"She is. I know it."

But Kaphiri was a hazard altogether different from any she had faced before.

Back in the well room, Udondi saw things in a more positive light. "If you can't get a link out of here, neither can the worm."

That was true. So it was possible nothing was known of our activities since we'd left the Kalang's western rim. If we could get rid of the worm before we left the Crescent's eastern spur, we might still stand a chance of slipping away undiscovered.

I laid out my sleeping bag beside one of the heating coils. Then I checked that my rifle was loaded. "How can we stop the worm?" I wondered aloud. "Would a shot to the head do it?"

Nuanez had heard the story of the worm from Udondi. "Depends on the design," he said. "Some mechanics have intelligence in every segment. Do you want to sleep in my bed?"

I glanced at his sagging mattress—"No thank you; this is fine"— and crawled inside my bag before he could insist.

Liam said, "The metallophores could still work. Or maybe we could take it in a noose."

"No," I said. "If you noose it, the worm would only split into segments and escape." I pulled the bag over my shoulders, grateful for the nearby heating coil.

"Maybe it could be noosed about the head," Nuanez said.

"It has only one set of eyes," Liam mused. "That probably means the intelligence is local to the head."

"So a head shot *might* work," I mumbled as a lethargy crept over me. The room grew distant, and yet I didn't fall asleep. Or if I did, it was only a half sleep in which the voices of the others continued to play inside my mind, their soft words wrapped around a whiskey smell. I guessed it was Udondi who'd produced the liquor, because I never knew Liam to carry it. I listened to their low voices, and after a while it was mostly Nuanez who spoke, his words building the shape of his life in my half-waking mind.

Long ago he had come to the Kalang Crescent with his lover,

and together they had made this temple around a kobold well they discovered freshly born from the ground. A lifetime spent in that horrible forest! I could not imagine it, yet Nuanez spoke fondly of his past. He had been happy, and I can only think his lover Mari had been happy too. There had been twenty-six children, though one daughter was lost to the forest mechanics when she was five. Nuanez still was bitter: "Kalang—whoever he was—was a fool to leave them here. Now it'll take a silver flood to be rid of them."

In time the children grew up and one by one they went away. "I hope some of them found lives out there," Nuanez said, a faraway note in his voice. "Anyway, none came back."

But Nuanez did not look old enough to have even one child. I wondered if he might be the youngest son after all, left on his own after some terrible accident, his loneliness driving him to re-create a life history of love and family bonds. "How is it you look so young?" I asked.

They all turned to me with startled faces. Then Liam chuckled. "Jubilee, I thought you were asleep."

"Not really."

Nuanez eyed me with that disturbing, speculative glint he had. "Do I look young?"

Udondi answered that. "Hardly a teen."

This pleased him. "That'll be a relief for Mari! She wouldn't want to come back to an old man. Ah, I miss her so much. She endured a lot to win the traveler's favor. He was a cruel one, with never a kind word for her, but she would always gift him the best room and the best food when he came to stay." Nuanez smiled sheepishly. "It's hard to believe, I guess, but we kept a fine house when Mari was here. Not like now . . ."

"Your house is warm," Udondi said, "and your hospitality unquestioned . . . but who is this traveler you speak of?" Was there an edge of excitement in her voice?

Nuanez frowned, struggling with the memory. "Did he ever have a name? If he did I don't remember it. We called him the traveler. Or we called him nothing at all. *He's here.* That's all Mari would say when I returned in the evening from tending the wells, but I knew who she meant. He had no need of a name.

"He came the first time not long after we moved here, but even then he knew his way in the forest. He showed me kobold wells I had not found before, and he ordered me to care for them. It made my circuit very long, but I kept them well. Mari wanted me to. The traveler knew many things, and Mari loved to learn new things. *Our wells must be very special*, she'd say. *To bring him back again and again.*

"Years passed between his visits, and when he came back he always looked just the same. Mari noticed it first. *He doesn't age*, she'd say."

This startled me, and my gaze shifted to Udondi, who answered my look with a slight nod.

Nuanez went on with his story. "Mari felt her own age growing heavy on her. She had spent ninety-one years as a wayfarer. She was past one hundred when she found me. She'd been through a lot and . . . it made her afraid. If she died and was born again, would she have to spend another ninety years in fruitless searching? She didn't want to die and lose what she had. So finally she gathered her courage and asked the traveler about his secret, how he had held on to his youth.

"He had always been a cruel man, but he showed her some kindness then. He told her he would help her, that she did not have to die. So she went away with him. He was going to make her young again, that's what she told me, and then she'd come back, and we'd be together always . . ."

Again Udondi and I exchanged a look, and I could see she thought this traveler was Kaphiri.

Nuanez did not notice. "She'll be surprised when she does finally come home, because I have found a way to get my own youth back, and I found it right here, in our own kobold wells. After Mari left, I had a lot of time, so I read her books, and I experimented with the kobolds and changed their configuration codes and finally I got what Mari wanted: an elixir to return youth."

I pushed myself up on one elbow, peering at his boy-face. "So you made yourself young again." But his youth was not the same as Kaphiri's. The player I'd met at Temple Huacho had none of the childish look or mannerisms of Nuanez. Kaphiri had seemed not so much young, as timeless, immune to age.

"She should have come back by now," Nuanez said, and his voice broke. His face scrunched up, so that I was afraid he would cry. "Why does it take so long?"

"Has the traveler never come back?" Udondi asked gently.

"Never. The road is dangerous, I know, and if something happened to him in some far land, then Mari might have become lost. That could be why she takes so long. But the goddess will finally guide my Mari home. I know it. The silver's aware of all of us. Mari told me it was so, and she grew up in the mountains, so she would know."

He snapped his fingers. "But I'm forgetting again! It's gotten bad lately. The traveler must have known something I did not, for he never forgot anything . . ." Nuanez tapped his forehead. "But me . . . I feel stuffed with memories. Too many memories. They make me fuzzy-headed. Sometimes I feel I don't have room in my head to think at all, but—" He stopped in midsentence, a distant look in his eyes as if he were off chasing some stray thought. Then he smiled. "Mari doesn't like me forgetting."

His bed creaked as he stood. He shuffled over to one of the cabinets behind the heating coil at the foot of his bed. Opening the plastic door, he bent over, and rummaged around inside. "Oh. Miracle. I've found it."

When he turned around, I glimpsed a flat, greenish object half-hidden in his great hand. "This was Mari's. When she was a girl in the mountains, it was the custom to make shrines to the goddess. If you left something valuable for the silver, sometimes something even more valuable was returned, so it was said. Well, Mari had a brother who was good at everything, while she was not so good. It sat hard with her, and one day she made a shrine and left her cat there. That cat was more precious to her than anything . . . except, I guess, beating her brother. She wanted the goddess to send her something powerful in trade for that cat. Well, she lost the cat, and all she got in return was this book." He handed a little palm-sized book to Udondi, who thumbed through it curiously. "Can you read it?" Nuanez asked hopefully.

"Not a word."

He sighed. "Neither could Mari. She never showed it to the traveler, or told him she had it, because she didn't trust him to let her know what it was about. But before we came here she used to show it to everyone she met, hoping someone could read it."

"Jubilee is good with these things," Udondi said, and she passed the book to me. I accepted it eagerly. The cover was green plastic, but each inner page was a wafer of green lettered stone, the black writing tiny, compressed. I bent over it, squinting in the poor light. I knew these letters! My lips moved as I sounded out the words. *"Sweet silver,"* I whispered.

"Do you have it?" Liam asked.

I nodded, feeling a sudden chill. "It's the same language used by the bogy in the ruined city."

"You can read it?" Nuanez asked in hoarse amazement. "What does it say?"

I turned a few pages, reading words where I could. "It looks like an index of configuration codes."

"For regrowing youth?"

"I don't think so. It'll take me some time to work the whole thing out, but here . . . and here. These seem to do with recalling memories."

His face fell in clear disappointment. "Oh, I have too many memories already. An old man's mind in a young man's body and no room left for thinking."

I frowned over the book. Had I misspoken? The codes had to do with recalling memories, yes, but not the memories of individual players. Rather, the memory of silver . . .

Could that be?

I glanced at Nuanez, knowing I should explain the difference, but I'd begun to covet the book. I held it against my chest. "May I read it?"

"You can have it! Didn't I say that? Mari intended to give it to the one who could read it. She got to thinking maybe that was the reason she'd been given the book in the first place—to hold on to for another. She traded her cat for it. She wanted it to mean something. Oh, Mari. You'd be disappointed to know it was only configuration codes."

After that the light was put out and the others slept, but I lay awake, thinking, still holding the book in my hands. Mari had traded her cat for it—the same as if I'd traded Moki. A powerful gift.

Was the silver aware? I riffled the book's crisp stone pages and a light fluttered from them. A greenish light.

My eyes went wide in surprise. I huddled deeper in my sleeping bag. Then I opened the book again.

The pages made their own light, a lovely, light green glow that left the letters standing out in crisp silhouette. I turned to the first page and read the title: *Known Kobold Circles*. There was an introduction before the listings of configuration codes. I rubbed at my eyes and told myself to close the book and go to sleep. But the introduction was short; only a few sentences. I decided I would read that, no more. Eagerly, I started puzzling out the unfamiliar words. The meaning I gleaned was close to this:

> *Ours is a world of tricks and complications. Who made it so no one can say, but all tricks must unravel in time if we work together, and share what we know. This book is dedicated to that end. Herein are summarized the findings of seventy-three temple keepers, all of whom dedicated many years to the puzzle of kobold circles.*

All the circles listed here are based on the Pythagorean series. No doubt other combinations of zero exist, but at the time of this writing they are unknown. New solutions should be reported to the keeper of Temple Choff-en-Oreone, for inclusion in future editions of this book.

Ki-Faun
5th day of Spider
this year 13,255

If Ki-Faun had counted years according to the same calendar we used, then this writing was more than eight thousand years old.

Forgetting my resolve to read only the introduction, I turned the page, puzzling over the lists of configuration codes. It was too bad Ki-Faun had not bothered to explain what a kobold circle was, or for that matter a Pythagorean series. Maybe my savant would know?

I stuck my head out of my sleeping bag to whisper a quiet summons. That's when I saw Moki standing over me, stiffly alert, his ears pricked toward the top of the tree trunk beside the heater where I had made my bed. I followed his gaze. Between the trunk and the collar that ringed the hole in the ceiling, I could just see the tiny head of the worm, glittering in the faint light of the drifting savants. Moki growled, and the worm's head emerged a little farther. It looked at us with its empty white eyes.

I reached for my rifle. Without sitting up I raised it slowly, slowly to my shoulder. Then I lifted my head, just far enough to peer along the sight. The worm didn't shy at my movement. It hung motionless against the tree trunk, its white eyes fixed on me . . . as if it was daring me to take the shot.

That first night Liam had shot it in the body, and it had immediately repaired itself, but I knew I could hit it in the head . . . and maybe that would finish it.

I held my breath; my finger tightened over the trigger—

Then, as if some ghost had whispered a warning in my mind, I realized what I was about to do. I would hit the worm, yes, and maybe destroy it, but the bullet would carry on into the trunk of the tree and then the forest mechanics would surely come.

I collapsed back to the floor, holding the rifle against me, my eyes closed and a cold sweat beading my skin. *Sweet silver.* I had nearly repeated my mistake of this afternoon. I could hear Liam again, his disappointment, *Learn to think first, Jubilee.*

He didn't trust me. I wasn't sure anymore I trusted myself.

I laid the rifle on the ground. Then I looked again for the worm, but it had withdrawn. I watched for it to return. Only after a long time, did I fall asleep.

Chapter

15

The table lamp was on again when Udondi nudged me awake. "Time to rise, wayfarer, the road awaits us."

"You found a road?" I asked around a yawn.

She grinned. "Where we step, that is our road."

I groaned and tried to wriggle deeper into my sleeping bag. "It's too early to quote classics. Are you sure it's even morning?" There was certainly no evidence of daylight in the temple's well room. The lamp on the table burned just as it had last night, casting the same illumination. I squinted at the tree trunks, but could see no sign of the sun winking through the narrow gap in the ceiling.

"It's morning by the clock," Udondi assured me. "And even better the rain has stopped. Do you feel all right today? Has the worm poison finished with you?"

I considered the question. I felt tired, hungry, sore, but what else could be expected? "I feel all right."

"Good. Come have some breakfast. We want to be ready to leave at first light."

I gave in, and crawled out of my sleeping bag. A glance around the room showed the other bags were already gone, packed on the bikes I supposed, along with the savants. Of Liam and Nuanez and even Moki, there was no sign. "How long has everyone been up?" I asked, collapsing onto the bench beside the table.

Udondi set a bowl of kibble in front of me. "Not so long."

They were babying me. She and Liam had probably been up for an hour, packing, and making plans. I scowled at the kibble. I didn't want to be the cargo, the human baggage on this journey.

Udondi chided me: "The kibble will not be improved, no matter the stern looks we give it." She put out a glass, and a pitcher of water. Then she sat down across from me. "You've been sick with the worm's bite. It would have affected any of us in the same way."

I nodded, though I couldn't help but think she and Liam would have shown more fortitude.

I commenced my duty with the kibble, while Udondi spilled three snub-nosed bullets onto the table. Picking up the first, she opened it at the base, revealing a hollow chamber inside the ceramic jacket. Next she took out the vial of metal-eating kobolds. With ceramic tweezers she carefully transferred seven kobolds into each of the bullets, sealing them shut when she was done.

"Going worm-hunting?" I asked.

She smiled.

Liam had been out with Nuanez, scouting about for the worm. He had hoped to try a head shot. But though Moki found scent trails that excited him, he did not find the mechanic, and Liam returned with his rifle unused.

Then it was time to leave.

Nuanez stood with us on the stoop, his boy-face looking all the more forlorn for the brave smile he tried to put on. "Take care on your journey," he told us. "It's a long way to the end of the eastern spur. Be cautious all the way. Don't make fires. Don't harm the trees." Then he turned to me, still with that questioning look in his eyes. "Keep that book close to you, Jubilee. And if you ever come back here, you must visit, and tell me if it was worth Mari's cat."

I thought my heart would break. "Why don't you come with us?" I blurted. "I think you should. We're not the perfect companions, I know. That worm's not a pleasant shadow, but you'd probably be okay with us to the edge of the Crescent. You could use my bike. I could ride with Liam."

"Jubilee's right," Liam said. "Come with us. Let the matchmakers help you find your Mari."

Nuanez shook his head. "I thank you for your kind offer, but I can't go. Mari and I, we made promises. She said she'd come back here, and I know she will."

We argued with him some more, but he had his faith and he would not come. So we left him some of our food packets as a parting gift, and we said good-bye. Afterward I thought of him as a kind of ghost, for although he was not dead he did not seem truly alive either. The past owned him, and he had not the heart to ask it to let him go.

We left Temple Li heading east, but after several miles we turned in a more southerly direction. This spur of the Kalang Crescent reached deep into the desert, and it was our plan to follow it for as long as we could, but first we wanted to find our way to the remote southern side.

The Iraliad was really two deserts. The northern expanse was renowned as a harsh land, with few settlements and no permanent highways, where the silver was said to rise almost every night of the year. But the southern basin was worse. The silver storms there were so bad that few players had ever survived it, and what little was known was mostly rumor. We reasoned that if we kept to the southern escarpment, there would be no highways, and no settlements below us, and the worm would have no way to make radio contact with its masters, and give us away.

We set out in the gray light of dawn, but it wasn't long before the sun joined us, glittering among the leaves and casting spangled shadows on the moss. With no mist among the trees it was not so easy for the worm to hide, and Liam and I glimpsed it shortly after we set out, sliding through a patch of sunlight. We both pulled our rifles, but it slipped away. Then at midmorning it was Udondi's turn to spot it.

She was riding ahead of me when she brought her bike skidding to a stop, so that I had to pull hard to the side to avoid hitting her.

She yanked her rifle from its sheath, snapped it up to her shoulder, and fired.

Hiss. Pop!

The worm was caught on the moss, less than fifty feet away. It bucked, its back rising a hand span into the air. Then it writhed, coiling into a tight knot, turning over and over until it vanished behind a tree.

Udondi slung her rifle over her shoulder and sped off after it. I followed. It took us only seconds to reach the site, but the worm was gone.

At least it had not gone away unscathed. Liam found a six-inch segment of its body, where one of the kobolds had attached. I found another, smaller segment a few feet away, and then a third. Udondi crouched over each, counting the kobolds. "Five," she announced. "There were seven in the slug. Damn. The other two will be lost in the moss somewhere."

"They might be with the worm," I said. "We don't know."

"No. It would have dropped more segments."

"Not if one reached the head."

She smiled—"Then we'll hope for that"—but I could tell she was only humoring me. She let the kobolds feed for a few minutes. Then she gathered them up and we went on.

We reached the southern escarpment just before noon. We knew we were close by the gleam of brilliant daylight growing steadily brighter beyond the massive trunks of the trees, until suddenly the trees were gone, and there was only sky.

Leaving our bikes, we walked the last few feet to the edge of the escarpment. A wind sailing up from the south poured over the cliff's edge, whipping my hair and chilling my face. I crept up to an outcropping of rocks that stood like a guardrail at the very edge of the abyss. Gingerly, I leaned over them—and found myself facing a sheer drop of at least two thousand feet.

Bile rose in my throat. I was looking *down* on the world, as a bird looks, as a bat looks. As if I were *flying* . . .

But players did not fly.

Beneath the cold touch of the wind my cheeks flushed with an unwholesome heat. *Players did not fly* . . . and yet there was something familiar in this height, in the feel of the streaming wind, as if I had known such a thing before, in some dream I dared not remember. I felt suddenly guilty, as if I'd violated some essential law . . . but I did not retreat from the edge. Instead I leaned even farther, gazing in wonder at the cliff's sheer face.

It looked unnatural, as if it had been chiseled by some giant hand. Here and there a few silver-barked trees clung to the rock, in defiance of the need for soil. Between the trees, moss and lichen grew in green streaks and silvery patches, but they did not soften the slope. Looking east and west I counted three waterfalls plunging in long spires of mist that turned to rain before they reached the land below. At the base of the cliff trees grew in a dense forest, but farther from the wall their ranks thinned, and soon they yielded altogether to grassy foothills that fell steeply away into a barren land of stone and brown dust. A brown haze veiled the basin, while storm clouds gathered on the horizon. Lightning flickered among them, and the streaming wind carried with it a faint growl of thunder. I was glad we would not be going down into those lands.

Liam and Udondi had retreated to the trees. I joined them, to find Udondi with her savant unpacked and balanced in her lap. "You see here," she was saying to Liam as she tapped at the screen. "The map shows rolling foothills, blending with the plateau. There's no hint of an escarpment like this. None at all."

Liam frowned at the display. "Well look over here, at the elevation measures on the western side. We came up that way, and it was a lot higher than it shows. Your map is wrong."

"You mean the Kalang Crescent isn't supposed to be this high?" I asked.

"Not according to the cartographers who pretended to map it," Udondi said in disgust. "Three different expeditions, according to the records, but they must have been copying each other's work because not one of them shows a cliff like this—" and she waved her hand at the escarpment. "Which means we can't rely on these maps to show us a way down."

"The northern edge of the Kalang is better known," Liam said. "And probably more accurately mapped. We'll find a way down."

"But finding takes time."

I crouched beside Udondi. "How old are these maps, anyway? Maybe it's just that the land has changed."

She frowned at me. "Enough that the entire plateau has risen two thousand feet?"

Well, it was true I'd never heard of land changing on such a scale. Still . . .

"May I see the other maps?"

She shrugged, and passed the savant to me.

I studied each display, not sure what I was hoping to find. On each one the southern escarpment was shown as a steep slope, but it was not vertical, and it rose no more than a thousand feet above the surrounding land. A thousand feet, at most. On one of the maps the height was only 740 feet, while on the other it was 870. I looked at the dates and my brows rose. "Udondi!" I called. She had returned to the cliff edge, where she stood, gazing east with her field glasses. "Udondi!"

This time she heard me over the streaming wind. I beckoned her over. Liam came too. "Time to pack up," he said. "If the terrain stays smooth, we might be able to put two hundred miles behind us by sunset, enough to bring us to the eastern tip of the Crescent."

"First look at this." I had the three maps displayed so they overlapped one another, with the southern cliff showing at the bottom of each. "The oldest map shows the lowest elevation . . . thirty-two hundred years ago. The newest map shows the highest. That one's nineteen hundred years old. The land *is* changing, but not so much as it seems. If it's been rising only six inches a year, that would account for the error in the most recent map."

Udondi and Liam traded a bemused look. "That's a clever idea,"

Udondi said diplomatically, "although I have never heard of such a thing in all the histories I've explored."

"The absence of silver argues against it too," Liam added.

That was true. Without silver, the Kalang should be unchanging.

"Anyway," Udondi said, "it doesn't matter why the map is wrong, just that it is. It will be a long way back if the cliffs prove to be this steep all around the eastern spur."

Liam shrugged. "We'll cross to the north side tomorrow, and then we'll know. But let's make what progress we can, while the light is with us."

With the coming of the afternoon, the weather changed. The storm we had seen to the south sent an army of clouds north to cover the basin, but they remained below us, hiding the desert beneath a white blanket that stretched to the horizon. I had never looked down on clouds before and I was fascinated by the slow, boiling motion of the mist tendrils as they rose, then collapsed again into the cloud bank.

Later, peaks came into sight far away to the south and east, their summits glittering faintly through the distance, like gems of white quartz cast on a field of wool. "That's called the Sea Comb," Udondi said, nodding at the distant points of white stone as we paused at a stream crossing. "A gulf of the southern ocean lies less than a hundred miles beyond them, and it's said those peaks comb the moisture from the clouds that come up on the southern wind, sending it back to the gulf in a thousand streams and rivers. The clouds that pass through those teeth are stingy with the moisture they have left. They cast a gloom over the Iraliad, but they seldom give rain."

I thought about the ocean, trying to imagine all those clouds as water. The fantasy delighted me. Maybe I should have been afraid, standing on that cliff edge, looking out on a vista that reached to the edge of the world, but I was part of that world, I felt my connection to it keenly. I wanted to throw my arms around it, and gather it all up and know it, for it was beautiful, and full of life and mystery, and these were things that called to my soul.

We continued east, and in the late afternoon we finally reached the edge of Kalang's forest. There was nothing gradual or natural about the transition. The trees simply ended in a last line of carefully tended giants, without a single sapling to mar the strict boundary between the forest and the wide grassland that stretched before us.

As we rode through that grassland we saw many herds of wild cattle, each shepherded by a bull that would snort and offer false charges if we passed too near. The land was badly overgrazed, and cut through with the colorful scars of exposed mineral deposits. I could not imagine how so many cattle survived there, but they looked in good condition. "So," Liam said when I mentioned it, "maybe they're tended by mechanics too."

We laughed, for even mechanics could not easily produce feed out of the air. Still, I looked around a little more warily after that, for if these herds were descendants of animals kept by the mysterious Kalang then perhaps they *had* inherited some ancient protection of their own.

The sun was behind us, low in the west and just on the verge of disappearing behind the gloomy line of the forest when we came unexpectedly to the eastern tip of the Kalang. Udondi, who had ridden ahead, stopped and gave a somber call back to us, her voice like a bird's cry on the wind. Liam and I hurried to join her, only to find that the sheer southern cliff had circled around in front of us. We were standing on a peninsula in the clouds, no more than a quarter mile wide, its apex marked by a rounded bluff that dropped straight down into the fog.

"The maps don't show anything like this," Udondi said, and her voice was soft with a restrained anger. If the map makers had been there, I fear they might have learned very quickly the exact height of that cliff. But they were long lost to history, and we could go no farther east.

So we rode around the bluff, and in that way came immediately to the northern wall. At first the cliff was as sheer as on the southern side, but after a mile the vertical wall gave way to great piers of eroded stone that stepped out into the cloud sea. Their slopes—the little we could see before they vanished in mist—were frighteningly steep and heavily eroded, covered with loose flakes and chips of stone so that the danger of landslide was very real. And still they seemed friendly after the stern impossibility of the southern escarpment. We could have tried to descend in a dozen different places, but all of them presented a considerable risk, so we kept going, hoping for something better.

At twilight we found it. The clouds pulled back, revealing a well-used cattle trail winding along the side of a great ridge. We watched a herd appear from out of the mist, lowing gently as they climbed the last half mile to the plateau.

"And if the native cattle choose to pass the night in the highlands," Liam said, "then I think we should too."

Udondi and I quickly agreed. In all that land we had seen no sign of silver, no follies, and no recent veins of beautiful ore. We felt safe camping there. Or we would have felt safe, if we didn't have to contend with the lurking threat of the worm.

We made our camp well back from the trailhead in case the cattle chose to use it in the night. I floated my savant, but there was still no signal. "That's the Iraliad," Udondi said. "Antenna towers go down all the time."

I couldn't help but worry—about my mother, about Jolly, and even about Yaphet. I was restless, so as evening loomed I set out for the cliffs, Moki at my heels.

To my surprise the clouds were breaking up, the greater mass rolling back toward the Sea Comb, while the stragglers evaporated in the descending night. There was little light left. Still, I was able to glimpse the land below. It looked to be a dry, jagged country, with little more vegetation than the southern desert I had seen that morning. Ridge after ridge ran east into darkness, each one cut by steep ravines that emptied into broad washes so smooth I guessed they were lined with sand.

Far, far away, where night had already fallen, a tiny light winked to life. Whose light? Few players dared the Iraliad and it was easy to think I looked out on the encampment of our enemies . . . but if so, why did they wait for us so far from the Kalang?

Within seconds a new glow appeared—silvery, nebulous—it sparkled in the washes, at first only a half-seen, illusory light but it brightened rapidly as twilight gave way to full darkness, and soon the plain was flooded with luminous silver. It rose as quickly as any silver flood I have seen, filling the gullies and climbing the steep slopes of the ravines until only the highest ridges and a few lonely pinnacles stood above it. Cattle, made tiny by distance, gathered on these islands, lowing forlornly to the twilight. Somewhere a coyote howled, and others answered it, and soon a symphony was rising from the lowlands and it was as if the silver itself had found a voice.

That sound got inside me. Or maybe it only wakened my coyote heart, but I found myself *hoping* the worm's owner was out there. Kaphiri might not be troubled by such an evening, but surely the same could not be said for Mica Indevar and the other players who followed him. The Iraliad was a dangerous place and not just for us. Perhaps the silver would swallow our enemies before ever they could find us. Perhaps it already had.

When I looked again for the distant light, I could not find it, though whether it had been taken by the silver or only eclipsed, I could not say.

Chapter

16

Liam had the last watch that night. He woke me with a gentle shake of my shoulder. *"Jubilee."*

"Is it morning?"

"Soon."

It was still dark, but I could hear a constant lowing of cattle all around me, and now and then the sound of a hoof striking rock. Udondi stirred sleepily. *"*Has something frightened the cattle?" she asked. "Why are they moving?"

"They make their way to the trailhead," Liam said. "Most of them probably go down to graze in the day." He was crouched beside me. I could just make out his rifle, cradled in his lap. "Are you both awake now?"

He spoke softly, but something in his voice gave me warning. I sat up, and Udondi did the same. "What's happened?" I asked.

"I've seen him."

"Seen who?" I searched my mind for possibilities. "Mica Indevar?"

"No. It was Kaphiri."

Liam told us then how he'd taken his rifle and walked out to the cliffs to look about. "The land below was flooded with silver, and I could see the tiny shapes of cattle, crowded onto the high ground. After a time one of the trapped herds began to churn in a sudden panic that drove some of the smaller calves into the silver. I thought a coyote might have been on their hilltop island, but no. The shape that came around from the back of the hill was no coyote. It stood tall, and it walked on two feet. A player."

"He was alone?" Udondi asked.

"Yes. Dressed in dark clothing. No more than a silhouette, despite the glow of silver. He walked around the side of the hill, and the silver lapped at his feet. He walked into it, as if it were only fog."

Shock was still fresh in his voice; it echoed my own. *"Kaphiri,"* I whispered, while fear shivered across my scalp. To think he had been here . . . "How long ago?" I asked.

"A few minutes. I lay on the edge of the cliff and watched to see if he would reappear. In only seconds he did. This time, right against the base of the cliff." In the darkness I could not see Liam's face, but I heard his harsh sigh. "Jubilee, I owe you an apology. I only half believed your story of Kaphiri. When I saw him reappear, across a gulf of silver from where he had been before, it seemed impossible, as if I saw a ghost. My mind froze, and it was many seconds before I remembered I had my rifle with me. When I did I moved swiftly, bringing it to my shoulder to aim. That's when he looked up at me."

Liam shifted, and a faint gray light from the east glinted in his eyes. "It all seemed unreal, like a dream. It made no sense. How could he know I was there? He couldn't have heard me, and so far above the silver, the darkness should have kept me hidden—"

"The worm," Udondi said. "Perhaps it watched you. Perhaps it warned him."

"Maybe." He stroked the barrel of his rifle. "Anyway, I hesitated. For a second or two seconds. Maybe longer, I don't know, but it was all the time he needed. He raised his hand and a tongue of silver rushed over him. I have never seen silver move so fast. I fired then, at the place he had been, but too late."

I remembered the confusion I'd felt the first time I saw Kaphiri. I could not blame Liam, and yet how I wished . . . what? That *I* had been the one on the cliff? Would I have done better?

"You did what you could," Udondi said gently. "To see him for the first time, and to know such a creature is real—"

"I knew he was real!" Liam hugged his rifle, his voice so low I could barely make out his words. "It was my brother's life he took. If I'd been faster, I could have put an end to him."

"It's something to remember," Udondi said. "Next time."

Liam rose to his feet. "He will come again. Maybe tonight. He'll look for us whenever the silver rises . . . and it rises almost every night in the Iraliad. We shouldn't sleep in the open again."

We had made our camp beside a low bluff, and this protected us from the passing herds, though we could hear them on every side. The bulls snorted and bellowed at one another and once I heard the thunder of running hooves followed by the crash of heavy bodies.

"It's said animals can sense the coming of the silver," Udondi mused as we ate a quick breakfast standing beside our bikes. "These cattle must have learned to retreat to the plateau whenever they sense a flood rising."

"It's too bad Moki doesn't have that talent," I said as I knelt, to feed some bread and bits of meat to him. He caught mice in the night, so I didn't have to feed him much.

"Are you sure he doesn't?" Udondi asked. "He's survived what? Almost twenty years in Kavasphir?"

"At a temple," Liam reminded.

"But it's true he never was caught out," I said, stroking the smooth fur of his back. "I never thought about it before, but he always does seem to know which nights are safe to hunt, and which better to stay at home." And after all, it was Moki who had warned of the silver that night Jolly disappeared.

Udondi knelt to feed him another snack. "He's been a handy companion."

Liam grunted agreement. "He keeps a good watch, but it's too bad he hasn't found the worm."

We rode our bikes out to the cliff edge, but there were so many cattle about we could not approach the trailhead. So we went a little to the west, to wait and watch as the giant bulls fought for the right to take their herds first down the narrow trail. We lay on our bellies at the edge of the escarpment while the eastern sky brightened, until finally the furnace of the rising sun climbed over the flat horizon, its rays painting long lanes of light and shadow across the land below.

In daylight the northern Iraliad looked even more austere than it had at twilight. Grass grew against the canyon walls and here and there I could see the deeper green of a tree, but I suspected the cattle would have a long trek to find enough forage. Where they would get water I could not guess.

Clearly though, we were about to enter a playground of the silver—for its mad creations were everywhere to be seen. False colonnades of gold decked the walls of many of the small ravines just below us. Farther away, a giant arch framed the mouth of a canyon. On a low slope of stone a mural had been laid, depicting a fantastic landscape so real it seemed as if one could step through it into another world—except the calves that skipped across its face remained in this one.

Elsewhere the exposed rock was shot through with veins of red and yellow minerals like lightning bolts, while the dry streambed spilling from one ravine was a stepped watercourse, architecturally precise but filled with drifted sand. Strangest of all, statues of gigantic god-men crouched in the shelter of every overhanging rock, or lay behind the ridges, their bows drawn as if they were hunting one another.

A gentle wind stirred, carrying a veil of dust to us from the cliff trail. I thought to look for other plumes of telltale dust that might be a truck moving at speed, or a posse of motorcycles, but I saw nothing. "It still looks blissfully empty," Udondi agreed as she studied the land through her field glasses. "No doubt Kaphiri has summoned his people, but they're not here yet."

"Maybe we'll have some hours to ourselves," I said. "This is a rough country, and if we can ride on hard soil, or stone, we might hide our tracks."

Liam lowered his own field glasses. "We'll never get free while the worm follows us."

Udondi nodded. "And even from a distance, we'll be easy marks the whole time we're on the cliff trail. It's too bad there aren't any clouds today to hide us."

I remembered the light I'd seen last night. Someone with a powerful telescope might want to sit far out on the plain, to get a good look at the entire wall of the plateau.

Liam boosted himself on his elbow, to look down at the progress of the cattle. "The last herds are starting now. When they're halfway down, we follow."

"Right," Udondi said. "Make a race of it. The less time we spend on the cliff, the happier I'll be."

Udondi went first, I followed her, and Liam came behind. The cattle trail plunged in steep switchbacks across the cliff face, so that a wall of rock rose always on one side while an abyss fell away on the other. The trail's surface was a mix of loose shale enlivened with buzzing flies and stinking dung, and our bikes slipped and skidded as we descended, sometimes bearing us perilously close to the edge. At first I made it a habit to pause at each hard turn and look around, especially to look back, searching the cliff face for the tell-tale glitter of the worm. We had not seen it since Udondi shot it with the kobolds, but none of us doubted it was around. Soon though, my attention was drawn by other things.

In the two days we'd spent on the Kalang Crescent, we'd seen no evidence of silver and as we began the descent it was the same: the trail wound down past iron-red, unchanged stone. But that ended some two hundred feet down. The natural stone proved to be a cap rock only, sitting primly atop an immense stack of transformed minerals. The first layer we passed was of glistening onyx studded with white seashells; below that, a stratum dense with veins of eroded opal; and then many layers of colorful sandstones pressed with the polished skulls of beasts I had never seen even in the playgrounds of the market.

All of it looked freshly formed—perhaps even forming still—each layer thrusting outward in lumps and bumps and crumbling knobs. It was as if the layers of transformed stone were being squeezed out of the plateau, forced out under tremendous pressure. The trail was littered with broken pieces of jade and onyx and sandstone and bone that had fallen away. Over the side of the trail, wherever the cliff lay back from the vertical, the loose stones clung in precarious balance, so that the whole slope seemed on the verge of giving way.

Of all the layers we passed, the most enthralling were the long veins of lettered stone. The trail was rough and commanded my full attention, yet I could not resist stealing a glance, and then another, at that treasure. Whole words, clearly legible, leaped out at me. I could have spent a lifetime there, happily decrypting the secrets of the past. I was so distracted that for many minutes I forgot to look behind. We were hardly a hundred feet from the bottom when I thought to pause and glance back—only to discover that Liam was nowhere to be seen.

"Udondi!" I called. "Hold up."

I searched the slope where the trail passed, but the light was all harsh sun and deep shadows, and at first I could not see him.

Udondi turned her bike around. She rode up beside me. Dust covered her face and her sunglasses. "He's there," she said, "where the trail crosses the top of that ravine."

Most of the ravine was so steep it was almost a dry waterfall, but near its top there was a ledge where the trail wound past. Liam was there, lying on his belly in the shadow of a large, flat stone of some rusting metal, gazing up the cliff face. "Where's his bike?" I wondered.

Udondi shook her head. "I don't—"

We both saw it at the same time: the worm, sliding down the

sheer wall of the cliff. It moved with the swiftness of water. It glittered like water too as the brilliant sunlight reflected off its scales. I watched it enter the ravine where Liam lay hidden. I expected it to slow or circle away as it drew near him, but it slipped past, unaware of him behind the rusting stone.

"Let's go," Udondi said, a sudden urgency in her voice. "Now!"

"But why doesn't he pull his rifle?"

"Rifles don't work."

Liam rose from behind the stone that sheltered him. He put his foot against a knee-high boulder, sending it bounding into the steep ravine. It exploded past the brush and knocked loose more boulders, along with a trickle of tumbled stone.

"*Sweet silver,*" I whispered.

Liam kicked more rocks, generating more tiny rock falls that went whooshing into the ravine, adding mass on top of the first bouncing stones so that within seconds the whole floor of the ravine was in motion. Small gray birds rose up from the slope as if they'd been shaken loose. Moki started to climb from his bin, but I put my hand on his neck as a sign that he should be still.

"Get back!" Udondi shouted over the rumble of stone. "This whole cliff face could go."

The thundering avalanche was shaking loose stones ahead of the flow and I thought she might be right. I started to retreat, but I stopped when I saw the glitter of the worm below us, in the lower reach of the ravine.

It was still well ahead of the tumbling rocks, but it was no longer fleeing downhill. Instead, it had turned. It was attempting to escape the avalanche by climbing the ravine's steep wall.

Moki saw it too and jumped from his bin just as I pulled my rifle. I shot from the hip, aiming not at the worm, but at the rocks just above it. The loose stone fountained, startling both Moki and the worm. They both hesitated. "Moki!" I shouted. "Come here!"

Udondi was firing now too. Her first shot missed, but her second kicked close to the worm's head. It reared back—and then the slide was on it. Its tail vanished under the tumbling rocks. Momentum spun its forward half around even as it dropped segments, and then it vanished inside a cloud of roiling dust.

Udondi whooped. "Got it!"

"*Moki!*" I called again, but he couldn't hear me. The rock slide was thundering past and I could feel the ground shaking under my bike. I slammed my palm against my thigh. "*Moki!*" Fear got the better of him at last. He gave up on the worm and came bounding back to me. I helped him scramble into his bin, at the same time glancing at the cliff directly above us, where a dozen tiny rock falls were skipping merrily downhill. "Udondi . . ."

"I see it. Come on!"

We raced our bikes then, starting a small rockfall of our own as we cut straight down to the next switchback. Moki hunkered low in his bin to keep from being bounced out.

The cow trail left the cliff through a steep tangle of stone and boulders left by past slides. Hooves had shaped the path into densely packed gravel—good traction for our bikes. The wheels became round and we sped toward the washes, the avalanche deafening behind us, spitting dust at our backs. Dust everywhere, and grit in our eyes so I could hardly see.

Then it was over. The rocks had spent their momentum. Birds whirled through the billowing dust, and for a moment I wondered if I'd gone deaf, the silence was so astonishing. Then a stray rock rattled, the wind whispered past my ears, and time began again.

I turned to look back at the cliff. Even through the dust it was easy to see that at least a third of the trail had fallen away, and there at the top of the slide . . .

"*Liam!*" I shouted. I grinned to see him, a tiny figure, gingerly working his bike around the unstable slope that remained.

Udondi laughed. "That'll do for the worm. I don't think even a mechanic can get out from under that much stone." Moki shook the dust from his head and sneezed, drawing a smile from Udondi. "This dust. If anyone is watching, they won't overlook it."

I had one more worry. "The trail's gone. How are the cows going to get back to the top? They'll be trapped down here."

Udondi considered this carefully. Then, "Hmm. We *could* stay to rebuild the trail."

I gave her a sour look, and she smiled. "Don't worry over it too much, Jubilee. I'm sure the herds have faced landslides before."

We waited in the shadow of one of the stone god-men for Liam to come down. As the dust settled, the transformed strata of the Kalang Crescent were revealed, glistening and glittering, scoured smooth by the avalanche. Wisps of silver curled ominously from the torn cliff face, evaporating in the sunlight. All was quiet now, and still I had the impression of a terrible pressure in the land, as if some great engine of silver lay trapped there, set to a task of endless creation deep beneath the Kalang.

Chapter

17

It was late morning by the time Liam found a way down, and the news he brought was not good. "I saw a plume of dust to the west. Ten, fifteen miles, maybe, back along the base of the Kalang. It disappeared after a few minutes but I don't doubt it was kicked up by a truck—one that was forced to slow when it hit rough terrain."

No one was surprised.

Udondi frowned at the sky, where clouds had begun to gather, just as they had yesterday. "We ride fast," she said at last. "There are refuge mesas in the northern Iraliad, way stations for travelers. If we can reach one, we might be able to defend it, and then the silver can take care of our pursuers."

"If Kaphiri doesn't interfere," I added gloomily, remembering the apparition Liam had seen last night.

"He's still a player, and he can die as easily as any other player from a bullet wound." She looked at Liam. "This time we'll be ready for him."

It was not a question, and Liam did not answer.

We rode swiftly, following the line of the Kalang to the east until that great plateau reached its sheer end. There we paused to look back at the cliff where we had stood late yesterday afternoon. How high it seemed, and far away! We had felt safe from the silver up there, but here on the plain I could see faint puffs of silver smoking from the cliff face even in the daylight, and I wondered how safe we had really been.

We had come to a boundary. On one hand the land descended to the terrible wastes of the southern basin. On the other it rose in a long, gradual slope to the high desert of the northern Iraliad. I was glad that was our direction, and I wondered if I would have had the courage to turn south, if Jolly had been waiting for me there.

We set off once again, riding fast, trying to keep out of the washes and on hard ground where we would leave few tracks. At noon we lay on a ridge top and studied the land to the north.

It was the darkest noon I had ever seen. The clouds made an unbroken ceiling, their gray bellies looming only a few hundred yards overhead. Beneath them the air was still and very clear, so despite the dimness of the day we could see for miles. After a few minutes Udondi spotted a thin billow of dust rising from behind a distant ridge. It might have been kicked up by cattle, or even a rockslide, but none of us believed that.

"Five miles," Liam said. "No more."

We returned to our bikes and resumed our flight. The sky continued to darken, until it seemed like evening, though it was only early afternoon. It was cold, and I could taste the moisture of the clouds in every breath, though they gave up no rain. Instead they had another effect: they sheltered the land from the corrupting rays of the sun so that silver began to appear despite the unnatural hour. Never had I seen the like before.

It started with a few frail wisps, curling to life within the shadows of the deepest overhangs. Wisps strengthened into luminous banks of silver tucked beneath the rocks. Before long, silver could be seen lying in the floors of the many narrow gullies that faced away from the hidden sun. Nowhere was it more than a few inches deep, but it made a blanket so dense and substantial that it looked as if it could be walked on. Even on the ridge tops the air was crisp with the scent of silver, and I began to fear a full-blown storm might burst into existence, though it was only afternoon. I wasn't encouraged to see Moki huddled anxiously in his bin.

Liam and Udondi were riding ahead of me, so I called to them. "We need to get to higher ground." After a brief conference they agreed, and we decided to make for a line of pinnacles, four to five miles ahead.

Speed mattered more than secrecy now. We gave up our resolve not to leave tracks and took to riding in the broadest washes, where the silver had not gathered yet, and our path was smooth. When the washes narrowed we rode high on the ridges while the silver thickened in every gully and overhang sheltered from the direct gaze of the sky. But our pursuers guessed our plan, or else in their own panic to escape the silver they elected to make for the pinnacles too.

It happened that we came down from the rough country into a broad, open basin that I took for a folly of the silver because it was as flat and smooth as a road, though it was immense: a mile wide where we would cross at its southern end, and many more miles in extent to the north. The pinnacles stood on the other side of that plain, higher than the tower in the bogy's city, rounded, wind-sculpted into flowing shapes like contorted gourds or hanging birds' nests. Their summits touched the clouds and while I had no doubt we could climb them, it wasn't clear if a way could be found to get our bikes up above the flood zone—but that was a chance we were forced to take.

I pushed my bike to full speed, gaining a little on Liam, who was ahead of me. Udondi was in front of him, maybe a quarter mile ahead. I saw her arm come up. She pointed to the north, then her thin cry arrived on the wind, *"There!"*

I looked around, past the billowing white dust kicked up by our tires, to see a speeding truck just emerged from the hills. It was hardly a mile away. A posse of bikers—eight? ten of them?—raced ahead of it along a line aimed to intercept us.

Against that number we were helpless on the open plain. Our

only chance lay in reaching the pinnacles first, in time to find some shelter where we could lie in wait for our pursuers.

My bike was already running all-out. All I could do was lean close against the handlebars to cut the wind's resistance. Moki huddled beneath me in his bin. The pinnacles were half a mile away. A quarter mile. I saw Udondi reach the shelter of the rocks. She disappeared among them.

By then I had almost caught Liam, but I was going too fast for the rough ground ahead, so I started to slow. That was when something slammed into my back.

My bike slid out from under me. White ground exploded under my hands in a billow of powder. No pain. Not yet. Dust swirled as I lay staring up at heavy black clouds, trying to recall what I was doing there and why I had been in such a hurry. Then Moki was dancing at my side, the hair on his back standing on end, and I remembered.

I rolled over and got up on my knees, wincing at a bruising pain in my back. What had they hit me with? Not a real bullet. My body was not torn. They did not want me dead. They wanted me because I could tell them where Jolly was; that was my value, but they were not going to collect.

I looked for my bike. It had skidded twenty feet. I started toward it, one stumbling step and another, until a rifle shot hissed into the ground at my feet. A real shot this time. I flinched back from the fountain of dust and stinging debris. I retreated again when another shot hit even closer.

That's when I finally looked around, to find two of the strange bikers were almost on me. Before I could think what to do the air exploded in a swarm of buzzing shots and to my surprise both bikers went down. *"Jubilee!"* I whirled around at Liam's shout. He had come back for me. A wall of white powder sprayed in the air as he spun his bike around. "Hurry up! Get on!"

I ran to meet him, vaulting onto the back of his bike. More shots buzzed past, from the pinnacles, I realized, from Udondi. We raced for the rocks. I pulled Liam's rifle from its sheath. Billowing white dust obscured everything behind us. Moki was a liquid red blur, running all-out, but he could not keep up with us. The pursuing bikes had fallen back too, but the truck—less vulnerable to Udondi's covering fire—had come up in their place. Its tires spit jets of dust as it closed on Moki.

I lobbed a wild shot at its windshield. Moki dodged to the side. Then we reached the shelter of the rocks and started to climb and I had to turn around fast and hold tight to Liam to keep from being bounced off.

But we had come upon the rocks with too much speed. The tires were still round; they couldn't grip the loose stone. The bike bounced, skipped; held its balance, then shot forward, climbing higher along the rim of a broad, west-facing gully. There was no silver in the bottom, though I could smell it on the air.

I glimpsed Udondi ahead of us, hunkered down in an outcropping of white rock that seemed to be undergoing a series of tiny, violent explosions as dust and rock splinters burst out at a dozen different points. Another volley of rifle shot exploded around our bike. I felt Liam flinch, then the front wheel of the bike jumped sharply. This time I was ready.

I kicked free as the bike went down and managed to land on my feet. But the embankment where I hit was dry and badly eroded. It gave way beneath my weight and I was sliding down into the gully, the bike following behind me so that I had to scramble to get out of its way. I didn't see Liam, and to my horror I found I'd dropped the rifle.

The gully was wide and shallow, its mouth opening onto the white plain so that when I looked up I saw the truck bearing down on me. I started to rabbit up the loose wall, but shots drove me back down. I went to ground behind the fallen bike.

What to do? I had no weapon, and no way to escape. Udondi was pinned down among the rocks and could not help me. Liam might be with her, or he might be hurt—and I had his bike, for all the good it would do me. And Jolly—Jolly was still days away, somewhere in the northern Iraliad, counting on me to find him. Would I ever find him?

What to do?

I could taste silver on the air. If these bikers didn't finish me, I thought, the silver would, but what to do? I lay there, unable to come up with a single solution, while the ground vibrated with the approach of the truck. Finally I could bear it no longer. I turned on my side and started popping open bins on the bike just to see what was there, to see if any of it could be useful. In the third bin I found Liam's savant.

Like a flash image in the market, I remembered the savant we'd pursued, the one we had thought was Kaphiri's. I saw it again, rising higher and higher into the blue afternoon sky above the highway until a tiny silver storm burst into existence around it.

Just a little silver storm.

But here on the edge of the Iraliad, beneath the gloom of heavy clouds, silver was already lurking in every sheltered niche . . . like a fire that smolders, waiting for any faint breath of air to stir it into a firestorm. Could I give it that breath?

I yanked the savant from its bin and slapped the wings open. Then I whispered to it. "Go. Over the truck. As fast as you can, and as high. *Go!*"

It shot off into the air. I expected to see it tumble as a bullet took it, but someone was firing again from the rocks above me and my pursuers had no time to devote to a harmless savant. I lay on my back and watched it sweep away toward the plain. It was only a hundred feet up when silver enveloped it in a small cloud of cool light that expanded rapidly, outward yes, but mostly downward, driving toward the ground with the force of a waterfall.

I heard a great scream of brakes, a roar of tires on dirt, the popping of stones. I raised my head to look and saw a flood of silver gushing around the truck's melted tires. Several of the bikers were down: frozen ghost-shapes wrapped in luminous death, melting into the shallow flood. Beyond them the plain was aglow with a blanket of silver only a few inches deep.

No one was watching me anymore.

I scrambled to my feet, heaving the bike back onto its tires. It started up at a word. I rode it back up the side of the gully, letting it find its own way. It slipped once, and I looked back to see the gully floor flooded with silver. But the tires caught again and then I was over the rim.

Liam must have heard me coming. He staggered from behind a rock. He had found his rifle, for he had it in hand, but half his face was covered in fresh blood. I fought a rush of revulsion. A player's blood is poison if it gets inside another's veins. But this was Liam. I spun the bike to a stop and he lurched onto the seat behind me.

"Uphill!"

"Where's Udondi?"

"I'm here." She emerged on her bike from the rocks where she'd sheltered. Her rifle was slung over her shoulder and she looked unharmed. "Let's go, before this silver consumes us too." With that she took off into the tumbled rocks that surrounded the foot of the pinnacles, and I followed, not daring to look behind until we'd climbed up some two hundred yards above the plain. There, just where the pinnacles properly began, we found a small, west-facing ledge. We stopped then, and looked back.

Silver was puddled in a shallow lake against the rocks. It did not reach as far out into the plain as I had thought, but it reached far enough. The truck was dissolved in it, sunk almost to its roof. The fallen bikes were gone, and of the players who had pursued us, I saw no sign.

"So, Jubilee," Udondi said in a wary voice, "have you become like Kaphiri now?"

I turned, to face her troubled gaze. I couldn't meet it long, for it was true: I had summoned the silver, and made it serve my own ends. How many players had I just killed? Eight? Ten? Did this balance my father's death?

"You had no choice in it," Liam said gruffly. "We'd all be prisoners now, or dead, if you hadn't sent the savant up. And Kaphiri would have Jolly back this very night. It's your luck we're still here at all."

My wicked luck, that made others fall in my place. Even my bike was safe. I could see it lying on its side out on the plain, covered in a drape of white dust.

But Udondi bowed to Liam's words. "You're right, I know. And it was my own wish that the silver would swallow our enemies . . . though I never thought to call it to that purpose. It's not a thing to be commanded. I fear there will be a cost."

I looked up sharply. "Where's Moki?" I had seen him last, fleeing before the truck. I dropped the kickstand and slid off the bike. *"Moki!"* My voice echoed off the rocks. "Udondi, did you see him?" She shook her head. *"Moki!"*

Tears were welling in my eyes when I turned to Liam. Hadn't he warned me to leave Moki home? Then I caught my breath as my gaze fell on his bloody face.

Liam said, "I haven't seen Moki since your bike went down, Jubilee. I'm sorry."

"But you're hurt. I forgot. Oh, Liam." His cheek was caked in blood and dirt, with fresh blood still seeping from behind his sunglasses.

"A rock fragment hit my eye. That's when I dropped the bike." Gingerly, he lifted away his sunglasses. I flinched. "That ugly?" he asked.

I nodded. The wound was a nasty gouge across his eye, the lower lid torn, the upper swollen so it could not close. The eye itself was oozing tears of blood. The sight of it frightened me, more so because I had open abrasions on my hands from when my bike had fallen. If our blood crossed we might both die.

Udondi saw my predicament. "Stay back, Jubilee," she said. "No need to take a chance."

So I held Liam's rifle while she examined the wound. "Can you see?" she asked Liam.

He shrugged. "It's a blur on that side."

"And no doubt very painful. Let's cover it, and tonight we can put together an elixir that will help it heal."

"Hold on," Liam said softly. "Look around. On the ridge behind you. Is that someone coming?"

Chapter

18

I turned and brought the rifle to bear on a hooded, sticklike figure in dull-colored clothes, angling down the boulder-strewn slope above us. My first thought was that one of the bikers had survived, but my quick offense collapsed when I sighted Moki trotting proudly in front of this desert apparition, as if intent on doing the introductions himself.

"*Moki!*"

He came bounding at my call, and I greeted him with a joyous hug, almost dropping the rifle in my enthusiasm. Fortunately Udondi acted with more thought, neither raising her weapon nor lowering her guard. Instead she called a cautious greeting. "If you are not one of those who pursued us on the plain, then well met."

"If I were one of them," the stranger answered in a throaty voice that identified her as an older woman, "I do not think I would be in fit condition to speak."

Udondi stiffened at this jibe. Her grip on the rifle tightened just a little. "We did not ask to be pursued, nor to be accosted."

The stranger stopped, still many yards away. She regarded us, her brown, time-weathered face looking out from the hood of a tunic that might once have been white but was now stained to the reddish-brown color of the Iraliad. She wore loose trousers and cloth boots of the same color, and an unused veil that draped her shoulder, but beneath her soft clothes I sensed she was as thin and hard as the pinnacles that towered over our heads—and in her height she echoed them too. My head did not reach her shoulder, while Udondi looked like a petite child before her. She said, "Your objection was strongly stated. Is it your way to summon the silver to your defense?"

Udondi's posture softened. "No. That was a desperate act. One I hope we never repeat."

"Still . . . it can be hard to forget such a weapon." Her gaze turned to me, where I knelt, cradling Moki. "Such knowledge can haunt us, following us even from one life to the next."

Her words stung. I wondered: *was* it possible I'd done such a thing before? I didn't want to believe it. "I saw another savant taken by the silver only a few days past. And the air was heavy with the silver's scent all this afternoon. That's why the idea came to me." But wasn't that how languages came to me as well? In the right circumstances, memories were stirred.

The desert woman nodded, as if she approved this new turn of my thoughts. "I am Maya Anyapah," she said. "Temple keeper here at the Sisters—" She gestured at the pinnacles. "Night is not far off and it's my duty to offer sanctuary . . ." Her lips pursed in a cool smile. "At least to the survivors. Will you trust *me*?"

Udondi glanced at Liam, who answered with an ironic smile: a rather frightening expression given the blood on his face. "I would like the chance to prove we are not brigands."

Udondi nodded. "Then, Keeper, we gratefully accept your offer of sanctuary this night."

Liam and Udondi went with Maya Anyapah, but after receiving instructions on how to find the temple, I took Liam's rifle and walked back down to the plain to retrieve my fallen bike. Moki went with me.

We skirted the pool of silver I had made. There was nothing left to mar its smooth surface, for the truck had been entirely consumed. I thought of it being returned by the silver in some far-off time, perhaps transformed to wood or quartz or jade. Few things leave the world forever; even players are returned when they are born again, but like the follies of the silver, they never return unchanged.

I walked out onto the plain. It was a folly too, as I had guessed, made of white, interlocking tiles the same color as the powdery dust. The walking was easy, and I had only a quarter mile or so to reach my bike, but it seemed much longer. Now that my blood had cooled, my body was remembering its traumas. My back ached where the soft shot had knocked me from my bike. My palms were skinned, and my shoulders and wrists felt as if they'd been sprained in my fall. The bike seemed very heavy, but when I finally got it back up on its tires it started easily. Moki scrambled into his bin, and after that it was a quick ride through the rocks to the temple door.

The Temple of the Sisters was built within the living rock of one of the pinnacles. From the front step, I gazed up at huge double doors of shining black onyx, carved in an intricate geometric relief. I could see no place to leave my bike, so I nudged one of the doors open and walked it inside, feeling truly like a brigand. I found myself in a large room lit with warm yellow ceiling panels. Hangings softened the stone walls, and across the carpeted floor pillows and low couches invited conversation . . . if only someone would linger long enough to speak.

The room was empty, but the other bikes were there, parked on a strip of stone floor, so I left mine beside them. Then I crossed to an arched hallway. The sound of voices encouraged me to push on to a kitchen where Maya Anyapah was recounting the temple's history as she tended Liam's wound at a massive slate table. In this way I learned the Temple of the Sisters was astoundingly old, 617 years, while its kobold well still showed no sign of the decrepitude that usually comes over a well of that age. Such was the power of silver in the Iraliad.

Udondi sat on the floor, cleaning her rifle beside a large fireplace where a bank of glowing coals yielded only an occasional yellow flame. When she saw me she sent me immediately out again to fetch the other rifles. I brought them, and my savant as well. My shoulders burned to carry even that little weight, my back ached, and I felt colder than I should have. That was the nearness of death, I think. I was not used to players dying. Especially, I was not used to causing their deaths, but I could not think what else I should have done.

The keeper offered me tea, but I was sad, and I wanted nothing to eat or drink. "Is there a high place where I can try to link?" I asked. "An upper room, maybe?"

"There's a stair to the very top if you want to climb that far. Sometimes the Tibbett antenna can be reached from there."

"You don't keep an antenna of your own?" Liam asked her. He sat hunched over a steaming teacup, a plastic patch over his injured eye.

"There was one. But antennas bring company. It's more peaceful, since a windstorm took it down."

"Do you live alone?" Udondi asked.

"No, no. We are a colony of old cessants, though my companions went off to Tibbett a few days past. Only the old man is here, in his room upstairs. He's almost two hundred twenty now, and he's gone very frail."

"Where is the stair?" I asked with some impatience.

Maya nodded at the door. "At the end of the hall, but it's a long climb."

"Don't try to reason with her," Liam warned. "She's set her mind to it. You won't persuade her to rest."

Udondi set her rifle aside. "I'll go with you."

"No," I said—too quickly. A faint blush touched my cold cheeks, but I was in no mood for company, even Udondi's. "Really. Stay here. I'll be down soon." I started for the door.

"Jubilee," Udondi called. I hesitated, glancing back. "Death is not an easy thing to face."

"I'll be okay." And I hurried from the kitchen before she could persuade me to stay. Moki chose to remain behind by the fire's warmth, so I got my wish to climb the stair alone.

The stairway spiraled up through the natural rock, opening on three more floors, each with a wide sitting room, and tall windows to the right and left set into the rock, admitting a wan gleam of late afternoon light. Hallways like the one below led away to private rooms.

Past the fourth floor the stairway narrowed, becoming as tight as a chimney and almost as steep as a ladder. If I had gone back for my bike (as I'd considered doing) I would have had to leave it in the last sitting room, for it would not have fit past those tight turns.

So I climbed on foot, and climbed and climbed, following a spiral of optical tubes set into the stairwell, and as my body warmed my back hurt less but it never stopped hurting altogether.

At last I saw gray daylight above me, and in a few more steps I emerged on a walled platform at the very top of the pinnacle. The wall was chest-high and damp, and as I looked over it I could see nothing of the surrounding plain, for I had climbed literally into the clouds. Fog wrapped the platform and I could just glimpse the boulder-strewn ground far, far below at the pinnacle's base.

I instructed the savant to seek a link to my mother, but there was no link, and I was so high already I didn't dare float it on a line. I felt close to despair. If only I could know my mother was well; if only I could tell her I was well too . . . though I didn't want to tell her what I had done that day.

I sat down on the wet stone, my back against the enclosing wall and the savant cradled in my lap. I tried to imagine myself back at Temple Huacho, and my mother, busy in the kitchen, or taking my littlest brothers and sisters on a walk through the orchard, but those scenes kept getting messed up with the memory of the bikers behind me on the plain, and of Kaphiri's shadowed face on that night he had come asking for Jolly, until in desperation I pressed my palms against my eyes to drive all visions away.

That's when my savant spoke in its soft old man's voice. "There is a call for you."

I looked up, wide-eyed. "I thought there was no link."

"There is none to the west. This call is from Yaphet."

Yaphet.

Suddenly I wanted to see him almost as much as I wanted my mother. "Open the link. Now. Please."

And as easily as that Yaphet was on the screen, looking at me with a stunned half smile. "Jubilee? I've tried to call you, every few hours, for days."

"We weren't in range of any antennas."

"I thought something had happened to you."

"We're okay. But you . . ." His cheek wore a dark bruise, and he had a cut over one eye. "You're hurt."

"No. It's nothing."

"You left home, didn't you?"

He nodded, his eyes charged with excitement. "I'm on my way to meet you."

"It's dangerous."

This won another rare smile from him. As if he cared! "I talked to your mother."

"You did? When? Is she all right?"

"The night I left home. That was the night after we talked. Two nights ago, now. I was worried when I didn't hear from you. She told me more about your brother Jolly—"

"Was she all right?"

"She was worried for you—"

"Did she say if anyone had come to the temple?"

He shook his head. "No. We didn't talk about anything like that . . . why? Something's happened to you, hasn't it?"

"Yaphet, there's no time to explain—"

"Yes there is. Look—" He gestured at his screen. "There's no limit on this call. Probably because there aren't any links beyond the Iraliad, so no one bothers to call. We're probably the only players on this channel. We can talk all night if we want to."

"I should call Jolly." I opened a second link, to the address Jolly had given me at Rose Island Station. A savant answered, and I asked for my brother, but the savant said he'd gone out. I left a message for him to call me.

It was getting really cold on the pinnacle now, so I sealed my field jacket and huddled close to the stone, cradling the savant in my lap, and we talked, Yaphet and I, while night descended on the desert. Night still reached him first, but it hurried on to me much faster than it had that first time we'd spoken. I learned how it had been for him, when he left home. At first he'd thought to just slip quietly away, but his conscience wouldn't allow it. So he did the proper thing and went to his father to speak his intentions and say good-bye.

It is an unnatural thing for a parent to have only one child, and perhaps that is some explanation for the row that followed. It was the worst that had ever fallen out between them. In his rage Yaphet's father beat him, but afterward he was so shocked by what he'd done that he relented and Yaphet was given his freedom. He seemed bitter over it, and sad, and angry, but also proud and pleased too. So many feelings, all at once, but then, that was Yaphet.

In turn I told him all that had happened to me, and it was both pleasing and disturbing to see him fret over the dangers I had visited. To be the object of his concern—that was a heady feeling, though at the same time I sensed in him the same strong protectiveness he despised in his own father. Not that I mentioned it. He was still too far away to bring his will to bear and I wanted only to bask in his affection.

So we talked.

At one point I heard footsteps on the stair, and I guessed Udondi had come to check on me, but after listening a moment she must have assured herself I was in good company because she retreated. I smiled, feeling content in that moment despite the cold and all the questions we still faced. I asked Yaphet if he would go back with me to Temple Huacho after we found Jolly and he said he would do that. It was a pleasant dream for us to share.

Darkness came, the clouds rolled back, and silver bloomed across the desert floor just as it had the night before. I stood beside the wall to watch the spectacle, while Yaphet watched it through my savant.

That's when I saw Kaphiri for the second time.

The silver had risen almost to the foot of the pinnacle when a slender, dark figure slipped out of it, glowing tendrils trailing from his body as if the silver was reluctant to give him up, this living folly. My eyes widened, and I stifled the cry that tried to rise from my throat.

Yaphet saw him too. "Jubilee—!" but I slapped the link off so Kaphiri would not hear and know that we were aware of him, for our best hope was to take him in ambush.

I darted for the stairway. My muscles had grown stiff in the cold, and the first downward jolt reawakened the angry bruises in my back. Each step was an agony. Still I hurried as I could, turn and turn, until the world itself coiled about me in a dizzy spiral.

At last I reached the wider stairway between the floors, and there I slowed, to keep my footsteps quiet. Udondi was in the kitchen. She had the rifles there. This was my thought as I stumbled onto the lowest floor. Liam must have heard me gasp, for he appeared at once from the kitchen.

"He is outside," I whispered.

And immediately there came the sound of a fierce pounding on the door.

Chapter

19

The pounding at the door was echoed in my panicked heartbeat. "Liam! He will bring the silver through that door. Quickly. The rifles. There are windows on the upper floors."

"What talk is this of rifles in my house?" Maya Anyapah demanded as she followed Liam from the kitchen. "You claimed to be innocent victims on the plain, but now you would murder a player who comes openly to my door?"

"It is the one we spoke of, Keeper," Udondi said. "And he is not a player like any other."

"Because he knows more of the silver than any other?" Maya asked.

"Do not let him in," Udondi warned. "The cost of your curiosity will prove too much."

I guessed this debate had gone on for most of the time I had been at the top of the pinnacle. Keeper Maya was tempted by what she'd been told of Kaphiri . . . but I had no patience for the argument. "Where are the rifles?"

Maya tried to keep me from the kitchen, but Udondi stepped between us, and I was able to slip past. The rifles were lying clean and reassembled on the table. I took all three, handing one to Liam and one to Udondi as I left the kitchen again. Maya looked on us in cold fury. "You *are* brigands," she said. "Practitioners of cold murder." Then she turned away, striding resolutely down the hall, toward the great room, and the front door, though by this time the pounding had subsided into silence.

"Stop her," I whispered to Udondi.

"No. Our only chance now is to beat her." And she darted for the stair with Liam right beside her.

I hesitated, but I could not bring my rifle to bear on Maya's stiff back. I would not. "If you open the door to him, you'll kill us all," I shouted after her.

Maya stopped, turning to look back at me. "You forget this is a temple. It has survived for six hundred seventeen years because the silver cannot enter here."

"It can. I have seen it happen."

"My house is my own," she said, and went on toward the front door.

So I left her, and galloped for the stair.

On the next floor the sitting room was empty. I glanced out both windows, but saw no sign of Kaphiri. Then I noticed a door at the end of the hall was open, where it had been closed before. I went to look, and found a bedroom, neatly decorated and brought to a comforting warmth by an electrical heater set into the wall.

In a reclining chair beside a tall window there sat an old man—older than anyone I had ever seen or imagined, his white hair reduced to wisps and his body shrunken, as if life had taken all he could give it, and more. A white afghan lay across his lap and his hands rested on this. They were marvelous hands, almost translucent white. His pale eyes glittered in amusement as he looked from me to Udondi, who stood with her back flat against the wall, craning her neck to look out the window.

The silver loomed only a stone's throw away, already as high as the floor on which we stood. Udondi had unlatched the pane and pushed it open an inch, admitting a current of cold air. It brought the scent of silver, to mix with the scent of temple kobolds. Udondi had the barrel of her rifle aimed outside, but when I looked her a question she shook her head. Under her breath she said, "The phantom has disappeared."

"And Liam?"

"He has gone to look for a better vantage in another room."

The old man said nothing, seeming pleased to be watching the drama playing around him.

Up through the window came the sound of the front door creaking open below us. Then Maya's voice, calling to the night: "Let it be known, this keeper welcomes all strangers to the Temple of the Sisters, but be warned that this night my other guests have murder in their hearts."

The old man looked at me with raised eyebrows. I could not meet his eye. "I'm going back up to the roof."

Udondi nodded. Both of us wanted to see the conflict finished that night.

Leaving her with the old man, I slipped from the room and trotted back toward the stairway. Liam intercepted me, startling me badly as he stepped out of a side room in his silent way. I whispered my plan to him, and he nodded. "I'll go too."

"Can you still shoot with that patch over your eye?"

"I can try."

But as we reached the stair we heard a faint scraping sound from the spiral above us . . . like a boot brushing stone? Maya was still at the front door, so that left only one other player whom it might be. I could not guess how he had reached the stair, but it did not seem a feat beyond his powers.

Liam must have shared the same thought, for we both flung ourselves into the stairwell, aiming our rifles up just as something slipped into sight around the spiral . . .

I cursed and almost dropped my weapon in my fight to keep from firing off a shot, for the intruder was nothing more than my own savant, making its slow way down from the roof. "A call for you," it said pleasantly.

I looked at Liam. My hands were shaking. "It's Jolly. I left him a message to call." I laid my rifle down, and took the savant in hand, whispering to it to link.

But it was not Jolly who came to life on the screen. I drew back in horror as I found myself face-to-face with Kaphiri. I knew who he was, for he still wore the same style of elaborate, starched clothing he'd worn that night at Temple Huacho. His long black hair was still pinned in sleek waves, and specks of silver still glittered around his eyes. But now his face was fully illuminated by the silver so that I could see him clearly for the first time: his pale skin, his blue eyes, his thin black beard. But for the color of his skin, he bore an uncanny resemblance to Yaphet. His face was as youthful, as beautiful, but his was the beauty of a knife, without softness or sympathy. When he smiled, I felt as if all the cold of the night had run into my spine. "I am warned you would murder me."

"You murdered my father!"

"Jubilee—" Liam tried to draw me away from the savant, but I shrugged him off.

"You're still here, aren't you?" I asked Kaphiri. "Surely you haven't gone?"

Liam understood me. He nodded and started up the stairs to get the vantage from the roof as we had planned.

Kaphiri seemed to watch him, though Liam did not pass within the scope of his view. "Do you send someone to hunt me?" His strange accent stirred a resonant memory in my mind. If he were to speak his native language, I would recognize it, I was sure, but he spoke only the language I'd been born to. "To resist me is more dangerous than you know. You might kill me, but I will still have my revenge, for you would then become the destroyer of this world."

What words were these? They made no sense. "I'm not like you! I called the silver only this once."

Confusion bloomed on his face. "You? How could *you* call it?"

He didn't know.

Kaphiri didn't know how or why his players had failed.

So let him wonder.

"You must leave us alone," I said. "Leave us alone, and you will come to no harm. We don't want this fight."

"It doesn't matter." He spoke softly now. "It has all been

decided for us." His blue eyes were hard and terrible. "Whatever you did today, your talent does not match mine. The silver will not harm me. Can you say the same?"

My mouth was so dry I could say nothing.

"I will not tolerate a pretender."

I shook my head. "It was a trick. I'm not like you."

"Even so."

"What do you want?"

"You. I must have you. I have wondered why I let you live that night outside your temple. It troubles me, and I would have my mind at peace. And of course I must have Jolly back. He is here, in the Iraliad, isn't he? It must be so. How long do you think it will take me to search each one of the handful of stations where he might be?"

I felt faint. Kaphiri could do it in one night.

Or could he? Why would he be here, questioning me, if it were that easy? "You're afraid to enter the stations, aren't you? You don't want to be known. Not yet. That's why you have your players silence any talk of you in the markets."

His head tilted thoughtfully. Whatever elixir he had used to extend his life, it had not left him slow of wit or confused, as Nuanez Li had been. "Do you love your home?"

I froze, for he had found my greatest fear.

"Ask that woman who travels with you what became of her family, her mother, her lover, her children. Truly, it's so much better to keep me happy."

Did he mean Udondi? Did she have a family once? I heard my voice, pathetic and pleading, "Don't hurt them. Please."

"Come outside."

"No."

"Come out now. Come tell me where Jolly has gone, and it will all be over so quickly. Jubilee . . . that is your name? I envy you. All of you who are not like me. Now come. I'm waiting just outside the door."

The link closed. I cried out. I shoved the savant away. What had he promised? What? That if I should give up my life and give away Jolly he would leave Temple Huacho in peace? But he had not *said* that . . .

I seized my rifle from the floor. *"Udondi-i-i!"*

She appeared at the end of the hall. "Jubilee?"

"Is it true you had a lover?" I shouted it, as if it were an accusation. "Is it true you had children of your own?"

An expression of shock came over her face.

"I thought you were a cessant!"

"I am now," she said softly.

I bowed my head. "He waits for me outside." I was afraid to go; afraid not to. He had promised me nothing . . .

"Will you go?" Udondi asked.

Now it was my turn to look stunned. "You want me to?"

She hefted her rifle. "If it draws him into the open . . ."

I stared at the weapon. "He told me if he dies, I'll take his place. I'll be the destroyer of this world."

"He toys with your mind, that's all. If he can seed doubt in you, you might hesitate. This is our chance, Jubilee. Likely our only chance. We can end it tonight, and stop any more senseless deaths. Your mother—"

"I know! I know." With shaking hands I leaned my rifle against the wall. It would not do to take it with me; I was supposed to be giving up.

Udondi passed me a knife from a hidden sheath in her boot. "Just in case."

I nodded, and we hugged. "Be ready," I whispered. Then I went down the stair on shaking legs.

I was afraid. So afraid. Sweat soaked my clothes and my chest felt hollow. I told myself that Liam was on the roof and Udondi was at the window. One or both would get a clear shot, no matter the direction Kaphiri came from, so long as I didn't stray far from the door . . . and I had no intention of doing that.

But surely Kaphiri was aware of this danger?

MEMORY

You might kill me, but I will still have my revenge.

Maybe he didn't care? But I couldn't believe that.

Maya stood beside the door, watching me with reproachful eyes. "Where is your weapon?"

"I have left it upstairs."

I stepped past her, and put my hand on the latch.

"What game is this?" she asked.

"I don't know."

I opened the door a crack. The silver stood off some sixty feet from the door, though its glow seemed strangely bright. Amplified by my fear? I did not see Kaphiri. Was he really here? Or was this only a game designed to break me?

"I am coming out." I could hardly hear my own voice. So I straightened my shoulders and shouted it, "I am coming out!"

I stepped onto the stoop. Immediately a pale hand, all aglitter with specks of silver, reached from behind the onyx door to seize my forearm. He yanked hard and twisted, and suddenly I was sprawled on the sand-strewn rock before the door. *"Udondi!"* I screamed, rolling to get back on my feet. How had he gotten behind the door? It wasn't possible. Udondi would have seen him from above. Why didn't she shoot now?

He loomed over me as I tried to rise, a phantom dressed in black. He chopped at my head. I ducked, but the blow proved a feint. Spinning quickly around he seized both my arms and twisted them behind my back so that I thought they would tear from their sockets. I collapsed to my knees, my head bowed. He followed me down. He was crouched behind me so I could feel the heat of his body. I had expected him to be as cold as silver, but it wasn't so. Why didn't Udondi shoot?

"Now, girl," he said softly, "your time is almost over. Tell me where my Jolly can be found."

He wanted an answer. So he eased his grip on my arms, allowing me to raise my head. I saw then the power that was his. Silver surrounded us, not just on the sides, but over our heads too so that we were crouched in a cave of silver that hid us from anyone watching from above. No wonder the silver had shone so brightly when I had looked out the door! That door was still ajar. I heard Udondi's voice from somewhere deep inside, shouting at me to stay inside; the silver had risen. She did not even know I had been taken.

All this passed through my mind in the space of a heartbeat. "Why are you doing this?" I pleaded.

I could feel his breath in my ear. Warm, and familiar. "It's what I was born for. The silver will not take me. Not until my task is complete."

"What task?"

"To bring about the end of this age." His grip tightened again, making me gasp. His voice softened. "I could almost think you were her, come again."

Her.

Udondi had told me of his past. "The woman who was your lover?" My words were only a pained whisper, but he heard me clearly. "If I were her, I would leave you again!"

He chuckled softly. "You are so very much like her. But now you must tell me, where is Jolly? So that we might finish this."

"I don't know where he is! I told him to run away! I don't know where he's gone!"

Now there was movement at the door. Kaphiri saw it and doubt touched him. His grip slackened. I reared back, and we sprawled together on the hard stone. He had my arms still in his grip. I twisted, trying to escape him. One hand came free but the other he held by the wrist.

Then he was not fighting me anymore. We knelt on the stone, face-to-face, while he stared at the scar that crossed the back of my hand, the one I had gained in the kobold well. With his thumb he traced its ragged line, while tiny sparks of silver followed that movement, jumping from his hand to mine. "What does it mean?" he murmured. "Who—?" He looked at me, his expression deeply troubled, and again I was struck by how much he looked like Yaphet.

It was a similarity I wanted no one else to ever see.

I reached for Udondi's knife with my free hand. Kaphiri saw the blade slide from my boot. He tried to block my strike—too late. The knife hissed through the starched fabric of his sleeve and struck flesh. Blood poured from the wound, as red as the blood of any player, but he did not release his grip on me. Instead he struck my hand. The blade tumbled, and he caught it in the air.

"Let the silver decide then, if you have a destiny."

He brought the knife's bloody edge against my forearm. I screamed, twisting away, more afraid of blood poisoning than of the silver itself but his will was sterner than mine. The knife cut deep, ferrying his blood into my body.

Then he released me. The knife clattered to the ground. He raised his hand to the silver, just as he had that night outside Temple Huacho, and the sparkles that seemed to always follow the motion of his hands were bright and vibrant. The silver rushed toward him, it spilled over him, while I scrambled out of its path, fleeing back to the temple doors.

They burst open and Udondi was there, her rifle aimed over my head. "He's gone!" I shouted, my bloody arm pressed hard against my belly.

I pushed past her, over the threshold. A wave of faintness took me and I went down on my knees. I heard Maya Anyapah say, "Their blood has crossed. She will surely die."

Then I felt Udondi's cool hands against my forehead; I heard her whispered plea, *"Forgive me, Jubilee, forgive me, forgive me,"* and I wondered why I had not let the silver take me after all.

Chapter

20

I should have died within twelve hours. Instead my blood fever stretched on through three days of delirium, or so the old man told me when I finally awoke. I opened my eyes to find him sitting at my bedside, his beautiful pale hands resting atop the afghan in his lap. The sun was just rising, its rays striking past a translucent window shade to illuminate his kindly smile.

"At first we were all frightened by the imminence of your death," he mused, his voice raspy as desert sand. "Then we were frightened you might live, it was so unnatural. I think now most of us have grown used to the idea."

"*Will* I live?" I whispered. I did not feel at all confident in that conclusion.

He smiled. "You'll live through this, at least. The fever has broken. All the savants agree that is a sign of imminent recovery."

"I thought there was no recovery . . . from a blood poisoning."

"Ah." He seemed embarrassed. "There is an exception. A *rare* exception. Very rare. That it should be you here, now, well, it would not be unreasonable to conclude this game you're playing is not entirely random."

"Game?" I croaked, struggling to follow his conversation.

"A figure of speech. I meant this contest you are engaged in with the traveler."

"The traveler? That is the name Nuanez Li used."

"That is the name he is known by in the Iraliad. I am told you call him Kaphiri, though where he came by that name I cannot say. He is old, older even than I am—far older!—though he does not look it. How I would love to know what he knows of the silver!" The old man's eyes twinkled. "Though I don't think I would survive that interview.

"But I am forgetting my duty. Maya put me to watch over you. Watching is what I do best these days. I don't sleep much."

His beautiful hands had lain so still in his lap I'd begun to wonder if he was somehow damaged and could not move them, but now he stirred, opening a compartment in the arm of his chair and removing a small device that proved to be a voice phone. "Hello, Maya," he said, with droll amusement in his voice. "Yes, she has wakened. Soup would be in order, I think, and the company of anxious friends. Nay, of course I am not talking too much. What a preposterous suggestion!"

His name was Emil, and in the short time I spent in his company I grew to love him. He was the oldest in a household of scholars who had come to live in the remote Temple of the Sisters so that they might study the silver without risking harm to anyone else. His companions had been gone to Tibbett, just as Maya had said, but they'd returned the previous evening, bringing life to the silent household. Emil reported that they were very interested in all of us, and Liam and Udondi had been made to tell their stories many times, and had been closely questioned. "You can be sure the eager young vultures want to question you too! But for today at least, I guard the door."

He did allow Liam and Udondi inside. Liam still wore the patch over his injured eye. He held my hand for a long time, looking pleased, but troubled too. Udondi remarked again and again on my luck, speaking a little too loudly. As Emil had said, my survival was unnatural. So what explained it? Looking on their worried faces, I guessed they knew something I did not.

"Why am I alive?" I asked at last. "You all know, don't you?"

The far corners of the room suddenly commanded their complete attention.

"Emil," I insisted, "you said there was an exception to the blood poisoning. What exception? You must tell me. Please."

His eyebrows did a zigzag dance. "Ah. Well. Your case is fascinating, you see, because you suffered harm from the traveler's blood, though you did not die."

"That's right," Udondi said. "You should have suffered no effect at all, if—" She caught herself. Her gaze met Liam's.

"If what?" I demanded.

She sighed. "If your blood crossed with the blood of your lover."

I must have misheard! But Liam confirmed it. "It's the only exception," he said gruffly. "A player cannot be poisoned by the blood of her lover."

I stared at him, trying to make sense of what I was hearing. "Kaphiri is not my lover."

"I know it."

"Yaphet is my lover!"

"Jubilee, I know it."

"Still, that is the only known exception," Udondi said.

I closed my eyes, hearing again his harsh voice: *I could almost think you were her, come again.* He had said those words to me. And he had looked like Yaphet. He had looked so very much like him . . .

"It doesn't mean anything," Liam said. "If . . . if there was something between you, you'd have sensed it . . ." He hesitated, waiting for me to deny I'd felt anything, but I could not. "Anyway, you should have suffered no harm, if it had been that way. As it was, you nearly died."

"But she had two lovers, didn't she?" I whispered.

"Don't think about that," Udondi commanded, though she might as well have ordered me not to breathe.

Still, there was good news to be shared. Jolly had called while I was feverish. As it turned out, he'd never received my message. It

227

seemed his rescuer, this Ficer Elmi, had heard a report of strangers in the town where Jolly first appeared—strangers with a lively interest in the odd incident of the boy who stepped out of the silver. Ficer Elmi had decided that an expedition into the desert was long overdue, so he and Jolly had spent the past few days exploring the ruins of lost, unmapped stations.

"Isn't that dangerous?" I asked. "If the stations are in ruins, surely it's because their kobold wells have failed?"

Liam shrugged. "This Ficer Elmi has apparently survived the Iraliad for a hundred twenty years. I've no doubt Jolly is safer with him than he'll be with us . . . uh, I'm not sure I said that right."

"Such confidence!" Udondi chided, but her smile didn't last. "Still it's true. We'll need to think hard on our next move."

To that end they planned to set out within the hour, to scout the land to the north looking for any sign of a new assault against us. "But you can't go on without me," I protested.

Udondi took my hand. "We're not. We're going north, not east, and we'll be back by tomorrow evening. That's how long you have to regain your strength. It's not much time."

I shrugged. "If you come back so late, we won't be able to leave until the morning anyway."

Liam scowled, the way he did when he was uneasy. "The scholars here think that maybe the silver will come late, both tonight and tomorrow night. We're thinking of leaving tomorrow in the evening, to throw off pursuit."

Travel the Iraliad at dusk? "Liam, that's crazy. If you're trusting to my luck—"

"Oh, no. Your luck's too harsh to trust, Jubilee. But these scholars—they've studied the flow of silver here for over a century. They're sure enough of their predictions that they came back last night after full dark had fallen."

We talked some more about it. I didn't like the idea of traveling at night, but they badgered me into a promise that I would at least consider it, and soon after that they took their leave.

I wanted to watch them ride away, but Maya came into the room and told me I must not raise the shade or show myself at any window. "Kaphiri may be watching, or he may have sent someone, to learn if you lived or not. Don't give away the truth. It's better for you if he thinks you're dead."

I should have been dead, but there was something monstrous inside me that had let me live.

"Do you believe us now?" I asked Maya as she turned to leave the room. "Do you understand why we did as we did?"

She stopped at the door and looked back at me. Wariness, or maybe regret, lurked in her eyes. Her tall, stern frame seemed a little stooped. "All the time you were outside," she said, so softly I had to strain to hear, "I was standing just within the front doors. I heard everything he said to you."

I couldn't think what to answer. She had been there, but she had not helped me. Maybe there had been no way she could help, and still . . .

I looked at the shade, at the sunlight streaming in, until I heard the door close.

Emil returned soon after that, shuffling in his time-weighted gait, a white shawl held about his shoulders. He sat beside my bed and asked after my health and we talked. I could feel his curiosity, but he was too polite to guide the conversation toward Kaphiri. So I did it for him: "If he was my lover, we should have known each other right away, but we didn't. Still, he suspected. The blood poisoning was a test."

"One you did not truly pass."

"Would he see it that way?"

Emil's thin shoulders rose in the slightest of shrugs. "He is far older than any player should be. Who can say what he thinks, or what pains his heart might still feel?"

"He hates her."

Emil nodded. "I'm afraid it's so. I met him once."

"You met him? Are you from Lish? I thought he was known only in Lish."

"In Lish they believe he is known only in Lish, but we have known him longer in the Iraliad. I grew up in the desert, and I returned here when my wandering was done. When I was a boy, it wasn't uncommon to see the traveler. My own encounter occurred when I was twelve. He came at dusk, to the gate of the enclave my father tended in Bakran. It was my duty that evening to seal the gate, so I saw him first. He told me he wanted to buy food, but he would not enter the enclave. I ran to report this strange incident, and some among the cessants were very excited. They went out to speak with him and I . . ." Emil smiled. "I listened at the gate.

"Ah, the traveler! He was not a man you could easily forget. Frighteningly intelligent. A natural scholar. He did not look it, but he was ancient even then, and it was apparent he had not spent his days in idleness. The cessants questioned him on many subjects, and the range, the depth of his knowledge, it astounded me, even then when I was twelve. But his bitterness was as obvious as his brilliance. He had examined life without embracing it, and for all I could tell, he loved nothing.

"At last one of the cessants asked the question that is always first in the minds of all of us who have been defeated by the great search: why are so many players condemned to a life of loneliness?

"The traveler answered with these words: *'Because this world was broken, along with the goddess who made it. We are all condemned to a cycle of death and birth and terrible loneliness, that can be stopped only by a final great flood of silver.'*

"In this flood the world will either be lost forever, or remade as new," Emil explained. "The traveler did not seem at all sure which it would be and he did not seem to especially care, so long as the cycle that had trapped him here was finally stopped."

After he finished recounting this story, we were silent for a while. I considered what I'd heard, but I was confused. "I like it here, in the world. Don't you, Emil? Why would anyone want it to end?"

"Ah, I like it here too," Emil said softly. "But it is hard sometimes. Very hard."

"Do you believe the world is broken?"

"Ah, well. Perhaps it *was* intended to work differently."

"Intended? Then do you think the stories of the goddess are true? That she was wounded in her war with the dark god?"

"It's hard to know. Still, the world was made somehow."

"I wonder why the dark god would wish to destroy it?"

"I cannot say."

"But if it's true, if the world is broken and the goddess cannot heal it, then it's up to us to try, isn't it? Isn't that better than hoping for its end?"

Emil accepted my words with a formal nod. "That is my belief. It's a good belief, and if it's any comfort, I don't feel we are entirely on our own."

"Do you mean . . . the goddess?"

He raised his eyebrows, but I was not at all amused.

"What good is a dreaming goddess, when her dreams are so wicked?" I demanded. "She should be dreaming of life! But in just these past days my father has been murdered. I have abandoned my mother to a dangerous position. I have caused the deaths of many men, and I have survived the blood poisoning of a monster. If we are not on our own, Emil, we might as well be."

Many players would have been offended at such an outburst, but Emil nodded, as if my words were worthy of careful consideration. "When you put it like that, it does seem a wonder you're alive at all."

"I'm a lucky player, or so others like to say."

"I've heard. And what is luck? Why do things happen as they do?"

I did not like the flavor of this question. "Things must happen one way or another."

Emil smiled, amused I think, at my resistance. "The scar on your hand," he said. "It saved you, didn't it?"

I raised my hand, to look at the scar I'd received in the kobold well. Emil was right. In another few seconds Kaphiri would have killed me . . . but he'd seen the scar, and hesitated.

"He recognized it," Emil said. "These scars are so very distinctive. So many fine lines and ridges, like the compressed writing in lettered stone."

Like writing? I examined the etches and loops of my scar. "I cannot see it as writing."

"Did the traveler ask how you got it?"

"No. He seemed to know."

Emil nodded; his eyes were sad. "I also know, for such things have happened many times before. Players are impetuous, and still it's a cause for wonder. History tells us not one in ten thousand will survive the kobold poison."

"That can't be right."

"Perhaps the traveler once knew a player with a similar scar."

"Emil—"

"It *is* a wonder you are still alive."

"So what are you saying? That I climbed down the kobold well seven years ago, so that Kaphiri would not kill me here, this year, at the Temple of the Sisters? That's ridiculous! Our roles cannot be that closely written."

He smiled. "Perhaps not. But the scar would be lucky no matter where, or when you met him, don't you think?"

"It was only chance that I met him at all. He did not come looking for me."

"And still he found you. Twice."

"He wants my brother."

Emil nodded slowly, and his thoughts seemed far away. "Mostly the silver seems to act without purpose, but sometimes it is otherwise."

"Nuanez Li believed that too." I told him of Nuanez, and the book he had given me, *Known Kobold Circles*. "It came out of the silver, and he and his wife believed it came to them for some purpose, though in the end the only purpose was to give it to me."

"That seems cruel to you?"

I nodded. It was eerie too, given the book's subject, and the language in which it was written—the same language used by the bogy in the ancient city. More than chance, as Emil might say. "The author hints his 'kobold circles' might be used to recall memories from the silver itself."

Emil's pale old eyes widened in a flicker of surprise. "I have heard of such things, but only in fantastic stories. This book claims it for the truth?"

"I have not had time to study it, but yes, I think so. It has lists and lists of code. Almost all of it is code. I'll show it to you if you like. Where is my field jacket? It should be in one of the pockets."

Emil took a great interest in my book. He could not read it. Neither could anyone else in that house of scholars, but they were eager to hear my translation. Once again, I puzzled over the words of the introduction:

> . . . Herein are summarized the findings of seventy-three temple keepers, all of whom dedicated many years to the puzzle of kobold circles . . .

"But what are kobold circles?" I wondered, looking around at the half-dozen scholars Emil had allowed to gather in my room. "That's what the author, Ki-Faun, never bothers to say."

"I can tell you what they are."

It was Maya who spoke. She stood on the edge of our little group, lurking near the door. Everyone turned to her in surprise.

"I saw a kobold circle once, in a road show, when I was a girl. At least, that's what the hucksters called it. They asked for very specific kobolds from the audience. When these were presented, they adjusted the configuration codes, claiming they must be set to the correct sequence of zeroes. When this was done, the kobolds linked together in a ball."

Maya cupped her hands, the fingers interlaced, leaving a hollow space between her palms. "Like this. No one had ever seen anything like it. At the end of the show—an hour or so, I'd guess, though I don't really remember anymore—the kobolds separated, but as they did they released a new kobold, one they had made together. This new kobold inflated into a balloon and blew away."

She shrugged. "Well, it was a comedy show. Probably there was some trick to it, some way of secretly introducing the 'new' kobold, though I never figured out what it was." A self-conscious smile flitted over her lips. "I tried for years to get kobolds to form circles, but I never succeeded."

How odd to think of this stern keeper trying to reenact a road show she'd seen as a little girl. "The coding sounds very specific," I mused, frowning at the next sentences in the introduction. "So really it's no wonder you had no luck with it. Here it says something like, *'All the listed circles are based on the—'* There's a word here I don't know . . . Pythagorean? Has anyone heard of it? I meant to ask my savant."

"That is a very old word," Emil said. "It describes a sequence of numbers obtained by adding the next greatest number to an accumulating sum . . . zero plus one to give one, one plus two to give three, three plus three to give six, et cetera."

I laughed in amazement. "Why would you know such a thing?"

"Well, to impress wild young wayfarers, of course."

"Oh. Well . . . is there any meaning to these . . . Pythagorean numbers?"

He shrugged. "They're interesting."

Someone asked, "What does the text say of them?"

I frowned at the page. "Just that all the listed circles are based on these numbers, then, *'No doubt other combinations of zero exist, but at the time of this writing they are unknown.'*"

"There, Maya," Emil said. "Did you set your zeroes in the pythagorean sequence?"

She shrugged. "It was all long ago."

It went that way for an hour or more as we read and discussed the little book. Before long I came to understand that a kobold circle was a means of procuring rare kobolds that could seldom, if ever, be found naturally in wells. If the book was correct, then a kobold created within a circle might be completely unlike any of those that had given rise to it.

In the road show Maya had described, the new kobold had been nothing more than a toy, but *Known Kobold Circles* implied wider possibilities. Its pages listed hundreds of formulas for producing kobolds, most with catalog numbers that would fit among the mysterious, empty pages of my mother's kobold libraries. Unknown kobolds—though Ki-Faun had included brief sketches describing what they might be used for. Most produced elixirs that were claimed to prolong life and health and even to cool the blood fever. ("We could have made use of *that!*" Emil chuckled.) But a very few seemed to have something to do directly with silver . . . Recalling its memories? That had been my impression on first reading, but now I felt less sure. Certainly the silver must have some means of memory. How else could it bring follies forward in time? Still . . . "I think these formulas are more about calling certain follies from the silver, than about calling out the silver's memory."

Even that was unheard of, as the general murmur confirmed.

It was a wonder to me, to think I might hold in my hands the instructions for a method of kobold culture unknown to even dedicated keepers like my mother. If the formulas proved true then I would know something of kobolds that my mother did not—and how astonishing that would be!

Chapter

21

Sleep did not come easily that night. I lay awake, listening, I don't know for what. I could hear a distant guitar, and closer, the soft scratch of kobold feet on the stone windowsill. The rich, cloying scent of temple kobolds pervaded my every breath.

A restlessness grew in me, so that after some time I left my bed, to stand watch at the window. From my room I could see the plain below the pinnacles. The silver was just taking form there, as a thin, bright sheen like liquid glass poured across the flat basin. I could feel its presence, as a strange new awareness in my mind. I could feel it, as if the silver had somehow become part of my mind. I felt it flowing past the rocks and swallowing them whole. I felt it rising.

Fear took me, and I retreated from the window, but it made no difference. My preternatural awareness continued, as if some outpost of my mind existed down there on that plain, looking, listening, waiting on my instruction while my familiar self trembled in the darkness of my borrowed room.

A terrible suspicion took root in my mind. *"No,"* I whispered. *"No. I am not him."*

But had some part of him gotten inside me, when his blood mixed with mine? Had that poison wakened something in me? Was this how Kaphiri sensed the silver? Was this how he felt?

A faint glitter caught my eyes and I looked down, to find my hands surrounded by tiny sparkles of silver. Horror washed over me. I was not like him! I dashed my hands against my thighs. *"Go away!"*

The vision snapped, as if in obedience to my command. My awareness collapsed, to become only a human awareness. Fatigue rushed over me, and I soon convinced myself it had been nothing more than a dream.

I awoke in the morning to find my strength returned and I refused to stay longer in bed. I repacked my bike and checked my rifle, and when that was done I spent some time translating the lists of configuration codes in *Known Kobold Circles* for the scholars of that house—a payment of sorts for the kindness they had shown me—but I could not keep my mind on it. I was impatient for Liam and Udondi to return.

By late afternoon the waiting became unbearable, so I slipped away from a discussion of the nature of silver, and with Moki at my side I climbed the long stairway to the top of the pinnacle to look for my companions. Maya had warned me not to show myself outside the temple, so I sent my savant to look over the wall, while I lingered in the stairwell.

The day was clear, and the savant had command of the land for miles all around, yet it reported no sign of movement. I told myself not to worry. Sunset was still more than two hours away.

I called Yaphet, but he didn't answer, so I left a message. I started to call Liam, then remembered I had destroyed his savant. So I called Udondi, but there was no answer. Next I tried Jolly, using the new address he'd given to Liam. No answer.

I grew annoyed. No one I cared to talk to ever seemed to be within reach. I understood the difficulties of communication in the Iraliad; I knew that a savant stored in the bin of a bike would be unlikely to catch a radio signal, but that knowledge did not ease my isolation.

After an hour or so I heard footsteps climbing the stairwell, and a few minutes later Maya appeared from below. "Ah good," she said, when her gaze fell upon me, crouched at the top of the stairs. "I was afraid I'd find you in the open. Have you sighted your companions yet?"

"No, and they should have been back by now. They wanted to leave again at dusk."

"There are many reasons they might be delayed. Don't worry too much." She sat on the stairs, unfolding a square of paper across her lap. "I've had a map made for you. It shows all the refuge mesas in the northern Iraliad . . . and it also charts several wild kobold wells. It might be helpful to know where they are. Not that the wells offer much shelter. Most are in the open desert, or in boulder fields. A few are in canyons, or on cliff walls. Still, you'd be safe from the silver if you camped at any of these sites, and it's unlikely anyone else will know of them."

I leaned over her shoulder, studying the map. The nearest wild kobold well was only fifty miles or so away. "So if Kaphiri has sent more players, they'll likely look for us at the mesas, and not at these wild wells."

"That may be," Maya said, "but if you camp at the wells you'll find no food or water or shelter from the elements, and no defensible positions. It's a trade-off, though it may be a worthwhile one. You'll have to decide as you go."

I nodded. "Thank you for all you've done."

"Too much and not enough," she said as she handed me the map. "We do ask this of you: make no copy of this map for your savant, and destroy it as soon as you have left this region. The life span of a wild well is fleeting, but the life span of expired information is not. In a few months this map will show only where wells used to be. I wouldn't want anyone to follow it to their death in the silver."

Dusk came and went, and still there was no word from Liam, but as the scholars had predicted, the silver did not immediately appear at the onset of darkness.

The scholars based their predictions on the rhythm of storms that arose in the Iraliad's southern basin. Little was known of the basin, except that silver seeped from it, even in the daylight. It was a low-lying, broken land, "As if the fist of the god had struck the world," Emil said. Like the other scholars, he believed some force or factor, hidden there beneath veils of silver, controlled the rise and fall of silver storms even as far away as the northern edge of the Kalang Crescent.

"Our histories tell us the goddess spun the world from a cloud of silver, and that the silver is her mind, dreaming the world into existence. But where does the silver come from? And how could the goddess control it? I believe some hint of an answer might be found within the southern Iraliad. That region is different from all others in the world, for the silver is never absent, and no player may go there, and live . . . except perhaps the traveler.

"Once, I tried to go there. I was already old, so there wasn't so much to lose. I was determined to discover what was there, even if I never escaped alive with the knowledge—but the goddess has no patience for hubris. I barely penetrated the rim of the basin, for the silver became a wall that would not let me advance. In that land you can *feel* the forces that made the world, still at work, endlessly building up the land all around. You came across the Kalang Crescent. Did you know that it grows higher every year?"

"We had guessed," I said, quietly astounded at this confirmation. "And we saw the southern desert, when we were on the Crescent. *I* have no curiosity to go there!"

"Wise youth! For myself, I decided that life was precious to me after all, and I turned for home, but it took me a hundred days to return a mere two hundred miles to these friendly lands of the north."

Emil sighed. "If we could but understand the factor of the southern desert, we would be so much closer to understanding the tide of silver now rising in the world . . . or so I believe."

The scholars had collected notes for centuries, but they could only predict the rise and fall of silver in a radius of some hundred miles around the Temple of the Sisters. Farther than that, their studies failed. This one night they could guide me. Then I would be dependent on luck once again.

Leaving my savant on the pinnacle, I retreated down the stairs to eat some dinner. When I returned half an hour later I found the stars out in all their glory, and a message from Jolly recorded on my savant. I cursed my timing. But when I sent a link Jolly answered immediately, his youthful face gazing from the screen of my savant with worried eyes. "They said you were sick."

"I'm over it now. Where are you?"

"It's an old station. I don't know if it has a name, but we're only staying here this night. We'll leave again in the morning. Ficer says to tell you we'll be at Azure Mesa by tomorrow afternoon."

I consulted the map Maya had given me. "That's only a hundred twenty miles from here!"

A gruff voice spoke from off-screen. "Ask her if that's not too far . . . now that we've crossed almost all the North Iraliad to meet her."

Jolly grinned. It was infectious. "I'll be there," I promised. "In fact, I'll be waiting when you arrive."

"If the silver allows it," the gruff voice amended.

"Yes," I agreed. "If."

Only 120 miles—a few hours by bike, if all went well . . . though things had not gone well for some long time. After Jolly had gone to have his dinner, I cradled the savant in my lap and considered.

Liam and Udondi still had not called. Did that mean they could not? If they had found trouble, it might mean trouble would find me if I stayed at the Sisters.

I could leave tonight.

Liam had been planning to set out tonight anyway. The silver wasn't expected to rise until late. I could set out, get as far as the first wild well on the map, and camp. That way I'd have a start on anyone who might come looking for me . . . and if Liam and Udondi showed up at the Sisters tomorrow . . . well, I'd leave a message with Emil telling them where I'd gone.

I took my savant downstairs. Emil nodded when I told him my plans, as if he'd expected as much. He summoned Maya. "She has decided to leave us this night."

"There are no safe choices now," Maya said. "You should have until midnight to reach shelter, but in the darkness you'll need to go slowly. You weren't planning to use a light?"

I shook my head.

"By starlight," Emil said. "By the light of Heaven." He clasped my hand. "If I were younger I'd go with you. As it is, I can only watch . . . but I'll watch well. The traveler will have no news of you from this old man."

"No, Emil. If he comes, you must tell him whatever he wants to know. He'll learn it anyway, and I would not have you or anyone else hurt."

His eyes were moist. "That task may be too hard for me."

I kissed his cheek. "Still I ask it of you." Then I whispered the name of the mesa where I was to meet Jolly, and I left him and went downstairs.

My bike was ready. I put on my field jacket while Maya made sure I understood how to find the first wild well. I thanked her, then I called Moki and put him in his bin. Maya opened the door for me. The Bow of Heaven glimmered overhead, giving me a little light. There was no sign of silver. I wondered if Kaphiri lay hidden somewhere among the boulder-strewn slopes. I desperately hoped it wasn't so; I didn't want him to know I lived. But even if he was watching, at least he would have no way to follow me except on foot. He would have no way of knowing where I went.

Maya set her hand on my shoulder. "Go slowly," she whispered, "and with great care. The Iraliad will not forgive any mistake tonight."

I nodded. Then I set out alone on the path she had shown me.

Coyotes were about that night, and for two or three hours they followed me, appearing as silhouettes on the ridge tops, or as dark shadows against the pale sand of a desert wash. When I first saw them I was frightened. But they did not attack, and when they vanished an hour before midnight I felt terribly alone.

It was only fifty miles to the well that would be my refuge, but the Bow of Heaven was stingy with its light and I worried I would lose my way so I went slowly, making sure of every landmark Maya had told to me. In this way I came to a wide plain.

In much of the Iraliad the land is a hard mineral soil, but the silver had made that plain a fertile place, and despite the rarity of rain, tough sedges grew knee-high, with waxy white flowers looking out among them, their petals agleam in the starlight. Far away I could see the dark shapes of mesas rising against the star-spangled sky, and closer, an ethereal gathering of white standing stones half-melted by the passing tides of silver, so that some stood on stems, looking like elongated white mushrooms.

I hurried forward, for this was the last landmark Maya had described. The well was supposed to be a mile beyond the standing stones—"No farther," she had warned. "You must be very careful. It would be easy to pass it in the dark."

It would be easy to pass it in the daytime too, I thought ruefully as I looked out on that plain. Maya had carefully described the well, but she had not mentioned the dense sedges. I was supposed to search a little north of east for the mound of the kobold well, but if her description was accurate, the mound did not stand as high as the sedges. I could see no hint of where it might be.

I headed out anyway. There was still no sign of silver, but I knew it could not be far away. The hour was late, and Moki—who had been excited at the scent of coyotes earlier in the evening—now huddled fearfully in his bin. I spoke soft reassurances to him as I watched my odometer measure the distance.

A mile passed, but I discovered no sign of the well.

I stopped and looked about. The sedges were so dense that even in daylight I might pass within ten feet of the mound and not see it. How could I expect to find it in the dark?

I had to find it.

Moki whined his fear. Faintly now, I could smell the crisp, clean scent of silver, and as I breathed that scent I felt something waken within me, just as it had last night when I stood by my window, looking out on the silver-covered plain. I could feel the silver, unseen and lying close against the ground, but rising into life . . . and into my awareness. *Stay back*, I thought. *Stay away*. Suddenly, sparkling motes were dancing around my hands.

Moki whined again—and then the silver emerged all around us, rising in a silent flood among the sedges, everywhere, except at our feet, and around the tires of the bike.

Stay back.

Moki panicked. He scrambled out of his bin.

"Moki!" I caught him with my sparkling hands just before he touched the ground. He shook in my arms. "Moki, stay with me." I held him against my chest, and slipped the bike into gear.

Back.

I leaned with my mind against the silver. I raised my hand in a warding gesture. The motes brightened, and I felt as if I had raised some larger hand that I could not see, one that *pushed* the silver back, pushed it away from my path. I felt it fall back. Not so much as a physical sensation, but as a kind of cool awareness sliding away from the pressure of my will.

Oh, it was a neat trick! But it was also a gift from Kaphiri, and I did not trust it. I had to find the well.

But how?

A well is made safe by the kobolds that grow within it. The first that emerge are always of the kind we call "temple kobolds" whether a temple is ever made around that well or not. They are similar to the kobolds my mother had used to call the silver during my father's memorial ceremony, but their duty is the opposite: the petals on their backs exude a sweet scent that somehow works to keep the silver away. I sniffed at the air.

Moki watched me and whined again, the fur on his neck standing straight and stiff beneath my hand. I set him on the ground, keeping my hand on him until I was sure he would not panic and run. He edged forward, sniffing at the air. He edged right up against the silver, and whined.

"Do you smell the well?" I whispered, rolling my bike up behind him. I held my hand out and *pushed*, and the silver retreated before us. "Find it, Moki," I urged. "Find the way."

He turned a little toward the south.

Push.

The silver rolled away from our path. Moki hurried forward and I followed. But when I glanced back the silver was rolling in behind us. I panicked. As if by instinct I raised my other arm and *pushed*, and the motes that clung to my hand brightened, and the silver fell away.

Why?

I didn't want to think too hard on it. I didn't believe this new power of mine would bear up under examination. What I had done was impossible, and if I thought too hard on it, surely it would cease to be, just as childhood fantasies fade when we enter the age of reason?

"Hurry, Moki," I whispered, and I *pushed* and a channel opened before us and closed behind, while the silver climbed as high as my waist, as high as my head. Then suddenly the sedges ended. We came to a mounded ring of barren soil a full nine feet across. Moki scurried over the mound and I pushed my bike after him. "Moki, you did it!"

In the darkness I could just make out the black circle of the well, hardly a foot across, at the very center of the mounded ring. I rode my bike to its edge. I could hear kobolds moving in the loose soil. I knew I must be crushing more beneath my tires, but what could I do?

I dropped the kickstand and slipped off, staggering to keep my balance, I had gone so weak with fear. All around the well, silver drifted as high as my head so I could not see the standing stones. But even with my eyes closed I could feel the silver, as if it were part of my mind, leaning on my awareness, waiting for me to invite it in.

I remembered the night Jolly had invited it in.

"Not me," I growled. "That's not me. Stay back! Please. Just stay away."

That night I did not sleep. The silver rose so high around me, it was as if I huddled at the bottom of a well of light. Far above, hundreds of feet as it seemed to me, there was a disk of blackness I took for the sky, but the glow around me was so bright, I could see no stars.

I waited for Kaphiri to step out of the silver. Did he know I was alive?

How could he not know? He had poisoned me with some splinter of his nature, but the silver remained *his* element. He existed somehow within it. He emerged from it whenever he desired, and surely he desired to find me? I held my rifle with bloodless hands, on guard all that night, but Kaphiri did not come.

What ruled his comings and goings? I didn't know, and not knowing, I worried he might be occupied elsewhere . . . at Temple Huacho, or the Sisters, or that he might have found Liam and Udondi, just as he had found my father.

That night seemed endless, but at last the dark circle of sky above my head began to lighten. I returned my rifle to its sheath, eager to be on my way. Minutes passed, gathering together until most of an hour had gone by, but to my consternation the silver did not break up. The sky had lightened just enough to show me why: heavy clouds lay over the desert and only a wan light reached past them—not nearly enough to drive the silver away.

I looked around at the pale, misty walls of my cage, and fury built inside me. Had I been betrayed? Why had no one warned me? If the scholars at the Temple of the Sisters could predict when the silver would rise, surely they also knew when it would subside? But they had said nothing.

And what of Jolly? Was he trapped too? Did the world conspire to keep us apart?

But I was *not* trapped. I could push the silver away, as I had done last night. I could hold open a bubble within the silver and go where I liked . . . if I dared. I wanted to go, but I was afraid. I did *not* dare. I could not bring myself to do it.

Frustration fed my anger. I cursed the silver. I dared it to take me. I shouted for Kaphiri to come, and threw handfuls of dirt into the mist. But while I succeeded in terrorizing Moki, my rage was a tiny thing, unmeasurable against the reach of the world and soon spent. Afterward, I gave into sleep like a tired child.

I slept for many hours. When I awoke it was to the howl of a cold wind against my cheek. The silver still surrounded me, but it was breaking up under the pressure of the wind. Tufts of it whipped across my sanctuary so that I did not dare to sit up above the shelter of the mound. Moki was of a similar mind. He huddled at my side, his tail thumping nervously in the dirt. I thought about taking him down into the well. The blowing silver could not touch us there, but my first experience in a kobold well still haunted me, or maybe it was the stunned look on Kaphiri's face when he saw my scar . . .

But I was saved from a decision by the sudden appearance of the sun. It broke past the fleeing clouds and the silver was immediately transformed. Its menacing tendrils became a thin mist, sparkling in a watery atmosphere, and then it was gone, leaving only the wind and the blowing dust.

I stood cautiously and looked about. The coarse sedges in that place had not been harmed by the flood, though the white flowers were closed now in daylight. Here and there in the near distance clusters of irregular standing stones glistened, looking as if they were made of fine leaded glass. But what caught my attention was a mesa standing far away on the flat horizon. It was a pedestal, narrower at its base than at its flat summit, for the silver had eaten away at its foundation for untold centuries. Its color was a light, bright blue, like turquoise, only a little darker than the afternoon sky. Azure Rock. Where I would meet Jolly, if only I could get there.

I whooped and whistled to Moki. It was late in the afternoon. No more than two hours of daylight remained to me, but that was enough.

Chapter

22

By the time I reached Azure Mesa the sun was directly behind me. Its rays shot through rips in the clouds to fall in mottled patterns against the mesa's blue stone cliffs—a lovely, bright blue like polished turquoise. Changed stone. Perhaps all of Azure Mesa was a folly. I wondered how long it had been there, and how long it would last. Its walls were badly undercut by the silver, and in places the overhanging rock had collapsed into hills of turquoise stone. Still, it looked solid enough to offer me shelter through the night . . . if I could find a way to scale its smooth walls.

A skirt of brush surrounded the mesa. Perhaps it had rained recently, for the brush was covered in a haze of tiny yellow flowers. I breathed in their dry, honey-sweet fragrance: a pleasant scent, but not nearly strong enough to hide the lingering scent of silver. Darkness would not fall for the better part of an hour, but that smell had me nervous. Almost panicky. I did not want to be caught out in the open again. I wanted to get up among the rocks, while the sun's light held the silver at bay.

But I also wanted to find Jolly.

I had seen no tracks as I approached the mesa, and the dust plumes that wandered the desert had all been tossed up by the fierce wind. Perhaps the morning's silver storm had kept Jolly from traveling. If so I would have another night on my own. I did not look forward to it.

Grimly I set about exploring the mesa, circling east around the brush, and after a few minutes I found a path. It was a sandy track that cut straight toward the base of the mesa. Eagerly I looked for the marks of tires, but if there had been any, they were gone now, smoothed away by the wind. "Jolly!" I shouted his name, but the wind took my voice away, and there was not even an echo in answer.

I followed the path. It took me all the way to the mesa's wall, ending beneath a vertical notch cut into the overhanging stone. There were handholds in the blue stone, making a sort of ladder that climbed to what looked like a narrow shelf some thirty feet overhead. Was this the way onto the mesa?

I could not believe it, for I could see no way to get my bike up that rock face. Giving up on the notch, I searched the brush on either side, and after a few minutes I found a second path, fainter than the first and nearly overgrown in places, but it circled around the base of the rock so I followed it—all the way around the mesa without finding any sign of another way up the smooth blue rock.

By the time I returned to the notch the sun was nearly on the horizon. The scent of silver was growing stronger, and Moki was starting to worry. I considered again the handholds that had been cut into the stone. I could certainly climb them and get myself above a silver flood, but if I could not also get my bike to safety, what would I do tomorrow? If I lost my bike, I would be afoot . . . and it might take me days to walk to the next refuge mesa. Could I do it? Fending off the silver every night? It seemed impossible. Even if I could manage that trick again, eventually I would have to sleep, and surely I could not fend off the silver in my sleep?

No. There had to be some true sanctuary here, or Maya would not have sent me. And Ficer Elmi—the stranger who had Jolly in his care—he would not have told me to come. So, leaving Moki to sniff out partridge trails, I started climbing.

Each handhold was deeply cupped and together they made an easy path. Soon I became all too conscious of my height above the ground. I hesitated at the last handhold, thinking that a snake might have come for the sun on this western-facing shelf, but when I peeked over the edge, I saw only one small lizard that fled at the sight of me.

Even if there had been a snake, I would have found the courage to fight it for possession of that shelf, for just to the right of the notch ladder, set back from the edge a few feet so it was invisible from the ground, was a steel post supporting a boom with pulleys and cable that looked in good condition. So there was a way for me to get my bike above the reach of the silver flood.

I heaved myself over the edge and spent a minute exploring. The ledge was nine or ten feet wide on its outer edge, but it narrowed toward the back. It reached fifteen feet into the rock, giving the impression of an alcove . . . an effect enhanced by the presence of a steel door set into the back wall. I leaned on the latch handle, and the door opened easily, swinging inward onto a cool darkness that bore the sweet scent of temple kobolds. My heartbeat quickened painfully. That perfume will always speak to me of home, and as I stood on that threshold I found myself torn between joy and loneliness.

Then optical tubes flickered to life along the walls, revealing the foot of a wide stairway littered with the beetlelike carapaces of thousands of dead kobolds. Spiderwebs hung from the ceiling, swaying on air currents too slight for me to feel. A veil of brown dust overlay it all. I took a step inside and dust rose around my foot. Peering up the stairway, I called Jolly's name, but without much hope. The only tracks in the dust were the tiny tracks of kobolds. Clearly, it had been a very long time since any player had entered Azure Mesa by this stair. I called again, but only an echo answered me, so I went back outside.

The ledge looked south and west across a desert plain studded with follies and standing stones, and here and there on the horizon, hazed by blowing dust and distance, the blocky silhouettes of other mesas. In all that land I saw no sign of movement, or of any purposeful plumes of dust of the kind that would mark the passage of a bike and I was glad, for the air had about it an opalesque quality, a shimmering density that I had never seen before, though some part of me knew it was an effect of silver, edging into existence. Night was not far off. Any player still on the road was in dire danger. My own position would not be secure until I brought my bike up from the desert floor.

So, working quickly, I swung the boom out over the edge of the shelf. Then I scrambled down the notch ladder to secure my bike to the dangling cable. Tucking Moki into my field jacket, I climbed up again while the sun blushed red, its disk melting as it neared the world. I set Moki down, then turned my attention to the cable. A hard pull and the bike rose from the ground. Gears locked behind the pulley so that the rope could not slide back. I hauled again, and in less than a minute I was able to swing the boom in and bring the bike to rest on the ledge. I unshackled it, and hurried with it into the refuge, but I did not close the door.

The sun was a thin arc of fire on the horizon. Its last rays penetrated the refuge, overwhelming the pale optical tubes. In that glare I unpacked my savant, determined to contact someone before I sealed myself away for the night.

I snapped the wings open and stepped outside—to find a new sound intruding on the stillness of the evening, a soft sound that I knew immediately: the hiss of tires moving at speed on a sandy trail.

I abandoned the savant and scrambled to the edge. East beyond the brush that skirted the mesa was a lone biker, riding fast so that a tail of dust spun up from the tires to glitter in the sun's last light.

Then the sun was gone. Twilight rushed in, and the biker became a shadow—a singular shadow—for this player was certainly alone.

Panic touched me. Kaphiri was the only player I knew who traveled without companions. Kaphiri . . . and myself.

I went back for the rifle. By the time I returned to the cliff's edge the biker had found the trail to the notch. I crouched in the shadows, huddling close to the rock, my hand on Moki's back to let him know we were hunting, and that he must be quiet. The scent of silver was very strong.

The biker reached the base of the cliff and stopped there, a darker shadow among dark shadows. He straddled his bike and looked up. "Throw down the cable," he said in a gruff voice that was not Kaphiri's, but was familiar just the same.

Moki whined, trotting to the very edge to look over while I swallowed my fear and did as I was told, swinging the boom out and releasing the cable. "Who are you?" I asked. But my mouth was so dry my voice was a whisper. He didn't hear me.

"Go on now," he said. "Find the notches on the wall and climb up." His words were not addressed to me, but instead to a smaller figure that slipped from behind him. I caught my breath, while Moki whined again. *"Jolly . . . ?"*

At the sound of his name he froze, one hand on the first notch.

"Go on up," the gruff voice commanded. "There's little time."

Ficer Elmi. I had heard him speak last night.

But Jolly did not climb up. "Is it her?" he asked, his voice glassed with fear. "You said it was only one player who came here."

"It was only one."

"Jolly," I said softly. "It is me. Jubilee."

He stared upward, but it was dark and I could not see his face.

"Come up," I urged. "Hurry."

The gruff voice backed me. "Be up, Jolly, now. Before the silver awakes."

Jolly obeyed, though he climbed hesitantly.

"Haul the rope," the old man reminded me.

I scrambled to do it. A fierce tug brought the bike swinging into the air. I shifted my grip and hauled again. "Hurry," I pleaded. "The silver is close."

"We've a minute," Ficer Elmi said.

The bike cleared the ledge. I secured the rope, then swung the boom in just as Jolly reached the top. Moki was frantic, bouncing around on the edge of the cliff and barking so that I feared he would slip over or that he would knock Jolly off. "Moki!" I shouted. "Back up! Back up!"

Just then a faint gleam of silver ignited on the flat below. Jolly saw it and twisted around. "Ficer!"

"I'm here," Ficer answered, his voice comfortingly close. "Just below. Now *climb*."

Jolly scrambled onto the ledge, and Ficer followed behind him. Moki was beside himself, barking and dancing, and I was fighting with the cable, struggling to get it unclipped from the bike, a task made hard by the darkness and my shaking hands. Ficer knelt beside me. His callused hands helped with the hasp. "It'll be heavy this night," he murmured. "Can you not feel the weight of silver in every breath?"

I could. "Why were you out so late?"

"We were to meet three, not one."

Jolly squatted among the shadows beside the door, cradling Moki in his arms. "We thought you might be him," he said in a voice so low I suspected he still wasn't sure.

"I'm not him. But things have happened. Come. We'll talk inside."

Chapter

23

Even before Ficer sealed the door, Jolly turned to me and asked the question I dreaded most. "Why were you the one who came, Jubilee? Where is my father?"

"He is gone, Jolly. Gone to the silver."

Not a flicker of surprise could I see on his face, only grief. He must have guessed the truth long before. Indeed, nothing else could have kept our father away. Now Jolly's gaze fixed me in a way I remembered well. "Tell me how it happened."

And I would have, there on the doorstep, but Ficer intervened. "We'll have time to tell our stories when we've settled in." He mounted his bike. "Azure is not a true temple and the kobolds are poorly tended. We'll be safer on the highest floor."

Jolly rode on the back of Ficer's bike, with Moki cradled in his arms. They went first, while I followed them up the wide stairway, lit from above by optical tubes that glinted against the blue stone. Dead kobold shells crunched beneath our tires, and the taste of dust was in my mouth. It was easy to think we were the first players to enter that refuge in a hundred years. All looked abandoned, yet the sweet scent of temple kobolds permeated the air.

"There is no keeper here," Ficer assured me when I questioned him on the matter. "Not in my memory, or the memory of anyone I have known."

The stairs climbed in three long flights to a chamber of startling size, as wide as the auditorium at Halibury, though the ceiling was so low I could have jumped and touched it. The air was fresh and for good reason: nine bell-shaped chimneys perforated the rock. I supposed they were made to bring air into the cavern, but they also served as excellent conduits of sand, for mounds of it were piled beneath each vent.

Ficer sat astride his bike, watching me as I studied the chamber, as if waiting on my reaction. He was a tall man, thin and dark and sun-wrinkled so that pale dust was trapped in the deep fissures of his skin. Even so, and even though his hair was silvery white, he did not seem old. This puzzled me, until I decided he was an artifact of the desert, as much as the clean stone and the blowing sand, and I left it at that. "This is the well room," he announced, when I refused to make any comment.

I smiled, sure he was having fun with me. Then I looked again at the mounds of sand on the floor. Was I supposed to believe each one was the mouth of a well? But I had never heard of a temple with more than one well. Even the oldest temple at Xahiclan was said to have only one, though it was vast in size.

Ficer smiled. "You don't believe me? Take a look."

I glanced at Jolly, but his face was turned away. My grief was older than his, and my curiosity was strong. So I dropped the kick-stand on my bike and ventured across the chamber—to find it was just as Ficer had said. The mounds of sand were not made by the wind blowing grains into the ventilation shafts. Instead, the shafts appeared to have been carved over centuries by the traffic of stone-eating kobolds flying up from the mouths of nine wells that perforated the floor.

"It's a natural wonder," Ficer said. "More so, because the wells die out every few years, but always they come back to life. No one can explain it."

I wondered how often Maya's scholars came this way, and if their theory of silver tides could say anything about this strange concentration of wells. "But why is there no keeper?"

MEMORY

"Azure is a strange place. A place to pass through. No one I know has ever stayed more than three nights. Too much history." He waved a sun-blackened hand, indicating the double stairway on the opposite side of the chamber, that rose without rails to the right and left. "There are chambers and passages all through the rock, enough room for a hundred people, or more than a hundred if they're not desert folk. But the only way into the refuge is by those notches we climbed. What kind of people would wall themselves in like that? Not a happy people, I expect. Not at all."

I looked around, and despite the large size of the chamber I felt a sense of entrapment.

Ficer nodded. "Some say the memory of those who made this place is still here, locked up in the rock. That's how it seems to me."

Though I had known Ficer only a few minutes, I could not imagine him being frightened by ghost stories. So perhaps there truly was something strange about this place. "There aren't any bogies here, are there?" I asked suspiciously.

"You know of bogies?"

"I met one."

He grunted. "Nasty things, spawned in greed. There have always been players who would try to protect the wealth of one life until they could find it in the next, and some, even worse, who could not endure the thought of others trespassing in the ruins of their estates, so they used bogies to guard them, even through the silver. But there are no bogies here. Just memories, and that's enough."

"We'll be all right, though?" Jolly asked, his voice hoarse, little more than a whisper, though when he looked up at Ficer his eyes were dry. "This one night?"

Ficer gave him a reassuring smile. "Sure we will. And tomorrow we'll do our part for the temple before we go."

"For the next player," Jolly said with a solemn nod, as if repeating a phrase he'd heard many times before.

"For the next player," Ficer agreed.

We laid our sleeping bags in a small side chamber. I shared out some of my dwindling supply of packaged food, while Ficer brought out dried meat and fruit. I didn't know how to ask the questions that were most important to me—what had happened to Jolly, where he had been, what he knew of Kaphiri. Also, I knew if I started asking questions, I would have to answer them too, and I was reluctant to say more about my father. There was a quality to Jolly's face, a fragility, that frightened me. I couldn't guess what he'd been through, or how much more he could bear. What if he blamed himself for my father's death? Kaphiri had come seeking him after all.

Jolly ate mechanically, wrapped up in his own thoughts, so it was left to Ficer to carry the conversation. In a quiet way he told me about himself, how he roamed the Iraliad, repairing the antennas that grew here and there on the mesa tops. "The silver is less an enemy than the wind. Fierce storms out of the southern ocean blow down the antennas more often than the silver takes them away."

When we were done eating I asked if there was a passage to the mesa top, for I wanted to call Liam, but Ficer shook his head. "This is not the night to be opening any door. But come with me awhile. There's something here you should see."

I started to my feet, surprised at the relief I felt at the prospect of leaving that room and my brother's silence. Only a latent guilt made me hesitate. "Jolly," I asked, without really meaning it, "will you come . . . ?"

He looked at me with some faint amusement. It was a look that made me shiver, for it seemed mature beyond his years. "I think Ficer wants to speak with you alone."

"There is no point in trying to be subtle around Jolly," Ficer announced as he clambered to his feet. "He'll see through it every time."

That was true. Jolly had always had an eerie knack for guessing the thoughts and intentions of other players, while I was hardly aware of my own heart. Still, I worried about leaving him alone. "Will you be all right?" I asked.

"Fine," Jolly insisted, his hand resting on Moki's back.

"There's nothing here to harm a player but his own conscience," Ficer said, "and no other can be a shield against that."

Jolly met my doubtful gaze. "That doesn't reassure you, does it?" My cheeks warmed, for he had seen through me again. "So. We'll be back in a few minutes then." And before I could diminish myself further, I followed Ficer into the hall.

The passage ran level for several hundred feet, lit by optical cables growing on the smooth walls. Beneath the strings of lights, dust and dead kobold shells were heaped in shallow banks, pushed there by passing feet. I glimpsed a few living kobolds among the debris. In such a strange place I expected to find strange kobolds, but there was no evidence of any variety beyond the familiar temple strains.

We passed many closed doors. Some were locked. Those few rooms that were open held only dust. It felt as if no one had ever lived there, or as if the abandoned kobolds had consumed everything except the rock itself.

Twice we passed other hallways, both running at odd angles to our own. Neither was lit, and I felt no urge to explore them when I saw the great cobwebs that hung like skeins of mist from their ceilings.

We'd been walking several minutes when the passage came to an end, widening into a round chamber with a single, massive door set in one wall. "That's a stairway to the surface," Ficer said. "If tomorrow the silver subsides, you can take your savant up and try your luck."

I didn't understand why I should wait. "We must be five hundred feet above the desert floor. The silver cannot have climbed this high."

Ficer nodded at a pillar of black metal set to one side of the door. "It's true the top of the mesa is only ten feet or so above us."

He laid his palm against the metal, which was damp with condensation. "This pole reaches up to it, through the rock and into the open air. Lay your hand on it."

I did, and felt a faint but frantic vibration.

"That's the teeth of the silver you're feeling," Ficer said, "chewing on the metal."

My eyes grew wide. "Do you mean the whole mesa has drowned?" Never had I heard of silver so deep.

"The same as last night," Ficer said. "Where did you stay?"

"At a wild well . . ." And hadn't it been like standing at the bottom of a luminous ocean?

Then doubt set in. "This pole . . ." I frowned at it. "It must have been here for many years. How has it gone untouched so long, only to be consumed tonight?"

Ficer ran his fingers through the condensation. "It's not so much that things go untouched by the silver. It's more that sometimes they're put back exactly as they were, and sometimes not. This pipe, it's been touched by the silver many times, and always it's been returned more or less as it began. Someday though, it'll be given back changed . . . or not at all."

I too ran my fingers down the column of metal and the cold of it seemed to reach all the way to my spine. "How is it the silver gave Jolly back?"

"That I don't know."

"I didn't want to tell him of my father's death."

"You had no choice."

"Still, he's been very quiet."

"He doesn't say much," Ficer agreed.

"You wanted to tell me something, didn't you? It's why we're here."

Ficer's gaze took my measure. Then: "It's the way you look at him, as if you're looking at a ghost or a phantom."

"*I* . . . ?" I was shocked. "That's not how I feel!"

"No?"

I had to look away. "But he is a ghost, isn't he? In a way."

"So I thought when I first saw him."

"How did it happen? How did you find him?"

He smiled at the memory. "If you were lost in a silver fog, looking out for players to be with, what sort of players would you be most likely to see?"

I shook my head, not at all sure what he meant.

"What is the one and only reason most players ever approach a bank of silver?"

"Oh . . . you were at a funeral, or a memorial ceremony?"

He nodded. "I was attending a funeral at Sentinel Mesa. They have a fair-sized enclave there, almost at the center of the northern desert. The body of the deceased was hardly committed to the silver when this boy stumbled out, all silver himself at first, as if the soul of the deceased had returned. It scared everyone. It's amusing now, to think on it, but it scared me too. Players don't like being startled. Makes 'em feel foolish later. I could see how the talk was going, so I took Jolly away from Sentinel before anyone could notice."

"I want to thank you for that."

Ficer accepted this with a slow nod. "I wasn't sure at first, but I think now it was the right thing to do. Jolly's a good boy . . . and if the silver has given him back, it's for a reason."

" 'Mostly the silver seems to act without purpose,' " I recited, " 'but sometimes it is otherwise.' "

Ficer laughed. "And where did you hear that?"

"From Emil."

"The old man of the Pinnacles? That one is worth listening to."

I didn't disagree. "So what is Jolly's purpose?"

Ficer's eyes challenged me from their deep setting among sun-wrinkled skin. "Maybe that's for Jolly to discover?"

I nodded, for it was true that each of us must find our own way. "I would still like to take him home."

"And maybe you will. But come. He's waiting, and he'll be worried if we're gone too long."

Chapter

24

When we returned, Jolly was huddled in a corner, with Moki in his lap. That sight affected me strangely, for it seemed as if I looked back in time at myself, alone in the corner of my room, holding on to a scream of despair until the silver was fully gone.

I moved my sleeping bag next to his and sat down. He watched me with wary eyes as if I were the silver itself. I leaned against the wall, looking out across the room so that he did not have to feel my gaze. I was not, after all, the Jubilee he remembered. I said, "I'm sorry for this strangeness between us. You were my older brother. That's how I remember you. My best friend. Now seven years have passed—"

"It has not been that long."

"It has, for me. Seven years." I tried to smile. "Ficer says I look on you as if you were a ghost. You must forgive me, Jolly, if it seems that way, but the dead do not come back to life every day, looking as bright as when they left. I think it will take some time to get my mind around it . . . though it doesn't mean I love you less."

He nodded, but his grip on Moki tightened. "Do you remember that night I called the silver?"

I could feel his dark eyes on me, and there was defiance in his voice, but I was not going to argue with him. I knew what he had done. Maybe, I knew how he had done it. "I remember it all."

He leaned back against the wall, his right hand obsessively

stroking Moki's neck. "You are a ghost too, Jubilee. The silver was there in our room. I knew it must have taken you too. How could you have escaped? I thought you were dead. That we both were, and I had killed you."

I turned to him in surprise. "*No.* The silver never touched me."

Ficer appeared in the doorway then, startling Jolly so that he shrank against the wall. "Getting jumpy again?" Ficer asked as he lay down on his sleeping bag.

Jolly smiled sheepishly. "Sorry." Then he glanced at me. "Did you see what happened that night?"

"Yes."

His next words were haunted with memory. "There is silver in all of us. Mama told me when a player dies, silver will leave the body, like a last breath. I was that wisp-of-silver. I *felt* like a ghost, floating, not solid at all though I was still me. Like being in a dream, when you can't touch anything, but I could see. I could see everywhere . . . that's how it seemed. Windows opened everywhere I looked. It was the world—at least I guessed it was. None of it looked like any part of the world I had seen before. But at least it was somewhere, and I was nowhere. I tried to get through the windows, but they kept slipping away. I didn't know how to move. I thought I would never escape."

Whether that time in the silver encompassed hours or days or the slow turn of seasons, Jolly couldn't say, but it was long. I think it was a different kind of time than passes in the world. Perhaps it was a kind of infancy, for like an infant that grows in strength and learns to walk, Jolly's helplessness gradually yielded to a new mobility. He struggled always to move toward one of these vistas that he called a "window" and finally he reached one.

"It was like being pushed into a painting of a landscape, only to find the land in the painting was the real world, while . . ." He waved his hand vaguely. "Wherever I had been . . . that was a dream. Though it had felt real enough when I was there."

"Where did you find yourself?" I asked when he'd been silent for most of a minute.

"Nowhere." He shook his head. "There was no one there. Nothing. It was an empty land"—he glanced at Ficer, stretched out on his bedroll—"a lot like this place, but by the ocean."

He had been terribly frightened and utterly alone. Wandering that strange coast he grew hungry and horribly thirsty under a pitiless sun. He hid behind rocks and watched as wild animals came up out of the water, great fat seals and giant sea stars with shining tentacles. A bull hippo chased him, giving up only when he scrambled up a cliff face where it could not follow.

"I stayed there three days. It rained twice and I had some water, but the sea snails I could pry from the rocks were salty and they made me sick. I thought I was going to die. It made me so angry. I didn't want to die. But I was sick. I could hardly stand up. When the silver came, the third night I was there, I tried to run, but there was nowhere to go. No more cliffs to climb. So the silver caught me, and it was just like the first time. The world slipped away and I could see it only through windows. I was a ghost again, looking through windows, with a different view everywhere I turned . . . but I never saw home."

Moki stirred, so Jolly set him on his feet. The hound stretched and yawned and wagged his tail, and we both watched, as if it was a fascinating thing to see. Then Jolly spoke again. "I thought everyone had lied to me." His fist clenched against his knee. "I was so angry. Furious at Mom, Dad, because they'd lied to me about the silver—"

"They didn't lie—"

"I know that! I know it now. But then, I thought it was the same for everyone, that the silver only took you away, it didn't kill you."

"But it's not like that . . . is it?" I longed for him to tell me that everything I knew was wrong, that players could return from the silver, but Jolly was wiser than that.

He shook his head. "Other players can't survive the silver. It's only me and . . . and . . ."

"Kaphiri?" I asked softly.

Jolly looked suddenly fearful. "You know him?"

"I've met him." I tried to keep my voice calm. "He's hunting you. And now . . . I think he's hunting me too."

Jolly nodded, and turned away again. I was afraid he'd stop speaking, so I pressed him with a question. "Jolly? How did he find you?"

"He didn't. I found him."

He described how he'd struggled once more to escape the silver by reaching toward the vistas he could see, the "windows" as he called them. It was hard for him to move willfully. It was so much easier to drift, and yet, as he strove for direction, he learned, and motion became easier. This time he chose carefully, before slipping through a window into the world.

"It was a better place," Jolly said. "A lot like Kavasphir, though there were animals there I never saw before, so I think it was really far away. But there was a stream with fish in it, and wild berries, and I set a trap and after a couple of days I caught a piglet." He shrugged. "It's better to hunt with a rifle."

So I would guess.

"Anyway, I stayed there many days. I didn't keep count. But I never saw another player. It was lonely, and I wanted to go home. So when the silver rose again, I walked into it."

That became the pattern of his life, for weeks at least. Perhaps for months. He would look for a place like Kavasphir, or any place that seemed familiar, or just a place where there was some sign that players might be nearby. But the world is vast, and he never found his way home.

"Then *he* came," Jolly said. "I saw him, far away in the silver. At first I thought I was only looking through another window, but there was something different about him . . . as if he was solid and everything else was mist. The other windows would fade in and out of existence, but he was solid. Not a window at all, but a player within the silver itself.

"A player . . . but he wasn't a ghost like me. He was real. *Solid.* Fixed in place . . . like the sea snails I'd pried off the rocks. That's what he was like. I went to him, but he couldn't see me. He was in the silver, but he couldn't see. You understand? I *was* the silver. He was still a player."

"You were transformed? And he was still untouched?"

Jolly nodded. "The silver would not take him, or touch him. That was his power, but it was a curse too. It made him angry, though I didn't know it then." His eyes had a distant look. "He couldn't see me, but I could see him. He was walking, and there was solid ground under his feet, but it was not solid for me. I followed him anyway, through a window and out of the silver." Jolly's smile was bitter. "He saw me then. I scared him. He looked *so* scared. But only for a few seconds." His face grew sad as he remembered. "He took care of me, and for a time I was happy that I'd found him."

They learned much from each other, Kaphiri and my brother. Though they both could survive the silver, their talents were not the same. When Kaphiri entered the silver, he remained a physical being. He could go only where he could walk within the fog. It was different for Jolly. His fate was like that of the metal pole Ficer had directed me to touch. The silver would dissolve his body, but he would not lose coherence. He would remain whole in the memory of the silver. He would remain aware. It was as if the silver's awareness became his, as if he shared the mind of the goddess. He could see through the silver, to places all around the ring of the world. He could reach through it: a ghost that might appear anywhere the fog touches.

Never before had Kaphiri imagined it possible to *ride* the silver. It was a talent he wanted for himself.

"I asked him to help me find my home," Jolly said, "but he had never heard of Kavasphir. So we went to a temple in high mountains where he kept his home.

"He told me that silver once was rare, and in those days people were less afraid of the mountains. Many temples had been built in the high places then, and people would come deliberately to see the silver. All those temples are gone now, except the one where Kaphiri lives, and almost no one comes there because they're afraid of the silver. But there was another player who lived there, a woman who kept the temple for him."

"And was she his wife?" I wanted to hear that she was, for then I would not have to suspect myself.

"He has no wife," Jolly said. "He told me he was a cessant, and Mari—she who keeps the house for him—she is a cessant too."

"Mari?" I asked, startled.

"Yes. Why? Have you heard of her?"

"I think I have." The wife of Nuanez Li had been named Mari, and she had gone off with the traveler, seeking to restore her youth. How long ago? I could not guess.

"Tell me more," I said, "and I'll tell you my story later."

Jolly nodded. "Mari was an old woman. Very old. She wouldn't tell me how she'd come to be so high in the mountains, but she was afraid of the silver. She would never step outside the temple walls, even when the sun was bright. So she was trapped there, a prisoner.

"She was always good to me though, and she never became angry. Still she must have been lonely when Kaphiri was away. I felt sorry for her. I wanted to find some way for her to escape. It wasn't Kaphiri that held her prisoner, you understand? It was the silver. So I hunted around the temple, wandering for miles, and made a map of all the wild kobold wells I could find."

He frowned, and his voice grew even softer. "I was afraid of the silver too. Kaphiri could find his way through it, but I could not. Not when he wasn't there. I needed him. I needed something solid to follow. I knew if I went back into the silver alone I would get lost again . . . and we were so high in the mountains there was no way I could walk out in the few hours the silver was away. Maybe, if I could move from wild well to wild well . . ."

He shook his head. "Mari didn't want to go. Kaphiri had been away for many days, but as soon as he returned she told him what I was planning. It made him angry. Whenever he was angry I would stay in my room, or if the sun was bright I'd go walking in the forest. But when Mari told him I'd been looking for a way out of the mountains he went crazy."

Jolly's voice dropped again until it was no more than a whisper. "He hit me." His hand rose, to touch the side of his head. "It made me dizzy and sick. It was night, and he took me outside, up onto the temple wall.

"That temple was on a cliff above a steep canyon. On afternoons when the sun was bright you could see to the canyon bottom where a thread of white water ran through forest, but most of the time there was only silver below us. That night the silver filled the canyon, flowing downhill like a wide, slow river just beneath our feet. Kaphiri said he would throw me into it."

My brother's eyes were haunted. He gazed at his hands, but he saw other things. "I didn't want to be lost again!"

"Jolly, it's all right."

"I was afraid."

"It's all right," I said again, but neither of us believed it.

"After that he brought other players to the temple." His voice took on a note of bitter triumph. "He guided them between wild wells! I learned that after—that he stole the idea from me. He had threatened to throw me into the silver, but after that night he was afraid I would jump, so he brought some of his cessants to watch over me."

Kaphiri had found a treasure in Jolly and he was not about to give it up. "All of us, we are like the kobolds," Jolly said. "We all have configuration codes. That's what I learned from Kaphiri." He looked me hard in the eye as he said this, as if daring me to argue. I did.

"Jolly, players don't have configuration codes. He was lying to you. We're not mechanics."

Jolly laughed—a cold laugh that frightened me because it reminded me of another. "You think you know." He jumped up then, and paced the room. Ficer watched him, propped up on one elbow. Jolly said, "Kaphiri knows more about how we are made than anyone else alive. Our configuration codes are hidden deep in our blood, in our cells, but they exist. Kaphiri studied the codes in my blood, the codes that made *me*. Then he copied the pattern as best he could, adjusting the codes in his own blood."

In his blood? I was aware suddenly of my heart beating. Kaphiri's blood had crossed with mine and now I was changed, as if some part of me had been rewritten . . .

Jolly said, "He learned to move through the silver as I do. He went to many far places, while I stayed in the temple with the cessants he'd brought to watch me. They were afraid of him, but they loved him. They wanted to be like him. Sometimes . . . I wanted to be like him too."

I nodded. There is an attraction in power. It's why a son wants to be like his father, or a daughter like her mother who she sees as being in control of life. How much more powerful Kaphiri must have seemed than any father!

"At first, he would never tell me where he went, or what he did," Jolly said. "But he would talk to the cessants, and when he was gone they would talk among themselves. I asked him if it was true, if he had brought the silver into enclaves where players still lived. He said it was true. It was his purpose."

"He told me the same. It's what he was born for."

"He said I was born for it too."

"No! You can't believe him. That's not true."

But the look in Jolly's eyes belied me. "You weren't there," he said. "You don't know what happened."

Dread stirred in my belly. I didn't know, but I could guess. "You called the silver into the temple, didn't you? Just like that night at Temple Huacho."

His face grew taut, as if he were seeing again some terrible vision. "The cessants saw it coming. They tried to carry me to safety, but the silver caught them anyway." There was grief in his voice, though his eyes were dry. "So I got away, but I still couldn't find my way home."

"You *have* found your way." I said it with conviction. "I'll take you home, Jolly. I will."

There was a distance in his eyes as he considered this. It was as if I'd become the child and he the adult with concerns I could not even conceive. "And what if he follows me there?"

I looked away. I didn't want him to see my own fear.

"He's looking for me!" Jolly insisted. "You know he is. You said it yourself!"

Moki shrank from his side, troubled by his anger. I gathered the hound into my own lap, burying my fingers in his soft fur. "Why does he want you, Jolly? He's already stolen your secrets. He's learned to move through the silver—"

Jolly cut off my protests with a quick slice of his hand. "You can't turn a metal-eating kobold into a temple guardian, can you?" he asked. His voice was soft and bitter. "Kaphiri made himself more like me, but he is not me. He can go where he wants in the silver, but he can't see anything until he's there. For him it's like stepping through a door between rooms. The rooms might be thousands of miles apart, but it's only one step for him. Only one step between the mountain temple and the enclave he would destroy. He can't see anything in between. He's blind to most of the world. Posses have gathered to attack his cessants, and he has never seen them. But I can see them. *I can see it all.* That's why I get lost. Everything is there at once, and it all gets confused . . ."

I came to understand it only slowly, that our senses are filters. We do not hear everything there is to hear, or we would be overwhelmed by the complexities of sound. We do not see everything there is to see, or our brains would fail trying to interpret every nuance of light. But in the silver Jolly was not protected by any similar filter. He perceived far more than his mind could make sense of, and so he could make sense of nothing . . . until he found

Kaphiri. Solid and unchanging, Kaphiri was the rock he could cling to while chaos rushed around him. It was the difference between a player who is swept away in a raging river, and one who stands upon a rock while the river sweeps past him, gazing at the debris that passes by.

"I am his eyes," Jolly concluded. "I see the world for him. I see his enemies."

It was very quiet in that refuge, with no sound of wind or water, or the night songs of birds. When Ficer stirred in his bedding, it seemed a loud noise. "So he needs you," Ficer said. "But he must fear you too. He must fear you could find some way to lead his enemies to him."

Jolly shook his head. "No. You don't understand. To do that, I'd have to go back into the silver, and then I'd be lost again. Jubilee—" He turned to me. "Don't you see? If I go home, he'll know it. He knows I'm from a place called Kavasphir. If he looks hard enough, he'll find it—"

Something must have shown in my face.

"Has he been there already?" There was horror in Jolly's voice. "Is that where you met him?"

I wanted to deny it, but I was not well practiced at telling lies. "He came. One night when I was sitting on the wall. He asked for you. I told him you were gone. I thought you were dead. I didn't know."

"And my father? Was that when . . . ?"

"No. Kaphiri had already found him on the road."

I told Jolly my story then, keeping nothing back, not even the story of the blood poisoning, which Jolly accepted with a look that had more of resignation in it, than surprise.

Should I have lied? Should I have tried to shield some of the truth from him? He was a child after all . . .

And yet he was not a child. He had been through the silver, and he had passed through other fires. Those experiences had changed him. Ficer was right in that. Besides, Jolly had a truth-sense too keen for me to evade. If ever I tried to pass lightly over a subject he questioned me, drilling down to levels of fact I hardly knew existed. I relived my journey that night, and it was late before we finally lay down to sleep.

Chapter

25

That night when we put out the light, I did not expect to sleep, for my mind was full with the day's events, each memory jostling for recognition and reflection. But sleep came anyway, quieting my troubled thoughts one by one, until all that remained in my awareness was a soft whispering, a murmur of voices with no apparent source unless it was my own ears, stunned by the profound silence of that cavern. Adrift between sleep and wakefulness, I listened, and gradually the whispering resolved into words, faint and garbled at first, and in a language I did not immediately know, but as it had so many times before, the knowledge of another language wakened in me.

Or I wakened into that knowledge.

I have dreamed often, and what happened then was no dream, though it was a kind of vision, for I wakened into more than just the knowledge of another language. I wakened into another life. *My* life, though it was not the one I had lived.

The whispering grew closer, surrounding me, faint ghost voices imploring me to do what only I could do. *Save us.* That was their plea. Their ghost fingers brushed my arms, my face, light touches like puffs of warm air. They whispered blessings. They touched my tears as if this effusion was a sacred liquid.

The fear in my belly was so hot I thought I would puke. I had already run away once. Now they begged me to go back.

I raised my head, looking up to meet the gaze of an old man, small and crooked as a crab that has spent most of its life living in borrowed shells. His complexion was dark, but his skin had a translucence to it, a smooth purity, as if he had never seen the sun. His hair was gone, but tendrils of beard remained, reaching past his knees like lichen that hangs from the limbs of trees. He sat in an ornate chair, a small throne really, for we were in an audience chamber of grand design such as I had seen only in market dramas, with high ceilings and immense windows of colored glass and all of its span filled with whispering ghosts begging me to do what I dreaded to do.

The old man was Ki-Faun. In my vision I knew this. He was the player who had authored a book of kobold lore. I had never seen him before, yet I felt as if I had always known his name. At the same time, I was not entirely that other me, for I felt surprise too. Ki-Faun, the author of my book? Yes.

I had not seen him before, but as I looked on him I was surprised by a sense of familiarity, and I began to realize that I *had* known him, but in another guise, or more likely another life altogether.

Surprise filled his eyes, and he leaned forward to look at me more closely, as if he was troubled by remembrances too. His old crab hands pinched at the armrests of his chair, and his eyes closed briefly. *"Not by chance,"* he whispered. When his gaze met mine again there was the faintest of smiles on his faded lips. "The knot is tied around you, milady, did you know it? All our fates circle around you."

I had no idea what he meant, but I knew what he wanted. "You want to blame me, but it's not because of me! He was something strange and wicked before I ever knew him!"

"We do not blame you," Ki-Faun said softly. "But we need you, just as we have needed you in other lives before this." He set a kobold in my hand. "We have reached the end of this age. We will either master the silver, or we will drown in it—"

"You think you can master it?"

"With the time that you buy us, yes. We are that close. Our fates circle around you."

"He will not want to see me again!"

An expression of such pain crossed the old man's face I thought he would cry. "Oh, no, milady, he will want to see you."

An anguished cry pierced my dream, and I awoke with a start, to find myself once again in the room at Azure Mesa that we had chosen for sleep. Faint light fell from my drifting savant, and in that illumination I could see Jolly sleeping peacefully beside me, but beyond him Ficer was calling out in a troubled sleep. Sweat shone on his face. My own clothes were damp and my skin was clammy. The scent of kobolds was strong in the air, and sweeter than the kobold scent of Temple Huacho.

I sat up, feeling my muscles limp, and trembling. I leaned against the hardness of the stone wall, thinking on my vision, and trying not to think on it, as if I were still two people: one that was me, and one that was me, in another life.

A life I had lived.

How to describe the horror this conviction brought? To know who I had been, what I had done . . .

He was something strange and wicked before I ever knew him!

Not for a moment did I doubt who "he" might be, and it was Ki-Faun's plan that I should return to him.

Most of the time we live an illusion. We put the worst possibilities out of our thoughts, and live as if evil is a neutered beast, incapable of the horrors described in stories of old. We see ourselves as strong, and lucky; the weakened beast is no more than a shiver in our spines on a blustery evening—and this is a good way for us to live. For to be fully conscious of the potential horrors of existence would quickly destroy existence, as a raging stream will level the mud castle a child has made upon its bank.

That night though, I saw with the clarity of a condemned prisoner. The world was broken, and had been, almost from the day it was made. The silver that should have served us was drowning us instead. The floods grew deeper with each passing night and enclave after enclave was falling to them.

No player had made this disaster. It was a flaw in the world itself. But one player there was who would hurry the world toward its conclusion.

Our fates circle around you. Ki-Faun thought he could master the silver, if only he had time, so I promised to do what I could to get him that time.

I flinched as Ficer again cried out in his sleep. But Jolly slept quietly, as if no unpleasant thought had ever brought a shadow to his beautiful boy's face.

My eyes started to close, but I forced them open again. I had no idea of the time, but I swore I would not sleep again that night. I would stay awake until dawn and then we would leave this ancient stronghold and my dream would fade and all would be as it had been . . . so I told myself. But the cloying scent of kobolds was in my nostrils, sweeter, and more intense than their scent at Temple Huacho, and my mind drifted. Though I clutched at my sleeping bag I could not keep myself from slipping away.

The stone walls of that room became the stone walls of a barren canyon that tumbled down to a desert plain, and the faint gleam of my savant became the gleam of a twilight sky. A cold wind moaned among the rocks, bringing with it the scent of silver, to mix with the scent of temple kobolds that arose from the wild well where I had made my camp. My sleeping bag was laid out and I had put a pot of water to heat on my little stove, but these were only gestures, done out of habit.

All around me, skeins of silver gleamed beneath the overhanging rocks, and there was a pearly opacity to the air that I knew too well. The kobold Ki-Faun had given me weeks before scrabbled within the prison of my clutching hand. *You must not crush it!* Ki-Faun had warned. *Not until the moment when he will breathe its vapors. There will be no second chance.* That I might breathe the same vapors was a possibility Ki-Faun admitted with real grief. *You are his guardian. It is not an easy task, but it is yours. The goddess herself made it so.*

The kobold could not escape its fate, any more than I could.

The evening's last light faded from the sky, but it did not grow dark, for silver gleamed into existence, seeping from the air. It sank to the ground all around the sheltering ring of my wild well. Once on the ground it gathered together at the lowest point of the defile and slid away downhill, like a phantom stream. I watched it pool in a vast lake on the plain below.

Some time passed. An hour. Maybe two and then I saw him, a dark figure, climbing up from the plain with a spritely step, the silver flowing harmlessly past his knees. He spoke to me, the memory of a memory, his warm breath tickling my ear as he whispered his dark philosophy like words of love: *We can be like them. The goddess who made this world and the god who pursued her . . . they were once as we are now, mortal, on another world in a far place. There they were tested, and some few among them climbed beyond their world and became more than human . . . We can do the same, you and I. We don't have to remain simple players. We can master the silver, and own this world . . .*

I hated him. Even then as I lay in his arms. And I hated the goddess and the god, who were swallowed by their own darkness, leaving the world broken. Why should I wish to be like them?

I was content to be human. To be human was to know the difference between good and bad, right and wrong, to live without a darkness in the soul. I understood enough of gods and goddesses to know that they were terrible, as the silver is terrible, and not human. Not at all.

Now he was back.

I watched him climb toward me up the canyon and the silver did not harm him because he had become a minor god.

He must not die, Ki-Faun had warned, *or the silver will be poisoned. And he must not live, or he will bring the silver into this enclave. It is a wicked thing we ask you to do, to erase the very memory of him from the world, but it's the only thing we can do. He must be removed forever from the cycle of birth and rebirth.*

Evidently his climb up the canyon was taxing him. His pace slowed, and as he drew near I could hear the harsh wash of his breath, though I could not hear the tread of his feet against the stone for his feet were hidden beneath the silver. I wondered if the ground he walked on was somewhere else altogether.

He looked ahead and he saw me, but neither of us spoke, not even when he reached the edge of the safe ground around the kobold well and stepped free of the streaming silver.

His shoulders heaved with exertion and in his dark eyes was an expression of mistrust and anger and pathetic hope that sickened me. Could he really believe I would love him again?

I saw that he could.

The kobold struggled in my hand, reminding me of why I had come. I stepped toward him. I tried to smile.

A rock skipped down the cliff behind me. He heard it too, and looked up. His enemies were uncountable, and any one of them would be grateful to murder him, but I could not allow him to die that way, not while there was still a chance Ki-Faun's plan might work.

"Get down!" I cried, but he was already moving, dropping behind the shelter of a boulder. I fell on my pack and dragged it with me behind the cover of another rock, as rifle shots bit at the sand all around us. I pulled my own rifle free of the pack. Then I leaned out just far enough to see the cliff face.

He had called the silver to his defense. An arm of it was flowing—impossibly!—*up* the gully wall, nosing behind boulders and sweeping into every cleft and cut. Someone shouted, in a language strange to me. Then six players appeared as if from nowhere. They charged down the slope, their guns firing wildly. I ducked back behind the boulder, clenching my rifle, listening.

It would not take long.

There was a scream, and then another. The chorus of shots was cut in half, and then it was cut again until only one weapon spoke. A man's voice shouted what must have been a curse. Then silence fell, save for my ragged breathing.

I turned to look at him.

He was standing, smiling faintly, with the silver behind him and all around. "You didn't know they were there, did you?" he asked. I shook my head. "I was careful not to be followed! I don't know how—"

"It doesn't matter."

We were both still alive. That's all that mattered.

His gaze fixed on something between us, lying in the sand. He frowned, stooping to collect a large kobold, the very one I had dropped when the shooting started. "What is it for?" he asked, looking at me.

I could not lie. "It's for you."

He regarded it thoughtfully. "And what will it do for me?"

I whispered the only answer I had: "It will end your pain."

"No, I think only you could do that." Then he cocked his arm back. I saw what he was doing and shouted at him, *"No!"* but he did not heed me. He cast the kobold in a powerful throw down the gully where it plunged into the streaming silver. Gone.

Then he looked at me with wounded eyes, this man who had brought the silver into a thousand enclaves. "They sent you, didn't they? Ki-Faun and his cohort, always so taken with their own cleverness, but they will not live long past this night."

He had never been one to lie. So I made my choice. Bringing my rifle to my shoulder, I fired.

Blood fountained from his chest. He collapsed first to his knees and then he started to pitch forward, but he stopped his fall with one hand against the ground. He looked up at me. There was confusion in his eyes, and cold horror. *Do you know what you've done?* he seemed to ask. *Do you know?*

I did. I was his guardian after all. I always had been.

Then he could no longer hold his head up. He sagged to the ground, his eyes reflecting the gleam of silver but with no life of their own. Silver seeped from his lips and nostrils, the silver that leaves the body at death—more and more of it. I was amazed at how much. I watched in fascination as it flowed across the ground, to meet with the ordinary silver of the night. Ki-Faun had warned against just this. *It must not happen!* But surely it was better for the silver to die than for the world to drown in a silver flood?

The two fogs met, and where they touched the silver collapsed, its light going out as it was transformed to a gray powder that sifted to the ground. The destruction spread outward, sweeping down the canyon, leaving the rocks covered with a fine, powdery ash and every gleam of silver extinguished.

The transformation reached the plain. Darkness rolled across that lake of silver faster than a bird could fly so that within seconds the only light left was that of the stars overhead and the pale gleam of Heaven's arch.

A warm hand touched my shoulder. "Jubilee, what's the matter? Why do you cry?"

I shoved that comforting hand away. "You ask me that? The world is murdered! *Again.* And you ask me that?"

Then I was back in the cavern of Azure Mesa, on my knees but still entangled in my sleeping bag, with Jolly all in a heap before me, looking up at me with frightened eyes. "Jubilee?" he whispered, as if testing if it was really me.

I closed my eyes. I could hear Ficer muttering, still trapped in visions of his own. "I have seen it," I whispered. "I have seen what happens when one such as Kaphiri is made to die. He did not lie, Jolly. He did not lie."

Chapter

26

That vision left my body as weary as ever I can remember, but I would not lie down again despite Jolly's urging. I would not risk a return to sleep and that nightmare world of vanishing silver. I felt trapped by my own history. Not for a moment did I doubt that what I'd dreamed was real. Somehow I had been allowed to recover a memory of my own past, to glimpse one of the lives I had lived. *Why?* So that I would not repeat the disaster of that night? Or so I would be prepared when I faced the same choice again?

I remembered the feel of the kobold in my hand. A kobold that would erase the very memory of a player from the world. *Any* player. What a horrible weapon Ki-Faun had made, and I had been ready to use it.

I started for the door. Jolly followed after me. "Where are you going?" He glanced anxiously at Ficer, whose sleep had quieted.

"I cannot stay here. I need air."

"But there is silver this night."

"I need to see it."

He did not ask why.

I took a flashlight from my bike and Jolly went with me, to the distant room with its steel pole. I pressed my palm against the cold metal, but I could feel no vibration. Had the silver receded? Moki was sniffing at the door that was set into the wall. I laid my palms against it. It too was still.

Jolly watched me with wary eyes. "This should lead to the surface," I said. "I don't think there is silver on the other side, but I cannot be sure."

"Will you tell me what you dreamed?"

"When we're outside. I need to see the silver first."

The mechanism to open the door was a large, polished wheel. I took it in both hands and glanced at Moki. He seemed eager to go out. So I turned the wheel.

It proved to be well oiled. I felt a heavy bolt slide back and then the door swung open an inch, admitting a breath of cold, clean night air. No silver came sweeping into the room, so I pushed the door wider, and Moki slipped outside. The beam of my flashlight followed him as he disappeared up a rising stone stairway.

Jolly and I were more cautious. We stayed long enough to gather some of the kobold shells that everywhere littered the floor, making a mound of them in the doorway so the door could not close completely and lock us outside. Then we went to find Moki.

The stairway was steep. After only a half-dozen steps I could see stars in a rectangle of sky above us. There was no glow of silver.

I knew there had been silver on the plateau earlier in the night: I had felt it bite against the steel pole. What had caused it to retreat? Fear hurried my steps until I burst from the top of the stairs, to find myself only a dozen feet from the southern escarpment.

That prospect was not as lofty as standing on the edge of the Kalang, but it was impressive enough. An ocean of silver lay upon the desert below us, an expanse that reached all the way to the faintly gleaming horizon. I went to my knees in relief. *"It's still here."* My vision had been of the past, yet I feared it spoke of the future too.

"You dreamed his death?" Jolly asked. He stood beside me, gazing out across that luminous sea, its glow reflected against his smooth skin.

"It was another life. An earlier life. Did Kaphiri . . . did he speak to you of his death?"

"Always, when he was angry. If he was killed, the world would regret it. That's what he would say. That he was a poison in the world, and the silver would not outlive him."

On the surface that might seem a pleasant outcome because silver is so dangerous, but silver is also essential to our world. Darkness and light rolled into one. Destruction and creation. Its loss would be a disaster.

"Did you believe him?" I asked.

Jolly's shoulders moved in a little shrug against the star-filled sky. "At first I thought he was just crazy. In the end, I believed everything he said."

I nodded. "In another life I saw it happen. I *made* it happen."

How many times had I made it happen?

You are his guardian. The goddess herself made it so.

I felt a weight upon me, as if I had come to this moment of understanding many times before without ever growing wiser. Was there no way out? How old was the world?

My hands began to shake.

We had already come so close to disaster. That night on the Kalang escarpment, when Liam had seen Kaphiri on the plain below. If he had brought his rifle into play a little sooner, it would all be over now. Or if I had been better prepared that night at the Pinnacles . . .

If we had succeeded in our murder we would have murdered the world. Maya had been right all along.

I thought of running away, taking my brother and disappearing so deep into the Iraliad that Kaphiri would never find us. But to do so I would have to forget about Liam, and Udondi, my mother, my brothers and sisters, and Kaphiri himself, who had been my lover in another life, I could not doubt it now.

Someday someone would kill him.

I had seen the ancient city, and the horrible bogy haunting it—

relics of an age without silver. Should the world be returned to such a time?

(Or should it be left to drown in silver flood?)

Why is it me?

Because we had been joined somehow, long ago.

Many minutes passed before I trusted myself to speak, but finally I glanced again at Jolly. Where his thoughts had ventured I cannot say, but I was remembering the words of my ancient lover. "Did Kaphiri ever speak to you of the goddess and the god?"

The wan light cast up by the silver exposed a look of sudden wariness on Jolly's face.

"Jolly . . . ?"

"I never said it!"

"Said what?"

"*He* said it. That we were gods."

"The two of you?"

He nodded.

So I told him of my dream: of Ki-Faun, and the kobold in my hand that should have removed the memory of Kaphiri from the world. I told him of my failure, and the final choice I had made.

"How closely did you look at the kobold?" Jolly asked. "Did you see its configuration code?"

"No. I didn't think about it. Not then. It was a horrible thing."

"But before? Is it possible you looked at it before? Is it possible you knew it? You lived through that night, didn't you? Is it possible you wrote it down?"

Was it? Might a record of my experience exist in a library somewhere? I shook my head. "I don't think I would have wanted such knowledge to survive."

"You have Ki-Faun's book."

"It does not speak of erasing memories."

"You might have another vision."

"Jolly, don't frighten me more!"

He crouched beside me, and it no longer seemed to me that I was older. "He is full of hate, Jubilee, and this can have no good end. If he lives, he will drown every enclave in the world in silver. If he dies, the silver will die with him, and that would be almost as bad. It was the same in your vision. He could not be allowed to live, and he could not be allowed to die."

"And still I killed him."

"To stop the flood! This time we must act while there's still a choice."

"And do what? I don't know what kind of kobold it was, Jolly, and even if I did, I would not use it. Don't you see? Ki-Faun was wrong. No matter how terrible Kaphiri is, only he can turn the silver back. Without him, we will all drown."

"Ki-Faun believed we could learn to control the silver."

A weak little laugh escaped me. "We can. Anyway, *I* can, though I don't think it will help us much. I can push the silver away, Jolly. It's something I've learned since Kaphiri poisoned me."

My brother accepted this without surprise. "It has to do with your configuration codes. They must have been reset by the contact with Kaphiri's blood. He had reset his own codes already, so he wasn't the same. Not an exact match for you anymore. I guess that's why his blood sickened you, but not so much that you would die."

So. Kaphiri had poisoned me, and I was not human anymore.

Moki returned from the dark, nuzzling in between us. I buried my fingers in his fur, realizing for the first time how cold the night was.

Jolly said, "I want to know what Ki-Faun knew."

"I don't."

"We need to read your book, Jubilee. I don't think we have a choice."

Chapter

27

We stayed on the plateau until the eastern sky grew light enough to show the weather. It was not an encouraging sight. Heavy clouds were moving up again from the south, and though the silver faded as the dawn grew brighter, it seemed reluctant to be gone altogether. I wondered if we should risk leaving Azure Mesa, or if we should wait . . . for a better day, or to give Liam a chance to catch up with us. I wanted to try again to call him but I did not have my savant, so we returned to the cavern to fetch it.

Ficer was awake, busily packing his gear onto his bike. He greeted me with a weary nod. "It was no pleasant night, was it?" he asked.

"I dreamed," I admitted.

"Everyone does, and it's never pleasant dreams either. It's the kobolds—that's what I think. They smell differently from your common temple kobolds, don't they? A perfume to trouble the mind. It's why no one lives here; why so few come to stay even one night—which made it the safest place for us to meet."

I hesitated, for it was rude to ask, but I could not help myself. "What did you dream?"

My question confused him. "Nothing I can remember. The memory is gone when you awake—at least that's how it is for most who visit here. Was it different for you?"

I looked away, knowing I had said too much. "I seem to . . . remember a little."

"And not a comforting little by the look of you."

I was groping for some polite way to deny the truth when he raised a hand. "Don't speak of it. I have heard that some few come here on purpose to dream. They claim it's the past that visits them." He shook his head. "If that's so, we all have wicked things to account for, I say, for I have never met one who slept peacefully here . . . that is, until now." His gaze settled pointedly on Jolly—a look my brother answered with a sheepish smile.

"What's this?" I asked curiously. "What do you speak of? Not just that Jolly slept well?"

"That underestimates it," Ficer said. "I awoke several times in the night, and while you were troubled, Jolly's sleep was always quiet. Like the sleep of an innocent? One who has never lived before would have no past lives to haunt him."

"You think this is Jolly's first life?" But how could that be? No one new had been born into the world since its making—or so I'd been taught.

"It's what *I* think," Jolly said. "It makes sense. I don't have talents like you, like everyone else. I don't know anything but what I've learned—"

"It hasn't wakened in you yet," I said. "That's all—"

"And I don't think I could be reborn into another life. How could I, if the silver always returns me as myself?"

"Jolly!" He was so young. How could he believe that he would live only this one life? That such thoughts could even enter his mind . . . it horrified me. That he could believe such things and still hold on to the sweetness that had always been in his character . . . it astonished me, so that tears started in my eyes.

"He is closer to Heaven than you or I could ever be," Ficer said gently, and though Jolly tried to protest, Ficer would not hear it. "He plays a different game, that's what I believe. He's on his way to a different end, same as the traveler that hunts him. What end that is I don't know, but I've heard enough stories of this traveler to know whose side I'd rather play."

"Is that why you've protected Jolly? To hinder Kaphiri?"

"Ficer helped me because that's who he is," Jolly said.

But it was more than that. Jolly could live within the silver, the realm of souls that other players visited only in death. Did that make him a god? Kaphiri believed it, while I . . . I pretended I did not.

"I must try to reach Liam," I said brusquely. And taking my savant I fled to the mesa top where birds had begun to sing to the new day. Liam's savant was destroyed, so I directed my calls to Udondi. But neither she nor Liam answered and my fears did not leave me, while the weather grew worse. Clouds gathered overhead, and patches of silver could be seen gleaming among the sheltering vegetation that surrounded Azure Mesa. I studied the horizon all around, but nowhere could I see a sign of dust that might indicate someone traveling in the desert. I wished desperately that Liam would come. I wished desperately for guidance. I did not know what to do. If only I knew where Liam was, and what had delayed him, then my own path might be clearer, but I was at a loss.

Should I wait for him to reach Azure Mesa? Should I try to find him? Or should I take Jolly and flee deeper into the Iraliad?

Yaphet was out there—likely only a day or two away, by now. I wanted to run to him, to meet him, to know without doubt that he was the one . . . but the clouds were growing heavier, and I could smell silver gathering on the plain below. I had told Jolly I could control the silver, but I had no confidence in my talent. It seemed foolhardy to do anything—and in the end that was my decision. I convinced myself that no one would risk travel on such a day.

I left my savant on the mesa top with a prerecorded message for Liam, and another for Yaphet, if either should chance to call. Then I went back down into the cavern, to find that Ficer had reached a different conclusion.

"What do you mean you're going?" I demanded when I found him astride his bike, on the verge of descending to the gate. "Where are you going? And have you looked at the weather? There is silver on the plain, and no sign of the sun—"

"Aye," Ficer said. "It's why I'm going now."

"But *why?* Ficer, where do you have to go that you must be there today? If the silver rises, you could die. Jolly—" I turned to my brother for support. "You must convince him."

"He won't listen," Jolly said softly. My brother looked as frightened as I felt.

"Ficer—"

"No," he said gently. "Don't argue more. I've lived my life in this desert, and I've traveled on worse days than this—"

"But you don't have to go—"

"That's not how I see it." He started his bike, its soft purr resonate against the stone walls. "They could be in danger at the Temple of the Sisters. The traveler knows you were there. I must see to that . . . and too, I must speak with the old man. There is too much here I don't understand."

"But Emil doesn't understand it either. None of us does. And—and—" I bowed my head. I didn't know what to do, what I *should* do. "I am worried for them too," I confessed. "And for you. None of you asked to be caught up in this."

"Neither did you."

That didn't matter. "We'll come with you."

"No," Ficer said. "You'll stay here, at least until the weather clears. Your duty is to Jolly now."

"But it may be I can keep you safe from the silver."

"Jolly said as much. But believe that I am safe enough. Stay here with your brother. It won't be pleasant, but it's the best refuge you'll find. I'll come back if I can, but don't wait for me once the weather clears. If your heart tells you to go, then you must go. Do you understand?"

So we went down to the gate. Jolly and I worked the winch, lowering his bike over the side while he climbed down the notch steps. Though it was day, the light was dim. There seemed to be no colors anywhere, and the scent of silver was very strong. Ficer called back to us once: "Set your savant to listen at dusk. I'll call if I can."

Then he was gone away.

———

MEMORY

The caverns seemed a haunted place after Ficer left, a grim prison of cold stone and memories, and the prospect of sleeping there another night had me in a quiet terror. It wasn't long before Jolly and I decided to flee to the mesa top.

It was gloomy there with the sun lost behind a ceiling of low clouds, but it was still incomparably brighter than the caverns. We stood on the cliff's edge and looked out across the plain. Silver glittered in every drainage and depression and for a long time we saw no sign of Ficer. Then Jolly spied a plume of dust far to the south, and we agreed it must be him, though it might have been a dust devil, or even a small landslide.

My savant had received no messages from Liam, Udondi, or Yaphet. I told Jolly not to be discouraged. We were not in the range of any working antenna, so any communications would be line-of-sight only, meaning the sender was no more than a few hours away. I tried not to show my own disappointment, tucking it away beside my terror of the coming night.

We spent the morning exploring a tangle of pocket canyons in the mesa top, while silver gathered ever more thickly on the plain below. There were dead kobold wells in almost every ravine, so that we soon learned to be wary of holes as we beat paths through the desert brush.

There were birds everywhere, and day-flying bats as well. A constant, mad twittering filled the brush, and each time we descended into a new ravine, Moki would charge ahead of us, sending a storm of winged creatures into the air. The flocks would circle just above the ravines, keeping low, as if they feared being seen, and indeed, after a while a hawk appeared overhead, and then Moki could not get the flocks to stir at all.

I wondered where the birds went on the nights when silver climbed higher than the mesa top. I imagined them spending the whole night on the wing, gliding in a luminous space between the bright silver and the ethereal gleam of the Bow of Heaven. With such thoughts in my mind I fell asleep in a nest of grass and I did not waken again until the evening.

We went to retrieve the savant, and to wait for a message from Ficer, but night gathered and no message came. The plain below us was a luminous sea, and overhead was only darkness. We stayed there until silver began to gleam among the ravines on the mesa top. Then we retreated into the cavern and sealed the door.

I made it my strategy to put off sleep as long as possible. To this end, I persuaded Jolly to explore with me the labyrinth of the cavern. He had not slept in the afternoon, and I could see fatigue on his face, but he set off gamely beside me. We took a flashlight, and picking one of the many dark tunnels that branched from our well-lit hallway, we set out to see what there might be.

Within a few steps the tunnel began to descend. That was no surprise, as we were encamped at the top of the caverns. Still, it made me anxious, for silver lay all around the plateau.

Shadows jumped away from the beam of our flashlight, while dead kobold shells crunched unpleasantly under our feet. Worse, the scent of their living relatives faded the farther along we went, and I soon began to fantasize that I could smell silver seeping into the cavern.

Then Moki hesitated, peering ahead into the darkness and growling.

Kaphiri. My heart thundered and my skin grew flush as I imagined him climbing up that tunnel from the sea of silver that surrounded our keep. But there was no sound of footsteps and I could not imagine how anyone could walk among the dead kobold shells without sound. So I edged forward and Jolly went with me, and in a few steps we came upon a chamber so broad our flashlight beam could not find the other side.

Cautiously, we entered that great space. The ceiling was high, maybe thirty feet, while the walls that stood within reach of our light curved as if part of a great circle. "Is it an audience chamber?" I wondered, remembering the audience chamber of Ki-Faun that I had seen within my dream.

Jolly said, "It's big enough to be a marketplace."

There was no evidence of either function. All we found within reach of the light was a broken bike, shrouded in dust and missing its wheels, lying forlornly beside a knee-high midden of bird bones. Moki growled over these things while we examined them. Then Jolly took the flashlight, and casting its light about, he searched the shadows. He did not have to say what he was looking for. I followed him, expecting to see the bones of the bike's owner materialize in the gloom. Instead the light picked out a purple pigment on the walls.

"Look at that," Jolly said. "Is it writing?" He edged forward, until the light revealed a scrawl of purple lettering covering the wall from the height of my head to the floor. "It *is* writing. Jubilee, can you read it? No, wait. *I* can read it."

Indeed, the script and the language were the same as ours. It had been done in a chalk of purple tint that had since acquired some moisture from the air so that it shone like enameled paint. "Look how the letters have begun to drip," I said. "This cannot be too old."

Jolly was eagerly deciphering the rough lines. "It's a journal. Look here. *'Today the silver subsided beneath the gate. I try not to hope for tomorrow.'* That is dated 'day twelve.'" Jolly scowled. "Does that mean a player was trapped here for twelve days?"

"For far longer than that, I would guess," I said, gazing down the length of the wall. The writing continued at least as far as the light reached.

It came to both of us then, that we might be trapped at Azure for many days, and it was as if the room grew colder, the walls harder, the reverberations of our voices a little more loud. "The longer we are here," Jolly said, "the better chance Kaphiri will have of finding us."

I nodded, but what could we do?

Jolly shone his light again upon the words. "There is day fifteen." He walked several steps along the wall. "And there is day twenty-five. *'A good day! The mesa top was clear of silver. The net worked! I have songbird for dinner! I am a mad man, to be so excited at such a thing. But who would not be mad, enduring night after night of these dreams?'"*

But by day thirty songbird had grown dull, and by day forty-five the flocks had thinned. Day fifty-one was the last entry. *"This night is full of stars. It feels like a lifetime since I have seen stars, but they have returned this night, and the Bow of Heaven with them, brighter than I have ever seen it. The sun will be bright tomorrow. I know it. May I never dream again."*

I touched the blank stone beside the writing. "He must have gotten away." Perhaps by saying it, I could make it so?

Jolly nodded.

Neither of us mentioned the mystery of the broken bike.

We returned up the tunnel to our encampment and made a small dinner. The food tasted odd, as if it were permeated with the heavy, sweet scent of the temple kobolds. "You can't eat temple kobolds," Jolly said thoughtfully, picking up a stray to examine the white petals on its back. "At least I've never heard of it." He tapped the hard shell. "It would be like eating stones."

"I think the petals might be poisonous."

Temple kobolds produced no food, no machinery, no hard goods, no medicines. All they did was to create a chemical shield against the silver. Until I came to Azure Mesa, that had always been enough.

My eyelids grew heavy, so I forced myself to my feet, determined to fend off sleep, for all night if I could. Fifty-one nights of Azure dreams. I could not imagine it.

"Jubilee, where is your book?" Jolly asked. "May I see it?"

It was still in the pocket of my coat, where it had been almost since Nuanez Li had given it to me. I'd had it out at the Temple of the Sisters, only so that Emil and the scholars could make a copy of it, though they could not read it. "It's here," I said, and I drew it out. But I hesitated in giving it to him, held back by a reluctance I could not explain.

"Jubilee?"

"I'm nervous tonight." I made myself hand him the book.

He sat cross-legged on his sleeping bag, studying the green plastic cover. Then he examined the pages of fine lettered stone. "I guess you'll have to read it to me," he conceded.

I sat beside him, accepting the book back though I did not open it. "I have a dread of this book I did not have yesterday. I suppose it's an effect of the dream."

I started to slide it back into my pocket, but Jolly stopped me. "Jubilee." He took the book again, but this time he laid it open in my lap. "If he dies, the silver dies with him. If he does not die the world will drown in silver flood. In your vision Ki-Faun believed he had found a third choice—to control the silver. I would learn that."

I swear Jolly opened the book at random, but there on the page that faced me was a formula for a kobold circle made up entirely of temple kobolds.

The wells at Azure Mesa produced only temple kobolds.

"Jubilee?" he pressed, when I'd been silent too long.

I looked at his anxious face, wondering what powers a god might have. Then I tapped the book's open page. "Here is a recipe. It's supposed to create a kind of . . . mirror, I think. *'Reflect the other self'* . . . ? I'm not sure, but we can try it, just to see if a circle might work."

It was late, but neither of us wanted sleep, so we went down to the well room and hunted for the required kobolds. All of them were common, and it didn't take long to gather the necessary kinds, returning with them to our little stone room.

It was a harder task to reset the kobold's configuration codes. We did not have the tools of a temple keeper—no magnification lens, no pick, and no decent light. But these were large kobolds, each the size of my thumbnail, so we were able to use a fine wire to tweak the digits.

There were six kobolds in all, and when their configuration codes were set as the book instructed, we put them together.

Kobolds generally seem aware of very little except an instinctive need to crawl, but this group was different. They did not clamber away in six different directions. Instead they crawled deliberately toward one another. It was eerie to watch them gather together. At first they made a tangle of twitching legs and glossy shells, but in less than a minute they had fitted together into a perfect sphere. Their petals were on the inside, locked away from sight, while their legs were folded flat against their exposed bellies

Several minutes passed and nothing else happened, so I picked up the sphere and turned it over in my hands. It looked like one of those balls that is a puzzle of blocks, each piece a different color, but linking perfectly to the next.

The book did not say how long this kobold circle might take to mature, though from Maya's description of the road show, I hoped it would not be much more than an hour.

It was already past midnight, and the very air of the cavern was working against me, its cloying scent like a potion drawing me down, down into sleep. I rubbed at my eyes and paced to keep awake while Jolly sat beside the sphere, watching it constantly, as if it were an explosive that might go off at any minute.

I swear I was asleep on my feet, ghost voices whispering again in my ears when Jolly gave a shout of triumph. I stumbled in fright and went down hard on my knees, producing a pain that brought me fully awake.

"Jubilee, look." Jolly had risen to his feet. He backed a step away from the kobold circle.

A faint mist of silver seeped from its seams.

Moki barked at it, dancing frantically backward to the door. "Jolly, get back!" I shouted. "Get out of the room!"

The silver gathered about the kobold circle, hiding it inside a cloud that shimmered and boiled as it spread across the floor toward our gear—and the bike.

"Jolly, wait!" I jumped for our sleeping bags, gathering them up with our other things. "Get the bike outside!"

He remembered the savant too.

We tumbled together into the hall, while the silver filled the room. It did not behave like ordinary silver. Instead of flowing outward, it rose up, trembling and shimmering as it progressed higher and higher, as if the particles that made it up were linking into threads—too small to be seen, but strong enough to weave a wall of light.

I watched its growth from the corner of my eye as I worked to get our gear stowed aboard the bike. The savant went in last. Then I mounted. "Jolly, get on."

"No wait." He pointed into the room. "Look."

The silver had reached the ceiling; its trembling had ceased. It had formed a luminous panel, with a texture that teased the eye, suggesting somehow a vast depth within that smooth surface.

"Jolly, let's go. We'll be safe by the wells."

But Jolly did not heed me. He crept closer to the door. "The kobold circle was supposed to make a kind of mirror." He glanced back at me. "I don't see anything reflected."

"Maybe 'mirror' was the wrong translation. Now come."

"But it's not growing anymore." He took half a step into the room.

"Jolly!"

"But what's that?" he asked. "Jubilee, do you see it? That shadow, near the center."

I saw it. A dark shape, like the silhouette of a player obscured by rain or fog, far away, but striding steadily closer, with a gait all too familiar.

"*It's him,*" Jolly whispered. He backed into the hallway. "How can it be him? How can he see us?"

"Maybe he can't."

"But he's looking at us!"

Indeed, the figure had drawn close enough that I could see his eyes. Their gaze was fixed on me. He gestured, as if commanding me to stand fast. "Remember the translation?" I said.

Jolly glanced at me, and nodded.

A reflection of the other self.

I reached for my rifle. "No," Jolly said. "It's too soon for that."

I pulled it out anyway. In my vision I had been the only one of his enemies who could get close to him.

"Jubilee, it's not time!"

"Then let him stay away!"

He might have heard me, for he hesitated. Confusion bloomed on his distant face. He looked about, but he no longer seemed to see us. His mouth opened as if with a shout, but no sound could be heard. Then he changed. It was not him anymore that we saw in the distance, but a woman. She walked on toward us, a woman of good height and strong build, dressed in a gown of gold and white. Her dark hair lay loose about her shoulders, and there was a glow on her face of some hidden vitality, a perfection of body and spirit that did not seem to be of this world.

As she drew near, Jolly grabbed my arm and whispered the most nonsensical thing: "Jubilee, it's you."

Meaningless words that I ignored.

"It *is* you," he insisted.

"Hush. It is the goddess."

The memory of her lay within me, a vague remembrance, but certain all the same. I dismounted from the bike and went to meet her, wondering if she would step from the panel of silver and into the world, but she did not. She stopped only a step away. We faced each other, and for a dizzying moment I could not tell which of us stood within the mirror of silver, and which stood without, for her world seemed far larger than my tiny cage of stone.

She did not speak, either in words or in visions. Instead she reached out, much as the bogy had reached out from the wall of the tower room in the abandoned city. But as her arm passed through the panel it changed: on her side she was lovely, but the hand that darted out to touch me was a tiny, wizened, blackened thing—the arm of a corpse subjected to a long, slow fire. I flinched back, but she was faster. Her palm brushed my forehead.

The contact lasted only a moment, but that was enough. I stumbled back. Vaguely, I was aware of Jolly, shouting at me to flee, but I could not. My body felt far away, a distant object that I watched from a place deep inside myself, while another presence looked out from my eyes, and spoke with my voice. "This is a chance I did not foresee."

The silver panel dissolved. In a few seconds it melted into nothingness so that I stood in an empty room, listening to my voice speaking words that did not come from me. "Do I still live within your memory?" it asked. "It was so long ago, when you were my hands and my eyes . . . before the war began . . . So much was lost. So much broken. And still this last battle will not end! It drains me, and I cannot heal."

My mind jumped with frantic questions. Was she in me? Was I in her? In those seconds I could not tell the difference.

"Don't you remember . . . ? Oh. Oh, no. I took that away. It was too horrible to remember. It's enough to know he came to unmake this world we had built. I drove him into the darkness, but some shadow of him exists here still. You sense it, don't you? *I* sense it." Her voice fell to a whisper. "He has left a wound in the world, and the silver gushes from it, like blood to drown all the land and sea. Some fragment of himself festers within it, like a poison, and it cannot heal. *I cannot heal, so that I too am become no more than a shadow.*"

A shadow strong enough to take me over! That was my thought, and I guess she understood it.

"You are my hands," she said gently. "From the first days it was so. You must be my hands again. Find this wound. A veil of stealth lies over it, but you must look past that, and remove this fragment of our enemy, and let us heal."

Then she turned. It was a clumsy movement and partly mine, for her presence was fading within me, dissolving like silver in the dawn's light. She felt herself slipping away, and fear—or maybe it was despair—caused my heart to quicken. *Hurry now.* "Where is the new one?" she demanded. "Where is he?"

He stood in the doorway, watching us with panicky eyes. "Jubilee?" Jolly whispered. "Is it you?"

The goddess frowned. "How is it you are still so young? Ah, but at least your *ha* has awakened. I see it all about you. You must waken it in the others. All of them. Teach them how. They have been children for far too long . . ."

Even as she spoke, I felt her slip loose, sliding past me, into that remote place where I had been, while I was pulled back into myself. She spoke once more, but in a soundless voice, rising up from memory. *"Remember! When the* ha *awakens, any player may speak to the silver and guide its function. But that will not turn back its advance. Do not make that mistake again!"*

Then she was gone.

I staggered, all my energy gone away with her. My lungs heaved, and flecks of silver glittered between my fingers and in the folds of my sleeves. I braced myself against the cold stone of the wall. "Jolly! Was she real? Or was she another vision?"

Jolly knew then that she was gone. He came to put an arm around my waist.

"She was real," he said.

"What is this wound in the world that she spoke of? If a goddess cannot heal it—"

"I know what it is."

Raw fear was in his eyes, and for many seconds the only sound in that room was my frantic breathing, for I knew too. I had seen the edge of it. It had been visible from the southern escarpment of the Kalang: a terrible region, hazed with dust, and lightning storms. "It is the southern desert."

Jolly nodded. "Kaphiri called it the Cenotaph. I don't know why. He tried to go there once. It's a great pit, with steep sides that go down and down into endless clouds of silver. He never found the bottom, and climbing out again, he nearly died of thirst and hunger."

"He tried to go down there?" It seemed an act of madness to me. "Why? Why would anyone?" I wanted a reason. I needed a reason. One I could believe in.

"Because he had learned there is a god there. Her enemy. Just as she said. A god from out of the darkness."

"But that's a reason to run away! It's not a reason to go."

"It was for him, but he failed."

"Of course he failed! How can any player do what a goddess cannot?"

Jolly considered this, as if he saw real merit in the question. "She *is* wounded."

That was true. I had felt her weakness.

She had called me her hands. I had been her hands in some other life. I had served her will. Was that why sparks of silver now danced between my fingers? "This is *ha*," I realized, raising my right hand to examine the glitter. "Or anyway, *ha* is the ability to survive this, to use it. Kaphiri wakened it in me . . . but who wakened it in you?"

"No one. It just came."

"I think Ficer was right. She made you for this—to waken on your own to the silver, and then to waken it in other players . . ."

"I don't know how to do that!"

"Can you learn?"

"I don't know."

"If you could—"

"If I could, then any player could learn to survive the silver. Our father—he'd be alive now, he'd be here, if—"

"No. Don't say that. Neither of us knew anything then—and even the goddess cannot turn back time." For if she could, surely she would have restarted this broken world? "Jolly, there's something else, something she told me after she could no longer speak aloud. She said that even though a player may come to control the silver, that will not turn back its advance. She said we must not make that mistake again. You understand?"

He thought a moment. Then his eyes grew wide. "Ki-Faun was wrong!"

I closed my eyes, trembling to think how perilous the chance had been. What if, in that other life, I had succeeded in his plot against Kaphiri? The world would be drowned. "Soon you'll learn to awaken the *ha*. When you do, you must tell everyone of this danger. Don't forget it."

"And you?"

I shrugged, feeling a weight upon me, the same as in my vision. The goddess had lied to me. I was not her hands. Hands were used for building; for creating new things. But that had never been my task.

"Can you sleep?" I asked Jolly.

He said he could not.

"Then let's go up to the mesa top, and see what the dawn will bring."

Chapter

28

That dawn was cloudless. A flood of silver lay on the plain, but it dissolved at the sun's touch, vanishing first in streaks and rays that lanced from the eastern horizon. Then the disc of the sun rose past a line of distant mesas, releasing a great wave of light to roll the remnants away.

Far to the south and west there were dark lines on the horizon that might have been storms in the southern desert where the Cenotaph lay, the wound in the world. Otherwise the day was perfect: clear skies and no wind to stir the dust, so that I felt we could see for a hundred miles in any direction.

In all that vastness, nothing moved. We waited for most of an hour, but no plume of dust marked the trail of a motorcycle. Where was Liam? It came to me that I might never know.

Finally, Jolly spoke: "I think we should go."

"Where would you go?"

"Anywhere! Just not here. Kaphiri will find us if we stay here."

Of course he was right. The Temple of the Sisters was only 120 miles away.

I sniffed the air, seeking the scent of silver, but all I could smell was the dusty odor of desert soil and the sweet perfume of blossoms from the brush in the ravines. I wanted to wait for Liam, but that did not seem wise.

It was easier to decide that we should leave than to know where to go. To the south lay the terrible lands of the Cenotaph, where the goddess had directed me, but I did not want to take Jolly there. North and east would bring us ever deeper into the wastes of the Iraliad, while west would return us to the margin of the desert. West was also the direction of home, though both of us knew it would be foolhardy to return to Temple Huacho. "He'll be watching," Jolly said, "waiting for me to find my way back."

I nodded. "It could be he will leave them unharmed, so long as he believes there's a chance you might go back." We both took comfort from this thought.

So we would not go home, but we decided to go west anyway, for that was where Liam had disappeared, and I wanted to find him. We went down to the gate. I was operating the winch, using it to lower my bike over the low cliff when Jolly called out. "Look there! Jubilee! A column of dust."

I made sure the bike was safely on the ground before I looked. To the south and west, perhaps thirty miles or more away, in a direction that pointed back to the Temple of the Sisters, a plume of dust stained the blue sky. I could not see its source, but it was more dust than the wheels of two motorcycles could raise, even if they raced flat-out. "Maybe it's a large herd of cattle?" I said, without much hope.

Jolly was more honest: "It's a convoy."

"They would have stayed last night with Maya and Emil and the other scholars. I hope no harm has come to them."

"Ficer went back there."

But Ficer had not stopped the convoy. How could he? He was just one man.

We climbed down the cliff face. Moki went into his box, while Jolly rode behind me. If we went west, they would see us immediately. So we turned east instead, setting off on the trail that circled the mesa. We went slowly at first, so as not to stir up our own revealing plume of dust, but as soon as the mesa lay behind us, I pushed the bike to speed. Our direction was north and east, a bearing that would take us deeper into the desert. It was also in my mind that with every mile, we were growing closer to Yaphet.

At first our progress was easy. The miles fell behind us as we fled across a smooth plain. But as the day advanced, the land rose in a rugged slope cut with shallow gullies and studded with a few far-scattered bluffs. It was a region made strange by its emptiness: we saw no follies, or deposits of exotic ore to indicate the presence of silver . . . though we knew silver had flooded this part of the desert only the night before. It was as if the folly constructed here was one of an untouched land.

Our progress slowed. Twice we found ourselves in dead-end canyons, not of any spectacular depth, but still with walls too steep to scale, so we were forced to retrace our path and find another way. It was after the second such doubling back that we sighted our pursuers again. From the vantage of Azure Mesa they had been only a distant plume of dust. Now that plume had separated into three, and I could see the metal glimmer of a truck at the base of each. They were not trying to hide their approach. Two ran parallel to our track, one to the east of it, and one to the west. The third truck was farther behind, but it followed our trail exactly. Even as I watched, it dropped out of sight, descending into the same shallow gully we had followed.

"They didn't bother to stop at Azure," Jolly said.

"I don't understand. How can they run so quickly and still follow our trail?"

"The middle truck, it follows our trail."

"But it's farthest behind."

"So they already know where we are? Is that what you're thinking?"

I glanced over my shoulder. There was a small bluff a mile or so to the east, and another, closer, to the northeast, but to the west there was no eminence for many miles. "Let's change direction. West and south will take us from the sight of any watcher on high ground."

So we descended again into the little canyon we had only

recently escaped, and we followed a branch of it west for many miles, until it became a shallow drainage between two low hills. At last we were able to look back: only to discover the convoy had not followed our trail to its farthest point. Instead, they had cut across the land, as if they'd known of our change of direction almost as soon as it was made. Not even two miles separated us now, and that gap was closing swiftly as the three trucks sped toward us. "They *are* watching us! But how?"

Jolly's voice was whispery with panic: "Look there." He pointed to the north. "That glimmer."

Almost lost in the shimmering heat was a metallic spark, but it was not a truck, for it floated high above the ground. I squinted. "Some kind of bird?" Then it caught the sunlight, reflecting it in a brilliant flare as only metal can. "Or a savant," I said, reaching for my rifle.

Jolly pulled it from the sheath and handed it to me. "Hurry! They'll be here in a minute."

I refused to look back at the trucks. *"Don't breathe,"* I whispered as I brought the rifle to my shoulder. Taking careful aim, I squeezed off one shot, then another, but to my consternation, neither found its target. A second later the glimmer descended from sight, disappearing into a low swale . . . and a cold confusion took me. I twisted around to look at Jolly. "Did you see that?"

He nodded, his cheeks pale beneath a frosting of dust. A savant is a small thing. When I'd taken aim with my rifle I'd judged it to be much less than a mile away. Farther, and we would not have seen it at all through the heat shimmers of that desert noon. But the swale where it had disappeared was two miles, maybe two and a half to the north—farther away than the pursuing trucks. "That was no savant," I said softly. "It was something larger." Much larger, though what, I could not imagine.

"Let's go!" Jolly's voice was breaking in panic. "Jubilee, *now!*"

I nodded, though I had no plan, no idea what to do except to run. I eased the bike forward. I was picking out a path on the crumbly slope when a muffled voice spoke my name from some-where close behind us: *Jubilee!*

I jumped in fright and the bike slipped. Jolly cried out, throwing his arms around my waist. The voice called again: *Jubilee!* An old man's voice, shouting as if from behind a pillow: *Jubilee!*

I recognized it then. "It's the savant."

"What?"

Again I stopped the bike. "Open the saddle box. Let it out."

"There's no time."

"Just do it, Jolly."

Furiously, he popped the hasp. The savant bobbed into the air, unfolding into its smooth wing shape. "A call," it said in its calm and formal voice. "From Yaphet."

Yaphet? His image coalesced on the savant's mimic screen. Dust smudged his cheeks and lightened his hair, and his eyes were hidden behind black sunglasses, and still I caught my breath, so much did he resemble Kaphiri. Jolly's hand squeezed my shoulder. "Jubilee, he looks like—"

"*I know.*"

But Yaphet's skin was bronze, and flushed with heat, while Kaphiri's face was cold and pale—and Yaphet stirred in me a different kind of fear. I hoped he was still far away, but I did not believe it, and his first words confirmed my hope was in vain. "Jubilee, I've seen you. I think it's you. Two players on one motorcycle? You're running west." He gestured with field glasses held in a black-gloved hand.

"Where are you?" I wasn't ready to meet him. Not yet. I wasn't ready to meet the trucks. It was all coming down too fast and I wanted to be anywhere but where I was.

He saw my panic and answered cautiously. "I'm here. A few miles north . . . or north and west of your position."

I looked to the northwest, but I could not see him. I had no field glasses.

"There's a second convoy, Jubilee, three miles or so west of me. It's moving to meet the other trucks."

I was aware suddenly of the dryness of my mouth in that desert air. "We're trapped then."

"Drop back to the south," Yaphet advised in a voice so flat it did not sound truly human. "It's not over yet."

We turned south. There was no sign of the dark line of storms I had seen that morning. The sky was brassy with a dust that blurred the sun but did nothing to mute its heat. I sniffed at the air, but there was no scent of silver anywhere. The sun was too bright, and all I could smell was dust and my own sweat.

Jolly kept watch behind us, twisting around every few seconds to see if anything had changed. After a few minutes he said, "I see that savant again—or whatever it is. It's moved farther east."

"Can you see the second convoy?"

"No."

A concussion struck my ears, a booming roar of thunder that I felt in my chest. There was a great rumbling of sliding stone, and when I glanced back, a cloud of cinnamon dust was climbing into the sky, from beyond a ridge to the northwest. *"Yaphet,"* I whispered, for he had been out there, only a few miles away.

Then I too saw the savant. It was much closer now, less than a mile away, and clearly, it was no savant.

It was a flying machine.

An impossible flying machine, soaring at least a hundred feet above the ground. I could see the dark shape of a player suspended beneath it, prone within a harness. I thought I could see a sparkle of silver along its wings. It passed behind an outcropping of rock.

My hands shook as I brought the bike to a stop. "Could Kaphiri order the silver away, even from a flying machine?"

"I don't know! Maybe he can. Do you think it's him beneath that wing?"

"Jolly, I tried to shoot him down! What if I had killed him?"

"We have to go. Now."

I hesitated. Yaphet was out there somewhere. Had he caused the explosion we had just heard? That night at the Temple of the Sisters I had told him everything. I warned him Kaphiri must not die, but did he believe it?

"Jubilee!" Jolly shouted. "We have to—"

The thunder of a second explosion overwhelmed his voice. Then the flyer reappeared, speeding toward us down the canyon we had followed. Something else moved on the ground beneath it: a thread of glimmering water some six feet long. It flowed around boulders and down shallow slopes, retracing exactly the tracks left by my bike, and suddenly I knew how the convoy had followed us.

I thought my heart would stop, but Jolly's reaction was the opposite. He had never seen a worm mechanic before, but I had described it well enough. "Go!" he shouted, and his fist hammered my shoulder. "Go now! Go now!"

But Yaphet was shouting too, and this time his voice did not come to us through my savant, which I had locked away again in my saddle box. Instead it reached us on the open air. "Get ready, Jubilee! Abandon the bike! There is no choice!"

Every word was clearly uttered, yet none of it made sense until I looked up at the flying machine.

It had overtaken the worm. It had run ahead of it, so close now I could easily see the face of the player suspended beneath it. It looked like Kaphiri, but it was not him.

Horror washed over me. We had only seconds before the worm mechanic caught us, but in that lost moment the threat of the worm meant nothing to me. All I could think was that this was my lover, in a flying machine. A forbidden flying machine. A wicked flying machine, with a glimmer of silver dancing along the leading edge of its long white wing. Yaphet lay prone in a harness beneath that wing, his legs splayed around the engine, with two white baskets on either side of him that held supplies. Only a psychotic would tempt the silver in a flying machine. A suicidal player or a murderous one. I knew the stories. There were many, and all were centered on a wicked player, his doomed machine sparkling with silver as it passed far above the influence of an enclave's defending kobolds, to descend among the houses, and ignite a silver storm.

This was my lover.

I knew then that there was no forgiveness for the sins and failures of our past lives.

I rocked the bike forward, sending it coasting down the slope, engaging the engine again as we rolled. Yaphet soared over us, his engine silent, the only sound an artificial wind passing over the white wing. "Jubilee! Stop. Look at me. You have to abandon the bike. The mechanic will have you if you stay on the ground, but it can't follow you in the air."

"No! Go away. I don't know you. I don't need you—"

But Jolly's desperation was different from mine. He reached around me and switched off the bike's engine. The wheels locked. The bike skidded and went down. Jolly jumped free, but I did not. My leg was caught beneath the bike and I slid with it down the graveled slope. I heard Jolly shouting at me to *"Get up! Get up!"* A shadow passed over the sun, and then Yaphet was beside me, heaving the bike off my leg. I scrambled to my feet.

That was when I felt the pain. I gasped as my knee gave out. But Yaphet was beside me. He caught me as I dropped. He took my weight, passing my arm around his shoulder—and as soon as I had my balance I punched him: hard in the chest and we went down together. For one full second he stared at nothing, a look of stunned disbelief on his face. Then I pushed him away. *"I hate you!"* The words rushed from my throat, an honest assessment in a desperate situation. I would have left him to the worm then, if I could. I tried to. I scrambled backward on three limbs. "Stay away from me!" I warned.

But his anger was the equal of mine, and he at least could walk. "The silver take you, Jubilee."

"Better the silver than you!"

He tackled me. I screamed as my knee was further twisted and then somehow he had my arms locked behind my back, his mouth beside my ear. I hated him for it, because it was the same way

Kaphiri had held me. But Yaphet's words were different. "You will live through this day, Jubilee, I swear it." And then he half carried me, half dragged me down the slope.

He had left his flying machine in the dry water course at the bottom of the little canyon. Jolly was already there, with Moki under one arm, and my savant under the other, climbing into one of the cargo baskets. "Jolly, don't!"

"Do you want to kill us?" he shouted. "Do you want to kill yourself? The worm can only follow us if we're on the ground. So get in. Get in! Our only chance is to fly."

Yaphet left me no choice. "Your brother's a lot smarter than you," he said, and he shoved me into the basket opposite Jolly. My head struck one of the struts. A different kind of pain. The sharp, fresh scent of silver tinged the air.

I had landed on a folded sleeping bag, but something brittle crunched beneath it as I shoved myself up on my elbows. What I had taken for a harness between the two baskets was really a solid platform suspended by fixed struts. Yaphet clambered over the engine and dropped onto it. The size of the flyer was such that his face was only inches from mine. "Look back," he ordered as the engine started up. I felt its vibration. I felt the wing begin to lift and I grabbed at the rim of the basket. "Look back!"

I did, and saw the worm. It darted up the slope behind us, following the track of my bike. The flying machine began to climb, lofting slowly into the air.

The worm reached my fallen bike. It turned immediately, tracking our path down to the canyon floor. We were twenty feet in the air, and twice that far away down the canyon when the worm reached the place where the flying machine had been. It stopped, its six-foot length sparkling in the sun like a stream of water that does not flow. Then it circled that place, around and around, faster with each circuit, like a mad thing. I felt the hair on my neck stand up. It never once looked up for us, as any living thing would do.

Then we soared around a bend in the canyon, and I couldn't see it anymore. I turned, to look ahead of us.

"You could unbalance us," Yaphet suggested, past the streaming wind. "You could shift your weight too suddenly, or jump out, and send us crashing to our deaths. If you want to."

Jolly worried I might consider this a good idea. "Jubilee, he doesn't mean it! Don't do it. Please."

I could not answer. A new clarity had come over me. If not for Yaphet, we would have fallen to the worm. If not for this wicked flying machine. "Why does the silver leave us alone?" I asked, without looking at him.

"Because we're flying low. Not even twenty feet above the ground."

We were lower than the canyon walls.

"And the sun protects us," Yaphet added. "If silver begins to bloom along the wings, the sun will burn it and stop it from growing."

"And if you go higher?" I remembered a day as bright as this one, when Udondi's savant had risen into the sky above the highway to Xahiclan, higher and higher, until a tiny silver storm burst into existence around it.

Yaphet said, "I won't go higher."

I did not want to look at him. I was afraid to look. So I kept my gaze fixed on the canyon wall, and still he was all I saw. Our bodies speak their own language, and mine was waking to one it had heard only faintly that night outside the Temple of the Sisters.

What if I hate him? I'd asked Liam that question on the day I'd first heard Yaphet's name, and Liam had answered honestly. *It won't matter.*

It was Jolly who broke a silence of several minutes. "Yaphet, was it you who set those explosives?"

I had forgotten the explosives. So distracted was I, I had even forgotten the two convoys.

"No, it wasn't me."

"It brought down a landslide, didn't it?"

"I couldn't see what happened . . . but it sounded like a landslide. Are you thinking it was your uncle?"

Liam? I had forgotten him too. I looked north, but all I could see was the canyon wall. "We have to go back."

Yaphet didn't answer. Neither did Jolly, for of course it would be foolish to go back. They both knew it . . . and so did I. Liam and Udondi would be furious if we did not use this chance to escape— and still I could not just leave them . . . "Jolly!" He lay in the other basket, his arm around Moki. "You have my savant, don't you? So call them."

Yaphet said, "We'll have to climb out of this canyon first."

"Then let's do it." We'd gone fifteen miles to the southeast, maybe more. "Both convoys are far away now. They won't see us." Not if we were lucky.

As we climbed to the canyon rim I found myself watching the wing for the glimmer of silver, but none appeared, and then we were over the plain. We stayed low, only ten feet above the ground, but the land was very flat, so that if anyone was looking, we would certainly be seen. I studied the land to the north and east, but there was no dust anywhere, no sign of a truck moving. Jolly put through a call to Udondi's savant, but there was no answer. "They could be in a canyon," Yaphet said.

He didn't like to fly in the open, so when he found a shallow stretch of lowland between two ridges, he guided the flying machine down into it. We were still heading generally southeast. Ahead of us loomed a rugged highland of steep canyons and wind-smoothed pinnacles. Goats moved on the barren cliffs. I took their presence as a hopeful sign. "There must be someplace in there to shelter from the silver," I said, pointing them out.

Yaphet nodded. "That's where we'll go."

We tried to reach the cliffs, but the winds were confused, darting at us in powerful gusts that pushed us back out onto the plain. We were working our way back to the cliffs once again, flying lower than ever, only a few feet above the rocky soil, when we heard two faint concussions, one swiftly following the other. I would have thought it my imagination, if Yaphet had not turned to look.

Far to the northwest, a huge dust cloud boiled silently into the sky—far too much dust to be caused by any convoy.

In the ancient city, the bogy had taken Liam for one of her warlords. I wondered if she had been right after all.

Chapter

29

We made our way at last into the highlands, succeeding in late afternoon when the winds began to die. We entered the mouth of a north-facing canyon where we had earlier seen goats along the walls. After half a mile, Jolly sighted a wild kobold well on the lip of a little pocket valley some three hundred feet above the canyon floor.

None of us wanted to fly that high, but time was growing short. The sun had already dropped behind the crags and the canyon was in shadow. We could look for a more accessible kobold well, but chance did not favor the finding of one so late in the day. So we agreed to try for the little valley.

Yaphet guided the flying machine in a tight spiral, keeping close to the cliff wall. He would glance anxiously at the valley, then back again, to the leading edge of the wing, alert for the first sign of a silver bloom. Jolly too kept a close eye on the wing, but I was distracted by a herd of brown goats that had stopped their browsing to eye us as we rose past them. They didn't seem to know what to make of us, for we did not much resemble the predators they were used to.

It was then, as I watched the goats, that a flicker of awareness stirred in my mind. Moki whined, and one of the goats snorted, scampering away on an invisible path that climbed the cliff face. The others followed after it, while I glanced up, confirming what I already knew: a glitter of silver had ignited on the nearest wing tip. "It has started," I said, loud enough to be heard over the wind.

Yaphet looked at me. Then he looked up, and his eyes went wide. He jerked at the controls, and the flying machine lurched. Jolly yelped, grabbing for Moki with one hand and a strut with the other.

"Hold on," Yaphet muttered. "We only have a few seconds. If we don't make the well—"

The tuft of silver expanded with astonishing speed, rushing along the wing's edge like a gleaming, glittering stream just escaped from its dam.

Yaphet saw it and leaned hard on the control stick. "I'm going for the cliff! There's no place to land, so get ready to jump—"

"No! Turn away! Turn away now!" There was no way we could survive a crash against the cliff face, but maybe we could survive the silver?

Motes glittered on the back of my hand and danced between my fingertips. My *ha* was awake. So for the first time, I invited it deliberately into my mind.

A liquid awareness filled me. The silver on the wing's edge boiled in my consciousness, becoming part of me, an extension of my will. Holding tight to a strut with one hand, I reached out toward the silver with the other. In the way I had learned, I leaned on it with my mind. I used it, like a glove that I could wear, and *pushed*, and it came away from the wing in a long thin skein of silver.

But silver will always sink to the ground. Detached from the wing, with nothing to buoy it up, the skein fell while we flew forward into it. Yaphet shouted, hammering at the controls so that the flying machine jerked upward, in a sharp turn away from the cliff. I dove half out of the basket and *pushed*, out and down. The skein passed just beneath my hand. It stirred an electric awareness in my skin so sharp I yanked my hand back, as if from contact with a flame.

Then it passed beneath us, brushing the belly of the plane and igniting a scatter of silver sparkles, but I commanded them away.

More motes formed along the wing, but these too I willed away. Then the cherished scent of temple kobolds reached me, and a moment later Yaphet guided us over the wild well and we landed gently in a little bowl of dry grass.

I could not wait to distance myself from the flying machine. I was climbing out of the basket even before it came to a rest. "Jubilee, wait," Yaphet said. "It's windy. If we don't anchor the plane—"

I stumbled on my swollen knee. At the same time, a gust caught the wing, dragging the whole flying machine a foot back toward the cliff. "Jolly, get off!" I shouted. "Now!"

Jolly's eyes were wide with fright. He shooed Moki out of the basket, then tumbled after him. Deprived of his weight, the plane skidded back again. Yaphet too scrambled free, but he did not abandon the plane. He grabbed a strut and sank in his heels. "Get the ropes!" he shouted at Jolly. "In the cargo basket. Help me tie it down."

I wanted to see Yaphet's flying machine tumble over the cliff. On the other hand, I did not want to be trapped three hundred feet above the canyon floor. Torn by these conflicting desires, I risked a quick glance around. The valley reached back only fifty feet or so. Really, "valley" was much too grand a word for it. It was more a gloomy little hollow, hemmed in by sheer walls of stone. Birds could reach us, and I guessed that goats could climb down from the ridgeline, but I did not know if a player could scale those cliffs— certainly the task looked hopeless for a player with a twisted knee.

So after a moment of indecision, I lurched after the flying machine and grabbed a strut, bracing my good leg against a rock. Jolly found the rope. He looped it around the central struts, and Yaphet secured the other end to a boulder. "Help me furl the wings," he told Jolly.

I had not realized it before, but the white wings were made of a metallic cloth, stretched upon a frame. Yaphet showed Jolly how to unclip the edge, and tie down the cloth so the wind would not catch it.

When the danger was past, I turned away from the hateful

machine. But I managed only a few stumbling steps before my knee gave out. I sank down in the dry grass, not knowing what else to do, or what to think. It did not seem hard anymore to accept the idea of *ha*, but I could not get my mind around the fact of a flying machine.

"Jubilee?" I looked up to see Jolly beside me, a furtive look on his face. "Is your leg badly hurt?" He sounded very guilty—as he should. He had dropped the heavy bike on my leg after all.

"My knee's swollen."

He cast a nervous glance over his shoulder. Then, speaking under his breath, "He is so much like Kaphiri."

"Has he threatened you?"

"No! He's angry though."

"Not with you," I reminded him. Then I nodded toward a stand of tangled brush that grew against the back wall. "Go and find me a walking stick, okay?"

I used the stick to hobble behind the brush and relieve myself. I had very little urine in me, which made me wonder how much water Yaphet had aboard his flying machine. All mine had been lost with the bike, and by the half-dead look of the vegetation in our little valley, I was certain we would find no water there.

When I came back, Yaphet was rearranging the supplies in the cargo baskets. He said nothing. He did not look at me. I asked about water. He had two gallons. He told me to sit down and he would get it. I hobbled the few steps to the rim of the valley, sitting beside the wide mound of dirt surrounding the kobold well.

From the valley's rim, I could look out of the canyon to the plain beyond. The dust cloud had long since blown away and shadows were running long. Very soon it would be dark.

I closed my eyes, feeling sick inside. Yaphet was my lover, I could not deny it. I felt as if I had always known him and always loved him. It didn't matter at all that I didn't want him. It didn't matter at all that he horrified me.

I listened to the rustle of the wind, to the fall of a pebble from the cliffs above . . . to the crunch of Yaphet's footsteps in the dry grass. I did not turn to look at him—I was too stubborn for that—but I knew exactly where he was by the sound of his steps.

He came and he stood behind me, handing a bottle of water over my shoulder. I took it, careful not to touch his hand. I drank.

"I wanted to tell you about the flying machine," he said, "but I knew how you would see it."

"Then why? Why did you do it?"

"I was born to it!" No apology in his voice. No shame. "I dreamed it, every night when I was little."

"I saw it in you. That first time we spoke. I saw it in your eyes. An obsession, though I didn't know what it was."

He crouched behind me.

I tensed. I still would not look at him, but I was brutally aware of his proximity, of his very gravity. "Don't touch me," I warned.

"You know it's never been that way between us."

I turned to look at him. I could not help myself. "Do you remember it?"

"Enough to know it." He slipped his sunglasses off with a black-gloved hand. "You're angry with me, Jubilee, but I'm not the only one with secrets. I thought Jolly did that trick with the silver, but he said it was you. Are you like him? Are you like *them*?"

With his face set in anger, he was Kaphiri's dark-skinned twin. "You are frightening my brother," I said softly.

He glanced over his shoulder, but Jolly had gone with Moki to explore the back of the valley. "He's not afraid of the plane."

"The plane?"

"The airplane. The flying machine."

"That's not what I meant. You remind him of Kaphiri."

Yaphet scowled, clearly hurt and perplexed that I would say such a thing. "You think I'm the same as him? You and Jolly would belong to him now, if I hadn't come."

That was true, though I wasn't ready to admit it aloud. I fixed my gaze on the plain, where glints of silver had begun to appear. "Jolly is terrified of him. He knows him well enough to be afraid. And I . . . I've met him too, face-to-face since we last talked, and . . . you look like him. Almost exactly like him . . . as if the two of you were made from the same memory of silver."

Yaphet considered this for many seconds. Then he denied it. "Players are not made in multiple copies."

"Well, you are. Or he is. You're like him. In many ways. But you're . . . you're different too." I had sensed a whispered connection with Kaphiri, but with Yaphet that connection was a clear song. I could never confuse one with the other, not even if they stood together, side by side. "You don't *feel* like him. Not at all."

I should have been more careful with the words I used. "Did you touch him?"

"What?"

I had never suspected such cold fury could inhabit Yaphet's eyes. "Something's changed in you, Jubilee."

"What do you mean? What's changed?"

"He touched you, didn't he? It feels like he did. Did he hurt you?"

I had been holding my breath. But I let it go in a sigh as I realized his anger was not directed at me. "He did touch me," I admitted. "And he hurt me. And he changed me too."

Our eyes locked, but too many thoughts were chasing around Yaphet's head and he could not meet my gaze for long. I half expected him to give it up and leave, but when he shifted his position it was to sit beside me—close beside me. His shoulder almost touched mine. His hand rested on his knee in a relaxed posture, but it was a pose. I could see white lines of stress in his dark skin. "Tell me."

So I did. First I spoke of the blood poisoning. Then I told him the story Udondi had told to me, of Kaphiri and his lover, and how she had left him for another.

In the evening's fading light, Yaphet's eyes were colored with a quiet fear. "These two lovers . . . they looked the same?"

"Udondi didn't say."

I spoke next of my encounter with the silver, on the night I left the Temple of the Sisters. He believed my story. How could he not? He had seen me push the silver away. But for Yaphet, belief was not enough.

"How could such a thing work?"

I shook my head. "You might as well ask, how does the silver work? What is it, after all?" The old questions, that had haunted me since Jolly disappeared, but Yaphet surprised me with an answer.

"The silver is a mechanism," he said, as if this were common knowledge. "A machine devised by the ancients who made this world. A device, and if we could relearn its use, we could control it, and make it serve our purposes."

I raised my hands, examining them thoughtfully. In the dusk, a few scattered glints of silver could still be seen between my fingers. "This is *ha*," I said softly. "Do you see it?"

When he saw what I meant, he reared back in fear. But then he leaned in again, to examine the specks. "How do you do that?"

"I don't know. It just came to me, after his blood poisoned mine. My brother, he believes we're like mechanics, that we have configuration codes, hidden away in our cells. Jolly thinks my codes were reset by the contact with Kaphiri's blood, and I was changed. He says Kaphiri reset his own codes; that he knows how."

"He does?" There was a sudden avarice in his voice. "Does Jolly know how?"

I had expected Yaphet to be offended—any sane player should be offended by the idea of human configuration codes. But he was not, and that offended *me*. "You've thought of such things before?"

His back grew stiff. He turned away from me. "I've thought of a lot of things."

"Do you believe we are mechanics?"

"Jubilee, I don't know!"

"And this desire I feel for you, is it a mechanism?"

He laughed and the sound was cold, with no humor in it. "Oh, yes. I'm sure that much is true."

I had not expected such an answer and it hurt me. I was surprised how much. Oh, but we'd had a fine first day. I'd declared my hatred for him, I'd struck him, I'd warned him not to touch me. "I think there was more pleasure in this for my mother and father."

"Your mother likely has a better temper."

"She does," I admitted.

"Jubilee . . . I'm sorry I keep offending you. I don't know if we're like mechanics. I don't know what we are, but I do believe there's an explanation for us, and for this world: a story that will explain why it exists and why it works as it does. If we could learn that story, then everything that confuses us would make sense . . . some kind of sense, anyway. Things like the silver . . . and the way we are made to love one another."

I have never been so conscious of anyone as I was of Yaphet in those lingering minutes. The blink of his eye. The slight rise and fall of his chest as he breathed. The tardy drag of his long black braid whenever he turned his head. Each tiny movement recorded itself in my memory.

"Yaphet?"

He smiled one of his rare smiles. "That's the first time you've said my name."

"I have not told you everything yet."

"Oh." He was silent a moment, staring down at the plain. "I guess you should, then."

So I described the vision that had come to me as I slept in the sanctuary of Azure Mesa. And then I told him of the experiment with the kobold circle. "It was called *'the mirror of the other self,'* and he was there, within it. But why was it him, and not you?"

"Did you want him to come?"

"*No!* Have you not been listening? He is *wrong.* There is something about him that is corrupt. It was so, even in that vision of my other life."

"But he was your lover."

"In another life! And even then it was a mistake."

"But it makes me angry! What's wrong with me? I've never felt this way before."

"I haven't either."

We sat in silence for some time, while the night gathered around us. Stars pricked the blue sky, while on the plain below silver filled the canyons, so that the dark land seemed infused with veins of luminous metal.

"Is that all?" Yaphet said at last. "Or is there more still?"

"A little more."

He made a groan of mock despair. "Say it, then. Let me have it all, for you could tell me anything now and I would believe it."

I snorted—"That's what you say now"—and I told him of the goddess and the task she had given me. He listened. He made no comment on it except to ask, "*Now* is that all?"

"It is."

He looked over his shoulder. I followed his gaze, to see Jolly, playing a game of fetch with Moki beside the flying machine. "I want you to be my wife, Jubilee. Now." He put his finger against my lips. "Don't speak! Because you'll say it's impossible, that we don't know what will happen to us tomorrow. But that's why I want you to marry me now. We are caught up in something, and maybe this time is all the time we'll ever have. Marry me now."

"But Jolly is here!"

"Just the words. Just share the words with me."

My mouth felt dry. "I cannot kneel. My knee is swollen—"

"Then we'll sit. Take my hand."

"All right." I laid my hand in his, but in that moment the awareness of silver stirred in my mind. I turned, to see a herd of goats hurrying down an invisible trail on the valley's sheer back wall. "There is a silver storm coming."

"How do you know?"

"I just do. We should bring your flying machine into the circle of the well." I started to get up, but my knee quickly reminded me that was not a good idea.

"Stay here," Yaphet said. "Jolly will help."

The flying machine was cleverly designed, so that Yaphet was able to collapse the wing. With Jolly's help he dragged the folded frame into the circle of the kobold well. The nose and tail stuck out beyond the mound, but we gathered handfuls of freshly spawned kobolds from the mouth of the well and scattered them about, expanding the protected zone.

When all the gear was safely within the circle, Jolly crept up to the precipice and looked over. "The canyon floor is flooded," he called back.

Yaphet went to look, and an expression of awe came over his face. "You can see it climbing. Does the whole Iraliad flood every night?"

Jolly answered, "Ficer said it's worse now than when he was a boy."

The goats snorted when they found us occupying their well, but they joined us anyway, and after a few minutes Moki gave up growling at them.

We were halfway through a cold dinner when the savant spoke in its cultured voice. "A call," it said. "From Liam."

"Answer it!" I had been sitting shoulder to shoulder with Yaphet, but when the savant settled in my lap, he moved back, positioning himself so that he could see the screen without being seen by those on the other side.

The image that formed was of stars, faint above a horizon limned with silver, "Liam?" I heard the scuff of a boot on gravel, then the tumbling bounce of a small stone. "Liam!" I called, louder this time.

"Jubilee?" His shadowed face filled the mimic screen, and in a moment the savant compensated for the lighting. He was dusty and haggard, his face thinner than I had ever seen it. The patch was gone from his eye, but there was a pink scar across his lid where the rock fragment had cut him. His eyes were red. From the dust, I told myself. The dust. "You're alive." His voice was a whisper of disbelief. "We found your bike. We thought—"

"I'm alive. And I'm free. Jolly is with me. Is Udondi—?"

"She's here." He looked away, calling to her. "Udondi! I've found Jubilee!"

A few seconds later her face appeared beside his. "Jubilee! Where are you? How did you—?"

I wasn't ready to explain. "Did you set the explosives?" I asked. "Was that you?"

Liam nodded. "Ficer is with us. He brought them from the Temple of the Sisters. We found your bike after. We thought you must have been with them, when—" He shook his head and stepped away.

Udondi looked after him with a troubled gaze. "I think this has been the longest day of his life," she said softly. Then she looked back at the screen and her gaze grew sharp, though it was not fixed on me. "Is that Jolly?"

I turned, expecting to see Yaphet, but it was Jolly who stood at my shoulder. He had come up silently while we spoke.

"This is my brother," I said.

Then another face crowded in beside Udondi's.

"Ficer!" Jolly shouted. "You came back!"

"Of course I came back. Didn't I say I would?"

We demanded their story first. Ficer told of how he had reached the Temple of the Sisters at midmorning yesterday, minutes ahead of a convoy of three trucks. "The drivers did not speak the name of the traveler, but it was clear who they served." He hid his bike and pretended to be one of the scholars and in that way the day passed. Dusk came, but Ficer would not risk suspicion by climbing the tower to send a message. "There is a cavern that opens on the white plain, that is used to garage the passing trucks. In the morning, when the drivers went down there, I tried to call you, but it was well past sunrise, and I think you were gone from the mesa top by then. Emil was very worried. He sent me back up the tower, saying that if I could not find you, I should try to find your uncle, and in that, at least, I had some success."

Udondi nodded. "We had already encountered that convoy. There were five trucks altogether—too many for us to stop, but we delayed them a day when we released the last of our metallophores into their engines. We spent that day in hiding, while they spent it repairing their trucks. But they also used the time to put up an antenna, and in the morning it was clear why. They had decided to split up. Only three trucks went to the Sisters, while the other two went north.

"We used the antenna to call ahead to Emil, and he told us you were gone, and that we should look for you at Azure. We cut the power supply to the antenna, and then we left, but it was a dark day, and by noon a great bank of silver drifted in from the west and we were forced to take shelter in a refuge mesa." She shook her head. "The next day was no better. We could not leave, and we could not contact you. It was maddening! To be trapped there, not knowing what harm you might be facing. But this morning the sun came out, and Ficer called, with word that you were still free. You did well, Jubilee."

"It was my luck." My usual harsh luck that I had lived, but only at the cost of Kaphiri's drivers, crushed beneath tons of stone.

"We are sheltering at Azure this night," Udondi said, "but on the mesa top, and not in the cavern, for the silver does not look like it will rise much tonight. I slept in the cavern once, years ago, and once is enough."

"What shelter did you find?" Ficer asked us. "Or have your gifts protected you from the silver?"

I said the truth, as much as I dared: "We found a wild well."

He gave me a strange look, and it occurred to me we had seen no wild wells in all those hills. But Ficer asked no more questions, and after, I pled fatigue, for Jolly and I had not slept the night before, and we said good night.

The viewscreen darkened, and Jolly and Yaphet became shadows in the starlight. On the other side of the folded flying machine, the milling goats were shadows too. "You left out a lot," Yaphet said.

Jolly agreed. "You didn't mention Yaphet. And you let them believe we were still in those hills."

"You think that was wrong? Should I have told them about the flying machine, Jolly? Or that my lover is mad? Or that he is the twin of Kaphiri?"

"We'll have to tell them tomorrow."

"We'll have to tell them when we see them. Not before."

"Do you really think I'm mad?" Yaphet asked in a troubled voice, so I couldn't help but smile.

"Well," I conceded, "maybe just a little."

Chapter

30

It was cold that night, so high up among the rocks, and Yaphet had only one sleeping bag. When unfolded it would cover two. He said that Jolly and I should have it, and he would watch until at least midnight. I was exhausted, so I accepted gratefully. When I woke again, it was to the glow of silver. I sat up abruptly, my heart pounding with the certainty that someone was drawing near. But when I looked about, all was still.

Jolly was still sleeping beside me, breathing softly beneath the folds of the sleeping bag. Yaphet was sitting with Moki on the folded structure of the flying machine, his hands clasped around his knees. He studied me curiously. "Are you truly awake?"

"I don't know." I glanced over my shoulder. The silver stood in a waist-high ring around the well. I could smell the goats, but they were huddled on the other side of the flying machine, and I could not see them. The Bow of Heaven glimmered overhead. "Did you hear something?"

"No. It's been quiet. Eerily quiet."

"Was I dreaming?"

"Probably. What did you hear?"

I shook my head. I had not *heard* anything . . . "I felt something."

I still felt it: a sense of someone drawing near, a presence, brushing past lines of awareness that had been laid down inside my mind, leaving them swaying with the evidence of passage, as a curtain will sway when it is lifted aside briefly, then allowed to fall back. I raised my hands, to find the *ha* sparkling brightly between my fingers. "He is coming."

Yaphet rose to his feet without hesitation, without doubt. "Where?"

I nodded toward the bank of silver that hid the precipice. "From the canyon."

He jumped from his perch on the flying machine. I scrambled to my feet, to find my knee much stronger for the rest. We waited, poised, watching the waist-high fog where it lapped over the rim of the canyon. Moki growled, and a moment later the shape of a man rose up from within the silver, exactly in the place I expected him.

At first he was only a silhouette of silver. Then his glistening shell dissolved, and Kaphiri stood before us, motes of silver glittering against his hands, and in his carefully styled hair.

His gaze moved from me, to Yaphet, then back again. He was careful not to move. "I have just discovered something," he said softly. "It seems that when the *ha* of your lover awakens, it becomes an unmistakable signal within the silver, one that requires no effort at all to follow."

"I am not your lover."

"Never again, it's true." He raised his hand, in the gesture I had seen before. The *ha* brightened between his fingers, and a tongue of silver swept over the rim of the well. It raced past his feet, rushing downhill toward Yaphet.

"No!" If there had been time to think I would have failed, but instinct moved me. I raised my hand to stop it. The lines of my awareness squeezed together—and the tongue of silver curled back as if it had hit a wall.

I looked up, to see my own astonishment mirrored in Kaphiri's gaze. "But that is not your talent!" He said it as if I had committed some social affront, as if I should take back the gesture, and apologize.

Yaphet was the only one of us not made dull by surprise. He sprang on Kaphiri, cuffing him behind the neck, unbalancing him.

"Keep the silver away!" he commanded as he followed Kaphiri to the ground.

Centuries must have passed since anyone had dared such a close assault against Kaphiri. He was completely unprepared. Dust puffed up around him to sully his fine clothes and he grunted as Yaphet pinned him with a knee in the back. Another tongue of silver darted toward him over the rim of the well. I shouted and

pushed

back

against the intrusion that tried to bend the lines of my awareness—and this time the tendril of silver dissolved.

But another followed immediately after it. And another, and then two at once, and then an explosion of tendrils, like a nightmare of worm mechanics darting toward Yaphet with their venomous mouths, but they could not break past my will. That's how it felt. The *ha* was my will, and while Kaphiri could command the silver that lay all around us, he could not force it past the defensive lines I had made.

Not that this was a measure of our relative power. I had no illusions about that. My connection to the silver had given me an insight into its behavior, and I understood, as if it had been explained to me in words, that a player's defensive gesture would always be stronger than an assault. That was one part of the silver's essential nature, for it had been made first as a gift, and only later corrupted into a weapon.

"You won't murder him!" I shouted at Kaphiri's prostrate form. "Not this night. I would let you die first—" Another flurry of silver tendrils reached for Yaphet. I blocked them. "Listen to me! *I would let you die.*"

He heard me. Perhaps he believed me, for the silver tendrils retreated, dissolving into the stillness of the ocean of silver that surrounded us.

Yaphet had Kaphiri pinned against the ground, but his head was turned toward me and there was such a coldness in his eyes, it frightened me more than the assault of silver. "Death is your role, *my love.*" There was dust on his lips, and when he spoke, I tasted it in my own mouth. "You have ended my life seven times already. Seven times that I can remember."

"How can you remember it?"

"Let me up."

I looked at Yaphet, and nodded, but Yaphet's anger was still hot. He brought his knee harder against Kaphiri's back, making him wince and grunt. "Swear that you will not bring the silver against us!"

Kaphiri's eyes were narrowed in pain, but he smiled even so. "I will not bring the silver against you," he said in a mocking voice. "Anyway, not this night."

Yaphet understood he would get no better answer, so he relented. Kaphiri sat up, slapping at the dust on his clothes. "You must forgive me," he said to Yaphet. "It's only out of habit that I hate you."

They looked alike. Yaphet stepped back a pace, studying Kaphiri with a wild look in his eyes that seemed part wonder, that such a thing could be, and also part fear, and fury, that such a thing could be. They looked so very much alike, but it was a surface effect . . . the similarity of a man and his reflection, and I was not fooled.

"Why me?" Yaphet asked.

Kaphiri shrugged. "It's hard to know. But then, you may have fallen far since the war." He glanced past me, and I knew he was looking for Jolly. I turned, to find the sleeping bag where I had left it, but my brother had slipped away. The goats snorted and skipped, shying away from the flying machine. They might as well have pointed to Jolly's hiding place.

"What will we do?" Kaphiri asked. "I cannot call the silver, and you are not ready yet to spill my blood." His mocking gaze returned to me. "Is it a stalemate?"

He was confident—and why not? I could not keep watch forever—I must sleep sometime—and then it would be easy for him to bring the silver.

"Jol-ly," he called in a mocking, singsong voice, "come home with me—"

"Leave him alone!" I cried, but he ignored me.

"Come home, Jolly . . . and maybe I'll let your sister live . . . at least until the final flood. The game finishes then for everyone."

"It won't finish," I told him. "It'll just start over again, when your death triggers the destruction of the silver!"

A sudden fey mood rose in him when I said these words. There was a sheen on his skin, and his eyes were wild. "Is that what you want? Shall I call the end of the silver now? Do you wish it yet again?"

"No," I breathed, and I backed a step away.

"Did you think the end of the silver was tied only to my death? It's not. I could summon it anytime. Cold murder isn't necessary, love, and I am not as stubborn as I used to be. Ask me, and I will destroy all the silver this night."

I could not doubt his claim, for at his words some connection closed in my mind and the world felt different. Harder, clearer. The uncertainty that had dogged me since leaving the Temple of the Sisters was gone, dissolved like the silver in my vision, leaving all the hard edges of the world exposed. "The goddess made you, didn't she?" I asked him. "She made you for this purpose, to call down the destruction of the silver at need. She must have trusted you so deeply."

I saw through his chilly smile. It was a false front, a painted animosity to disguise the fragile architecture that lay beneath. "She made me only when she could not find him." He thrust his chin at Yaphet. "It seems that in that age he had been swallowed by the silver, so she devised me instead, adding in some skills he lacked." There was such a gleam of hatred in his eyes as he said this, that I thought he would not be able to contain it. I felt the pressure of it in my own head. Then Kaphiri sucked in a sharp breath, like a swimmer returning from a deep dive, and his shoulders relaxed. "Sometimes I wonder if I remember it rightly," he added. "Was she the one who made me? Or was it the other?"

"The dark god?" I asked.

"No matter. I serve neither of them now." And he sat on the

ground, arranging the folds of his garments around him. "Come. Sit with me."

I would not sit, but I crouched nearby. Yaphet remained standing.

Kaphiri looked at me. "These are the last days. You sense it, don't you? There is only a little time left before the world drowns . . . unless you choose to stop it again."

"That should be *your* choice! It's what the goddess made you for."

His smile was bitter. "And I obeyed her, that first time." He looked down at the dusty ground. "I was naive. Do you know what follows the destruction of the silver?"

I nodded, for I had seen the city.

"You *don't* know!" Kaphiri barked. "Not until you've seen a hundred thousand players starve to death."

Nothing was the same. I faced a murderer, but I could see the horror of death in his eyes.

"Barely a thousand survivors left in the world," he said, his voice so soft I had to strain to hear him.

"How can you remember it?" Yaphet asked.

"I have learned to remember."

"Tell us how." He could not disguise his eagerness. Yaphet loved knowledge best. He always had. I knew it, though I could not remember how I knew or why.

Kaphiri knew it too. "Would you learn how?"

Yaphet nodded.

Kaphiri's expression turned to disdain. "Even if you remembered every word ever spoken, you would have no victory. The goddess is using you . . . using *us*. She always has."

I knew it was true. "I am going to the Cenotaph."

Shock overtook his features. He looked at me with haunted eyes. "Where have you learned of that place? Why would you go? My love, there is nothing in the Cenotaph. Nothing you can touch."

"There is a god there. Or some fragment of a god."

"He will not help you."

"I am not sent there to seek help. He is the cause of the floods.

The goddess has said that the world will not heal until he is removed."

"The goddess? Has she visited you?"

I nodded. "She said that I am her hands, and this fragment of the god must be removed."

"By you?"

I shrugged.

He started to laugh, but his humor turned suddenly to anger. "You cannot defeat a god! Even a fallen one. Think on it! If the goddess herself cannot eject him, what hope is there for you?"

"I don't know. None, maybe, for me alone."

"You won't be alone," Yaphet said.

Kaphiri threw him a dark look. "You are always so eager to play their game."

"And what alternative should I take? Should I refuse to play? Should I be like you and wish for the night when we all drown? Let us all die! Why not? If it will spite the goddess."

"You mock me, but I will answer you anyway. There is an alternative." He nodded toward me. "She has never dared it, but it's real all the same. The only way to bring our malice to bear against the gods who made this world is to become as gods ourselves."

I caught my breath, for these were the same words he had whispered to me in my vision—and that I had rejected. I rejected them again. "If you knew how to do that, you would have done it already."

"But I don't know how . . . though I might still learn, with your help. Will you help me? This time?"

My heart was beating hard. What he asked repulsed me. To become a goddess, to hold the power of life and death, and to wield that power with none stronger to say if I am right, or if I am wrong. It horrified me. "We don't need more gods and goddesses. They have done badly enough by this world already."

Yaphet touched my arm. "Jubilee, think. Will you always make this same answer?"

"What do you want me to do? Do you want me to help him?"

"If you have never helped him before, then *yes*. Do it differently this time! Do anything! Because there may never be another chance."

But this turn was already different. Yaphet had never spoken to me like this before. Never.

He turned to Kaphiri. "What is it you want from her anyway?"

"A small thing. The smallest thing. I want her to translate our past. My love——" He reached toward me. I thought he would touch me, and I shied away.

He laughed at my childishness, but his laughter could not hide his pain. "You did not always find me so repulsive! You loved me in other lives. But the bond between us has faded, for I have changed, and you have not. I have remade myself! But in doing so, I've left you behind. We can never be true lovers again."

"We never were," I whispered.

"You say that, because you don't remember. But you haven't forgotten everything, have you? You still remember the language spoken when the world was made. I know you do."

"And what use is that?" Yaphet asked.

Kaphiri mocked him. "We are always so hungry, aren't we? Insatiable!"

"And impatient!"

"I know it." He turned again to me. "If you would dare to face our past, to understand it, then help me. For lifetimes I have gathered documents and written manuscripts, in languages left over from the ancient world. Thousands of pages, my love, and I cannot read more than a few words of any of them! But you can. These languages live now only in your ancient mind. Come back with me. *Teach* me."

"No, Jubilee, don't!" Jolly shouted.

I had let myself forget about Jolly. I saw him now, crouched beneath the folded wing of the flying machine.

"He'll trick you, Jubilee. Don't do what he wants. Please don't."

Kaphiri crossed his arms over his chest, mocking the posture of a weary parent. "I have said only the truth."

Through every turn we had played, through every lifetime, I had

always refused to help him . . . and the world had never healed.
Always, we had been caught in the cycle of silver flood and silver
drought. "Where is it you would have us go?"

"Jubilee, *please.*"

"South," Kaphiri said. He turned to Yaphet. "You will come
too. We need you. Or anyway we need your flying machine, for
my temple is far to the south, among the peaks of the Sea
Comb."

Jolly crept out from under the wing. "Jubilee, say you won't go.
You can't go with him."

I wanted to refuse. I wanted to send Kaphiri away, and take Jolly
home, and have my father back, and see my mother, but all those
were impossible things.

Yaphet watched me, a hungry gleam in his eyes. "Think about
it, Jubilee. We can't let him go, and we can't let him die, and you
can't watch him forever. This is the only answer."

All was quiet. No wind blew, and no bird called. The world lay
still beneath a heavy blanket of silver and still I felt as if I was
hurtling forward. "We'll go."

Yaphet's fist clenched in triumph, but Jolly cried out in fear.

"Jolly!" I knew how afraid he was of Kaphiri. "We will take you
to our uncle first—"

"No," Kaphiri said. "We leave tonight, and Jolly comes with us."

Yaphet looked scornful. "We can't fly at night."

"With me, you can."

I did not doubt it. Sprawled on the ground outside the Temple
of the Sisters, I had looked up at an auditorium of silver arching
over my head. It was no great stretch to think the architect of that
magic could keep even a flying machine safe.

"We will go tonight," I said. "But we will take Jolly to my uncle
first. Hurry now, before I change my mind."

We set about getting the flying machine ready, while the goats
shied from us, frantic to avoid both our presence and the wall of
silver that lay all around. Into the cargo baskets went our few pos-

sessions. Then Kaphiri drove back the silver, far enough that we could spread the wings.

Was it real? So I asked myself over and over again, for the night was weighted with the strangeness and inevitability of a dream.

Jolly came out of hiding, but he would not let Kaphiri come near him, nor answer him in any way.

At Yaphet's direction, we carried the flying machine to the edge of the precipice, and the silver fell back before our advance. The air was calm, and the stars were bright despite the luminous glow of the flood.

I huddled with Jolly in one of the cargo baskets, and we cradled Moki between us. "Please don't do it," Jolly whispered. "He'll hurt you. You know he will."

"Not tonight."

I watched Kaphiri as he made a nest for himself in the other basket. Then Yaphet crawled into the pilot's sling. He yelled at Kaphiri to make a path through the silver that lay beyond the cliff, and the silver rolled back as if some god's breath had blown upon a cloud of cold smoke. The engine started. Then the plane rocked forward, and with a sickening lurch, dropped from its perch on the cliff's edge. I cried out, sure we were all falling to our deaths. Then the wings crackled as air filled their hollows. The nose of the flying machine nodded upward, and slowly, slowly we began to climb.

The canyon was filled with silver: a great gleaming river flowing between islets of sharp stone. We followed its current to the plain. I had wondered once what it was like to be a bird, forced to fly all night above a world drowned in luminous silver. That night I learned. It was cold! Bitterly cold in the high air above the world, and dreamlike: the dream of some ancient god bent on defying all the rules of the world.

It was a brilliant night. The Bow of Heaven glowed, without dimming the stars around it, and the world was ablaze with silver. The only real darkness was cast by the plateaus of two distant mesas, one to the east, and one north: Azure.

We could see it easily; the night was that clear. Yaphet brought the flying machine round in a smooth arc, and a wisp of silver danced along the wing's edge. I pushed it away and Kaphiri laughed, as if at a child's clever trick. He made no move to fend off the silver, leaving it all to me.

It took only a little while to reach Azure, but we did not go all the way to my uncle's encampment. How could I explain to Liam what I was doing? I was fairly sure there were not words in any language to convince him that a bargain with his brother's murderer was the right thing to do.

So we studied the mesa from afar, until we sighted the camp, and then we set Jolly down a quarter mile away from it along the mesa rim. Yaphet did not even touch down. He slowed the flying machine, bringing it almost to a stall a few feet above the ground. Jolly and I shared a long look. I did not believe I would see him again. "Take Moki," he whispered. Then he dropped from the cargo basket and fell into the brush. An explosion of birds took flight, and then we were away from the mesa and over the plain again. I heard a shout from the plateau. It sounded like my name. Moki turned to look, but I did not.

Chapter

31

It was my task to guard Yaphet, but my vigil failed during that long flight south. I fell asleep, waking only when Yaphet shouted some question and Kaphiri answered that we should bear west. My face and hands were numb with cold and I pulled Moki's small body close to warm them.

We were very high. The silver-flooded plain lay far below us, unbroken by any peak or pinnacle, but ahead there were mountains.

I had seen the Sea Comb from afar, but only as we drew close did I understand the expanse of that range. The part standing above the flood was twice as tall as the Kalang: a wall of sharp, ice-coated peaks raised against a dawn sky of liquid blue-gray.

As the dawn brightened, the silver rolled back, uncovering a land as strange as any I have seen. A city of glass towers sparkled in the foothills, carpeting the dry slopes and filling the valley floors for mile after mile. The glass towers were black, or gray, or blue, standing impossibly high and thin. Some of the buildings crowded one against the next, but where there was space between them, the ground sparkled in broken glass. As we passed over I saw why. Every few seconds a great windowpane would pop loose from one of the towers and drop, turning and flashing in the muted light, until it struck the ground, bursting apart in a high-pitched, crashing explosion of sound. It seemed to me that if the wind blew hard, the towers themselves would be toppled.

The glass city did not belong in our world. I was sure of it. The architecture was wrong. The towers were too tall, too thin, too fragile for our gravity . . . but the gods had come from another world.

I wondered: How does a player become a god? What *is* a god? What qualities might define one? If we could learn to command the power of the silver, would that make us gods? Or was that only a first step?

The city fell behind us, and soon after that the desert began to yield to an upland of shrubs and small trees, that grew greener and more lush with the increasing elevation. The ground no longer seemed far away, for the land rose steeply, while we only slowly climbed toward the middle peaks. Then Kaphiri guided us into a canyon, and suddenly the mountains surrounded us.

We flew between the canyon's narrow walls for perhaps five miles, and then at Kaphiri's direction we climbed above the canyon rim. A temple compound was perched there on the very edge of the precipice, and at once I recognized it as the temple Jolly had described. The defensive walls were massive, at least forty feet high and twenty wide, surrounding a courtyard and a central temple building, all of it built of a melancholy gray stone. Beyond the temple was a lovely green meadow edged in forest, with high peaks in the distance that glistened white with ice.

As Yaphet brought the flying machine around in a broad circle I looked again at the forest edge. Silver lingered there, in patches sheltered by the shadows of the trees, and between the silver I thought I saw players wandering in slow groups as if searching for something. But I wasn't sure. Maybe they were some kind of strange, upright animal, for they seemed small and hunched, with heads too large for their bodies, but before I could decide, they disappeared, shying away from the wind-rush of the flying machine.

Then we were over the canyon again, and a moment later the temple's massive wall was rushing up below us. Yaphet had chosen to land on the wall that faced the canyon. I glimpsed staircases rising up to it from the courtyard, and saw that only a shallow curbing offered protection from the precipitous drop. Then the wings flared, rolling back to embrace the air just as the wings of a bird will, and we floated gently down the last few feet, landing with only a slight bump.

Immediately, I rolled out of the cargo basket and staggered to my feet. It was as if I had been half-asleep all night, enthrall to some bizarre dream, but in that moment I wakened fully to my situation, and horror filled me. I was standing on the wall of Kaphiri's temple, his stronghold, where he had returned again and again over many lifetimes in his long and bitter struggle with the will of our flawed goddess. Why had I come? What had moved me to abandon Jolly, and Liam, and Udondi to flee south with my father's murderer? I wanted to discover that I had been swept up in a dream, another vision, but that dawn had too much of reality about it. I was stiff with cold, and exhausted, and hungry, and in desperate need to answer a particular call of nature.

Moki whined and I picked him up, the warmth of his small body so tender against my cheek that I knew it was no dream.

I stepped to the edge of the wall. Silver still filled the canyon. It flowed downhill in a great, silent river, roiling and tumbling past the foot of the temple wall without ever quite touching the stone. I breathed in the sweet perfume of temple kobolds, mixed with the sharp scent of silver, and it seemed to me that temple was strong and well defended. But then I stepped around the wing and I saw that the wall had been breached by the silver at least once, for a strange folly of blue glass had replaced some of the stone. The folly started at the top of the wall and plunged down into the courtyard, looking like the spillway of a steep mountain stream. I was tired, and it was hard to focus on the translucent mass, but it seemed to be filled with swooping shapes and swirls as if some edgeless, unstable geometry was trapped within it.

Kaphiri came round the flying machine. He saw where I looked. "That is Jolly's monument," he said. "Seven players were taken when he called that flood over the wall. And every night since the silver follows that path into the temple grounds."

I turned away, for I could not bear to think of Jolly, so far away, and lost to me again.

Within the walls, the courtyard lay like a dark skirt around the central temple building. That building stood three stories high, each story smaller than the one below so that it had the look of a stacked cake. Its dark windows cast a brooding gaze toward the vistas beyond the walls.

Memory stirred in me. I felt the tremor of an old fear rising in my consciousness, a terrible dread, and suddenly I knew with absolute certainty I had been in that place before. "Yaphet—" My mouth had gone dry, so that I could hardly speak. I turned to look for him—but what I saw made my voice leave me entirely.

He had called Kaphiri to him, and they worked together to furl the wings, while Yaphet explained the mechanism of the flying machine and its steering system, speaking gently, as if the two of them were brothers. *But they were not!* I could feel the difference between them . . . though it did not seem as profound as last night.

The night's cold had settled in my bones and I shuddered, but to the east the sky above the mountains blazed with the light of a hidden sun. As Yaphet finished furling the wings, the sun finally showed itself, rising over the eastern slopes to spill its warmth across the temple walls and the flowing silver in the canyon— which sank away into the shadows—and against my jacket, and like the silver, my fear receded, though it did not go away.

The sound of our footsteps made a forlorn tapping as we crossed the empty courtyard to the tall temple building. The wide grounds were tiled in a herringbone pattern of gray and blue brick, and nowhere did I see a stray leaf or any gathering of dirt or dust, or sprouting weed between the tiles, so that it seemed we walked inside an electronic market, and not in the true world. An explanation of this perfection was not long in coming.

The temple was made of the same gray stone as the walls. Wide, arched windows looked out into the courtyard, and between them were tall doors of shining platinum. They opened at our approach, and their motion stirred to life a creature that had been crouching on the step: a mechanic, mantislike and the height of my hand. It scuttled aside on four legs, while holding two front limbs close to its body—one pincered, one armed with scissored blades. Its machine eyes looked at us from a triangular head mounted on the end of a snakelike neck.

I stared back at it, mouth agape, for it was exactly like the mechanics on the Kalang Crescent, whose endless task it was to protect the forest. The traveler had visited that forest often, and Nuanez Li had seen his little daughter killed by these things.

"You're Kalang, aren't you?" I asked Kaphiri. "You are the player who left the mechanics in the forest."

He glanced at the mechanic, a look of melancholy in his eyes. "That was another life. My name was Zha Leng, but it changed with time, as all things do."

"You left the mechanics to guard the wells, didn't you? Not the trees!"

He shrugged. "If the trees cannot be cut, then no one should have reason to settle near the wells."

"Nuanez Li lived there. He lives there still!" But I bit my lip, regretting the words as soon as they were spoken. Perhaps Kaphiri didn't know Nuanez was still alive, or that he had found his own unending youth in the wells of the Kalang.

But Kaphiri's interest proved to be only philosophical. "If he still lives on the Kalang Crescent, then he'll likely be the last player alive in the world, for the silver may never conquer that plateau. Not that Nuanez would ever notice the difference!"

He laughed, but it was a laugh full of bitterness, delighting in the harsh ironies of the world.

We mounted the front steps, and passed through the open doors into a great room, neatly furnished with couches and tables and chairs, all meticulously clean. Across the room, a grand stairway led up to the next floor, while on either side gloomy passages gave access to other ground-level rooms.

A woman appeared from one of these hallways. She was white-haired and stooped, and she clung to the shadows, as if reluctant to show herself. I guessed her to be Mari, the woman who had cared for my brother when he was a prisoner in this temple. Mari, the lost wife of Nuanez Li.

Jolly had described her as a kindly player, but she did not extend us any welcome. When she spoke, it was in a soft, furtive whisper, as if she feared drawing the attention of a wicked fate. "How long will *these* last?" she asked Kaphiri, gesturing at me and Yaphet with her chin.

"No longer than the rest of us," he answered. "For all things must end, Mari. All things. Even you."

We were in the household of my father's murderer.

I had come to help him learn more about our shared past, and about the lost science of becoming a god. I brooded over these ironies as we sat down to a formal breakfast, in a room hung with paintings and projections of ages long past.

Mari served us. She would allow neither myself nor Yaphet to help, and while we were at the table she refused all attempts at conversation. But when I was returning from a visit to the scupper I encountered her in the hall. In her whispering voice she asked about Jolly, and I assured her my brother was well, but this news did not bring her any particular pleasure.

"Seven players died when Jolly left this temple." She glanced over her shoulder, as if to assure herself Kaphiri was still at table. "Did you see the folly that has broken the courtyard wall? Jolly left that to us, to remember him by. A knife thrust, that's what it is. A wound that draws the silver into the yard night after night, like bacteria seeking flesh. This temple won't stand much longer."

This last was pronounced with vindictive satisfaction.

"Do you want to see it fall?"

She bent closer to me, and her voice grew even softer. "I came here long ago, because he told me I would not die—not if I stayed within these walls—and he did not lie. I have lived and lived and lived! I have been old longer than anyone else has been alive. Even him!"

"You are older than him?" I asked incredulously, thinking of Nuanez, living alone on the plateau of the Kalang.

"So you know about him?"

I nodded.

"He kept himself youthful, but I have always been old."

"Not always, surely."

She looked away, and there was a tremor in her lip. "Whatever existed before . . . that is lost to time. I wonder how many lives he has lived, since I lived with him? I wonder how many lives he has spent searching for me? But there will be no more lives after this one."

I did not tell her that Nuanez too was still living the same life. I didn't think she would believe me. How could she let herself believe? If she had stayed with Nuanez she might have regained her youth . . . or Kaphiri might have murdered them both for nosing into his secrets.

Yaphet and Kaphiri had been deeply involved in a discussion of flight when I left the table. That discussion was still ongoing when I returned. I listened at the door, but their conversation was hard for me to follow. They spoke as if they knew, or guessed, what was in the other's mind and perhaps they did, for Kaphiri had been made as a copy of Yaphet, and it came to me that they likely shared a vast measure of memory kept within the silver.

Their similarity frightened me, but their growing sympathy troubled me even more. As I listened, I could not say with any certainty which was Yaphet's voice, and which belonged to Kaphiri. I told myself this confusion was only a result of my exhaustion, for I had not slept well since leaving the Temple of the Sisters, but I decided against rejoining them. Instead I resolved to explore the temple on my own.

I set out with that purpose in mind, but the dread of that place that had stirred in me upon our arrival was still strong. Fear seized me as I started to climb the grand staircase to the second floor, so I went outside instead, with Moki following at my heel.

The sun was warm and the air cool. I did not see any mechanics about.

I circled the courtyard, and in that way came to the temple gates. They were three times my height, fitted beneath a horizontal span of stone. I knew Jolly used to walk in the meadow beyond the wall, and climb the ridges around the temple, but in his stories he had never mentioned the strange creatures I had seen lurking on the forest's edge. Instinct warned me against them, and I did not dare to open the gates. Instead I climbed the nearest stairs, thinking to look for the creatures from the safety of the wall.

I spied them almost immediately: a band of five just at the edge of the trees, and this time there was no doubt in my mind. Though they walked on two legs and in every general way resembled men and women, they were not players. They were too tiny and too lithe, and gravity did not seem to chain them, for they would bounce and float at every step, sometimes drifting several inches into the air. They were ephemeral too. They began to disappear, one by one. I would look away, and when I looked back one more would be gone, reappearing sometimes a little farther along the forest's edge.

Moki growled, and I turned, to see Kaphiri coming up the stair. "Where is Yaphet?" I demanded.

"In the paradise of my library. He will not miss us for a little while."

"I feel as if I have been in this temple before."

He came to stand beside me. "You have been here before."

Across the wide meadow, the creatures paused in their random wandering. They looked toward the temple, and one cried out in a high, strange voice something that sounded like *La-zur-i*, with the syllables all drawn out. Another took up the cry, and another, and there was nothing of friendliness in the sound.

"It sounds like a malediction," I said, feeling shaken.

"I think it's a name." He watched the forest creatures with an expression that was part amusement, part contempt.

"Are they bogies?"

He nodded. "Though they don't seem to be attached to any ruin. They came out of the silver only a few days ago, but they have already demonstrated some skill with poison darts. They seem to have assumed the task of murdering me."

Startled, I stepped back from the edge of the wall. "You alone?"

"It's a hard assumption to test. There is only me and the woman here, but she does not come out on the walls." His brow wrinkled. "Still, I think it is only me. Some kind of vendetta, I suspect. They believe I am this *Lazuri*—"

"We should not be standing on the wall."

"There are mechanics in the meadow. We are safe enough."

"Are you Lazuri?"

"It's not a name I remember using. But come. There are more interesting sights than this."

We walked around the wall until we came to the side that looked down over the canyon.

On our flight south, silver had covered all the desert, but the sun had been at work since dawn and the silver had burned away. I looked down into the canyon and saw a thread of water sparkling within a forest far below, but my gaze did not rest there long, for the vast Iraliad lay before us. There was no wind, so no dust had risen to haze the view. We were high in the mountains, and through the crystalline air I could see farther—I could see more—than I ever had before. The desert glowed in the morning light, warm yellows and tans and rust red colors, with bright sparks of reflected light hinting at the presence of follies and precious veins of silver-spawned minerals. Far to the north—a hundred miles? two hundred?—the plain dissolved into a haze of blue distance.

All this came to me in a glance, before my attention was seized by the great pit of the Cenotaph. I had glimpsed its storm-wracked edge once before, from the southern escarpment of the Kalang, but now I saw it clearly, and I shuddered.

The goddess had called it a wound in the world, and that was what it looked like: if the golden desert was the world's flesh, then the Cenotaph was a great bullet wound.

It was a crater, fifty miles or more across, its rim a chaos of colored sand and slag—pink and putrid green and black and a poisonous, electric blue—with thin mists of silver steaming here and there from vents and fissures, sparkling brightly before dissolving in the sunlight.

Lying within the pit was a lake of silver, and it was boiling. Even at such a distance I could see great bubbles rising up from its surface and bursting, throwing drops of silver in all directions. How large must those "drops" be, if I could see them?

Kaphiri said, "It is the pressure of sunlight that makes it bubble. At night it is still."

"I did not know it was so close."

For several minutes I could not look away, but finally I raised my gaze, to see the dark, blocky mass of a distant plateau beyond the pit. *"The Kalang,"* I whispered, but my memory of that place felt borrowed, as if it was the memory of someone else . . . someone I used to be.

"What would happen if you hurled a stone into the mud?" Kaphiri asked.

I gave him a puzzled look. "What kind of question is that?"

"A straightforward one, so think on it. What would happen if you hurled a stone into the mud?"

I scowled, annoyed that he would toy with me. "I would not do it, for it would dirty my clothes, with the mud spattering everywhere."

He nodded. Then he looked again over the plain, to the distant clouds of silver steaming from the great pit of the Cenotaph. "A god was cast down to the world like a stone, and we are all dirty still. How are you going to fix it, my love? When even the goddess will not dare to try? And why is it you?"

Chapter

32

I could not answer Kaphiri's questions. I was too tired to do anything but wander aimlessly and worry. "You are no good to me like this," he said, and he led me to a bedroom Mari had made up.

When I awoke it was deep in the night. Through the window I could see stars, but they were pale in the sky, their light faded by the gleam of silver from beyond the temple walls. Moki stirred beside me, and I gave him a quick hug. "Yaphet?" I whispered, hoping he had come to the room while I slept. I listened for his breathing, but all was silent.

Fear drove away the last of my sleepiness. I was supposed to protect Yaphet, but I had hardly seen him since we arrived. All that day and night I had left him to Kaphiri's mercies. Quickly I rose, and found that I had slept in my clothes.

I did not know where the light might be, and I didn't want to spend time looking for it, so I groped my way to the door. It was not locked.

In the hallway the light tubes were dim amber, emitting hardly enough illumination to reach the floor. The hallway looked the same in both directions, but I knew to turn left. I had been asleep on my feet when Kaphiri brought me to my room, and I should not have known my way around his temple, but I did. I knew that wide hallway, and the turnings I would have to take to reach the great room. Even the echo of my footsteps I had heard before.

I passed the kitchen and went on, until I came to the great central hall with its tall doors to the courtyard. Moki whined to go out, but I did not dare let him, fearing the mechanics that patrolled there. So I called him with me as I approached the grand staircase.

Ever since I'd arrived, a strange, remembered fear had lived within me. It grew suddenly stronger as I set foot on that stair. The steps were made of massive blocks of the same gray stone used in the walls. I had climbed them before. I knew their number. When I reached the top, I paused to gaze warily across a wide landing at a closed door. I knew that door. I knew its bronze gleam, and the raised scene worked into its surface, of a sun rising beyond the horizon of a ring-shaped world. The door must have weighed several hundred pounds, but it was perfectly balanced. At a touch it swung soundlessly open . . . and my memory failed.

There should have been a wide audience chamber on the other side of that door. There should have been a raised dais at the far end, and a chair of rank, and whispering ghosts with fingers like leaves brushing my arms and begging my help . . .

For I had walked through this temple in that vision I endured at Azure Mesa.

But instead of an audience chamber, I found the library. I stood with the door propped open, staring at a bookcase that stretched from floor to ceiling, every shelf on it crammed with paper and parchment manuscripts, and leaves of lettered stone, and relics.

I wandered the length of the bookcase, trailing my fingers on the spines of the manuscripts to assure myself they were real.

An aisle opened at the end of the row, with scattered tables pushed up against the wall. Many more bookshelves lay beyond the first.

I walked past them, and as I made my way around the last one, I knew where I was. The raised dais was gone, and the chair of rank. In their place stood a long table holding a scattering of manuscripts. Three chairs were placed around it. Two had stacks of lettered stone piled in their seats. The other held Yaphet, sprawled in sleep upon the table. I wanted to wake him, to tell him what I knew: that we were in the house of Ki-Faun—in my mind's eye I could see him sitting exactly where Yaphet sat: his old, crab body hunched in his chair as he watched me with a pained gleam in his ancient eyes that I could not understand—but I knew Yaphet must be exhausted and I did not want to interrupt his slumber.

Moki had disappeared somewhere among the stacks, so I had no warning. I turned my head and Kaphiri was there in the shadows.

So forlorn was his expression that I thought our time was over. All hope seemed gone from his eyes, and with it his fiery ambition to become a god, so that nothing was left to him but to call the silver into that room to consume us all—except that it would not consume him. I think that was all that held him back—the knowledge that he would be left behind.

He said to me, "You have been here before. Do you remember?"

"I do."

He nodded at Yaphet. "And do you remember him? No?"

I was unsure what he was asking.

"It's just that he returns so naturally to the habits of his past, I thought you would know him."

I studied Yaphet and, slowly, I began to see that room again with the eyes of my past self. I saw age fall upon Yaphet, so that his body withered and his lush black hair vanished and tendrils of beard trailed like strands of gray moss from his chin. "It was him," I said, astounded at my sudden knowledge. "He was Ki-Faun." I turned to look again at Kaphiri. "Or was it you?"

"It was him."

Of course, for I had been sent to murder Kaphiri.

"Will you come?" he asked me, and when I hesitated he added, "There is nothing to fear. It's only your memories that I desire now."

We walked into a room of ghosts. From outside the closed door I could already hear their whispering, and when the door opened their chatter was like the streaming of wind in treetops.

They were savants. Hundreds of them, some floating near the ceiling, some hovering just above the floor, or at every level in between. Some were wing-shaped, others spherical, while many more were flatscreens. Some of these were fixed to the walls, or sitting like decorations on the shelves. They spoke to one another in languages I had never heard before, carrying on conversations that never slowed for the drawing of a breath.

"Are they sane?"

Kaphiri shrugged. "Speak to them and find out."

Where should I start? There were so many, it would require years to know them all, but the silver was rising, and I feared we had only days left, at best. Just a few days to learn the ways of goddesses and gods. But if any players had ever known such things, surely they would be the most ancient, those who had lived when the world was first made?

"Which is the oldest?" I asked. "Do you know?"

"That one never speaks."

"I would see it anyway."

He shrugged and slipped into the chaos of drifting savants. I expected him to select one of the decrepit ones hovering near the floor, but instead he reached for a translucent wing that hung in perfect stillness and stability near the ceiling. It looked to be made of some substance like glass, but with a greater purity, and clarity, than I had ever seen. The wing was as long as my arm, and two inches in thickness at its widest point. Colors burst to life within it when Kaphiri took it in his hands. He gazed at them, and his face grew more stern, and colder even than it had been before. Then he gave it a shove. The colors disappeared as it left his hands. It glided across the room, angling toward me as if it understood its destination, and it did not wobble, though it bumped against several other savants along the way.

I caught it and pulled it close, gazing into its glassy body, but the colors that had appeared when Kaphiri touched it did not immediately appear for me. "How do you know it is oldest?" I asked, for there was nothing worn in its appearance or quaint in its fashion. If he had told me his kobolds had assembled it only yesterday, I would have no reason to disbelieve him, and I would be much impressed with his art. Even without color, it was a beautiful thing.

"Languages grow and change, you know this?"

I nodded.

"Even though I may not understand a language, it is still possible to see its relationship to languages that surround it in time. The similarity of words and grammar and symbols . . . I have traced many languages back through time. Among the oldest of them that I can still understand, there is mention of savants like this one, and even then they were considered relics. If this savant were to speak, it might use the oldest language in the world, the one that lies at the root of them all."

Colors had begun to wake in it now, and at the same time I felt the electric presence of the *ha* stir against my hands. "What is happening?"

"It knows you through the *ha*." He allowed himself a smirk. "That was how I acquired it. It was supposed to be ancient, but all the scholars who examined it could not get it to awaken. They were certain it was broken, or else a fraud. It was only by chance that I discovered otherwise."

"Why would it respond to the *ha*? Was it made by you, in another life?"

"I wondered the same. But no. It dates from the beginning, eight centuries at least, before my first life."

I lowered the savant, to look at him. "I was taught we were all created in the beginning, that we all lived our first lives together."

"Not quite all of us."

"You then? And Jolly? But what do the two of you share? You are not alike. You are *not*. Except the silver doesn't take you."

"And the *ha* is awake in us."

"And in me . . ." I gazed again into the mysterious glass of the savant, seeing lines of colors warming within its depths. "The goddess said we were children, that we've been children too long. Jolly is to teach other players to awaken their *ha* . . . I think it's why he was made . . . But it was you who wakened the *ha* in me."

"I did not plan that."

"Oh, I know. You thought it would kill me." I saw symbols forming now in the savant's glassy heart. Vaguely, I heard the first stirrings of an ancient voice, whispering down through time. "This is what I think, that in the first years, the *ha* must have been awake in all players, or anyway, all who were not children—"

He stiffened. "Is it whispering?" he asked incredulously. "Can you hear it?"

I could. At first it spoke so softly I could barely distinguish the words, but I knew immediately that its language belonged to me. *"I have it,"* I whispered, and Kaphiri stepped closer. I felt his tension as a pressure in my mind, and it was at once frightening and amusing. He needed me. He knew it now, without any doubt attached.

I bowed my head, bringing my ears closer to the sound. There was a space in my mind that was dark. I had never been aware of it before: a great, sleeping mass of memory, now waking, bit by bit, as if each word muttered by the savant was a spark of light illuminating another word in a language I had spoken before I knew any other. They were *my* words, and the voice I heard was my voice, speaking to me across time, from out of another life.

I shuddered, and vaguely I was aware of arms around me, steadying me as I sank cross-legged to the floor. I was listening to a monologue, the recitation of a history, but no sooner did I understand this than the voice fell silent. I ran my hands over the savant; turned it over in my lap, but no image appeared in its glassy surface. Then I looked up, to discover that someone new had joined us in the room.

She was an image of course, some kind of projection, for I could see through her to the drifting savants beyond but—

She was myself.

An older version of myself to be sure. She looked the age of my mother, and her fashion was not mine: her dark hair was pinned up in a dignified style that astonished me, and she was dressed in a formal gown of gold fabric, its pleated skirt accenting her height. And still I could not doubt that she was me.

As stunned as I was, she looked more surprised. "How can this be?" she whispered, in the language I knew so intimately now. "Do I look on a projection of myself?"

"No," I answered, my tongue still unfamiliar with the words now so bright in my memory. "This is *my* life, and you are a savant."

"A recording . . . that's right. I was recording our history . . . though why, or for who . . ." She shook her head. "It was an act of vanity. But why are you so like me? Or anyway, like the girl I might have been?"

"Because I am you—don't you understand?—in another life."

"*Another* life? This one has not been enough?"

"You are not so old."

"Am I not? Nine hundred years in the service of the goddess, and I was never a child. Now she has brought us all to ruin! And yet if that's so, why are *you* here? It should have ended. It should have ended this night. How can you be here?"

Nine hundred years? My mouth was dry, so that at first I could not speak. I wondered if this persona was sane. "Why . . ." I swallowed, trying to get some moisture in my mouth. "Why did you think the world was at an end?"

"Because it is broken! It is flooded with silver. Most players have already been taken." She raised her hands, and the *ha* sparkled between her fingers. "Only a few of us are left to hold it back. Too few. We cannot win."

"But the world didn't end," I said. "Anyway, not yet."

"Is this the same world?"

"I think it is."

"What is your name?"

"Jubilee."

"That's different from mine. I am called Selma."

I shrugged. "We are not born with any memory of our past lives. We don't remember our past names."

"Then how do you know you lived before?"

"The talents of our past return to us . . . and also, a memory of our lovers."

"Indeed."

"Is this new to you?"

"Very new, though it smacks of the goddess. Did she finally return? Is this how she sought to set things right?"

"I don't know."

Selma turned half away, a distracted, angry look on her face. "The silver is memory. Do you know that?"

"I have heard it said before."

"It is the memory of the world, from its creation. The memory of the creation is still in it, and maybe, it even holds a memory of the minds of the god and the goddess who together made this world—though none of us left has the skill to bring her whole out of the past. I do not know what has caused the silver to flood, unless the god has won, and decreed that the world will be returned to chaos, so that he may stage the creation again."

"The god?" A sullen anger ignited in me. "The god had nothing to do with the creation. This world was made by the goddess alone. The god pursued her. He came out of darkness to destroy her work."

Selma did not answer this for many long seconds. Her hand clutched at her gown, and she frowned, pacing first a step away, then a step closer. "Is that what you were taught?" She turned to study me more closely. "Well, time has passed. It's only to be expected that the story would change."

I did not want to hear such words. One by one my ideas of the world had shattered, beginning that night I watched Kaphiri make his way up the road to Temple Huacho. I felt unbalanced and angry, and I did not try to hide it. "She is the wounded goddess. She was nearly destroyed when she warred with the dark god."

Selma nodded, and there was a great sadness in her eyes. "That much is true."

True? How could anyone ever know what was true? But my curiosity won out. Selma was ancient. She spoke as one who had lived in the beginning of the world, and I wanted to know what she knew. "Please tell me the story, as you learned it."

"I did not learn it. I lived it. But I will tell you."

For several seconds she was silent, gathering her thoughts. Then she began to speak:

"It is not true that the god pursued her from out of the darkness. They came together. Please do not think too highly of them. They were beings of great intellect and great power, but also of great arrogance. They were lovers. But as with any arrogant creature, they were also competitors. They set out to create a project together, a world of their own, where they might play games until the end of time. Would you ever presume to make a world, Jubilee? No? Ah well, neither would I.

"But together the god and the goddess created this world. They spun it out of the mass of a lifeless planet that had the misfortune to form too close to its sun, so that its atmosphere was a thick blanket of poisonous vapor over a surface hot enough to melt soft metals. They tore that failed planet apart, and with its debris they built a new world in the shape of a ring because it was an efficient design, with more surface area than the planet they had destroyed, but still with room in the long core for the machinery of their creation.

"And their new world was beautiful. No one could deny that.

"So they invited people from other worlds to come play in their creation. They even made avatars that they could inhabit when it pleased them. These avatars were ordinary players in all respects, except that one resembled the favored form of the goddess, and one resembled the god, and they would host these deities on rare occasion."

She was telling me about myself. It was not a truth I wanted to know, but how could I deny it? The goddess had come to me. She had inhabited me. She had used me as her avatar. "Then you—"

(. . . and me too . . .)

—were made as a toy?"

"That description is painful . . . but not unfair."

"And you were not born of parents?"

"I have said I was made."

"Then you were a mechanic? You were never human at all? And I . . . I am the same as you."

"No, Jubilee, you misunderstand both your own history and the skill of the goddess. I am no mechanic, and neither are you. The goddess would never inhabit a simple mechanic. I am human—though I was made and not born—and if you are the same as me, then you are utterly human too."

"And Yaphet?"

She looked at me closely. "Is this the name of your lover?"

I nodded, too frightened to speak.

"They made him too. But all the other players they brought from other worlds."

I wondered how many other worlds there might be, and how a goddess might move between them . . . but the silver was rising, and there were many things I needed to know.

I told her, "There have been two more players made since the beginning." I glanced over my shoulder, and Kaphiri was still there. He met my gaze, but he looked confused. I realized then that Selma could not see him, for if she could, she would have surely called out to this avatar of her lover. And he could not see her, or he would be looking at her, and not at me.

Turning back around, I told her of Kaphiri, and of Jolly. She seemed mystified by this news. Then I described how the goddess had come to me, warning that some fragment of the dark god was hidden in the Cenotaph, and that I must find a way to remove him, and heal that wound.

Selma looked stunned, and shaken. "Then the war is not over."

"I guess not."

"And the flood is caused by the god after all."

"It's what she said. But how is it you didn't know this? If you were there in the beginning?"

"I do not have the sight of the goddess. It's been many centuries since she came to me. I thought the war long past."

"But you must know how I can heal the wound in the world? You must have ideas?"

"He is a god, Jubilee."

"But surely he is broken? Surely he is less than a god now?"

"She did not tell you what to do?"

"No! She is wounded, and very weak. Players say the silver is her fever dream and only rarely is she conscious."

Selma did not answer; she did not even move. She stood there frozen, so that I feared the ancient machinery she inhabited had failed. *"Don't go,"* I pleaded. "Not yet."

Her eyes blinked, and they were shining with tears. "Jubilee, you have explained so much to me."

"Then return the favor please, and tell me, why was there a war?"

She answered with a long, sad sigh. "You and I, Jubilee, and your lover Yaphet, and my lover, all of us are ordinary players. We are not the goddess and we are not the god, and their sins are not our sins. Do you understand this?"

I nodded, though I was too dazed by then for any true understanding.

"Their arrogance betrayed them. They became jealous of one another, and they began to argue over whose world this really was, for the god had made its mechanical structure, but the goddess had given it beauty and life. Their conflict grew violent, and the goddess sought to evict him from the world. In retaliation, he told her he would dissolve the biosphere, so that he might build it over again and prove he could bring beauty to a world as well as she. The players they had cajoled into populating their world were forgotten, no more than discarded toys, their lives of no value in the schemes of our failed deities."

"So they fought?"

"And both lost."

"And the world was broken?"

"I thought the world was finished. But looking at you, I know it lived longer than I expected. Do you know the age of the world?"

"Many tens of thousands of years, I think."

Again she looked stunned. "So long? I recorded this persona on what I thought would be the last night of the world. It was an act of vanity, or of anger. A great flood of silver had consumed the land, a flood that dwarfed all floods before it. I did not think any players would survive that night."

"The goddess found a way to turn back the flood."

"By the look in your eyes I will guess this cure was almost as evil as the affliction."

"She caused almost all the silver to be destroyed, and the players died of hunger and war. Only a few survived it, but of those few some had lovers, and there were babies. Still, it must have been hundreds of years—maybe thousands—before all the players could be reborn, and by then the silver was on the verge of flood again. This cycle has happened many times . . . at least seven times that we know of . . . because the wound has never been healed. But how can I make a god—even a wounded god—leave the world?"

"I do not know."

"But you must know! She lived within you, didn't she?"

"She did not tell me how to murder her."

Murder.

Murder again.

"Death is my role," I whispered.

"What are you saying?"

I was speaking to myself as much as to her. "It's what Kaphiri told me. Death is my role."

"Jubilee, do you know how to murder a god?"

I shook my head. But then a new thought came to me, and though it repulsed me, I could not let it go. "Tell me, did the goddess make the kobolds? Do you know?"

"What is a kobold?"

"They are beetle-like mechanics that grow in the ground wherever a plume of nutrients awakens the kobold motes that are everywhere in the world."

"I have not heard of mechanics like these."

I nodded. "I am not surprised, for it is said they did not exist at the beginning of the world. They were made later, in a time when the world was on the verge of starving to death . . . by a player who could survive the silver."

"Like this Kaphiri you have described?"

"Maybe it was him. But I think it was someone more clever."

Fiaccomo had defied death in the silver, seducing the goddess and stealing her creative powers to bring the first kobolds into the world. So it was said. Ki-Faun twisted this gift, making a kobold that could erase not just a player, but the very memory of that player from the silver so he never would be born again . . .

Was the goddess aware that players had stolen this knowledge from her mind? Did she guess what might be done with it?

Death is my role.

My heart was beating hard, and it took some time to understand that the voice calling my name was a real voice, and not the whispering of some ancient version of myself. "Jubilee," Yaphet crooned, his mouth beside my ear. "Come back to me. Come back, please."

I shoved the savant away, and I turned to him, crying against his shoulder and whispering, *"I'm afraid. I'm afraid."* Over and over again. I did not want to know what I knew, or what I had to do. I did not want anything but to hide in Yaphet's arms.

We spent the remaining hours of that night together. All those who have lovers will know how it was between us. There is no choice in love. Though we were in the house of Kaphiri, and though my heart was sick with fear, we had comfort between us, and I still treasure those hours above all others in my memory, which has grown very full indeed.

Chapter

33

I slept through much of that next day. Sometimes I sleep just to avoid being awake. A waking mind must face facts and make decisions. I wanted none of that. I wanted to sleep forever, but in the afternoon my conscience stirred, and I wakened.

Instantly I felt cold, for Yaphet was gone.

I knew where he was. In my imagination I could see him in the library, poring over ancient slices of lettered stone, or electronic documents that might have been written by himself, lifetimes ago.

I called Moki and he appeared from under the bed and I petted him for a few minutes, but it did little to calm me. In the vision I had suffered at Azure Mesa I had spoken with Ki-Faun, who was Yaphet. His words re-echoed in my mind and I felt their weight like a curse: *The knot is tied around you, milady, did you know it? All our fates circle around you.*

He had been so old I had not recognized him as my lover, but he knew me.

He had put the kobold in my hand. I wondered if that memory lay somewhere beneath the surface of Yaphet's mind . . . and if so, how far beneath the surface?

There was a knock at the door, and I stood and dressed, though I did not hurry, knowing he would wait.

He had been made in the image of Yaphet, and Yaphet had been made to resemble the god, and I was an avatar of the goddess, a container for her to play in, when she was in a playful mood.

We were not them. We were only players, made to look like them. But perhaps we had also been made to share some aspects of their personalities? The god had designed the mechanical structure of the world—which went far in explaining Yaphet's passion to know, to analyze, to understand, and to defy . . . and also why he frightened me even when I loved him.

But where was the explanation for *me*? The goddess had given life to the world, but death was my role. Maybe I was that part of the goddess that had made war against her mate.

The knock sounded again at the door, louder, and this time I answered it.

Kaphiri waited in the hall, his eyes shadowed by a sullen anger. I had not seen him when Yaphet retrieved me from the room of the savants, but he was back now, and wanting to know what I knew. I could see it in his eyes.

I told him, "Terrible things can be done in the heat of anger."

"And also when it is cold."

So true. Cold anger had eaten at him for thousands of years. It had led him to murder my father and countless others, and it had planted in him his ambition to become a god. I said, "I know why the bogies are trying to kill you. It's because you were made to look like the dark god."

"Do not toy with me."

"It is what the ancient savant told me. I have already warned Yaphet."

I told him everything then, for I saw no advantage in hoarding the information. He and Yaphet were both brilliant, and I desperately hoped one of them would find a better solution than the one that had come to me.

Evening had fallen by the time Kaphiri left me. I thought of going to the library, but I dreaded that place, so I wandered into the courtyard with Moki for company. I could smell the silver beyond the walls, though I could not see it yet.

In the corner of the courtyard, the glass folly glowed and flickered as if illuminated shapes moved within it. I thought of Jolly in this courtyard, calling the silver to him over these towering walls. "Come, Moki," I said, and we wandered closer to the glass spillway. The shapes within it looked like ghosts. They turned to gaze at me, with faces that were not quite faces, their eyes like hollow sockets. Moki whined. I reached down to comfort him, but he was gone, fleeing back to the open temple door.

My own retreat was more dignified, but it was a retreat, just the same. When I reached the temple I turned back, to see a wraith of silver flowing down the glass spillway to settle on the courtyard floor.

A luscious scent of cooking had infiltrated the temple. I followed it to the kitchen, and found Kaphiri again, sitting at a table of rose-colored jade. Mari was at the stove, fussing over a pot of stew. "You'll be hungry," she announced. "Sit down." And she set a bowl before me.

Kaphiri did not eat, or maybe he had eaten before I came in. As Mari put my bowl down, he gave her a hard look. No word passed between them, but she turned sullenly away, and after taking a moment to check the stove, she left us alone.

"Look at me," he said.

I did, and saw a version of Yaphet, older in the ways of the world and bitter. Terribly bitter.

"You want me to believe that players were no more than toys in their eyes, but the god and the goddess must have been players once, on another world. Did the savant say nothing of this?"

"She did not. And I do not understand you. How can you still want to become a god, knowing what they did?"

"Tens of thousands of players in this world think I am a god now."

"And you know they are wrong. You have learned to command the silver to destruction, but not to creation. You have never learned to command it to bring forth what you choose. If you want to be a god, learn that! It is said Fiaccomo created the kobolds. Your talent is similar to his, but what have you ever done except wipe away the world?"

For a long time he said nothing. He seemed to be looking inside himself, but if he found an answer there, I never learned what it was.

I had finished eating and was feeding the leftovers to Moki when he spoke again. "You are right. Destruction is always easier than creation. It's what you've always chosen. Will you choose it this time too? To destroy the silver is an easy thing. Ask me, and I will do it. Now. This night. And in the next few years most of the world will starve to death or die in warfare. That, my love, is the choice you've made over and over again."

"What else should I have done? I am not the goddess. I cannot create a world. I've never been confused on that point."

"So will you choose it now?"

"I don't know! Maybe it will come to that."

"If you do, you will send us all around this same circle again, and this choice will face you in another life . . . and what reason is there to believe you will ever choose differently? So that again and again and again you make us relive this nightmare."

"It is not my fault!"

"But you could end it so easily, by doing nothing at all. Stay here and wait for the last night. Let the silver drown the whole world, and there will be no survivors to give birth to us ever again. The gods will be defeated then, and their great project will be only an empty folly, lost among the stars."

My eyes stung, and suddenly I wanted my mother desperately. Should I let the silver drown her world? Should I murder *her*? I blinked back my tears, and asked him what I had not dared to ask before. "Have you already murdered my mother?"

He shrugged. "I went back to that place you lived, but it was gone. The hills were empty."

A fierce ache filled my throat, so that all I could do was whisper.

"There was only one temple in Kavasphir. Did you go to the right hill?"

"The road was there, and the raspberry bushes, but on the hill-top there was only a ring of golden standing stones."

Kaphiri had murdered thousands, but never had he lied to me. I laid my head down on the table, but I did not weep. Once—it seemed so long ago—I had crawled to the edge of the Kalang, and peered over a sheer precipice, where waterfalls vanished into mist long before they reached the ground, and the world had seemed grand and wild. Now it had become a cold, hollow thing.

"I need you," I whispered.

He leaned closer. "What did you say?"

There was a note of desperate hope in his voice, but it did not move me. I was done with compassion, and I was done with waiting. Why wait? I knew what to do.

Ki-Faun's kobold had been made to erase the very memory of a player from the silver, removing him forever from the world. Might it do the same thing to a god?

Selma had believed that within the silver was a memory of the minds of the goddess and the god who made the world. If I could remove all remembrance of the dark god, would he be gone forever? And would his flood of silver cease?

I lifted my head, and turned to meet Kaphiri's gaze. "I need you to go into the Cenotaph with me."

The hope in his eyes died. Anger took over, announcing itself with a short and bitter laugh. "I have already gone there."

"But you did not find the god."

His fist slammed against the table. "You cannot fight a god! *I* cannot. *You* cannot. Not unless we are gods ourselves, but you won't help me there. I know you won't, no matter the promises you make."

I felt no fear of him. I should have taken warning from that, but my mood was as fierce as his. "These are the last days! You said so yourself. There isn't time left for all the studies you would have me make, but it doesn't matter. I know what to do. I just need you to come with me. You have a power over the silver—"

"Enough!" Such an anger filled his eyes! A murderous rage. He stood, slamming back his chair so that it went tumbling across the room, while Moki darted into the darkest corner. "If you choose to go, then your decision is made. It will be the flood."

He strode toward the door.

"What do you mean?" I rose to my feet. "Wait! Where are you going?"

"Into the silver."

"No!" I charged after him, and grabbed his arm. "If you will not come with me then at least stay here! The end will come soon enough."

He was no taller than me, but he was stronger, and better skilled in mayhem. He caught my hand in the lightest of grips and twisted—

—and I went to my knees, crying out in pain.

"I won't go again into the Cenotaph," he called over his shoulder. "Not until you have shown me how to become a god."

"I don't know how!"

He paused at the great bronze doors. "Then learn. There is still tonight. And for you, at least, there will be a tomorrow."

He stepped out into the courtyard. I ran after him, but now he was running too, sprinting to the pool of silver that seeped from Jolly's monument. I screamed my pleas that he should come back, but he reached the silver, and it rolled over him, and even now I do not know how many enclaves fell to him that night.

I was sobbing when I reached Yaphet in the library. I choked my story out to him. "I provoked him. I didn't intend it, but I provoked him, and now he has gone into the silver to do murder. I could not stop him."

"Hush, my love. How could you stop him? If you tried, he would only call the silver over you."

"I should not have made him angry. I should have lied to him, told him what he wanted to hear." My gaze fell upon the long table. Last night it had been almost empty, but now it was covered in neat stacks of lettered stone. "What are you studying?"

He smiled apologetically. "Anything. Everything. It's fascinating. I could live here for a hundred years."

"You did live here for at least that long. This was your house, Yaphet, in another life. Can't you sense it?"

He looked around at the tall stacks, then back at the table. "I know my way around, but I have no memory of this place. None." He looked at me. "Do you?"

"Yes. Fragments come to me."

"I wish I could say the same. It's what I want most: to recall the memories of my past lives."

"That talent has not made Kaphiri happy."

"He doesn't have you."

I could not answer him. I was cold inside, and hollow. "I told you of my vision at Azure Mesa."

"I remember. You saw your past then too. When you ended Kaphiri's life, it caused the silver to be destroyed."

"I had planned to end his life in another way."

I watched Yaphet closely, looking for any spark of remembrance, but all he recalled was our conversation. "That's right. You were going to use the kobold the old sage had made. It was supposed to erase the memory of him from the silver, but that part sounded like a magic spell to me."

"That old sage was you, Yaphet. And I want you to re-create that kobold for me. I want you to do it tonight."

He told me it was impossible, and then he set to the task, moving between the shelves with a certainty that must have come from Ki-Faun himself. Near dawn, he stopped beside me with a puzzled look. "I choose manuscripts without knowing why, and they are the right manuscripts. Some part of me remembers this place, and the things I must have done here . . . but I can't remember *being* here. It's eerie." And then, as an afterthought, "I found the recipe for the kobold you wanted."

"You did? Where is it?"

He tapped his forehead. "Here. It was too dangerous to write down, so I memorized the formula for the kobold circle. The memory came to me, as I was scanning other texts on the subject. I hope we can find the right kobolds. Have you been to the well?"

"No."

"Neither have I. Not in this life anyway, but I know where it is. Come on, I'll show you the way."

The well room lay beyond the kitchen. The well itself was a wide hole, maybe twelve feet across, and deep. I dropped a bit of stone down its dark throat and listened, but I did not hear it hit bottom. Yaphet said, "This well must be a thousand years old, or more."

"That would make it even older than the well at the Temple of the Sisters."

"Both are close to the Cenotaph. I wonder if it feeds their longevity?"

"I think it does. I think it's the engine beneath the Kalang as well."

There were interesting kobolds alive in the mound, but the four we needed all came from the drawers of a vast kobold cabinet. We wakened them and reset their codes. Then we put them together and immediately they formed a smooth, interlocked sphere.

Yaphet studied it, turning it over and over in his hands. "This is awkward." He frowned at the kobold circle "Doesn't this seem like a cumbersome procedure to you?"

"So long as it works."

"But what are kobolds, really?"

"Yaphet, please," I said, in no mood for his musings.

"But they're mechanics, seeded by the silver. Tools."

"Yes, of course they are. They are a knowledge stolen by Fiaccomo from the mind of the goddess."

Yaphet smiled. "They are tools we use to create the things we need—but why do we need tools? Why can't we create these things directly from the silver? It should be possible, if only we knew how."

I felt the hair rise on the back of my neck, for wasn't that the definition I had given to Kaphiri for a god? "Do you know how?"

"No, of course not. Not yet. But it's something I wanted to talk to you about. You use the *ha* to manipulate the silver, or anyway to push it away."

"Even if I could call it, that is not the same as creation. Even Kaphiri cannot do that, and he's had centuries to experiment."

"But before the *ha* was awake in you, you could not push the silver. It wouldn't matter how many experiments you ran, or how much you tried, it couldn't be done. It would be like trying to speak when you had no voice. So what if there is another level of the *ha*? What if this level you've found is only the level of an apprentice or an adolescent? What if there is another level that can be awakened too?"

It frightened me to think of it. I did not want to know more. I knew too much already. "Would you want it?" I asked him. "If such a door opened, would you step through it? Even if it took you to another world?"

He looked away. He looked guilty. "I would still want to be with you."

"You would go." The comforting scent of kobolds was heavy in the air, and I was remembering how sweet life had been when I was a child, in the years before Jolly was taken. "I'm afraid all the time . . . but you're not. You're like Fiaccomo, in that. If the silver swept over you, you'd embrace it. You'd make love with the goddess, and bring some great gift back to the world. I never used to believe the old stories, but I do now. I wonder if you were Fiaccomo, in another life?"

Yaphet blushed. Even past his dark skin, I saw his color rise. "No. I know that's not true. It wasn't me."

"It could be true," I insisted.

"I don't want to guess at things like that."

"Kaphiri doesn't guess. He remembers his past. Yaphet, if we could do that . . . We are older than he is. Our memories would go back farther. Maybe, back to the beginning of the world, to the days when we knew how to use the silver."

Yaphet looked suddenly guilty. "He told me how to do it. He was happy to share all the details of it . . . how to make the kobold circle, and what it felt like to have the past fall open."

I was stunned. "And you have not tried it? Why not?"

"It nearly killed him, to remember that much. His mind was overwhelmed. Months passed, and he couldn't think straight, and finally he stumbled into the silver and that helped him sort it out. He keeps his memories there now. Only some of it stays with him when he's outside."

"And we cannot go into the silver."

Yaphet nodded agreement. "And still I might take the chance . . . except you're right. We are older than Kaphiri. Far older. You talked to that ancient savant. Her one life was so very long. If you remembered what she remembers, would you have room for anything else? And among all that knowledge, would you be able to find the one fact you're looking for?"

I smiled a fuzzy smile. "You make it sound like it would be easier to just ask her how to reach the next level of the *ha*."

"Ask her?" A fierce scowl darkened his brow. "Actually, I hadn't thought of that."

So we ran to the room of savants, taking the kobold circle with us, for we had no way of knowing how much time might pass before the new kobold emerged. But the ancient savant would not waken. Yaphet examined it, but all he could say was that its power system must have failed. "The shock of powering-up after so many millennia. It's amazing it worked at all."

I held the lifeless glass shell, furious at the thought of the knowledge it contained, locked away forever.

"Okay," Yaphet said. "So we'll have to remember it some other way."

But a sense of urgency had come over me. "What time is it? Has the dawn come yet?"

"Long since."

"Then where is Kaphiri?"

We went to the kitchen. Mari was there, but she said he had not come back.

"I thought he would return at dawn."

She shrugged. "Sometimes he is gone for days."

"It is always night somewhere in the world," Yaphet said, and his face was grim.

It made me shudder, to think of Kaphiri following the night around the ring of the world. I had thought his rampage would end at dawn . . . but what was there to stop him now except exhaustion?

I looked at Yaphet. "We need his talents. We must make him come back."

"How can we?"

"I'll call him. When the silver rises tonight . . . I'll seek him. I've felt him through the silver before."

So we waited out the day. I slept for part of it. Yaphet did not sleep; he said he could not. There was an energy burning in him, and he spent all that day at study in the library, but he did not learn how to awaken his *ha*. Near dusk we ate a quiet meal in the kitchen, with the kobold circle on the table before us. "Do you still plan to call him?" Mari asked, standing in what I had come to think of as her place, beside the stove.

"Yes, as soon as the silver has risen. We're going to leave after that. So I want to thank you for your kindness . . ."

She shrugged. "If you come back, I'll be here."

"We won't be coming back."

"So sure, are you?"

"Yes."

I felt the weight of the book, *Known Kobold Circles*, in my pocket. Almost as heavy as the weight of my conscience. I reached for the book. Yaphet caught my hand, and we traded a look. "She should know," I said softly. He could not meet my gaze. So I pulled out the book and showed it to her. "Nuanez gave this to me because I could read it."

Her face went slack. With a trembling hand, she pulled out a chair. Then she collapsed into it, steadying herself with a palm against the table. *"Nuanez?"* she whispered. "How is it you know that name?"

"I stayed in his house. I spoke with him. He's still waiting for you, Mari, in the forest of the Kalang. He's still there, waiting for you to come back."

I went on to tell her all I could remember. She listened, asking no questions, her face locked in frozen grief. When I was done, she sat in silence for several minutes. Then she excused herself, saying she had chores to do.

"I wonder if that was a mistake?" Yaphet asked when she was gone.

I wondered too, but Nuanez had been waiting so very long. "Maybe she'll return now?"

I hoped she would.

I reached for the kobold circle, picking it up yet again to examine it. Many hours had passed since it was formed. I had looked at it a hundred times without discovering any hint of change, but now dark lines appeared between the joined kobolds. I cried out in excitement, and over the next hour Yaphet and I watched as the kobolds were pushed apart by some force within the sphere. Lifelessly they fell aside, and at last a new kobold crawled with slow determination from the ruins of the sphere. I stared at it and felt cold, for it was the same kobold I had seen in my vision: a large, glossy, silver specimen, with a carapace like a lozenge, and six strong legs, but no head, no eyes.

Yaphet picked it up.

"Don't crush it!" I warned.

"I won't."

"Its vapors are the harmful thing."

"I know."

He had a case for it in his pocket, and he put it in that. Then he handed it to me. "We should go tonight," he said, "whether Kaphiri returns or not."

I slipped the case into the pocket of my field jacket. It was our plan to use the flying machine, to get as close to the Cenotaph as we could. We hoped to land near its rim. Then we would walk down into the pit, and perhaps it would take us only a day or two to reach the bottom . . . but Yaphet had not found his *ha*. "We need him," I whispered. "I cannot fend off the silver by myself."

"Every night, thousands more die."

"I know."

"Last night—"

"I know! I know it. Please don't say it."

"I'm sorry."

"We'll go. But let me call him first. Let me try."

We found a cloth bag in one of the cabinets, and I filled it with bread and cheese and rations. Yaphet took several plastic bottles from another shelf and filled them with water from the tap. Then we went outside.

Chapter

34

Night had come to the mountains, though it was not full darkness yet. The sky still had some blue in it, and only the brightest stars showed. From the direction of the forest we heard the plaintive call of a night bird, but within the courtyard all was still. Not a breath of wind stirred, and I did not see even a single mechanic as we crossed the tiles. Moki trotted ahead of us, his ears pricked and alert, but he did not seem worried. We climbed the stairs to the top of the wall, and every breath that we drew was laden with the sweet scent of temple kobolds.

We paused to look down into the canyon. A river of silver ran through it. It was still far below the wall, but I could feel it, streaming past the lines of my awareness. I closed my eyes. The silver was in me. It was in all of us, but in me it was awake. The *ha* was a new sense, one that reached beyond taste and touch, beyond sight and scent and hearing. This new sense reached out into the night, riding on thin lines of detection, and almost immediately I felt him. It was just as Kaphiri had said, that night when he came to us. The *ha* of one's lover makes an unmistakable signal. I clutched Yaphet's hands. "He is far away."

"Call him."

He was not truly my lover, but I called him anyway. My desire made a tremor in the silver, a wordless wanting. I felt him startle. I felt his anger run back to me, following on the same lines of connection, his cold resistance.

"Look," Yaphet said.

Our joined hands sparkled with the *ha*. It ran up his arms, and mine.

"I can feel you," he whispered. "I can feel the flowing of the silver."

"Is it awake in you?"

"I don't know . . . but I can feel him too."

"And he feels you . . . but he's not coming. Yaphet, he's not coming . . . is he?" The connection I felt with Kaphiri was so strong it hardly seemed possible that he could refuse . . . and then he was gone, vanished from my awareness.

"He has gone into the daylight," Yaphet said.

"He won't come back."

I felt stunned, and frightened, and for a long time I stood there, just holding his hands. When we finally let go I thought I would see the *ha* dissolve from his hands, but it stayed with him. It sparkled in his hair. He held his hands up, gazing at them in wonder.

"Maybe we don't need him?" I asked.

Yaphet shook his head. "I think we do . . . but we can't wait."

So we prepared the flying machine, first unfolding the wings and stretching the canvas tight across the frame, then dividing our supplies between the flying machine's two cargo baskets. In the canyon, the silver was rising, climbing swiftly nearer the temple wall. I could feel the lines of its structure, vibrating with information, but the structure I saw with my eyes and the structure I felt were not the same thing. The second was vaster, reaching far beyond my sight. I searched for Kaphiri within those lines, but he had hidden himself away.

I turned my back on the canyon. Yaphet was busy checking the wings. I still did not see any mechanics, either in the courtyard or on the walls, and that seemed strange to me. I was about to say something about it when Moki growled.

I looked up. Moki stood at the tail of the flying machine, gazing back along the length of the wall, toward the stairway we had ascended, and the hair on his back was raised, and his teeth were bared.

Silver lit up the canyon, but in the courtyard the temple walls cast black shadows. I stepped forward, straining to see what Moki saw. It could not be Kaphiri. He was still far away. "Is it a mechanic, boy?"

A black shadow slipped from the blackness on the stairway. Another followed close behind it, and another, and another still. They were humanlike, but hunched over, like awkward animals scampering on all-fours. At the same time, they weren't human at all. They were too tiny by half, with hairless heads and huge eyes that gleamed and flashed in the starlight. They whispered to one another:

La-zur-i. La-zur-i. La-zur-i. La-zur-i.

Like the hissing of snakes.

There had been no mechanics in the courtyard or on the walls. I understood then that there would be no mechanics in the meadow either. Kaphiri must have somehow ordered them in, opening the way for the bogy army to carry out their vendetta— against Yaphet. "Yaphet, *run!*"

More stooped figures joined the first four. One raised a thing like a stick to its lips. I turned to flee, and a dart smacked my shoulder. Its tip stuck in the fabric of my field jacket, but did not pierce it. Another dart whistled past my ear. "Yaphet!"

He dropped to the ground, and the tiny missile passed over his shoulder. In an instant, he was on his feet again. "The flying machine!"

"Leave it! They want to kill you. Run. Run!"

He grabbed the dart that had stuck in my jacket, and he hurled it back at them. "Go back!" he shouted. "Back into the silver!" But they did not heed him. Already they were swarming past the tail of the flying machine.

Moki had given up his defense. He darted past us. "Come on," I yelled, and this time Yaphet gave in. He grabbed my hand and we ran together along the wall.

Where was the next stairway? I knew there was one by the temple gate, but that was on the other side of the complex. Had there been another in between? We had to get off the wall. We had to get back into the temple. The mechanics would surely be there, hidden away in some chamber. If we released them, the bogies would be driven back.

"Jubilee, wait!" Yaphet grabbed my hand and we stopped together, staring ahead at Jolly's monument. It blocked our escape: a tentacle of blue glass reaching from the top of the wall, down into the courtyard. In the canyon, the silver had not yet risen high enough to touch the base of the temple wall, but the folly had made its own silver. Fine veins of it flowed over the monument, a nerve plexus of tiny streams, joining, parting, glistening, collecting in a slowly growing pool of silver on the courtyard's tiled floor.

If we tried to climb over it, we would surely be consumed.

The bogies were a stone's throw behind us, and the walls were too sheer to climb.

"Mari!" I screamed, desperately hoping she would hear me. "Release the mechanics! Release them now!" But there was no response from the temple. Not even a light.

I did not see a way out for us. But Yaphet still harbored a hope. "Call the silver," he said.

"I do not know how."

"Call it."

I looked again at the onrushing shapes of the bogies. One of them paused, to raise a tube to its mouth. I lifted my hand, and the *ha* sparkled brightly between my fingers. The silver in the canyon brightened. I felt its proximity, and the lines of influence reaching from it to my beckoning hand, seeking a connection . . .

A tendril of silver shot up from the canyon, hurtling straight toward us. I cried out, stumbling backward, but Yaphet stayed rooted in place. He raised his own glittering hand, and he warded the tendril away. It went swirling around us, and as it passed, it slowed and it expanded, billowing into a wall of luminous fog that divided us from the bogies, hiding them from our sight.

MEMORY

We were left standing in a ring of silver. Its diameter was wider than the wall, so we could see down into the courtyard, and the canyon, and to my relief there were no bogies on either side. I turned to Yaphet, throwing my arms around him and kissing him—"You did it! You did it!"—while Moki danced at our feet.

Then a bogy scuttled out of the silver. I saw it from the corner of my eye and fell back. It raised a tube to its lips. *Phwat!* A wasp buzzed, and Yaphet's whole body snapped backward. His hands rose spasmodically, to tear at a black dart dangling from his throat. Then he plunged over the wall, into the courtyard.

"Yaphet!" I dropped to my belly, in time to hear the sickening *thunk* of his impact against the tiles. Clinging to the edge, I looked down, to see him forty feet below me, his crumpled form illuminated by the glow of the silver that pooled at the foot of Jolly's monument. I wanted to go to him, but the wall was too sheer to climb, and I could not bring myself to jump. A mob of bogies appeared out of the shadows by the temple. They swarmed over Yaphet, ignoring my screams of rage. They were like ants, swarming over a choice morsel. I could not even see his body. Then, as if they had become one creature, of one mind, they moved toward the pool of silver. One of them touched it, and the silver flowed over all of them, billowing madly up the wall so that I had to ward it off to keep from being consumed.

Some part of me died with Yaphet. We'd shared lifetimes together, and I knew I must have lost him before, but not like this. He had been taken away by phantoms from out of the silver, and only the god or the goddess could have sent them.

In my heart I was sure it had been the god. He was a brooding remnant within the Cenotaph, still at war with the goddess who had brought life to the world. He must have taken Yaphet, believing him to be Kaphiri—for only Kaphiri could turn back the flood of silver that would soon drown all the world. When the final flood came, life would be erased from the world, and the dark god would finally have his victory.

Except the god had been mistaken. Kaphiri still existed.

A coldness settled in my heart, and I whispered a vow of vengeance against the builder of the world.

Moki whined and waggled. The silver that surrounded us could not stand against the vapors of the temple kobolds. It was swiftly steaming into nothingness, so it was no trick for me to push the remnants away.

No bogies remained on the wall, or in the courtyard, or anywhere in sight. With Moki at my heels I walked past the flying machine. It was still poised, ready for its journey to the Cenotaph. I made sure it was anchored, so no stray wind could blow it away. Then I made my way down the dark stairway to the temple, where I found Mari, standing in the doorway, her hands kneading at the fabric of her skirt. "I heard your cries," she said.

"Yaphet is dead."

"I know."

"Where are the mechanics?"

She would not meet my gaze. "I thought he would come back this night," she whispered.

Her words stirred a terrible suspicion. "What are you saying?"

"I thought he would come back this night," she repeated, her voice faint, and hollow.

"Did *you* remove the mechanics?"

A violent shaking seized her hands. She turned away, withdrawing into the shadows of the great room.

"You arranged it so he would die," I whispered.

"He told me Nuanez was dead! Long dead."

"But it's Yaphet who's been murdered!"

"I thought he would come back this night!"

"He will," I said softly as a scheme took shape in my mind, a structure for my vengeance. "I will force him back."

In the pocket of my field jacket I still carried the book *Known Kobold Circles*. I took it with me to the well room. Consulting its pages, I collected the same kinds of kobolds Jolly and I had gathered at Azure Mesa, and within an hour I had a kobold sphere. I put it into the pocket of my field jacket. Then I went to the kitchen, and took a knife from a drawer. In a closet I found a spool of thin rope, and I cut a section of that and took it with me to the court-yard. I set the sphere down on the tiles, at a point equally spaced between the temple and the wall. Then I sat back to wait, with Moki nestled at my side.

The night was quiet. No wind blew, nor did I hear any night birds. Overhead the Bow of Heaven gleamed faintly, while the sil-ver cast up its luminous glow from beyond the walls. I remembered the statues we had seen in the sandy desert washes at the eastern foot of the Kalang, stony warriors waiting in silent ambush, and I felt a kinship with them, for a great patience had come over me.

Near midnight the sphere began to steam with a mist of silver, faint at first, but swiftly growing. I picked up Moki and stepped back a pace, but I did not try to flee.

I had translated the name of this kobold circle as *'The mirror of the other self,'* but it was more a portal than a mirror, and it had almost brought Kaphiri to me once before.

I watched the silver rise in trembling threads that fused into a panel. Its texture teased my eyes, suggesting an endless depth, as if I looked across time as well as space; but if there was structure there, I could not see it. To my eyes it was only a vastness of possibility.

I should have been afraid, but my anger would not let any such benign emotion surface.

"My love," I whispered, searching the silver panel for some shadow, some trembling of his presence. Even if he had withdrawn himself from the silver, the silver still existed inside him, just as it existed inside all of us. He could not escape my whispering voice. *"My love, come home."*

In only a few minutes I found him. He appeared first as a dis-tant smudge that grew quickly larger, until I could distinguish his dark garb, and his confused gaze as he turned to look over his shoulder.

He was not alone.

He had his hand in a raptor-grip on the shoulder of a smaller figure beside him, a wriggling figure that slipped free even as I watched, eluding Kaphiri's clutching hand, to vanish into mist. "Jolly!"

I screamed his name, but he did not hear me. He was already gone. Safe into the silver, I hoped, but at the same time I reeled under another dark blow of despair, for Jolly had been with Liam and Udondi—and what hope could remain for them, if Kaphiri had come upon them in the desert?

Kaphiri heard me cry out. If he had been unsure of my identity, he knew it now. He turned toward me, and taking one long stride, he stepped through the panel and into the courtyard, almost before I was ready to meet him.

Almost.

I had made a loop at the end of my rope. As he stepped through, I charged him, and thrust the rope over his head and pulled it tight. He smelled of sweat and smoke.

Without air he panicked. His hands went to his throat; then he tried to pummel me, but I had slipped behind him. I pulled the rope tighter still, and he went to his knees. I was shifting my grip to finish the job when a small hand touched mine. "Jubilee! Please don't kill him! Please don't!"

I looked up, stunned to find Jolly beside me. "You found your way here." My grip eased, and Kaphiri drew in a whistling breath.

Jolly nodded. The *ha* glittered brightly around his hands, his face, and in his hair. "I learned how to do it. Now please, let him live."

My anger flooded back. "Why should I? Hasn't he killed Liam too? And Udondi?"

"No! They're alive. Kaphiri didn't find us. It was me. Liam wanted me to stay at the Temple of the Sisters, but I couldn't. I went into the silver, looking for him. Liam is alive. He's coming south to find you. Jubilee, please. Let him live."

I could not deny my brother. My grip eased, and Kaphiri coughed and fell forward onto the tiles. "Yaphet is dead," I said.

Jolly blinked hard, and coughed himself.

I nudged Kaphiri with the toe of my boot. "And this one swears that Temple Huacho is gone from Kavasphir."

"I'm sorry," Jolly whispered.

"I am sorry too. But I am going to end it, Jolly. I am going to make sure I never face this choice again."

He looked at me in confusion, and dread. "What do you mean? You were going to kill him . . . Jubilee, you aren't going to let the flood come, are you?"

I felt incredulous at his question. "You ask me that? I am not him. And anyway, Kaphiri is only partly to blame for this."

I crouched beside him. Guilt touched me as I listened to his wheezing as he struggled to draw air through his damaged throat, but I pretended I did not feel it. "You said you would call down the destruction of the silver if I asked. So, I am asking."

"No!" Jolly cried. "She doesn't mean it."

Kaphiri raised his head, enough that I could see his eyes. "She means it," he said in a rasping whisper.

"So do it. Destroy the silver." I tightened my grip on his leash. "Or I will do it myself."

"Why?" Jolly said. "Why do you want this?"

"Because he will not accompany me into the Cenotaph, and I cannot fend off the silver that boils from that pit. Not by myself. So let him tear away the veils and I will make my own way into the pit, and I will destroy whatever I find there."

"How?" Kaphiri whispered.

I stared at him, offering no answer.

"But you . . . have . . . a means?"

I nodded.

"Then I'll help you."

"You will go into the pit? Tonight? And you will fend off the silver?"

He nodded. "If it will mean the end of a god, I will do anything."

———

I tried to convince Jolly to stay behind at the temple, but he would not. "If you leave me, I will only follow you through the silver. You are so easy to see, now that your *ha* is awake."

Kaphiri soon recovered enough that he could walk. I kept the leash on him. We crossed the courtyard, and climbed the stairs to the top of the wall.

Jolly had hurried ahead to the flying machine, but he came back. "Look down, Jubilee. There is a fire in the temple."

I looked, to see red flames flickering behind the window nearest the well room. The fire spread with astounding speed, invading the kitchen, and then the great room. The doors flew open, and Mari stumbled out, embers smoking on her skirt. She turned back to look at the building. Then she looked up at us. "Your library will soon be gone!" she shouted. "I won't keep your refuge anymore."

But with the well destroyed, there would be no refuge for her either. "Come with us!" I called after her as she strode off across the courtyard. "We will fend off the silver as long as we can! Mari!"

She did not hear me over the roar of the flames, or she would not.

"Mari, we will take you to Nuanez when this is done!"

She rounded the temple and disappeared. I wanted to go after her, but I had Kaphiri under the rope.

Jolly had no such hindrance. He darted back down the stairs, then sprinted across the courtyard, following Mari's route around the building.

I saw her again on the other side of the temple, hurrying toward the gate. "She has lived too long," Kaphiri said.

I knew he was right. "Jolly!" I screamed. "Come back! Come back now!"

Mari reached the gate. She was an old woman, but she still had her strength. When she pulled on the latch, the tall gate swung open and a tongue of silver reached through. For a moment, Mari stood silhouetted against its luminous glow. Then it swept over her, just as fire roared up through the temple roof.

"Call your brother back," Kaphiri croaked. "The night is growing old."

The flying machine was ready, but neither Jolly nor I could fly it. Only Kaphiri had learned the techniques from Yaphet. He claimed the pilot's platform. I squeezed in beside him, so I could continue to hold his leash. "Aren't you afraid . . . ," he rasped, "of what you might feel . . . ?"

I did not think I would feel anything, but I was wrong. His warmth stirred in me a corrupt desire, but it was not so strong as my hate. "I will strive to bear your proximity," I whispered.

He chuckled. "And I will do the same."

Jolly took Moki with him in one basket. I had already balanced the other with food and water, so Kaphiri brought the engine humming to life.

It should have been Yaphet beside me.

Kaphiri touched the controls and the wings flexed; the engine's hum climbed in pitch.

Yaphet was gone.

I did not look back. Neither did Kaphiri. The banks of tiny propellers whined, and we lurched forward, lifted hesitantly, and then swooped down into the canyon. I cried out, for I thought we were falling. The silver rushed up toward us, and I reached out to ward it away, but before I could form the thought it parted beneath us as if an invisible plow had carved a furrow in its luminous surface. The wing tips skimmed the silver, and gleamed a moment with its light, and then the light fell away, and the river of silver sank below us as it flowed down the canyon to the plain. We soared on at the same altitude, and the wind was loud in my ears, but even so I imagined Yaphet calling, crying my name into the night.

Chapter

35

The mists over the Cenotaph had quieted in the night, and I could not tell with any certainty where it lay, for the silver had risen in a uniform fog, obscuring all the plain. I was studying its misty surface, searching for some sign of the pit, when we chanced to pass close to a small circle of open ground. I had only a glimpse before the clearing fell behind us, but that was enough to make out stones and sand, looming gray in the silver's glow, and against them darker shapes that I could not identify with any certainty. I clutched Kaphiri's shoulder and pointed back. "What was that? Was that a kobold well?"

He arched his neck to look, but we had already gone too far. So he put the flying machine into a steep bank, and we turned back, descending at the same time.

On this pass we flew directly over the open ground. It was a kobold well—the largest I had ever seen. The black circle of its mouth was twice the wingspan of our flying machine, and around it was a ring of soil at least twenty feet high. Three players stood on the inside slope of the soil ring, their faces turned up toward us. Their bikes waited a few steps away, and there were sleeping bags on the ground.

Kaphiri started to take the flying machine down. "No," I said. "We will fly on."

"Players do not come this far south! I will know who they are!"

"I know already."

Those upturned faces had belonged to Liam and Udondi and Ficer, but I would not risk a reunion. I trusted neither Liam's temper, nor Kaphiri's tolerance. "Fly on," I insisted. "Whatever they have come for, it cannot matter now."

Kaphiri relented. He guided the flying machine up, and away to the north.

Liam's voice called after us, carrying eerily in the still night. *"Jubilee, we will follow when we can."*

Kaphiri glanced at me, a grim smile on his face. He knew now who these wayfarers were. "His chance will come only if we succeed." This seemed to please him, though whether by the anticipation of our success, or our failure, I could not say.

The sameness of the silver confused my mind, but Kaphiri seemed to see through it. He pointed out the pit to me, and laughed when I could not see it. Then he turned the plane and began a tight spiral that took us quickly closer to the mist. When the silver lay just beneath the belly of the plane he warded it off. We continued to descend, turning round and round, while the silver rose above us, and then closed over our heads.

We still flew in a tight spiral. I knew this because the wind of our passage roared past my face, and the wings flexed and dipped. But with the sameness of the silver all around it felt as if we had been caught and suspended in a place of endless luminosity.

Then a wall of darkness emerged from out of the homogeneous glow: a steep, crumbled slope of transformed stone.

Kaphiri hissed. He leaned on the guidance stick and the plane rocked to one side. I looked down the length of the wing to see Jolly's terrified face below me. Then the other wing clipped the wall. The canvas tore, and the struts collapsed.

The plane dropped. I closed my eyes. I could not help it, but at the same time I pushed at the silver beneath us. There was an impact. The air was knocked from my lungs, my teeth snapped together, and every part of my body felt as if it had been torn from its proper placement. There was a terrible scraping sound and a sense of motion. I heard Jolly cry out, but all I could do was hold on and *push* as hard as I could against the silver that crowded my awareness.

I did not lose consciousness, for I was always conscious of the close press of the silver. I was aware too of Moki's menacing growls, but only when his growling turned into a high-pitched yelping attack did I open my eyes.

Kaphiri stood over me. He had removed the leash from his own neck and was attempting to place it over mine, but little Moki had already savaged his hand.

I reared back, kicking out at him at the same time, but my reflexes were slow, and he dodged easily. I seized stone from the jumbled slope and flung it after him. It was a keen throw, but too late, for Kaphiri stepped into the silver, and was gone.

"Jolly?"

I turned to look for him, and was stunned to see the remnants of the plane. It lay all around me like a smashed skeleton. The pilot's platform had broken in half, separating from the engine, which lay downslope, only inches from the wall of silver. The crumpled wings were draped across a chaotic slope of stones and dust and layered ground that reminded me of the eastern slope of the Kalang. "Jolly!" I called again. Moki had been with him, and Moki had survived the crash, so Jolly had to be somewhere close by. "Jolly!"

This time I heard a muffled answer. *"I'm here! Over here! Help me get out."*

I followed his voice and found a narrow crevice splitting the slope. A slow-running flow of silver seeped through it, shimmering two meters down. Jolly straddled the flow, his feet and hands propped against the crumbling wall.

"Help me," he said when he saw me peering down.

I gave him my hand. That was all the help he needed to scramble out and onto the slope beside me. We collapsed together, spending a minute just looking at each other. His face was bruised, but I saw no blood, and he would admit to no broken bones. Moki crawled between us.

"We've done well, don't you think?" Jolly said, and I couldn't help but laugh.

We were in a chamber of silver, on an unstable slope that fell away to the abode of a wicked god, and my head hurt, and I was thirsty. "At least it's not dark."

"Are you holding the silver off?"

I nodded. "It's certainly not *him*. But I can feel him out there. I can feel his *ha*. He's not far away."

Jolly raised his dusty hands. The *ha* sparkled brightly between his fingers. "I think I can hold off the silver too. We should be all right, so long as one of us is awake."

"Do you know how far it is to the bottom?"

He shook his head. "A long way, I think." Then he added, in a frightened whisper, *"I'm scared."*

I glanced upslope, but after a few feet, the only thing to be seen was silver. "We could try going back."

"Back to what? The silver is rising. There's no way out."

"There is for you—"

"No."

"Jolly, you could make your way back to Liam—"

"No! I'm scared, but I'm not leaving you. I'm not. We came for a reason, and there's no going back. Not even for me. Jubilee, if the final flood comes, it will only be me and him alive in the whole world. That's what I'm scared of, more than anything. So we have to go on. There's no choice, and no other way out."

So we scavenged the wreckage, and after a few minutes we found some water bottles and the bag of food I had packed. Sharing the weight of these things we set off downslope, trading off between us the task of pushing the silver away.

At first the air was very cold. My breath condensed in little gray clouds. I had never seen that before. Neither had Jolly. We played with it for a while.

It was hard walking. The slope was steep and covered with loose stones that rolled away under the pressure of a foot. We both fell down several times. I was afraid one of us would twist an ankle or break a leg, and then what would we do?

I didn't want to think about it.

So we pushed the silver away ahead of us, and let it close in behind, and after a while we came to a precipice. It was a cliff of hard white stone, full of tiny air bubbles. I'd never seen anything like it. It felt as slippery as soap, and when I scuffed at it with my heel, it crumbled.

I stood on its edge, pushing with all my will against the silver, for I wanted to know if the drop was ten feet or two hundred. The silver rolled back, and I saw that it was more than ten feet down. It was at least twenty, and maybe a lot farther. Remembering the southern escarpment of the Kalang, I felt a little queasy. I stepped back from the edge.

"Let's follow the cliff," Jolly said. "Sooner or later we'll find a way down."

On the cliff's edge, the walking was easy. Maybe the escarpment had pushed its way into existence only recently. It seemed that way, for its lip was bare of the loose stones that covered the slope above. We followed it for a long time. As we walked, I kept glancing over my shoulder, partly because I knew Kaphiri was somewhere close by. His presence burned within the net of awareness that is part of the *ha*. I knew he could sense me in the same way, and I feared he would emerge from the silver while our attention was turned away—though exactly what his intentions might be, I didn't know. He wanted the death of the dark god, but I suspected he wanted my death too.

Another part of my edginess was due to the voices that began to whisper to me. For a long time I wasn't sure they were real. They sounded distant, like someone calling, who is almost too far away to hear. I couldn't make out any of their words, but I heard them speaking in the turning of a stone under my foot, or in the wash of my breath, or the ticking of Moki's nails.

I started remembering things too. Flashes would come to me, perfectly clear recollections. I was feeling bored, watching a baby play. I was driving a truck. I was reading a manuscript, or tending a kobold well. Perfectly ordinary recollections, except they weren't mine. They did not even belong to some version of me in another life. I was seeing into the lives of other players, and that seemed wrong somehow, though I could not stop it.

I wished they would all shut up and leave me alone.

I described the effect to Jolly, and he looked at me in evident relief. "It's happening to you too? Thank goodness! I thought I was losing my mind."

"It's like we're breathing in memories." I stopped and shrugged out of my jacket. "I was cold when we started, but it's gotten hot."

It got hotter still. Heat soaked through the soles of my boots. I started to get scared about it. Then it was cold again. Just like that. Like stepping through a door. But when I walked back a few paces, it was still cold. The heat was gone, and it was cold that stung my hand when I touched the rocks.

"Have you noticed there are no follies here?" Jolly asked.

I looked around, and realized it was true. There were no follies like those we were accustomed to seeing. "I wonder if the voices are follies, and the memories?" Flashes of substance from out of the chaos, unmade as soon as they were formed, except where we passed. In our bubble of stillness we held them for a while in our senses.

It was hot again when Jolly finally found a break in the cliff face. It looked like part of the white rock had dropped away in an avalanche, leaving a cleft at the top. I guessed there would be a skirt of debris below, but we couldn't see it.

"It looks rough," I said.

"So maybe if we keep going, we'll find a paved road to take us down?"

"Well it's not impossible."

He grinned. "You realize, if we were stronger, we could *will* a road into existence."

"Or another flying machine."

"Or our father."

Or Mama. Or Yaphet. "We'd be gods, if we could do that."

We made our way down the cleft. The stone walls played strangely with my vision. From the corner of my eye I would see the outline of a window, or the shape of a watching player, but when I turned to look, there would be only white stone. I might have passed it off as an illusion, but Moki was nervous. He would stop and growl at nothing. Then dart ahead and growl again.

We had been walking several minutes when I slipped on a rock. I caught my balance with a hand against the white stone. In the moment I touched the rock, a burnt black hand reached out of it to grab my arm. I yelped, and flailed wildly, while Moki launched into a storm of barking. The arm dissolved like a soap bubble.

"What was that?" Jolly demanded, and his eyes were wider than I'd ever seen them.

"A bogy, I think."

They were hideous and they haunted the walls. As we descended they appeared every few minutes: a fire-blackened hand reaching for us, or a burnt face pressing out of the rock. The faces spoke, asking always the same questions: *Will you stop him? Will you? Can you?* They were the fevered whisperings of our wounded goddess, but they were not her, so we made no answer, but hurried on, and when the cleft ended and we found ourselves on the apron of debris left by the avalanche, we felt relief, for the bogy-haunted walls were behind us.

We had no way to measure time. We were deep within the Cenotaph and neither the sun's light nor the light of the stars could reach us. In the pit the illumination was always the same: a beautiful silver glow that turned Jolly's face gray and made Moki's coat look whitened with age.

All I knew was that we had been walking for many hours. We both started to stumble, but neither of us called for a rest until Jolly almost slipped over another precipice. Even then he did not want to stop, but I insisted he lie down for a time and close his eyes. Moki curled up beside him, and they both fell quickly asleep. I walked circles around them to keep myself awake.

When that grew dull I opened my senses, deliberately seeking Kaphiri's presence. He seemed far away. My heart went cold as I imagined the wickedness he was doing: summoning the silver into enclaves, or trapping wayfarers on the road. I tried to summon him back. He heard my desire, and for a while he seemed to heed me. His presence grew stronger. But he did not come to me, and soon exhaustion led me to give up the duel.

Jolly woke, and we walked on for several hours more. Then it was my turn to lie down and sleep. I closed my eyes, but sleep didn't come. I longed for sunlight, the more because I did not believe I would ever see it again. I consoled myself with memories of sunlit days, and blue skies, and green meadows.

When I stood up again, I was suddenly conscious of every bruise and trauma I had received since the fall of the flying machine. "Remind me not to seek my ease again," I said to Jolly through gritted teeth. We shared out most of our food, and drank half the remaining water. Then we set out again.

Eventually, we found the bottom of the Cenotaph. We knew it immediately. All the tumbled stones and dust of the slopes stopped at a hard boundary, and the ground became level and smooth. Its color was white, even in the sheen of the surrounding silver. Even so, it did not seem to be entirely *present*. At least, I could not quite focus my eyes on it. It was as if the surface was constantly shifting up and down by tiny fractions of an inch . . . or as if it was saturated with silver slowly boiling on a microscopic scale, forever bubbling in mindless acts of minute creation. When I stepped out on it, I half expected a column of silver to erupt around me.

That didn't happen, but the ground felt springy, bubbly, and sometimes we would sink in it to our ankles, and sometimes we would seem to be walking just above any visible surface.

After a few steps the silver closed in behind us, and we could no longer see the slope we had just descended. There was only the silver, and the uncertain ground. We walked, but with nothing to measure our progress, we did not seem to be going anywhere. Or more accurately, it felt as if there was nowhere to go, that all places were one place, and the world was empty, save for us.

After we had been walking for some time, Jolly came to a stop, and I beside him. The silence in that place was extraordinary. It rang in my ears. "How can we know what direction to go?" Jolly asked softly.

"I don't know." I kept my voice low too; it seemed necessary in that place. "We could be walking round in circles and not know it . . . but I had thought to find the center. Kaphiri said this pit was made when the dark god was hurled from the sky and struck the world . . ."

"And that would put him at the center . . . ?"

"It's only a guess. But we know he is here somewhere, for the world has never been able to repair itself. The dark god has kept it from healing."

So we walked on some more, but after a few minutes Jolly stopped again. "I can sense a presence." This time his voice was no more than a whisper.

I answered in kind. "Kaphiri?"

"No." He stared off into the silver.

I followed his gaze, and not just with my sight. Kaphiri burned in my awareness as a dread beacon, but as I looked, I too discerned the essence of another within the silver, faint, elusive, yet somehow familiar, a memory, perhaps, of another life. "Is it the god?"

Jolly shook his head. "No. It's not him. It's *her*. The goddess. She's here, Jubilee."

Memories are elusive. We might struggle to recall a song or the name of a player, but come up with nothing until someone sings a teasing note, or utters the first syllable of the forgotten name. Then recognition floods in. When Jolly named the goddess, I knew it was so: the presence I sensed was her.

"Has she come to help us?" I whispered.

"How can she? She is wounded."

"Where is the god?"

"I don't know."

"He should be here."

"I can't sense him. Can you?"

I shook my head. "But he must be here. She said he would be here." The goddess had sent us into the Cenotaph to find him. She was our ally. I took Jolly's hand. "Perhaps she has come to show us the way. We will find her first. Then we'll find him."

So we gave up trying to guess at the direction of the center, and we followed her presence instead.

Sometimes I could hardly sense her. Other times she seemed to be all around us, existing at once in every direction. "Are you there?" I cried out in frustration. "Are you here? Where are you?" Her gravity pulled me in circles, and only when Jolly grabbed my hand and steered me in a straight path would I remember to walk on.

We walked and walked, and I began to think we would walk forever through that flat, featureless terrain. At the same time I worried the goddess was a being of mist only, so that even as we sought her, we pushed her away when we pushed at the silver.

Then at last we came upon the edge of a folly.

The silver rolled back, revealing a complex landscape, like a miniature city, though the tallest towers were only knee-high. There were no windows or doors in the "buildings," at least none that I could see, for each of them was encrusted in a sheath of some colorful growth, lumpy and uneven like the mold that will grow on bread, but in strident colors of bright green and pink, red, yellow and electric blue. I decided they were more like blocks, or oddly shaped boxes, than buildings.

They stood in clusters, some arranged in perfect squares, but most of them irregularly shaped, with narrow aisles of smooth white ground wedged between each group.

We stopped on the folly's edge. "My lady," Jolly called, "are you here?"

There was no answer.

I stepped forward, and tentatively, I touched a nodule on one of the mold-encrusted blocks. It looked like a solid thing, some kind of organic mineral, but that was illusion. At the first pressure of my finger the nodule burst with a tiny *pop!* I had heard that sound before. I yanked my hand away as a spurt of glowing silver slurry shot straight up into the air. Only a tiny droplet touched my finger, but that burned with a fury, and I turned away, my hand pressed against my belly and tears starting in my eyes.

Kaphiri felt it too. All this time he had been a distant presence in my awareness, gnawing on my consciousness like the pain of some deep wound that I could not reach, or comfort.

Suddenly he was aware of me. I felt his sharp surprise, his panic, as he turned away from whatever wicked deed had occupied him.

Jolly threw his arms around me, crying out in a high, frightened voice, "Jubilee, are you all right? Are you all right?"

"I will be." The pain was easing. I looked at my fingertip, and it was livid red. "Do you remember when we climbed down the kobold well, and I broke into the vein of liquid silver?"

"This is the same thing?"

I nodded. "We must walk very carefully now. Do not touch the blocks, for they will burst at the lightest pressure."

He nodded nervously.

"And, Jolly, Kaphiri is coming back. He knows we are close to the goddess now."

I went first through the aisles, and Jolly followed behind me. The goddess was everywhere in my awareness and I could not tell which way would bring me closer to her center, so I just followed the easiest path. A sense of haste was upon me. Kaphiri was drawing swiftly nearer, and I wanted to find the goddess before he could come. So our cautious walk soon gave way to a hurried jog, and then to a scuttling run, but that was the limit of our speed. We could not push the silver away any faster than that.

The blocks grew higher as we advanced, until their average was waist-high, with the tallest towers reaching to my chin.

Then suddenly the pressure of the silver vanished. Some will far greater than mine seized the luminous curtain that hung so close around us and flung it back so that we could see for a quarter mile in any direction, even straight up, though silver still made a ceiling far above our heads.

We stood on the edge of an open space, like a white courtyard fronting a great temple . . . or anyway, I wanted to think of the structure that stood there as a temple, though it was like none I had ever seen. Imagine a great sphere that has been half-crushed and split in two, so that only a small remnant of its shell is still intact. That remnant rose in an arch a quarter mile above my head. Within the amphitheater-shell of the arch, layer upon layer of the mold-covered blocks were suspended on laminate shelves curved in the same arc as the shell. Clouds of silver steamed and billowed from the rim, rushing down the back of the shell in a great, glittering flood. We should have drowned in it, but the will that had made this bubble of open space somehow held it off.

A small, blackened figure huddled on the threshold of the temple, its head bowed as it wept over a moldering burden cradled in its lap.

It did not seem possible that such a creature could be alive, for it looked like a burnt corpse, its hair and clothes seared away and its flesh like charcoal, withered and cracked. But it *was* alive, and as we approached, it looked up at us with eyes that were lenses of luminous silver. Its mouth opened, showing a blackened tongue, and the blackened stumps of teeth. "I cannot fix him," it whispered. "I don't remember how."

I looked more closely at the burden it cradled in its lap and I realized that beneath the encrustations of colorful mold it was the body of a man. I fell to my knees as dread blossomed inside me. "Who is he?" I whispered, for the burnt creature held the corpse close and I could not see the dead man's face.

"It is my lover." As if to prove this, the tiny arms eased their desperate hold and the body shifted, rolling slightly, so I could see the face.

Colorful molds blossomed across his cheeks and eyes and within his mouth and nose, but I knew him anyway. I had always known him. "Yaphet."

My chest heaved, and suddenly there did not seem to be enough air left in the world for me to breathe. I could not bear to look upon his face being consumed by the dreadful growths that thrived in that place, so I looked up at the burnt creature instead. "What have you done to him? And *why*?"

"I have killed him. He is dead now, and the war is over."

I knew her then. This burnt creature was the goddess, or some manifestation of her. When she had come to me at Azure Mesa she had seemed beautiful . . . until she reached through the mirror, and then her lovely arm had been transformed into the blackened arm of a burnt corpse.

"Where is the dark god?" I demanded.

"This is him," she insisted, cradling Yaphet's body. "The last fragment. I have murdered him at last—my own lover—and our war is over . . . but why is nothing changed?" She looked at me with her luminous silver eyes, and I felt as if I looked into empty windows.

"Explain it to me!" she demanded. "He is dead, but nothing is changed! I am still wounded. I tear out the flawed parts of myself and rebuild, and rebuild, but I cannot heal! Is there some fragment of him remaining still? Is there an avatar I have not found yet? Is there an avatar that *you* have not found? Why are you here? Why have you come? I sent you to find him! I sent you to remove him from the world!"

I felt Jolly's hand squeeze gently against my shoulder. "She is wounded," he said. "She does not understand."

"Neither do I."

"It is not the dark god who festers in the Cenotaph, Jubilee. It never was him. He is gone. Long gone. It is the goddess who is left here."

I looked up, to the towering shell of her temple. Torrents of silver poured from its shattered rim, rushing forth to flood the world.

"Is that *her*, then?" I whispered, nodding at the shell. "Is that the seat of her mind?" For she was a goddess, and I understood that the blackened corpse huddled before me could not contain the mind of a goddess, that it had to be only a manifestation, an avatar, a concentration of her dreams.

"I think she is some kind of a mechanic," Jolly said. "And this great structure is the last fragment of her mind."

She was listening to our words. Laying Yaphet gently on the ground, she stood, and looked with us at the great arch, and the vast layers of blocky mold that it sheltered. Her anger had passed, and when she spoke her voice was soft once again. "I am wounded. I know it. This war consumes me, and my memories slip away."

She had murdered Yaphet because he was made to look like the dark god. Her mind was so far gone she could not tell the difference. She was broken . . . by the war, or by her fall to the world, I did not know, but clearly there was so little left of her that she could not repair herself, or even comprehend how far she had fallen—and still enough of her mind remained that she must try. The Cenotaph boiled with her efforts, churning out vast clouds of silver: the fever dreams of a goddess flooding the world.

"He is gone," she whispered. "But it won't end. Why won't the war end?"

"Would you have it end?"

She had sent me to the Cenotaph for that purpose, after all. She had commanded me to be her hands, to find the wound in the world, and to remove the fragment of deity that would not let it heal.

I reached into the pocket of my field jacket and felt the hard shape of the kobold case Yaphet had given me, with the deletion kobold inside.

Did the goddess know, on some level, what I had come here to do? Had she planned it? Had some splinter of her crumbling self given me the book *Known Kobold Circles*? Had she deliberately left the memory of this kobold on the surface of Yaphet's mind? I hoped it was so.

"Jolly, I think you should go now."

"No. Not until it's over."

"That could be too late."

"I'll chance it. I'm not running away again, Jubilee. Now go. Do it while you have the chance."

So I turned my back on the burnt avatar, for it was only an interface to the goddess. Her mind was my target, and that existed within the maze of moldering blocks and towers that filled the broken sphere. I opened the kobold case and removed the solitary specimen. Its silver body gleamed, and its strong legs moved against my palm just as they had in my vision. If I were to crush it, its vapors would erase me forever. That was the promise Ki-Faun had made, but I had no intention of erasing myself. The goddess was the target, and only the goddess. I still hoped to be born again into a world that would never suffer the threat of silver flood.

My hand closed over the kobold. Would it be enough to hurl it into the depths of the sphere? Surely the impact would crush it, and then its vapors could do their work . . . but if its shell failed to break, how would I ever find it, to crush it myself?

In the midst of my hesitation, Kaphiri came.

Moki gave first warning with a sharp, frantic bark. Then Jolly shouted, "Jubilee! He is here. He is here. Hurry and release it!"

I turned, to see Kaphiri newly emerged from the silver. Jolly tried to stop him, but he threw my brother to the ground.

I should have hurled the kobold then, but hatred is stronger than reason. It is stronger than good intentions. In that moment I discovered that what I truly wanted was revenge against this man who had been made by a broken goddess, and who had brought so much misery on the world.

So I held on to the kobold and waited for him to come.

He stopped five feet from me. He smelled of smoke, and his fine clothes were stained and torn. His hair had fallen loose and it was gray with ash, but there was wonder in his eyes. "You have found the god." His gaze wandered up, to the high rim of the shell and the torrents of silver that gushed down its sides. "You have walked right to his dark heart. My love, I never thought it was possible . . ."

"The goddess commands that I end the war."

His gaze fixed on me again, and it was hard. "Do you still serve her?"

"Only in this last thing . . . and she has done all she can to aid me."

He looked at the great shell. He looked at me. Doubt showed in his eyes. "To aid you? How? She has not made you a goddess?"

"No, and she never will. We are only players, my love. Accept it."

"Then what aid has she given to you?"

I opened my fist to show him the kobold. I wanted him to know.

He recognized it, and the shock made him stumble back a step. "*No, my love!* Throw it away! You must throw it away now—"

"Oh, I will." I turned, intending to hurl the kobold into the heart of the goddess, but he was faster than I.

He caught my wrist. He unbalanced me, and we both went down. "You will not destroy yourself." He clawed at my fingers, his nails tore gouges of flesh from my hands. "I will not live forever without you! I will not! I will not!"

I tried to throw him off, but he was stronger—or more desperate—than I. Oh, how I regretted my hesitation! Why had I not thrown the kobold while I had the chance?

His knife appeared out of nowhere. It flashed with the speed of a worm mechanic, plunging straight through my wrist. I screamed, and my hand spasmed. The kobold spilled upon the ground. He yanked the knife out of my flesh, and swept up the kobold. Then he was on his feet, glaring down at me. "You will not leave me this way!"

He turned, and aiming at the bank of silver that surrounded us, he cocked his arm, ready to throw the kobold away, just as he'd done in that other life.

But in this life Moki reached him first. Jolly's little hound had a long grudge against Kaphiri. He leaped on him, sinking his strong teeth into the back of Kaphiri's knee, and Kaphiri went down. The kobold burst within his palm. I saw the silver vapors leach out between his fingers. He saw them too, and his eyes went wide. He stood up and hurled the remains of the kobold as far away as he could, but he had been turned around, and the fragments flew into the great shell. The burnt avatar of the goddess wailed. She leaped upon his back, driving him to his knees, but it was far too late to stop the kobold in its work. A brilliant silver fire spilled across Kaphiri's hand. I did not wait to see more. I grabbed Moki and scrambled away, while a horrible scream erupted behind me, and a wailing that I knew must be the avatar.

I did not look back again until I collapsed beside Jolly on the edge of the open ground. Blood was pumping from my wrist, and I could not feel the silver at all. Only Jolly's will kept it from collapsing around us. He put his arms around me, unmindful of the blood—"Come on, Jubilee. Come on"—and we retreated together. A few steps only, and then he had to stop and *lean* against the silver. I used that chance to look back.

They had become a pillar of incandescent fire. Within the shell of the temple many other white fires blazed. They drew the silver to them, as true fire will pull in oxygen. Fat streams of luminous mist raced past us, swirling into the conflagration, and causing it to burn brighter and brighter so I thought I would go blind with its brilliance.

I turned away, and I did not look back again.

The silver streamed past us for only a few minutes. After that all became quiet and calm again. So at least we knew we had not set off the destruction of the silver, though what we had accomplished was less clear. I did not doubt Kaphiri was gone forever, but the goddess was vast, and I wondered if our white fire had consumed only some small part of her?

There was no way to know, and neither one of us had the courage to suggest going back. So we continued our retreat, creeping for hours across the spongy ground, with Moki in between us.

The silver was never more than a few inches away. Jolly struggled to push it off, to hold it back. It yielded to him only with great reluctance, but it did give way.

At one point we stopped, and Jolly made a bandage for my arm, using the fabric of his shirt. I looked in his eyes, and saw his exhaustion, and I knew his thirst must be the equal of mine. But we had no water. We had no food. "Maybe you should sleep," Jolly suggested. "And when you wake up you'll be stronger. You'll be able to help me hold off the silver."

But I was afraid to sleep. I was afraid Jolly would give in to exhaustion too, and then the silver would roll in. Or that I would bleed to death. If I was going to die, I wanted to know it. So we pushed on.

I do not know how much time passed like that. It might have been only an hour, or many hours, I cannot say. Consciousness was slippery, and time did not seem to matter.

But sometime later Jolly spoke again. "Jubilee? Is something happening? Look around. Is the silver changing?"

I looked up, surprised to discover that we had left the flat floor of the Cenotaph. We were clambering up a slope of tumbled stone. "How long have we been climbing?" I whispered.

"I don't know. Not long, I think. But look at the silver. Is it my eyes? Or is it changing?"

I looked. The silver was still wrapped close around us, but its light seemed different. Warmer. No longer was it a featureless fog, for I could see swirls and currents running through it. "Is it thinning?"

"I don't know." He sat down on the loose slope. "I'm so tired."

"I know." I raised my good hand. The *ha* still sparkled between my fingers. "If you want to sleep, I think maybe I can hold the silver off."

"Okay."

But he didn't sleep. Neither did I. We sat together, and after a while the silver started brightening again, but now its light seemed tinted warm yellow. It was a familiar hue, though at first I couldn't think where I had seen it before, until finally the memory came to me: it was sunlight.

As the silver cleared, the slope around us came into view: a waste-land of crumbled minerals, and flows of transformed stone. There was not a weed, or a blade of grass, or a trickle of water anywhere to be seen.

Then the last of the silver above us gave way, and suddenly sun-light fell upon us and we could see all the way to the top of the Cenotaph, and to a brilliant blue sky beyond.

"*Oh,*" Jolly said.

I could not manage even that much. All I could do was to stare up at a towering wall that was certainly equal in height to the southern escarpment of the Kalang. "We can't climb that," Jolly whispered. "Not without food and water."

Water. Already my throat was dry and horribly swollen. "Maybe we'll find water."

"Okay. Maybe."

But neither of us made a move to start. We waited, while the sun chased away the silver that still lay below us. In only a few minutes we could see all the way across the vast crater of the Cenotaph, to the far wall, blurred by distance. I studied the white floor of the crater, but I could not see the ruins of the goddess's temple.

"Maybe she really is gone from the world," Jolly said. He lay back, and after a few minutes he pointed at the sky. "Look there," he said. "A hawk flying."

We watched it until it passed out of sight over the rim of the Cenotaph.

"We should go," Jolly said.

So far we had climbed only a hundred feet or so above the crater floor, but I felt a little stronger for our rest, or maybe it was the comfort of sunlight. Anyway, I made it to my feet and we pushed on, not because there was a hope of getting out, but because there was nothing else to do.

We had been going only a few minutes when I started to hallu-cinate. I thought I heard voices calling down the cliff walls, familiar syllables echoing against the rock: *Jol-ly-ly-ly! Jub-blee! Jub-blee! Jub-blee!* Sounds that rippled over the stone.

Moki pricked his ears and stared upward. Even Jolly stopped to look, scowling at the terrible walls. "Did you hear that?" he asked me.

"You mean Liam calling?"

"Yes."

"I thought I imagined it."

"Well then, I imagined it too."

Even in my fevered state of mind that didn't seem likely. "So call out to him."

Jolly drew a great breath. Then he bellowed at the top of his lungs, *"Un-cle!!! We're here. We're here!"* and it made such a cacophony of echoes that a flight of doves took off from the crater rim, and I feared a landslide would start among the loose scree.

But when the last of the echoes died away, Liam called out again. *"Stay where you are! We'll come get you!"*

Then I heard Udondi whoop and Ficer bellow.

"They're all here!" Jolly shouted, and I returned his smile.

Epilogue

We made our way back to the Temple of the Sisters. I rode behind Liam, my arms around his waist and my cheek pressed against his broad shoulders. It took us three days to reach the Sisters, and we camped twice on high ground and only once by a kobold well. The silver still appeared each night, but only as a low mist in the ravines and along the lower slopes of each desert rise.

We stayed seven nights at the Sisters, and I spent most of my time there writing down my remembrances. It was Emil who suggested it, for I could not speak of all that had happened. It hurt too much even to try, but he said I should not keep it inside.

So I started writing. I started in the middle, with all that had happened since I'd left the Temple of the Sisters, and by the time we were ready to leave, I had a draft for Emil to read.

After that we continued north, skirting the foot of the Kalang. I thought of Nuanez in his forest, and I told myself that someday I would visit him, but I did not have the heart for it just yet.

After two days we reached the desert highway. Or at least Ficer said we had reached it. I could not make out a road unless it was that the ratio of rocks had fallen off somewhat.

Ficer left us there, heading east back into the desert, while we turned west. By the afternoon, the invisible highway finally became a true road, and we followed its switchbacks up a long, steep slope, until by evening we had left the Iraliad behind.

Udondi said there had once been a temple where the road met the edge of the great desert basin, but it was not there when we passed through, so we camped another night.

Evidence of silver storms was everywhere. The road to Xahiclan had mostly been erased. Now and then there were follies marking where it had once run: arches and huts, and once, a wilderness of blocks hauntingly similar to the miniature cityscape we had found in the Cenotaph. We met no other travelers.

On the third day we found a long section of intact road. The miles fell behind us, and by late afternoon we reached the broad river valley where Xahiclan once stood.

The enclave was gone.

I had been there only once, but I remembered fondly walking the long, tall wall that skirted the river, and the merry streets with their crowded buildings, bright with lights at night and the heady scent of kobolds. I wondered if Kaphiri had murdered the city, or if the rising silver had simply overwhelmed it, but it seemed likely I would never know.

We camped again that night, and then we pushed on to Temple Nathé. All that day again we met no other travelers, and I dreaded to find that Nathé's walls had fallen too, but when we finally reached the valley's head, the temple was there, gleaming white in the evening's light, and as we drew near, players appeared upon the walls, and the gates swung open in welcome. The voice of the keeper, Elek Madhu, carried down to us in the fading light. "Welcome! Welcome to Temple Nathé. We had begun to fear we were the last players left in all the world."

"Not the last. Not quite," Liam called.

And then another voice called down to us, a voice I had known since before my birth. "Liam? Liam, is that you?"

"*Mama!*" I slipped off the back of Liam's bike, and raced through the gate, and I met my mother just as she reached the bottom of the stairs that descended from the wall. I fell into her arms, and for the first time since Yaphet was taken I cried, and for a time I thought I would never stop.

MEMORY

My mother's sister, Auntie Som, and all my own brothers and sisters were safe at Temple Nathé too. Emia and Rizal, Jacio and Tezoé, and Arial and little Zeyen, both of whom had not even been born when Jolly disappeared. They were frightened of Jolly. He looked younger than Rizal, but there was a gravity about him that did not belong to a child, and the *ha* still sparkled across his fingers. Only my mother did not seem to mind. She took his hands and gazed at them a moment, then she held him close and kissed him until he cried too.

Later that evening she told me the story of how she had come to be at Temple Nathé, and she warned me that I must acknowledge a debt of gratitude to someone I despised. It seemed that after we left Mira Indevar unconscious on the steps of Temple Nathé, the Ano truckers took it as a good excuse to leave him behind. "I don't know exactly what he did after you left," my mother said. "But after many days he made his way to Temple Huacho, as you feared. He was not alone. There had been silver storms in Xahiclan, and some of his companions seemed to be refugees, but they weren't unhappy about the trouble. They muttered that the same would come to Huacho, and on one night someone left the gate open, and the silver filled the orchard, and pressed against the temple walls. That next day I left."

"They drove you out?" I could not imagine my mother ceding Temple Huacho to bandits.

"I had already lost Kedato, and Jolly, and you . . . and I knew they would not stay long, though they might poison the well." She gave me a sheepish look. "I almost poisoned the well myself, they had me so angry. In the end, though, it didn't matter. Sometime after I left, the silver came upon them. I don't know how it happened, but there is nothing left there now."

Kaphiri had said the same thing. He never had lied to me. Now he was gone forever and that was a joy to me, not only for the wickedness he had done . . . but because some part of me was afraid I might have been tempted by him.

Yaphet's death had left me nearly empty. Just the thought of him would open a great wound in my heart. I tried to put him out of my mind. I wished fervently that I had never found him, never met him at all, for then I would not own this pain.

My mother assured me that I was young, that Yaphet might have been born again already, but there were not so many players left in the world that this seemed likely to me.

And I had another fear. Yaphet's body had been taken by the goddess. Had she captured his memories too? Each of us has an essence—that part of us that is kept in the silver until we are reborn into the world. If the goddess had held on to that part of Yaphet, then he is lost to me forever. No matter how many lives I live, I will never find him. I will never find another lover.

A thousand years from now, will I be as angry as Kaphiri? Will I be as hateful?

Temple Nathé finally has some new guests this night. Three wayfarers have arrived from the north, and they report that many enclaves along the coast are still intact. This is excellent news, and Liam has decided to go there. Udondi will go with him, as well as my brother Rizal and my sister Emia, who have both decided to seek for their own lovers in the wide world.

I will be leaving in the morning too. My mother and I and my Auntie Som are going back to Kavasphir. We will see if the well at Huacho still exists, and if it does not, we will search those hills until we find another. I will help my mother to rebuild Temple Huacho, though I don't think I'll stay for long. Three years. Maybe four. Then Jolly will be a man and it will be time for him to leave.

I'll go with him. He won't call it wayfaring, for he does not believe there is a lover anywhere in the world for him, but he has a mission, just the same. He is the last gift of the goddess. He is here to awaken our *ha*, so that we might live in the open, with no fear of the silver.

That is how the god and the goddess intended us to live, when they first dreamed of the world, in the lost and ancient past.